Praise fo

"I read Jessie and Calen's book with my heart in my throat, at times, my eyes burning with tears. It is a gripping, heartbreaking, and ultimately, life affirming, step-by-step account of how mental illness can shatter a family, but also how that family, through love and resilience, can not only survive, but triumph. I have deep love, respect, and awe for this book and my two heroes who wrote it."

Glenn Close
Award-winning actress and mental health advocate

———

"Jessie and Calen have laid bare and vulnerable the often lonely and misunderstood path of mental illness. Their book serves as a sensitive companion and a window into the world of severe psychosis. *Silence You* is not a journey for the faint of heart; but those brave enough to come along will find themselves with a deeper well of compassion for those who suffer, survive, and triumph through these infirmities."

Robert Munjal, MD
Associate Director of Inpatient Psychiatry
St. Patrick Hospital, Missoula, Montana

———

"*Silence You* takes readers on a family journey of mental illness and substance use disorder, rife with guilt, confusion, frustration, love, and healing. The multiple character viewpoints are felt by so many trying to navigate the struggles of mental illness. This realistic story increases knowledge and compassion, both of which are indispensable as we strive to improve our medical system."

Colette Kirchhoff, MD, FAAFP
Board Certified Family Physician, Hospice and Palliative Physician
Associate Clinical Professor, Department of Family Medicine
University of Washington School of Medicine

"With immersive and often-terrifying authenticity, mother-son team Jessie Close and Calen Pick transport readers inside the brain of a young man experiencing hallucinogenic schizoaffective disorder. Protagonist Oliver Moore's paranoid thoughts and audiovisual hallucinations are sprinkled throughout this auto-fiction in startling and alarming ways as he and his family, including his alcoholic mother with bipolar disorder, attempt to navigate this debilitating and difficult mental illness. A must-read for all who care about someone with mental illness."

Jodi Hausen
Award-winning freelance journalist focused on disability issues

———

"*Silence You* is a riveting accounting of the struggles and suffering experienced by one family impacted by mental illnesses. In intimate detail, Jessie Close and Calen T. Pick share the vivid mind-altering experiences of schizophrenia and bipolar disorder. Through the genuine compassion of these gifted authors, this book nurtures understanding and empathy for others."

Beth Sirr, RN, FNP
(Working with patients in hospitals and diverse community settings for over forty-four years)

SILENCE YOU

SILENCE YOU

A NOVEL

JESSIE CLOSE

WITH CALEN T. PICK

CRP

CENTRAL RECOVERY PRESS

LAS VEGAS

Central Recovery Press (CRP) is committed to publishing exceptional materials addressing addiction treatment, recovery, and behavioral healthcare topics.

For more information, visit www.centralrecoverypress.com.

Publisher: Central Recovery Press
530 S 6th Street
Las Vegas, NV 89101

29 28 27 26 25 24   1 2 3 4 5

Library of Congress Cataloging-in-Publication Data

Names: Close, Jessie, author. | Pick, Calen T., author.
Title: Silence you and the other cave paintings : a novel / Jessie Close
with Calen T. Pick.
Identifiers: LCCN 2024029711 (print) | LCCN 2024029712 (ebook) | ISBN
9781949481921 (paperback) | ISBN 9781949481938 (ebook)
Subjects: LCGFT: Novels.
Classification: LCC PS3603.L683 S55 2024 (print) | LCC PS3603.L683
(ebook) | DDC 813/.6--dc23/eng/20240708
LC record available at https://lccn.loc.gov/2024029711
LC ebook record available at https://lccn.loc.gov/2024029712

Photos of Jessie Close and Calen T. Pick used with permission.

Every attempt has been made to contact copyright holders. If copyright holders have not been properly acknowledged please contact us. Central Recovery Press will be happy to rectify the omission in future printings of this book.

Publisher's Note
This is a work of fiction, though many of the characters and events mirror some of the challenges the authors faced while navigating the landscape of mental illness. The authors hope presenting in this genre will help readers learn about and understand the daily struggles confronting those with mental health disorders.

Original cover art by Calen T. Pick from his collection.

Cover design by The Book Designers. Interior design by Sara Streifel.

For

Thomas Louis Pick

and

Bettine Moore Close

AUTHORS' NOTE

Silence You began twenty-three years ago as a project in writing about Calen's lived *experience* with schizophrenia and Jessie's alcoholism and bipolar 1 disorder.

We fictionalized some aspects for dramatic purposes. We hope readers will learn about mental illness and recovery through our story.

CONTENTS

1

THE GREEN CREEP

Inside a dark city night, the red reflections of neon signs pop more than any other color; Montana April has arrived, with rain erasing most of the dirty snowdrifts in the gutters, the streets, and on the sidewalks. April light can be white, flat. The fields surrounding the city are still dormant and won't come alive again until the end of May, the creeping green an emerald suddenness that catches everyone off guard.

The population is beginning to feel the vibration of spring's approach. April is the month, in Montana, that makes it easy to forget which way the seasons are moving; the brown vegetation could be the precursor to spring or fall. It's a confusing month for those who live in the cities as they can't readily see the calves in the fields or the newly arrived pelicans on the rivers. Bozeman is like any city: asphalt, tall buildings, and neon.

A black Acura Integra, crimson taillights glowing, drives back and forth on Main Street. A total of five teenagers are in the small car; Oliver's younger brother, Peter, is driving. Three are crammed in the back seat, including Oliver, his pale face framed by the window, his ·eyes staring at the city buildings they drive by. Music thumps, the bass audible to people on the sidewalks and nearby cars. The mood, except Oliver's, is one of mercurial joy.

The girl next to Oliver raises her hand to ruffle his thick, wavy hair, but stops, her hand midair. Oliver's hands are grasped between his knees, his broad shoulders are immobilized between the window and the girl he doesn't want to touch.

The girl notices his jaw, clenched so tightly the muscles are visible. She glances down at his arms and sees they're trembling. Oliver's body is rigid. The girl leans away from him, alarmed.

Peter, lanky, long blond hair in his face, begins pounding on the dashboard in time to the music. They arrive at the top of Main Street; Peter makes a U-turn in the Best Western parking lot then pulls back out on Main, their fifth pass up and down the city street.

Peter turns up the music and yells to Oliver, looking for him in the rear-view mirror. Peter sees his brother and is stunned by the disturbing turmoil in Oliver's eyes. He sees the dark rings under Oliver's eyes as though he dipped his little finger in ash then smeared the ash under his eyes.

Peter turns down the music, still looking at Oliver in the mirror.

"What's goin' on, bro?"

"Take me home," he answers.

"Are you sure?"

"Fuck you!" Oliver leans forward again and tells the rear-view mirror, "Fuck ALL of you!"

"What the hell are you talking about? FUCK you, too, man. FUCK YOU!"

Oliver punches the back of Peter's seat causing everyone else in the car to flinch. "Let me OUT OF HERE!"

"Goddammit, Ollie!" Peter screams at him. "I'll take you home." Peter's hands grip the wheel, he tries to look at everyone else.

Oliver is a bomb, the fuse short.

Peter drives fast, turning the car at breakneck speed toward their mother's house. He pulls into the driveway and jumps out.

"GO!" Peter opens the door for Oliver.

Oliver pulls himself out of the Acura, away from the girl, away from his friends. He begins to apologize to Peter but sees fear and embarrassment on his brother's face. Oliver turns away from him too.

Oliver, Peter, and their little sister, Wren, live in town with their mother, Elizabeth. Their home is close to Main Street. The west side of the house is bordered by a busy road, the east by a creek and north and south by high fences.

Oliver, when he turned eighteen, was given the loft above the detached garage, away from his mother, Peter, and Wren. The loft is narrow, the walls sloping inward to form a long, upright triangle, windows at each end. The only straight walls are short, maybe two feet tall, with accessible storage behind them. There is no light behind these small, upright walls, only a long and dark space. If Oliver wants to stand up straight he has to stand in the middle of his domain. A steep ladder is the only access to his loft; the ladder folds up by pulling an attached rope that curls the ladder up to the loft creating complete isolation, Oliver's desired effect.

Out of the car, he lights up a smoke, opens the gate to the house yard and walks up the back door steps. When he enters the house he hears the television in the living room. He walks down the hall and enters, sees his mother on the blue couch, feet up, next to Wren, Elizabeth's accustomed drink in hand. Both his mom and Wren are in their flannel pajamas. Jack, the Border Collie, jumps up instantly and approaches Oliver, sitting in front of him, his tail swishing back and forth on the wood floor.

Oliver makes no sound, his cigarette smoke curling against his arm. Elizabeth notices her eldest son.

"Ollie! You're back!" She smiles and pats the couch. "Come on in!" She sees the cigarette. "But please don't smoke in here, okay? Take it outside."

"Ollie!" Eight-year-old Wren runs to him. She hugs his stiffened torso, hanging on for an instant then reaches down to Jack who licks her face and follows her back to the couch.

Oliver remains motionless, arms hanging down, one hand holding his cigarette, the other in a fist, his eyes colored black by huge pupils, staring.

Elizabeth swings her legs off the couch, puts her feet on the ground. "What's wrong?" She stands, slightly bent, puts her drink on the coffee table. "Oliver?"

Oliver doesn't move. He stares at her.

"Speak to me." She walks over to him, extends her hand to put it on his shoulder.

Oliver's eyes finally meet Elizabeth's. She sees only his huge pupils and a look of hatred.

Oliver suddenly bolts; he runs down the hall to the back door, opens it, slams it shut, and is gone.

"Damn it!"

Cigarette smoke hangs in the air.

Oliver's outbursts are becoming more frequent and troublesome. Elizabeth and John don't know what to do.

Oliver stands at the bottom of his ladder to the loft. He'd left the ladder down before leaving this evening to be with Peter. The ground floor is the garage; dark, cold, unfriendly, and it smells of gasoline and wet mold. His mother rarely if ever parks her car in here. Peter's been after Oliver to help him clean this place out so they can use the garage for the Acura, but they never find the time to do that and, even if they did, they wouldn't know what to do with all the accumulated paraphernalia—an old bike missing handlebars, ripped, over turned furniture, and even an old, rusted clothes dryer. Standing by the ladder, the dark crept into Oliver, a cold spear of fear envelopes him. He thinks he sees something move or perhaps the dark itself moved.

He climbs up into the hole and opens the door. He forgot to leave a light on when he left. Oliver reaches the top of the ladder, fumbles for the switch, and finds it. He thinks about how good it would be to have Jack, his dog, up here in the loft with him, but even though Jack can climb up the ladder, it's difficult bringing him back down.

Jack doesn't seem to mind being over in the house; he sleeps with Wren now.

Oliver sits on his futon couch. An upside-down wooden box serves as his coffee table where cigarette butts spill over the sides of a shallow, green aluminum ashtray. He stubs out his smoke then sits; nothing else. He stares at the slanting wall in front of him. He reviews the evening. He doesn't move. His eyes, hugely dilated, stare into the evening past, the ride, the kids, the girl. The girl. He lies down on the futon and stares at the ceiling.

Elizabeth had spent a relaxing evening at home, happy the boys were out together. She was worried about Oliver, but when he'd decided to accompany his brother, a rare occasion of late, Elizabeth placed all worry on the outside of her heart and determined to enjoy her evening with Wren. She'd called her ex-husband, John, to tell him that possibly the recent medication, Seroquel, was making a change in Oliver. John shared Elizabeth's hope and was equally grateful to hear that Oliver was out with Peter and some of their friends. He had experienced Ollie's strange behavior as of late, knew Oliver isolated up in his loft, and mostly refused to speak to them.

Elizabeth covers her face with slim fingers, her wedding band mark tanned over after many summers. She knows she has to confront Oliver in his loft. She listens for any noise of Peter. Nothing. She walks upstairs to investigate. She looks in his room. Nothing. Her battered sheepskin slippers crack on each step down the uncarpeted stairs.

"I can't do this," she tells the sound. "I can't do this; I can't." She walks back into the living room, light reflecting off her dark hair. She reaches for her drink, the ice has melted, and chugs it.

"I'm going out to talk to Ollie," she tells Wren.

The little girl's face is glued to the television, one arm draped over Jack whose silky black and white head is resting in her lap, seemingly content to stay with her.

"Did you hear me?" Elizabeth asks Wren.

"Yes." Wren doesn't take her eyes off the TV. "Can we get a snack? Me and Jack?"

"Of course, sweetie." Elizabeth's heart sinks. She wants to stay inside with her little girl.

"Okay, okay, okay." Elizabeth walks down the hall, stops in the bathroom for a hair tie, pulls her hair back into a ponytail, then proceeds out the back door and into the garage. She feels fear and anger, a mix not purely recognized; the vodka tempering each into a ball in the pit of her stomach. Her shoulders tighten.

"Ollie?" She looks straight up the ladder where light pours out from the loft. She puts one foot on the lowest rung, hangs on to the step at her eye level, and begins her ascent. A pain stabs her stomach. She smells cigarette smoke. "Ollie?"

No answer, not even a whisper of sound. She stops mid-ladder, thinking she hears Peter outside. No. The door to the loft is open. At the top of the ladder Elizabeth cranes her neck to look down the length of the loft. She sees that Oliver has painted on the walls, in red. SILENCE YOU is written in big black letters. She climbs up, pulling herself inside the loft. She doesn't see Oliver at first then she notices his shoes sticking up from the futon couch.

"Ollie?" She walks closer.

Oliver is on his back staring up at the ceiling. He doesn't move.

"Oliver, say something!" She folds her arms across her abdomen, bends forward slightly, nausea grabbing at her.

Their eyes meet as he turns his head slightly. There is no gray blue around his pupils, only black. The darkened circles under his eyes and his blank expression shock her; his hollow cheeks and tight mouth scare her. She stands up straight, keeping her eyes focused on his. A glimpse of something flickers across Oliver's face.

"Are you hungry?" Immediately, Elizabeth feels the fool for asking.

Ollie sits up, puts his shoes on the floor. He stands, bent at the waist, and switches on the TV, then lights a cigarette from a crumpled pack of Camels.

"Ollie?" Elizabeth hears herself whine, wishes she was back in the house. "I need to know what happened tonight."

"Nothing." Oliver blows smoke in her direction.

"I don't think nothing happened!" She hears her strict voice, the one she hates, the one that takes so much effort. "Where is Peter? What happened tonight to make him drop you off?"

"Get out."

"Excuse me?" Elizabeth's heart pounds, hard and heavy in her chest.

"Get the FUCK OUT!!" Oliver's face is pale, almost white, his eyes black, piercing as a blade of steel, terrifying. Not her Ollie.

"Don't talk to me that way," Elizabeth says, quietly. Her heart is pounding harder, her limbs are shaking.

"Get OUT of my room!"

Elizabeth can barely stand, her body is cold, her chest now tight. "Don't you DARE speak to me that way! Who do you think you ARE?"

"Get OUT!"

Elizabeth backs away, riveted by Oliver's eyes. "Okay. I will, okay." A strange terror grips her as though this son of hers is possessed. "I'm GOING!!" she screams back at him.

Oliver sits back down, kills his cigarette, stares at the TV. Elizabeth doesn't see him move again as she backs away to find the ladder. She closes the door, keeping him behind it. Her legs take her down to the garage and back into the house. Once inside she doesn't bother looking for her old drink glass but reaches for a new one, clinks ice, pours straight. The glass shakes violently as she lifts the vodka to her mouth.

"Mommy?" Wren stands behind her. "Is Ollie all right?"

"No, he's not all right, and I need you to go to bed."

"What's wrong with Ollie?"

"He's not okay. Come on, bed!"

"But Mom . . ." Wren pleads.

"Now, come on!" Elizabeth hears her own harsh voice but doesn't know how to stop it. She wants to think only about Oliver right now. She doesn't want to go through the whole bedtime ritual required by her eight-year-old. "Let's go."

Elizabeth takes Wren's hand and leads her upstairs.

"I don't want to go to bed right now!"

Wren's voice grates on Elizabeth's raw nerves.

"I'm sorry, sweetie, but you in bed is what needs to happen right now."

They walk into Wren's room. Elizabeth picks her up and puts her in bed.

"But I haven't brushed my teeth!"

"That's okay. One night won't hurt." Elizabeth pulls back the covers. Wren climbs in. Elizabeth tucks her in.

"But Mommy, I don't want to go to bed like this! You haven't even read to me!"

"I know, but you have to. Ollie's not okay. You just have to."

Elizabeth turns out the light but leaves the door open. "I love you. I'm so sorry."

"I'm sorry too, Mommy."

Elizabeth walks back down the stairs. After a moment she picks up the phone.

2

THE ATTIC

After Elizabeth leaves, Oliver stands again. He paces the loft, long steps, hard on the wood floor, his arms moving, his face contorted with grief and fear. His TV is on, sounds coming at him, enveloping his body, terrifying him, speaking nonsense, the music orchestrating his every move, thoughts bombarding his brain, his body, his loft.

You. Are. A. Piece. Of. Shit

Oliver feels eyes watching, feels hatred. He knows where the cameras are, the ones watching him.

You don't know anything. You're stupid!

Oliver stops pacing. He looks in his jacket pocket for his knife. Finding it, he moves the one chair in his loft to the middle of the room. Earlier, when lying on his futon, he'd seen a small black crack where the drywall came together at the peak of the ceiling. Oliver starts working on the crack, jamming his knife in between the drywall, scraping and cutting to find the camera he knows is there.

It's in there, watching you.

Oliver pulls himself as close as he can to the crack, white dust falling on his face, his hair. The camera is secreting itself further into the darkness, moving away from Oliver's knife with every sharp scrape, denying Oliver any glint of its glass lens.

You can't even find it. You're a FOOL!

Oliver gets down from the chair, his neck aching, his eyes filled with dust. He wants to go into the house but his mother is there, maybe Peter. He wants the TV to stop talking to him, wants the camera to stop watching him, wants to be able to touch the girl, speak to his friends again. He picks up the chair and smashes it into the TV. Nothing. He pushes and the TV falls off its table on to the floor, silenced.

You think that's going to work, you idiot?

Oliver walks over to the TV. He notices a sharp bit of light behind the grate, below the knobs. He picks up the TV, places it back on the table and peers into the black grate. Nothing. Nothing! There was NOTHING! He gets his knife and begins cutting the plastic, sawing off black hard pieces. A hole, big enough for his finger, emerges from his work. Terrified, he sticks his index finger in the hole and feels mesh. No glass. No lens.

You're crazy! Now look what you've done to the TV.

Oliver pulls his finger out of the hole but catches it on a jagged piece of plastic. A small line of blood oozes out of his skin.

You are human and they are not and there's nothing you can do about it!

"FUCK YOU! LEAVE ME ALONE!" Oliver kicks the futon frame then lights a cigarette. He wants to cry but he can't.

Elizabeth's hand shakes as she dials, the phone in one hand, her drink in the other. The phone rings and rings and rings. She almost hangs up, her heart still pounding, then John's voice comes on the line.

"Yes?"

"It's me. Ollie is worse. He's getting violent; he was screaming at me, he's up in the loft. Peter dropped him off and . . ."

Elizabeth's hysteria irritates John, especially so late in the evening. "Calm down. It can't be that bad. Maybe something happened while he was out."

John's sensible words and steady tone wind up Elizabeth even more.

"No shit something happened! I don't know what it was. He won't speak to me, he just screamed."

"Liz. Calm down. Leave him alone. Peter will be home soon and you can ask him, okay?"

"No! I can't stand knowing he's up in that loft being so crazy! What if he comes in here? What am I supposed to do?"

John sighs. "Do you want me to come over?"

"Yes. I do." Elizabeth closes her eyes, feels some of her fear dissipate.

"Okay. I'll be right over."

Elizabeth hangs up, puts her drink down. She wishes she could cry. The pressure inside her won't allow it. She turns on the news for distraction. She sits on the edge of the couch, feet planted on the floor.

Oliver stops screaming, sucks his finger, tastes the blood with its thick metallic taste. He lights a cigarette, sees his knife lying on the floor, thinks about extending the line of blood on his finger.

Not yet.

He begins to pace again, back and forth, his footsteps comforting somehow, stomping louder and louder; he can't hear his thoughts now, back and forth down the length of the loft, turning quickly at each end to keep up the noise. He swings his arms, keeping time with his legs. There is no end to his pacing, no end in sight as he drowns out his thoughts, as he dodges the camera in the ceiling and the camera in the TV.

It's behind those dark walls, the space where you keep your duffel bag.

Oliver jumps at the voice. He drops his cigarette, covers his ears and keeps on pacing, stomping louder and louder, stomps on his cigarette, stomps until the loft trembles. He begins to hum, feels the resonance inside his head, knows he won't be able to hear the voice if he keeps this up.

It's back there you fool, it's watching you.

Oliver hums louder, howling, almost wailing. He paces toward the far end of the loft, toward the TV, then turns abruptly to prevent breaking his tempo back toward the ladder. This pacing seems to calm him.

John knocks on Elizabeth's front door. He watches through the door window as she approaches, her ponytail disheveled, her once beautiful face tired and slack and he spots the drink in her hand.

As Elizabeth approaches to let him in she sees John framed in the door window; open collar, crisp maroon shirt, his handsome face, blond hair trimmed just right, dimples, and cleft chin.

She opens the door to let him in. "Drink?"

"No." John's reply barely hides his scorn. "What's the problem? Where is he?"

They enter the kitchen.

"Excuse the mess." Elizabeth feels a pang of guilt, sees her kitchen through John's eyes; her sink piled high with dishes. She can hear the gritty floor under her slippers, she sees the table covered with crumbs. "He's up in the loft. You won't believe his eyes, John, they're crazy and scary and he screamed at me."

"What were you doing?"

"Me? Nothing! I was trying to talk to him!" Elizabeth slams her drink on the counter, spilling some liquid on her hand.

"For God's sake Elizabeth, you have to control yourself!" John pulls a dishrag off the rack above the sink and hands it to her.

"Thank you. And I can't control myself. Something is horribly wrong with Ollie."

"Let's go see him."

"I don't know if I can again, John."

"Liz, please pull yourself together, okay?" John leaves the room, starts walking down the hall. He stops, waiting for Elizabeth.

"I can't, John. I have to stay here with Wren."

John snorts. "She's asleep, Liz."

"I don't think so."

John opens the back door, slams it shut. "Jesus Christ," he mutters to no one. Dark envelopes him. He stands on the back steps looking up at the loft. He sees light and shadows, moving. He steps onto the lawn and crosses to the garage. It's pitch-black inside and he doesn't know where the light switch is. He hears noise above him, loud noise moving back and forth. He walks slowly and carefully across the garage floor. Groping with his hands he finds the ladder. Grabbing a rung with both hands, he begins to climb.

"Ollie?"

The noise doesn't stop.

"Oliver?" John opens the door and climbs the last rung, stepping high onto the floor of the loft.

Oliver is pounding the floor with his feet, his fists pushing into either side of his face. His back is to John who watches as Oliver reaches the end of the loft then changes direction. He stomps back toward John, unaware of his presence.

"OLIVER?"

The boy stops. He drops his hands to his sides. Terror flickers across his features, then fades. His eyes remain frightened but slowly take on the black aspect of anger, fear, and rage.

"What are you doing?" John's shock lodges in his throat.

"Nothing." Oliver's response is almost a whisper.

"Are you okay?" John remains standing by the door.

"Of course I'm okay."

"Then what are you doing?" John steps further into the loft, toward Oliver.

"I'm pacing! Just walking!"

"Well, that's good." Very slowly, John walks closer to Oliver. He stops in front of him.

Oliver takes two steps back.

"You frightened your mother this evening."

"So?" Oliver's response is sharp.

"You shouldn't yell at her."

"So she called you?"

"Yes."

"And what are you going to do about it?"

John's eyes narrow. He hears the anger in Oliver's voice. He collects himself; his initial shock fading into the stern persona of father.

"What do you think I should do about it?" John keeps his voice calm, almost soft.

"Nothing."

"Why are you home early?"

"I wanted to come home."

"What do you think Peter's going to say about that?"

"Why should I care?" Oliver moves further away from John toward the futon couch and TV.

John looks around the loft. He notices that Oliver has been painting on the walls. Red. And black. The letters are so huge they dwarf the TV.

"Why are you painting on the walls?"

"Why not?" Oliver stands in front of the TV, staring at his father.

John sighs. "Do you think the Seroquel is helping?"

"What?"

"Are you taking the medication Dr. Ritter gave you?"

"It makes me tired."

"Is it helping?

"Helping what?" Oliver hangs his head, his hands stuffed into his pockets.

"I think it would be a good idea for you to see him tomorrow if we can get you in." John hears the authority in his own voice but feels the panic in his gut as he speaks to this son he doesn't recognize.

Don't listen to him you piece of shit!

"DAMMIT!" Oliver yells, surprised by his own outburst.

"Ollie. Listen to me!" John steps closer to Oliver, his tone imploring, his hands reaching out to his son.

Oliver opens his eyes wide. He backs away from his father, further into the corner, up against the TV.

"What can I do?" John backs off, wants to flee, anything but this. "Where are your pills?"

Oliver stares at his father, unresponsive.

"Where are your pills?"

Oliver frowns. He points to the windowsill behind the futon couch.

"Have you taken one this evening?"

"Yes," Oliver lies.

John throws up his hands. "Then I just don't know. Maybe you'd better try to get some sleep?"

"Okay."

"I'll call the doctor tomorrow."

"Okay."

"I'll let you know."

"Okay. Bye."

"I'll see you tomorrow."

Oliver sits gingerly on the futon couch. His father turns to walk down the length of the loft. He doesn't turn again until he's reached the top of the ladder.

"Do you want the door closed?"

Oliver doesn't look at him. "Yes."

The door closes, then opens. "And don't yell at your mother!"

"Okay."

After John leaves, Oliver lights a cigarette.

John makes his way back through the garage, across the lawn to the back door. He knocks, but lets himself in. He hears the TV in the living room; looking in, he sees Elizabeth on the couch with Wren both wearing matching pajamas.

"She couldn't sleep," Elizabeth tells him.

"Happens." John walks into the room.

"Sit." Elizabeth sits up straight, her arm around Wren.

"No, I'd better be going."

"Please sit. I don't like you standing over me, and I want to hear how it went with Ollie."

"I think he's okay, for now. I do think he needs to see Dr. Ritter tomorrow though, if we can get him in." John sits in the armchair. "How are you, sweetie?"

"Good." The little girl looks tired but makes her way over to her daddy's lap. "Ollie's okay isn't he?" she asks once buried in his arms.

John and Elizabeth look at each other.

"He's just fine, Wren," John tells her.

"Tell me how he was, John."

"Not . . ." John looks from Wren to Elizabeth.

"She lives with him, John. She sees what we see."

"I know, but . . ."

"Did he yell at you? Did he speak to you?" Elizabeth shifts her position on the couch.

John sighs. "No, he didn't yell at me, and yes, he spoke to me. I don't know what it is about the two of you together."

"He's not okay."

"Well, no, he's not, but I don't think you should fight with him."

"I didn't provoke him, John."

"I didn't say you did, Lizzy. I'm just saying I don't think you should fight with him."

"Daddy?"

"Yes?" John voice is tight.

"I want to go to bed now." Wren rubs her eyes.

The front door slams. Peter walks in.

"Peter!" Wren runs to him and he picks her up.

"Hi, you little weasel!" Peter looks wild, his shirt is untucked, his jeans so long he's standing on the cuffs.

"Look who's here!" Wren points to John.

John stands, a big smile on his face. He walks over to Peter and Wren and gives the two of them a big hug. "It's good to see you."

"You too Dad." Peter puts Wren down. "Hi, Mom. What are you doing here, Dad?"

"I came over to see Oliver." John's energy fades at the reminder.

Peter throws himself into the battered armchair. "He was such an asshole tonight! What's his problem?"

Wren crawls onto the couch and Elizabeth's lap.

Elizabeth raises her voice. "He's not an asshole! He's not well!"

John sits on the edge of the couch. "I think something's very wrong right now. I don't think we even know what it is. We have to hang in with him. I'm taking him to see the psychiatrist tomorrow."

"Why did you drop him off early, Peter?" Elizabeth asks.

"Because he started screaming 'fuck you' and punched the back of my seat and he wanted to come home!"

"Did you do anything to upset him?" John asks.

"No! We were driving around having fun! Where does he get off doing something like that? He was screaming that he wanted to go home so I brought him home!"

"Okay, calm down." John rubs his forehead with one hand, thumb out. "That was the right thing to do."

"No, really, Dad. Why would he act like that?"

"I don't know, Pete. I don't know." John sits, his back hunched. "All I do know is it's not Ollie, it's not the Ollie we know."

Oliver tries lying down. He faces the window near the futon couch then sees the pill bottle sitting on the windowsill. He sits up, slowly, and reaches for the pills. He opens the childproof cap, tipping the bottle. Fat white round pills fall into his palm. He slopes his hand toward the floor, then moves his fingers open. The pills clatter to the floor. He stands and crushes them under his shoes.

You don't need this fucking crap.

Oliver likes the crushing sound and is disappointed when each and every pill is now powder in the floorboards.

That was NOT your dad. That was one of them.

Oliver is terrified. That man had seemed to be his father. Oliver had almost given in, had almost collapsed into the man, had almost told him about the cameras that were watching him, watching the man, but he hadn't. Now he was glad of it. Both those people, the people who had come up to his loft, had asked him about going out this evening with Peter. And he didn't know why he'd gone out with Peter. He didn't know why he'd agreed to get in the car with Peter and those people. He hadn't understood what they were saying. He hadn't been able to break their code. Maybe it wasn't Peter. He doesn't know.

Oliver lies back down on the futon couch. He pulls a blanket up and over his shoes. He closes his eyes and tries to sleep.

3

CONJURING YOUR VOICE: THAT MAKES NO SENSE

John returns to Elizabeth's house the next morning. He parks and makes his way directly through the garage to the loft ladder.

Halfway up the ladder he calls, "Ollie?"

No answer. He ascends to the door and opens it, stepping inside. Oliver is standing in the middle of the loft, lit cigarette in his hand.

"You ready to go?" John scrutinizes him.

"Where?" Oliver looks distracted. His face in daylight is as ghostly as it was last night.

"We have a 10:30 appointment with Dr. Ritter, remember?"

"No." Oliver stares at his father with such intensity that John takes a step back.

"Yes, we're going. Come on." John doesn't know what to do if Oliver won't come with him. "Come on with me, Ollie." John's voice is calm.

Oliver's expression changes suddenly. "Okay."

John waits as Oliver looks around the loft for something. He doesn't know what Oliver's looking for but just as quickly as Oliver's search began it ends and he walks to the ladder. He follows his father down to the garage, out the gate, and into John's waiting SUV. He gets into the passenger seat. They pull out onto the street.

"Fasten your seat belt," John tells him.

Oliver sits bold upright, doesn't respond.

"Ollie, put on your seat belt."

Oliver puts on his seat belt but stays rigidly upright, his hand on the door handle.

"You're having a hard time right now, aren't you?"

Oliver is silent. He doesn't look at anything as they drive toward the doctor's office; he keeps his face pointed straight ahead.

"You don't have to say anything to me, but it would be polite."

The car turns left onto Main Street.

Oliver glances at his father. "I'm okay."

The car pulls into the hospital parking lot. The landscaped grass is still brown, the trees bare.

"Let's go." John gets out, waits for Oliver. "Did you eat this morning?" he asks.

Oliver doesn't answer. He begins walking toward the glass entry doors. He stops, fetches his cigarette pack from a breast pocket and lights up.

"You can't smoke in here, Ollie." John's voice is low, frustrated.

"I know that." Oliver tells him, his eyes black, dangerous. He walks through the automatic doors.

"Oliver, STOP!" John's control cracks.

Oliver jumps. He drops the cigarette.

"Pick it up and take it outside."

Oliver's movements are awkward, he trips, he stares only at John's feet. He picks up the burning cigarette and walks back out the automatic doors. A small woman with white hair stares at him from the bench near the entrance. She slowly shakes her head. Oliver puts his cigarette into the ashtray. He leaves it there, still lit, and walks back into the hospital.

I know these people know who I am.

They find Dr. Ritter's office. John opens the heavy door and holds it open as Oliver passes him into the waiting room.

The receptionist greets John, glances at Oliver. "I'll have you see the nurse first since Dr. Ritter is in with a patient right now."

"That's fine." John turns away from the receptionist. "Let's sit," he says to Oliver.

"I'll stand."

"Dad?"

John looks at Oliver so thin, gaunt, and sad. "Yes?"

"I'll sit."

"Okay. Here, next to me." John pats the chair next to him, metal arms separating them. He can feel the thickness in his voice, can hear it. He's hyper aware that he's sitting in a psychiatrist's office with his first born, the son who's no longer tall and proud, no longer laughing, barely talking. This son who had to miss his high school graduation ceremony, who no longer has any friends. Oliver won't feel any of this, only detects it on himself at arm's length. Otherwise . . . John's not sure what the "otherwise" would be. He thinks about Elizabeth, her drinking, and the chaos in her home. Maybe it would be better, he thinks, if Oliver lived with him.

"Oliver Moore?" A nurse stands in the reception window framed by the glass, hundreds of color-coded files behind her. "Come with me."

"Come on, buddy," John tells his son. "Do you want me to come with you?"

No. Too dangerous. Too many of them in one room.

"That's okay." Oliver follows the nurse around the corner.

The nurse brings Oliver into a dimly lit room.

"Just make yourself comfortable, Oliver." The nurse speaks his name. She knows his name and begins to ask him questions.

"What seems to be the problem, young man?"

Oliver sits in this chair now, this blue one, the other was orange.

"Do you know why your dad wanted you to come in today?"

Oliver stares at his sneakers, the same ones that crushed the fat round white pills. He doesn't know what to say.

"Yes."

"Can you explain the problem to me? The reason you're here?"

Oliver swallows and swallows—it seems at least ten times. He can't get his saliva around the lump in his throat. He thinks about why he's here. This doesn't make any sense. Why is he here? Because his father, or at least that man who says he's his father, brought him here.

Maybe you should tell her that you're sad.

"I'm sad."

"Why are you sad, Oliver?" The nurse's expression is one of sickly-sweet concern.

"Because no one will leave me alone." Oliver shifts in the blue chair, feels how cold the steel arms of the chair are, feels carpet under his shoes.

"Have you been taking your medication, Oliver?" the nurse asks, now frowning, now smelling like disinfectant and the alien she is.

You better get this one right. They'll lock you up and then they'll kill you if you don't get this one right!

"Yes."

"Well, that's good." The nurse stands and reaches for a blood pressure cuff, her stethoscope dangling from her neck like a small round eye ready to see Oliver inside out.

Oliver trembles with the effort to hide, his hands sweat, his jaws ache. He holds as still as possible as the nurse wraps his arm with the blood pressure cuff, as she places that small, round eye on his vein. Maybe this is where they begin to kill him.

"Do you know the Lord?" the nurse asks him.

"What?" Oliver whispers and pulls away from her.

"Hold still, please." The nurse doesn't look at Oliver but she frowns, listening to his pulsating blood. She finishes, doesn't mention the Lord again, allows her stethoscope to dangle. "Good. You're pressure is fine. Up a tad but nothing to worry about."

Oliver's hands begin to shake. He knows what he heard. The nurse doesn't seem to remember, has not repeated, the strange word.

"You seem just fine, Oliver." Her voice is somewhere above him, her enunciation crisp and irritating.

Oliver clutches his hands together to hide any trace of fear. This woman is evil. He feels her all around him, pulling him into red, down into black. And he knows she's trying to trick him. He's glad it won't work. He's relieved he heard her code before it was too late.

"You can wait for the doctor in here." The nurse begins to leave. She slips Oliver's file into a small rack on the outside of the door. "Do you want your father to join you?"

"No."

The nurse closes the door. Oliver allows his hands to shake now, free of each other. He stands and begins to pace in small circles inside this room.

They're trying to keep you out of the Real World.

Oliver hears a hand on the doorknob. His body slam's back down in the blue chair. He grabs the cold arms.

Dr. Ritter walks in. "Hello, Oliver. Follow me to my office."

The doctor's broad face and babble seem to take up the entire room.

"Come on." Dr. Ritter is standing in the doorway waiting for Oliver. The door is held open by one of the doctor's fat hands, his wrists disappearing into tweed sleeves. The open door relieves some of the tautness trapped in this room; it whooshes out, alive.

Oliver pushes himself away from the blue chair, his hands releasing the steel arms, and follows the doctor. They walk down a short hall, chairs and a table covered with magazines making some chaos of the orderly office. Dr. Ritter ushers him into his office at the end of the hall. A huge desk sits under the only window, two stuffed and wide armchairs face the desk and Dr. Ritter's tall chair. Dr. Ritter's chair has wheels and sits on a stem that allows it to move forward and back.

Oliver feels panic in the pit of his stomach, feels his body getting hot, his face red.

Watching from the waiting area John sees Oliver and Dr. Ritter head toward the doctor's office. He's been waiting for this moment as his curiosity has been piqued by a book that's sitting up high on a shelf next to the receptionist. The book's spine tells him it's the Physician's Desk Reference for Prescription Drugs. Feeling suspicious, John walks over to the receptionist. "May I look at that book please?" He points to the PDR.

"Which book?"

"That one." He points again.

"Oh certainly!" She stands and lifts the heavy book off its shelf. "Here you go. Have at it!"

John takes the book and returns to his seat. He opens the book, sees it's alphabetized and quickly turns to Seroquel.

"Sit down, Oliver." Dr. Ritter's voice is changed inside this room; soft, compassionate, close to the heels of menacing. He closes the door.

Oliver chooses the armchair closest to the door.

"My nurse tells me your blood pressure's fine." The doctor picks up a pen and opens Oliver's file. "You're taking your medication, so what seems to be the problem?"

Oliver stares at him; tries to not stare at him. He almost replies out loud but bites his tongue.

Dr. Ritter pulls his chair on wheels close to Oliver who notices the red veins in his eyes.

"Are you hearing voices, Oliver? Or smelling bad smells?"

Oliver sits still, holds himself in what he supposes is the right way to hold himself. He says nothing. And more nothing.

"No" Oliver takes a deep breath. "I'm not."

Dr. Ritter moves away to look in Oliver's file. The turning pages slap each other until the doctor places the file, flat and open, on his desk and he makes a notation with a scratching pen.

"How's the medication? How's it making you feel?"

"Fine."

"Are you taking it every day at the same time?"

"Yes."

"What time is that?" Dr. Ritter turns his huge face and stares at Oliver.

Oliver remembers crushing the pills, the satisfying crunch, last night. "At night."

"That's no good, Oliver." The doctor's face expands even more. "You have to take one of those 200 milligram tablets in the morning and another 200 milligrams at bedtime. Do you understand? If you're not taking 400 milligrams per day I'm not surprised you're feeling a bit disconnected." Dr. Ritter pushes on. "Are you still confused, at odds with your parents and life in general?" The doctor continues to stare at Oliver. "Your father told me you yelled at your mother last night, which is why he brought you in here today."

Oliver wants to close his eyes to shut out this face who won't shut up, won't stop prying into him, sniffing at him like an animal. Oliver pictures his loft but keeps his eyes open.

"Why did you yell at your mother, Oliver?"

Oliver searches his mind, hears many reasons but doesn't know which answer will keep this face at bay. He feels the armchair swallowing him up and he fights panic. He knows he can't tell this doctor, this face who says he's a doctor but who isn't, that he was terrified by the woman who said she was his mother. He knows he can't give any reason that will allow this creature to kill him or lock him up. He wants to tell someone, if there is a someone somewhere, that he wants all to be how it was. He wants to tell someone how it is, now, but he knows he must not. He hopes his expression isn't giving anything away.

"She was bothering me," he tells the face, words rushing out of him. "She came up into my loft and was bothering me."

"That's no reason to yell at her." Dr. Ritter shuts Oliver's file. "Your parents are concerned about you, Oliver. I think we're on the right track. Keep taking the Seroquel, and take it as prescribed this time and I think your depression and confusion will abate, okay?"

An ocean of relief floods through Oliver. It was over.

"Okay."

"I have to ask you, again, since you're eighteen, if I may discuss all this with your father."

"I guess so." Oliver wants to stand up and walk out of here.

"Is that a 'yes'?" Dr. Ritter opens one of his drawers in his desk.

"Yes." Oliver stands, won't wait any longer. He walks to the office door and opens it. Dr. Ritter shuts his desk drawer and follows him.

Oliver walks into the waiting area and sees John sitting there, a huge book in his lap, but continues out the door, through the hospital hall, and out to the parking lot. He finds his father's SUV, leans against it and lights a cigarette. A chilly wind swirls around him but he welcomes it to take the smell of Dr. Ritter's office off his skin and out of his hair.

The doctor sees John sitting with the PDR. "Is everything all right?" he asks.

John stands, holding the PDR. "No, everything is definitely not all right," says John. "I'm going to have a word with you in your office right now!"

The two men stand, facing each other.

"What's the problem?" the doctor asks John.

John doesn't answer. He carries the PDR down the hall to the doctor's office. He sits in the chair closest to the door and opens the book to Seroquel.

Dr. Ritter enters the room. "Mr. Moore, I really don't have time for this. Patients are waiting."

"There's no one out there. Don't bullshit me, Doc."

"I don't have to discuss this with you. Oliver is eighteen."

"And he's very sick. I want to hear from you how sick you think he is before I put in my two bits."

Dr. Ritter looks unhappy. "I think his ADD is making him confused. It's a shame he can't tolerate Adderall because, if he could, I think it would help him."

"He couldn't handle it." John, annoyed, refuses to engage in this old story once again. Oliver hadn't done well on the stimulant. Elizabeth had finally timed his reaction to the little blue pills, discovering that twenty minutes after Oliver had taken one he was talking a mile a minute and was nervous and irritable.

"I understand, John." Dr. Ritter looks at his watch. "I think his manic-depressive symptomology overlays his ADD. I'm just saying that his confusion and distraction, his lack of concentration, is typical of ADD. I'm hoping the Seroquel will alleviate the symptoms of both. We'll see. He needs to take his medication twice per day and he's not. I can't help him if he doesn't take his medication."

"That's it?" asks John. "That's your professional opinion?"

"Yes."

"You think Oliver has bipolar symptomology with ADD?"

"Yes, Mr. Moore."

"What does that mean? Is he bipolar or not? I lived with his mother who fits the diagnosis of bipolar for twelve years, unmedicated except for booze. Oliver does not seem bipolar to me."

"Well, he may be a little psychotic. A patient can have psychotic features within manic depression, bipolar if you like to call it that."

"Whatever," says John. "I want you to listen to this, Doctor, and then you tell me why you have my son on this medication." John looks down at the PDR, on the page open to Seroquel.

"Why is this drug prescribed? Seroquel combats the symptoms of schizophrenia, a mental disorder marked by delusions, hallucinations, disrupted thinking, and loss of contact with reality." John stops reading and glares at Dr. Ritter.

"What are you thinking, Doctor? Do you think Oliver may be schizophrenic? You're saying now he 'may be a little psychotic'? You don't even know what you're doing, do you? Did you put him on Seroquel just to cover your ass in case he's schizophrenic? If you really think he's bipolar why isn't he on mood stabilizers and antidepressants like his mother should be? He can't tolerate Adderall because he's probably NOT ADD but you just keep pushing it and pushing it! Is that your favorite diagnosis?"

"Mr. Moore! You're going to have to leave now!" Dr. Ritter gets up and opens his office door.

"Tell you what, Doc, you're FIRED!" John drops the PDR on the floor. It lands upside down, the pages bent up inside the binding. John leaves the office and runs out of the hospital to find Oliver.

Oliver is still leaning on the SUV, waiting. He watches as John bursts through the hospital doors and hurries toward him. He notices how slim John is, how well-groomed and familiar. He feels an echo, like a déjà vu but internally—a memory of once looking very much like this man.

John reaches Oliver and puts his arm around him. Oliver is taken back by the abrupt physical touch. He pulls away and fumbles for another smoke. John isn't offended, not after what he just learned.

"Let's go to your mom's house," he tells Oliver. "It's lunch time."

Oliver doesn't respond but does get into the SUV.

"I need more smokes."

"We'll stop and buy some," John tells him, not caring about cigarette smoking. Not now, maybe never. "Maybe we could pick up a couple of sandwiches too," he adds. "Are you hungry?"

"No."

"I'm not really hungry either."

The two drive into town.

4

LOSE THE DUCK

Oliver doesn't say a word on the ride back to Elizabeth's house; he stares through the windshield, barely moving his head. John glances at him several times, panic growing in his heart. They find Elizabeth in the kitchen, cleaning up the mess in the sink, the sleeves of her blue sweater pushed up past her elbows.

"I think Oliver should come stay with me for a while." John speaks quickly as though he's screwed up his courage to push through the inevitable reaction to this statement.

Oliver reacts with surprise. "Whattaya mean, go with YOU? I don't want to go with you!"

"I think it would be best, Ollie. I think you need to be inside the house, out of your loft, and your mother doesn't have enough room for you here, unless you want to room with Peter."

"He doesn't mind the loft." Elizabeth turns away from the sink, her hands dripping soapy water on the old, dirty white linoleum floor.

Oliver sits hunched at the kitchen table, his black Joe Boxers showing over the top of his jeans. He stares at the surface. "I belong in the loft," he mumbles.

"You can stay in your own room. It'll be fine." John's tone leaves no room for argument. He leans on a kitchen chair, over Oliver, a protective move on John's part.

Oliver's stare is unseeing. This man's hands look like his father's, but . . . His head slowly sinks onto his arms.

"You could have discussed this with me first," Elizabeth says quietly. "You don't need to make decisions without discussing them with Ollie and me, John."

"There wouldn't be a discussion, Elizabeth." John looks at his own hands and Oliver's lowered head. "There would only be an argument." He pauses. "I think this has to be as I say, right now."

"What did the doctor say? You didn't even tell me that." Elizabeth's voice begins to rise.

John takes Elizabeth by the arm and walks her into the living room.

"What are you doing?" she asks, pulling away from him, her hands still wet.

"I need to tell you something out of Ollie's ear shot," John tells her.

"Why?"

"Could you just listen for a minute, please?"

"I will, sorry."

"When Ollie and I were at Dr. Ritter's, I looked up Seroquel in a book called the Physician's Desk Reference and discovered that this particular medicine is prescribed for schizophrenia."

"What?"

"I confronted Dr. Ritter about it who, first of all, insisted that Oliver is ADD and had bipolar symptomatology but when I brought up the Seroquel he said that possibly Ollie was a bit psychotic, that you can be psychotic and bipolar at the same time. Have you ever heard of that?"

"Jesus, John. Yes, I have heard of that but Dr. Ritter should have been more straightforward with us."

"That's what I think. I fired him."

"Good."

"I don't know what we're going to do now, what doctor we can trust, but for now I'll take him to my house for the night."

They walked back into the kitchen.

"Do you want me to collect your things?" John asks the back of Oliver's head.

Oliver doesn't raise his head, keeps it glued to his arms on the table. "I'm not going with you." His muffled voice is hard as it hits the table inside the cave of his arms.

"Yes, you are. Right now. Get up!"

Elizabeth walks over to Oliver. "This will be good, Ollie. Just for tonight."

John begins to say something but Elizabeth holds up her hand. "It'll be good over there. You'll have a real bed, a real bathroom."

"Maybe." Oliver's muffled word is taken as an affirmative.

"I'll take him to my house. We can come back for his things if he needs anything," John says quietly.

"I have to go back to the store for a while," Elizabeth says, the sharp edges of her voice erased.

"I can handle it. I took the whole day off." John takes Oliver's arm, gently.

"No." Oliver keeps his arm rigid, frozen.

"Come on, let's go." John keeps hold of Oliver's arm until the boy raises his head. "We need to go."

Oliver stares at John, then at Elizabeth. He gets to his feet, slowly, doesn't object any more to his father holding his arm. He walks outside with him.

Elizabeth follows them to John's SUV, leans in the window and puts her hand on Oliver's shoulder. "It'll be okay, sweetie."

Oliver turns his head to stare at her. She doesn't recognize him. She can see only a thin bit of blue in his eyes, the rest is huge black pupils.

"I can follow you in my car," she tells John.

"No, Lizzy. We'll be all right." John puts his key in the ignition, starts the motor, and pulls away from the curb.

"Oh my God," Elizabeth whispers as she watches them go. "This can't be happening." She follows John's car with her eyes for as far as she can see it, her arms clutched to her sides, tears streaming down her face. "Oh my God, Ollie!!"

The word "schizophrenic" reverberates in her brain.

"What does that mean?" she whispers to the empty street. "What the hell does that mean for Ollie?"

John's home is everything Elizabeth's isn't. It's clean and orderly, the precise picture of an older bachelor. The kitchen, living room, and bedrooms are all on one floor, carpeted throughout. Oliver sits down in the living room in a teal green armchair, the back taller than his head. Light pours in from a floor to ceiling window behind the chair. Oliver shades his eyes with one hand, his other elbow on the stuffed arm. He watches the stones that make up the fireplace, all different shapes, how they rise to the ceiling, one on top of the other, moving slightly; his eyes move back down to the fireplace opening, a black screen covering a mouth of darkness. He closes his eyes, still sees the shapes.

John walks into the living room, his footsteps quiet on the carpet. "How're you doing?"

Oliver jumps at the sound of John's voice. He takes his hand away from his face.

John is standing very straight, his arms at his sides. "I'm going to Safeway to stock up on groceries."

"I'll come with you," Oliver whispers.

"No. You hang out here, okay? I won't be long. Try to rest, watch TV, relax." John turns and walks away.

Oliver notices the rug fibers, how they lie flat where John stood. He watches as the fibers stay flat, watches as they try to rise to obliterate the man's prints. He raises his eyes to the quiet room and spies the kitchen through a doorway. He pushes himself out of the armchair and walks into the kitchen where the rug changes color and height.

Fishing a cigarette out of his pocket, he puts it in his mouth; he pats his right pants pocket, finding the blue Bic lighter. He lights it, sees the flame move over the tip, sees the cigarette catch fire. He breaths in the smoke, feels it in his mouth. He watches the flame of his lighter until it's hot in his hand, the flame standing yellow on blue. Smoke envelopes his face.

They're here too.

Oliver grabs the cigarette out of his mouth and looks behind him. He notices one of the cupboard doors is open slightly. The hair rises on his neck and with a rush of adrenaline he slams it shut.

"Fucking bastards!"

Holding his cigarette between his teeth, Oliver opens the offending cupboard and pulls the contents out onto the floor; soup cans, cracker boxes, spaghetti, tomato sauce all come crashing down. Once the cupboard is empty, Oliver peers into it. Nothing.

"Fucking SHIT!" he screams out loud. "I KNOW there's a camera in here!"

He picks up each item pulled from the cupboard and throws them back in, then slams the door shut.

John decides to swing by Elizabeth's house after finishing up at the supermarket. Her car is gone when he arrives. He climbs the ladder to Oliver's loft, grateful for daylight, and pushes open the door. A strong scent of Oliver and cigarettes greet him. He views the disorder and realizes he forgot a bag for Oliver's things. Searching for Oliver's duffel, he finally finds one behind the small wall near the TV. He places the duffel bag on the futon couch and begins to pick up a few of Oliver's clothes off the floor. He scans the surface of the TV table, the floor. The TV catches his eye. Bending close, he notices the mangled grate. A small shiver of dread runs up the back of his neck. He spots Oliver's knife lying next to the TV. John inspects the floor, sees the white dust, the pill bottle. He notices the chair standing in the middle of the loft and sees drywall slivers and chunky dust on it and the floor. He searches for the source. Avoiding the red and black paintings on the walls, his eyes move up to the crack in the ceiling. John's fear mounts as he notices the area where Oliver hacked at the crack in the ceiling.

"What the HELL?"

"Dad?" Peter's voice calls up from below, echoing in the garage.

John freezes. With an effort, he calls back. "I'll be right down, Pete, okay?"

Too late. He hears Peter climbing the ladder. "Damn!"

Peter hoists himself up into the loft. His face is flushed from the walk home from school, his eyes bright, the smile on his face infectious. He looks down the length of the loft.

"Where's Ollie?"

"I took him to my place for now, instead of keeping him in this." He gestures at the chaos around them. "Hey, shouldn't you be in school?" John looks at his watch. It's only 12:30.

"It's Tuesday. I don't have any afternoon classes until 2:00." Peter survey's the loft. "I haven't been up here for a while." His voice is quiet.

"Yeah," says John. "I don't think your mother or I really noticed the mess when we were up here." He picks up Oliver's knife from the TV table and pockets it.

Alarmed, Peter walks further into the room.

"Wow." He examines the paintings on the walls then walks to the futon couch and looks down at the white dust dirtying the floorboards. He quickly shoves his hair out of his face. It falls back, instantly. "What's this stuff on the floor?"

John glances over at Peter. "He must have crushed his pills."

John is riveted by Peter's alarmed expression.

"What's wrong with him anyway?" Peter asks.

"We're not sure."

"He's just so damned negative, Dad. He wasn't ever like this before, like, shutting everyone out and getting so angry about things. Our friends don't tell me but I know they don't want him around anymore. He's not who Ollie used to be."

Peter's grief and confusion silence John.

"What were those pills supposed to do anyway?"

"I'm not sure." John hears his own ignorance about what is happening to Oliver. And now there isn't even the semblance of a doctor to consult.

"He told me they only made him tired and dizzy," says Peter quietly. "I'm not surprised he didn't want to take them."

"He told you that?"

"Yeah, about a week ago."

John observes his sixteen-year-old; the light in Peter's eyes now gone, the smile erased.

John explains, "Ollie needs help, he needs a good doctor who will help him and medicine that he'll take."

"But he doesn't like taking medicine, Dad."

"I know, but what else are we going to do?" John's voice rises with frustration. "I don't know what else we can do. Maybe being at my house will help."

"Here." Peter hands John the empty Seroquel bottle. "And here." Peter picks up Oliver's dirty blacked framed glasses from the TV table and hands those to John also. "He may need these."

John pockets the pill bottle and hears it hit Oliver's knife inside his jacket pocket but puts the glasses inside an inner pocket for safety. He looks at Peter's face, anguish distorting his easy smile.

"You know, Pete, there are other illnesses that require daily medicine like diabetes and epilepsy and . . ."

"Yeah, but what is Ollie's illness? It's like he's crazy in the head!"

John sees how he stepped right into this. "No one seems to know yet. In the meantime, I'd better get back to my house and make sure he's all right."

"Can I come stay with you and Ollie?" Peter asks.

John busies himself with Oliver's duffel bag. "No, Pete. Not this time. You stay here and help out your mother and Wren." He stops packing the duffel to look up at Peter. "Actually, that would be a big help to me, and I'm not bullshitting you!"

Peter walks down the length of the loft and secures a foothold on the ladder. He looks back at his father as he leans over Oliver's duffel bag, stuffing in more dirty clothes.

"Okay?" John calls after him.

Peter doesn't answer but climbs down the ladder and walks to the house, Jack jumping up on him once he's inside the yard.

"Hi, Jack!" Peter roughs up Jack's silky coat. The dog follows him into the house.

John stops packing and finds a moment's refuge sitting on the futon couch. From this perspective he can see the gash in the TV, the paintings on the walls, the cuts in the ceiling. He holds his head in his hands, trying to still his panic. Schizophrenia. How could he ever tell Peter that his big brother might be schizophrenic? He just won't. Maybe Oliver isn't. He won't jump to any conclusions, especially because he isn't sure what schizophrenia is. He stands and grabs the duffel bag. Before lowering himself to the garage, he switches out the light and slams the loft door shut.

5

BROTHERS IN ARMS

Peter had his own special language when the boys were very little. When he spoke neither John or Elizabeth understood what it was he was trying to say. Oliver did. Oliver translated Peter's fast little words into English. When Peter needed something, Oliver would take his hand and they'd stand in front of Elizabeth. Their tiny hands made one fist. Oliver used to say, while holding Peter's hand, "We need . . ." anything from a Popsicle to a blanket.

Their cowlicks stood up straight on their heads, like antennae, streaming backward when they ran.

At only eighteen months apart, Oliver didn't want Peter at first, wanted Elizabeth to "put him back," but then couldn't do without him. They were two peas in one pod, two boys of one mind.

Elizabeth and Wren are home when Peter enters the back door. He can hear Elizabeth in the kitchen, can smell something cooking, probably spaghetti, or at least, he notices, something with garlic. He walks up the stairs, dragging his backpack full of books. The backpack bumps and scratches its way behind him. He opens his bedroom door and drops the backpack just inside.

Wren hears him from her adjoining room. "PETER!"

"Hi, Wren."

She stops in Peter's doorway. "Can I come in?"

"I guess so." Peter is standing in the middle of his room.

"What's wrong?"

"Nothing." Peter flops onto his bed.

"We're having spaghetti for dinner!"

"Big deal. We always have spaghetti."

The little girl frowns and sits in Peter's chair. She commences to swivel, only her toes touching the floor.

"What's wrong?"

"Nothing, Wren." Peter retrieves a small exercise ball from his bedside table and proceeds to squeeze it intensely.

"I don't believe you."

"Did you know that Ollie's gone?" Peter asks her.

"He is? Whattaya mean?"

"Dad took him to his house."

"Why?"

"Because he's crazy."

"No he's not!" she yells.

"Yes he is, Wren. He's fucking out of his mind!"

Wren sits very still, she stops swiveling in the chair. They glare at each other.

"I don't think so," Wren whispers.

"You mean you can't tell," Peter says.

Wren gets up and walks over to Peter, she stands over his head that is resting on the pillow. "What's gonna happen to him?"

"Who cares."

Wren's lower lip begins to tremble. "I do."

Peter throws the ball against the wall; it ricochets chaotically. "For fucks sake, Wren, you don't have to cry!"

"Aren't you gonna miss . . ."

"NO." Peter feels something break loose within, has to bite down—hard—to keep his tears trapped inside.

They both hear a soft knocking on Peter's door. Elizabeth peaks in. "Dinner's almost ready."

Wren uses their mother's interruption as a cue to leave. She runs past her mother, back to her room. Elizabeth lets her go.

"I heard you two talking," she cocks her head to one side.

"So?"

"You don't have to be rude."

Peter sits up.

Elizabeth steps further into Peter's room. "This is hard on all of us. I, for one, will miss him, but this may be better."

"Why?"

"Because maybe Dad can keep a closer eye on him." Elizabeth is afraid Peter will hear the uncertainty in her voice. She tries to sound hopeful, resorts to burying the issue. "So, in the meantime, let's eat."

Peter looks at her as though she'd uttered an obscenity. "I'm not hungry, Mom."

Elizabeth notices Peter's jaw, the muscles in his face are working hard, like John does when he's upset. "Okay, I'll save some for you. How much homework do you have?"

Peter hangs his head and wishes Oliver was here right now to handle their mother's intrusion. They could lock the door, smoke a bowl, and blow it out the window. They could laugh and talk their own language. Even though she understood the words, Elizabeth never did catch the meanings.

"Could you just leave me alone?" Peter asks.

Elizabeth pauses, ten beats. "I'll be downstairs." She walks away, making sure she closes the door behind her, quietly.

Elizabeth remembers driving the gang of five twelve- and thirteen-year-olds to the convenience store down the street. The five boys piled out of her Suburban, pushed through the double glass doors of the store as one gang and a few minutes later she saw them, through the window, lined up by the cash register, jostling each other, laughing, grinning, clutching their drinks and snacks. Elizabeth remembers wondering what would happen to each of those boys and now, looking back, she saw that she never thought, in a million years, that Oliver would be the first to crash and burn.

Oliver. Oliver's charming smile, his twinkling blue-gray eyes, his love of people. Oliver's teachers told Elizabeth that when they wanted to be severe with him, mostly always because he took socializing too far, they couldn't: Oliver smiled and without exception they forgot what they were going to say.

Even when Oliver was small, preschool small, he held forth with words and charm. His Montessori teachers would tell Elizabeth and John that Oliver needed reminding that he was supposed to be reading. He would sit, they told his parents, in the window on the carpeted ledge, and talk. And talk! And laugh his infectious laugh. The other students loved his talking. Frankly, the teachers loved Oliver and everything dear about him.

Throughout his preschool years and elementary school years Oliver was a model child. He was fun and considerate. He was cute, then handsome. It was in middle school that something began to take hold of him, not just the typical flip-flopping moods of youth but something sinister, something not Oliver.

John and Elizabeth didn't know what was normal. Oliver was their first born. They had no idea how an adolescent was supposed to act. When Oliver turned thirteen he fulfilled some of the horror stories they had heard about young adolescents—he was rude, had a bad temper, and a foul mouth. But still, he could be terrible one minute then their sweet, charming boy the next. By fifteen his temper was violent, his rudeness off the charts. Elizabeth began calling John at all times during the night and day. Oliver scared her. She didn't know how to handle the vagaries of his moods. There was no handling him.

"I'm sure you're exaggerating, Liz," John would say or "I'll talk to him. It couldn't be all that bad!"

Back then, when there were no doctors, no help was sought because John and Elizabeth didn't know they needed help yet. Back then, Elizabeth didn't want to get up in the morning. Wren was three, Peter eleven, and Oliver thirteen. Elizabeth found herself more and more frequently flying into rages; every morning she'd swear to herself that she wouldn't rage, but she did.

And Oliver. Oliver began obsessing over just about anything. When he decided he wanted something, his pestering became physical. He kicked and punched; one time punching the garage door when Elizabeth told him he couldn't have something he wanted. His knuckles bled from the punch. Elizabeth can't remember where Peter was during those days; maybe watching, standing to the side. Peter became invisible. When Oliver wasn't demanding attention, Wren took it all. There was nothing fair about it.

And Oliver had an awful time with homework. Elizabeth would find him in his room making fantastic things out of macrame or drawing instead of getting his homework done. It was then that Elizabeth took Oliver to see Dr. Oswald who classified Oliver as ADD and started him on Adderall.

Oliver is huddled in the teal armchair when John returns with the duffel bag. Oliver's face is turned into the back of the armchair and it seems he's studying the fabric. His legs are pulled up, feet tucked under. John call to him but gets no response. He drops the duffel and walks over to Oliver.

"Hey."

Oliver is rocking ever so slightly, his whole body is rigid and he won't look up at his father.

John takes in Oliver's frozen form. "C'mon, let's get you set up in your room."

No response.

"Ollie?" John bends down over Oliver's shoulder and peers into his son's face. He hears Oliver's shallow breathing. "Hey son, can you get up? Can you follow me?"

Slowly, Oliver moves his eyes and looks at John; there is no recognition, not even a flicker. Oliver's pupils are huge, black, deep. John is alarmed. He touches Oliver's shoulder, expecting him to react. Nothing.

John leaves the duffel bag and walks to the kitchen. He leans his back against the sink.

"Oh my God, please tell me what to do," he prays quietly. His gaze moves over to the cupboards opposite the sink. He sees something that looks like red sauce dripping from a partially open cupboard door. He opens the cupboard and discovers a broken spaghetti sauce jar and cans piled up near the back.

Oliver feels evil in this place. He unfolds himself from the high-backed chair, places his feet gingerly on the rug. His hands grip the arms of the chair as he slowly pushes himself up and off. His feet feel far away as he takes one step, then two, then another, heading to and out the front door. Once outside, late afternoon sun hits his face. He pulls his sunglasses out of his right jacket pocket, his watch cap out of his left. The sidewalk meets the stairs from John's house. Oliver feels good, considering. He feels as though he's escaped. He turns right. Up ahead he sees a man pulling a large, blue garbage can down his steep driveway on Oliver's side of the road. He thinks he hears John calling but isn't sure and besides, he knows he'll be in danger if he answers.

"What the hell?" John looks back into the living room and discovers that Oliver is no longer in the chair. He walks down the hall to Charlie's room. Nothing.

"Ollie!!!!" John yells and then goes out into the yard and yells again. Nothing. Desperation churns in the pit of his stomach. He wants to scream and pound the ground with his fists but he knows he has to keep it together.

Oliver crosses to the other side of the road. He can feel the man looking at him. He walks as slowly as possible to pass the man so the man won't notice him. But as soon as he's in line with him the man turns to ascend his driveway and disappears into his house.

John heads left, certain Oliver would walk up the steep street, not down. He calls and calls then stops to listen. He only hears the noise of a garbage can being dragged to the road but that noise is behind him. He peers between the houses on the street, hoping to see Oliver in the shadows. Nothing.

Oliver sits on the curb and stares. He takes a cigarette out of his shirt pocket, lights it, tips his head back to blow the smoke upward into the sky. He feels the scratch of grit under his sneakers, feels the hardness of the sidewalk on his rear.

John walks a few more blocks then heads back down past his house and finally spots Oliver. As he gets closer to Oliver he calls out. Oliver holds up his hand, palm toward John, gesturing for John to stop; John does not stop.

"Come on, Ollie," John says, trying to keep his voice steady. "Let's go back to the house."

"I can't," Oliver answers.

John is amazed to hear Oliver respond. "Why?"

"I have to stay here."

John tries a different approach. "What's going on?"

Oliver turns his head quickly and looks up at his father. John can't see through Oliver's sunglasses but can feel surprise emanating off him. "You know what's going on!"

"Really? What would that be?"

"I can't tell you," Oliver says with finality. He stays seated.

Oliver's mouth now seems sealed shut but John realizes that he was able to elicit a glimmer of response from him. He remembers what he read about schizophrenia in Dr. Oswald's office, among other things was "loss of contact with reality." There was certainly no mistake about that.

All of a sudden Oliver gets up. John moves in, puts his arm around Oliver's shoulders and turns him around. Oliver glances up at the windows above him in the houses that look down on this street. He sees someone peering from behind a curtain. Fear kindles rage.

"Fuck off," he mumbles but keeps his eyes on his sneakers.

John asks, "What did you say?"

Oliver glances at John's face. John sees Oliver's lips move, sees him forming words but can't figure out what he's saying.

Oliver looks back up at the window and sees the person still there. He can barely make out an expression but is sure of the individual's anger and hatred toward him. The night is almost dark and the suspicious, backlit figure casts a frightening shadow.

"What do they want?" Oliver whispers.

"I can't hear you," John says and leans closer to his son.

"I didn't say anything."

"Okay, Ollie, you're okay." He puts an arm around him.

John senses resistance, grief, heaviness through the arm around Oliver. He hears Oliver's sneakers dragging on the loose gravel. "We'll get home, have dinner, rest, okay?"

Oliver says nothing more, just drags his feet step after dragging step. He stops looking back and focuses on the ground, allowing John to guide him. They get to the steps that lead up to John's house but Oliver stops on the first step.

"Come on," John says.

Oliver's eyes travel up the stairs to the house. The stairs seem so very steep. He feels as though he's being asked to climb a mountain. He puts a foot on the bottom step and stops.

"Come on," John says again, still gently.

Oliver steps up one more step then one more then another until he's at the top. He looks at John and doesn't want John to say anything, which he doesn't. They both walk into the house.

"I'll make some dinner," John tells him. "Are you hungry?"

"No."

John wants to lecture Oliver about eating, about how thin, no, how gaunt Oliver is. But he doesn't say a word. He's beginning to understand what it is that has this hold on Oliver. It's huge, dark, and dangerous, and John knows he can't compete with it.

John crosses the living room and switches on the TV. Oliver is back in the teal armchair. Everything about him looks relaxed except for the fact that his feet and hands are pounding out an internal rhythm on the chair arms and rug. He looks at John, suspicion in his eyes, and stops moving. The sound of CNN fills the void between them.

"All right?" John points to the TV.

Oliver nods.

John steps into the kitchen and looks in the fridge for something to eat. Maybe, he thinks, he could entice Oliver with something like chips and dip. He pulls a bowl down from a cupboard, fills it with potato chips, fetches a smaller bowl for dip and scoops it out of the half empty jar he found in the fridge.

In the living room Oliver watches the news on TV for about five minutes before the terror begins.

Abruptly, he hears the announcer say his name. He sees this talking head point to him, tell him he's a fucker. Oliver puts his hands over his ears and closes his eyes. He can still hear the voice so he moves his head back and forth, which helps.

John carries the bowls into the living room, eager for at least a couple of hours of normalcy. If he and Oliver can sit together and watch TV then maybe Oliver will get some of the rest he so desperately needs.

Oliver is no longer semi-relaxed. He's leaning back in the chair, his head is moving back and forth, rapidly, his hands over his ears and his eyes are closed. John puts the bowls down, quickly, and calls to Oliver who doesn't respond. He can't think of anything that's changed except for the TV coming on. He turns it off then sits and waits, his elbows on his knees, hands in a fist in front of his mouth. Oliver isn't stopping. John stands and walks over to his son. He takes Oliver's wrists and pulls his hands away from his ears, saying, as he does this, "Ollie, it's okay now. The TV is off."

Oliver's eyes open, meet John's.

"It's okay," John tells him again. "We don't need the TV on."

Oliver's arms relax even though his expression remains frightened.

"Look, I brought something easy to eat," John says. "Do you want some?"

Could be poison.

Oliver shakes his head.

It takes all John's resolve to not badger Oliver into eating. Even if it's chips and dip. John is hungry and wants something a bit more substantial but he's not willing to leave Oliver for a second. Not now. The two of them sit together, quietly, Oliver in the teal chair, John on the couch. The only noises are the infrequent sounds of cars passing the house and the little quarrels of birds bedding down for the night outside the tall window. John tries some chips and dip but the crunching is too loud so he stops. He doesn't know what to do.

It's still only around 9:00 and too early for bed. He stands and crosses the living room to the bookcase. He chooses a book and returns to the couch. He's afraid to say anything to Oliver in case his voice or words set him off. He's afraid to leave him in case he decides to run off again. John sits quietly and reads, but not really. He can't keep his mind on what he's reading. Perhaps it isn't too early for bed.

"Ollie?"

No answer.

"How about we go to bed. It's been a very long day."

"No." Oliver rises from the teal chair and walks into the kitchen and out the back door. He sits on the edge of the patio and has a smoke.

John is right behind him and sits next to him, but not too close.

If I go to bed, thinks Oliver, he'll leave me alone.

"I'll go to bed," Oliver says out loud. He stubs out his cigarette on the cement pad.

Both John and Oliver stand up and enter the house.

"I put your things in your room. You can unpack."

Oliver goes into his room, his at-his-father's-house room. He picks up his duffel bag and dumps everything out of it onto the floor. He kicks the pile around a bit to spread it out then walks across the hall to the bathroom. He doesn't close the door to use the toilet. He remembers he and Peter talking about how convenient it was at their father's house because there weren't any females around. He feels himself smile a small smile from the memory.

Peter thinks you're crazy.

Oliver feels his smile fade. He walks out of the bathroom and begins to walk a circle around from the hall to the kitchen to the living room to the hall to the kitchen to the living room. He passes the bedrooms each time he walks through the hall and sees John changing into a t-shirt and long pajama pants. He keeps walking, faster and faster.

John notices Oliver walking but doesn't say a word. He hears Oliver mumbling to himself as he walks, sees Oliver hunched over, his hands stuffed into the pockets of his jeans.

He begins to count each time Oliver passes his door. He sits on his bed, the bedside lamp on and a book on his knees, outside the covers. The book is open but, as before, he isn't able to read. He suddenly hears the back door open and slam shut. John jumps off his bed and follows Oliver outside.

He's sitting, as before, on the edge of the patio, smoking. His limbs are restless. He takes long drags on his cigarette and blows them out, hard, switching the cigarette from hand to hand, his legs bouncing with energy, his head nodding as to an internal tune.

He looks manic, John thinks. He's not going to be able to sleep, he thinks, which means I won't be sleeping either. He doesn't think that making any suggestions to Oliver will help matters. Oliver isn't amenable to suggestions anyway. John feels that as long as he can stay close to him he has a chance of making sure Oliver doesn't run off again or hurt himself somehow. But then what? Where was he to go for help?

Oliver gets up and walks around the yard. He looks up at all the lines on the telephone poles as though he's trying to figure something out. He looks at John's roof. John hears Oliver speaking again but can't figure out what it is he's saying.

Just as abruptly as he walked out of the house Oliver runs back inside. He runs into the hall bathroom, slams the door shut and locks it. John, even though he's right behind Oliver, is not aware of where Oliver has gone to inside the house.

Oliver stands in front of the mirror in the bathroom. He reaches out with his right index finger and touches the cold glass. He pushes, his finger bends at the first joint, turning the tip white. The glass does not yield. He stares at his reflection until he's dizzy.

You're a wimp; you can't even kill yourself!

Oliver places his right palm on the mirror above his face.

He then pulls back his hand away from the mirror, resolve coursing through his body, makes a fist, and punches the glass as hard as he can.

6

SEVEN YEARS BAD LUCK

John hears Oliver's scream and runs to the bathroom. He kicks the locked door open so hard that it hits the toilet and bounces back, almost hitting John.

Oliver is standing, holding his arm. He seems calm as he watches the blood drip off his fist.

Christ's blood is different from everyone else's blood, the alien blood, the Real-World blood . . .

Thin shards of glass have pierced his skin between his knuckles. The mirror is shattered in the pattern of a spider web. Big and small fragments of glass litter the sink, the counter, and floor. John reaches for Oliver who backs up against the wall. His pupils are huge and he's whispering to himself. Then he starts to scream, "FU-U-U-U-U-U-CK" the word loud and drawn out, while he holds the wrist of his bloody fist.

John grabs at Oliver but he pushes his father out of the way and runs to the kitchen, John right behind him. Oliver stops and stares at the closed cabinet door where he'd thrown the jar of spaghetti sauce.

John, keeping his voice calm, says, "Ollie, let's get you to the hospital."

Oliver lunges forward and opens the cupboard to see the red sauce and broken glass.

It's all broken...

Oliver looks at his bloody fist.

John finally breaks. "OLLIE!!!" he screams, "STOP!" His chest tightens, his heart pounds.

Oliver looks at his father, his expression haunted, the high energy abruptly drained away.

John puts his arm around Oliver and steers him outside to his car. Oliver drags his feet, his eyes on his bleeding fist, his other hand still holding the wrist of his bloody hand.

John drives fast, not caring whether he's stopped or not. They pull up to the hospital's emergency entrance. John turns off the engine and tells Oliver to "stay" while he runs around the car to help him out. Together they walk in through the electric doors, whooshing open then closing behind them.

"I need help!" yells John when they get to reception.

A nurse appears. "What seems to be the problem?"

"My son, he has glass in his hand."

"Here, I'll take him. Here's a wheelchair, right here." The nurse hovers.

"No, no, you can't take him, trust me."

"You have to deal with paperwork first, sir."

"I know that but you don't understand."

"Yes, I'll take him into that room," she points, "and begin cleaning his hand and you can take care of the paperwork first."

John's fear breaks through and he yells at the nurse, "I HAVE TO STAY WITH HIM! Please, you don't understand!"

"Sir, sir, calm down. You can put your son in this wheelchair and keep him next to you while you handle the paperwork, okay? Will that work?" Her tone was now soft and reassuring.

"Yes, yes, I'll do that."

John wheels Oliver over to a cubicle where a coordinator sits. He starts the process with her.

Oliver holds his wounded hand and looks around, cringing slightly, his pupils still huge, his demeanor frightened.

"How old is your son?" the cubicle woman asks.

"He turned eighteen last June."

"Then he must sign himself in."

"Excuse me?"

"If he's eighteen he's an adult and has to sign himself in."

"But he has glass in his hand, how is he supposed to do THAT!?" Panic overtakes John whose own hands are shaking. "You don't get it," he tells her, "he can't."

"I'm just telling you like it is. He could sign with his left hand."

John stares at her. "You're kidding, right?"

"No, I'm not."

"He can't even understand what it is he's signing."

"You can understand for him, I can give you that. Why don't you fill out the forms, then ask your son to sign when you're finished, okay?"

John glances at Oliver who's staring at the woman.

"All right. We'll try that."

John looks at the forms and groans. He glances at the huge white clock on the wall and discovers it's now almost ten. He turns his chair to face Oliver. "Hey, how're you doing?"

Oliver, very slowly, turns his face to look at John and says nothing.

"He has finally brought me to a place where the people in white will transport me into the Real World." Oliver whispers to himself.

You must maintain a thought pattern or they won't transport you.

Oliver can see that all the people are busy getting ready to kill him; they're conspiring to capture him. It's so obvious!

They're going to take your blood and then they'll know for sure how evil you are.

"Ollie?" asks John.

Oliver is not there.

"I'll just get this filled out and then the doctor will get the glass out of your hand, okay?"

Oliver only continues to stare at John. He sits motionless and whispers; what it is he's whispering John can't tell. Oliver's wounded hand is elevated by his other hand holding on to it. Blood has dripped down to his elbow and dried; the fist of his left hand is also covered in blood.

John looks through his wallet for their insurance card. He leans sideways into the desk to keep an eye on Oliver while he fills in the interminable forms.

"Hey," John looks at Oliver. "You need to do something for me so we can get that glass out of your hand." He holds a pen out to Oliver who stares at the pen, then looks at his hand. The shards of glass are still sticking out. He looks up at John. He does not recognize him.

"I need you to sign on this line, sign your name. This says they'll take care of you if you sign here."

Oliver looks at John again, terror in his eyes.

"It's okay, really. We need to get that glass out of your hand and we can't do it at home."

Oliver looks through the back of the cubicle at all the people in the emergency room, the white curtains, and central desk and lights above the examining rooms, and waiting wheelchairs. People are walking and talking and he can see that they're watching him, watching to see what he's going to do. Nausea overtakes him and he begins to slip sideways in the wheelchair. John puts his hand on Oliver's shoulder. He's holding the clipboard that's holding the form.

"Come on, it's all right, you can lie down as soon as you sign this damned paper."

Oliver takes the pen in his wounded hand.

"You can use your left hand if that hurts too much," says John.

Oliver stares, not comprehending what John is telling him. John shows Oliver which line to sign.

"Both your names, Oliver Moore."

Oliver looks at his father, baffled.

"Oliver Moore, that's what they want."

"Will they let me into the Real World?"

Silence.

They'll let you in if you sign.

The shards of glass move as he shapes the letters of his name.

John pushes Oliver into the emergency room. The nurse is waiting and leads the way to a small room to the left of the central desk.

"Would you like to lie down?" she asks Oliver.

"Yes, he would," answers John. "How long will it take to see a doctor?"

"Not too long."

Both John and the nurse help Oliver out of the wheelchair and onto the examination table. His body is rigid and cold.

"I'll fetch some warm blankets." The nurse bustles out of the room.

"That was a brave thing you did, signing yourself in," John tells him after the nurse left.

John sees that Oliver is moving his lips and staring up at the ceiling. He moves closer to Oliver and tries to hear what he's saying.

"Blue square, red circle, blue circle, red square, blue square, red circle, blue circle, red square . . ."

"Oliver, look at me." John feels himself go cold, numb. "Ollie, look at me," he says louder. "Come on, you can look at me can't you?"

The nurse comes back into the room and proceeds to cover Oliver with blankets. He continues reciting the tiles near the ceiling.

"The doctor will be with you very soon," she tells John.

"Thank you." John sits in the chair next to Oliver and taps mindlessly on the stainless-steel tray next to him.

Oliver hears the tapping and knows it's code; code for keeping him out of the Real World. He doesn't know who this man is, the one who's tapping, but he knows he's dangerous.

Oliver's bloody hand is lying next to him under the blanket as though he can't feel it. John worries that the glass shards will catch on the blanket. He stands and pulls it back and carefully picks up the wounded hand and places it on Oliver's stomach, on top of the blanket. Oliver's wounded arm is as stiff as wood and he resists John's touch.

"Mr. Moore?"

"Yes?"

"I'm Doctor Farrell."

The doctor, a man in his thirties, short and blond, stocky, holds out his hand to John who shakes it. The nurse is two steps behind the doctor and begins setting up the stainless-steel tray with bandages and instruments.

"What have we here? Young man? You hurt yourself?" Dr. Farrell walks over to Oliver and glances at the bloody hand.

Oliver continues to stare at the ceiling, continues to recite the tiles. The doctor glances at John. John shakes his head. The doctor looks at the form on the clipboard in his hand.

"Oliver? Can you look at me?"

Oliver speeds up his recitation, louder.

"I see here that he's taking Seroquel," Dr. Farrell addresses John. "How long has he been taking it?"

"Well, I just discovered that he hasn't been taking it. He's become much worse over the past few days. I don't know what to do . . ." John feels his throat tighten. "He's been staying in a loft above the garage, and we haven't checked on him as much as we should have. I just don't know what to do! Do you think, doctor, that he could be schizophrenic?"

Dr. Farrell puts his hand on John's shoulder. "Let's get his hand cleaned up then see where to go from there. How did this happen? Was he with you?"

"Yes, he punched a mirror."

"I see. Do you know why?"

"No."

Dr. Farrell turns his attention to Oliver.

"Oliver, let me look at this hand." He picks up Oliver's wounded hand that's stiff with tension.

"You can relax. I'm going to start by extracting these pieces of glass, all right?"

Oliver stops reciting "red square blue circle" and glances at the doctor. "No." He pulls his hand away.

"It'll be okay."

"NO!!" Oliver screams and launches himself off the examination table. He lunges at the doctor who sidesteps him.

John stands frozen to one spot.

"Call Security!" Dr. Farrell barks at the nurse.

Oliver grabs at the metal tray and all the instruments go flying. He looks crazed, his pupils are completely dilated making his eyes look black. He uses the tray as a shield and comes at the doctor again.

Dr. Farrell meets Oliver head on and holds the tray with all his strength. Oliver drops the tray and grabs the doctor's coat, spins him and slams him up against the wall. John steps in and holds on to the back of Oliver, trying to pull him off the doctor. Two uniformed security guards run in, pulling on latex gloves. They tackle Oliver; he pulls away from them, his shirt ripping in the process.

Dr. Farrell yells, "HALDOL!" to the nurse who is already there with a full syringe.

"I'm not who you think I am!!" Oliver backs up to the wall, his face flushed, his eyes black glass, feral.

The doctor grabs the syringe and approaches Oliver who focuses on the needle. The security guards lunge at Oliver again, they grab his torso. Oliver knees one of the guards in the stomach.

"Get him DOWN!" the older security guard barks. "Down on his stomach!" They kick his legs out from under him and sit on him. Dr. Farrell joins them on Oliver's legs. The younger guard kneels on Oliver's shoulders, making it impossible for him to turn his head; his face is smashed into the linoleum.

They're trying to keep you out of the Real World! They work for the devil!

Oliver keeps screaming, struggles with both his arms, trying to pull them both free. He tries to reach around one of the guards, tries to reach the gun on the guard's hip. The guard grabs Oliver's arm and pulls it above his head.

"Please don't! I don't want to die, no, please, THEY'RE HERE. THEY'LL KILL ME!"

"What are you DOING?" John screams and pulls on Dr. Farrell's shoulder.

The doctor looks around at John. "We have no choice!!"

"Oh my God! Please DON'T HURT HIM! Christ! You're breaking his NECK!"

"No, they're not. I have to have him still so I can give him this shot!"

"What is it?"

Dr. Farrell doesn't answer. He's kneeling now on Oliver's thrashing legs. "There!" He sinks the needle in through Oliver's jeans. "He'll calm way down in about five minutes."

"Oh God!" Oliver is yelling. "Oh God! Help me. PLEASE GOD HELP ME!"

A patient is standing in the doorway where Oliver is looking, unable as he is to look anywhere else. The patient in the doorway is old, his hair is white and he's leaning on a cane. John sees him. He sees Oliver screaming to this man, calling him God. Then the old man disappears down the hallway.

"NO! DON'T LEAVE ME, GOD! PLEASE HELP ME!"

Oliver's body begins to visibly relax.

"Can't you get off him now?" pleads John.

"We're just making sure, sir," says one of the guards. "These guys have more strength than you think!"

"What do you mean by 'these guys'"? asks John.

The security guard looks over at Dr. Farrell.

"What he means," says the doctor, "is that psychotic strength can be more than normal strength."

"Why?"

"Probably the adrenaline. Who's been taking care of your son?"

"Dr. Ritter."

Dr. Farrell shakes his head.

"What?" John asks.

"Ritter should have monitored Oliver more closely. Seroquel is a heavy-duty drug. His condition, as you have just seen, is completely deteriorated."

A nurse brings a gurney into the room. The doctor helps the security guards lift Oliver, settling him on his back, arms at his sides, feet together.

John stands by Oliver's head for a moment, leaning down to whisper to him that everything will be okay. Oliver does not respond. He now seems unconscious.

The nurse walks in with clean instruments for doctoring Oliver's hand. Dr. Farrell unfolds the sterile towel as the nurse swabs the wounded hand with antiseptic.

Dr. Farrell continues: "Oliver is a very sick boy. Even if he hadn't signed himself in, I'm afraid I would have had to commit him anyway. As it stands now I'm going to recommend he be committed to the psychiatric ward, which is a locked facility, for observation and the beginning of treatment. Since he's eighteen, I'll sign papers for an involuntary commitment. You and your wife will want to look into facilities that are longer term for him, private or state facilities. Unfortunately, psychiatric care comes down to your wallet, just like everything else, but psychiatric care seems to be the most difficult to find and the most expensive to pay for.

"I'm not a psychiatrist. Oliver will be cared for by our in-house psychiatrist and his staff."

John backs up into a chair. He puts his face into his hands. "I don't know what to do, what to think, where to turn."

"It's best to get this straight from the get-go, Mr. Moore. Your son will have a better chance at a normal life if you know what you're dealing with."

"And what is that?"

"I'm not a psychiatrist and hesitate to diagnose. Oliver's symptoms could indicate several psychotic illnesses. We'll know more after observation, and I'll leave that to the resident psychiatrist."

"Can't you take a stab at it?"

"No. I don't want to do that. Okay, that's it for the hand!" Dr. Farrell stands, rips off his latex gloves, and turns to the nurse.

"We'll take him over. Thanks."

He turns to John. "Let's wheel him over to the ward." He sees the confusion and defeat on John's face and demeanor. "He'll be all right. It's a long road ahead, but he'll be fine in the end."

"You think?"

"Ritter should have told you more."

"He told us Oliver has ADD and is possibly bipolar."

"And he prescribed Seroquel for that?"

"Yes. And just so you know, I fired him."

"That's a good start!"

Oliver's right hand is now bandaged. They push him on the gurney out of the ER and in and out of corridors, over a glassed-in breezeway to an ominous door. They stop. John notices a camera outside the door looking down on them and a small, meshed window imbedded in the door at face level. Dr. Farrell pushes a red buzzer button.

"Once we know that Oliver is settled, I'll call the resident psychiatrist. His name is Dr. Bruce, and I'll pass my notes on to him. He'll confer with me, speak to you and your wife, and examine Oliver, okay?"

"Okay."

A nurse opens the door and they push Oliver through.

"I have to tell you one more thing, Mr. Moore." Dr. Farrell goes on. "I'll inform the staff here to keep Oliver in restraints until Dr. Bruce sees him."

"What does that mean?"

"That means his hands and feet will be buckled down in leather straps."

John goes pale.

"It's for his own safety, as I'm sure you can understand after seeing him in the exam room."

"Yes, if you have to. I don't really have much of a say."

"No, you don't. I'm sorry."

"I do have one question, Doctor."

"Yes?"

"How often do you see this in patients who come into the ER?"

"Probably more times than you would think!"

"What does that mean?" John asks.

"It means that mental illness, severe mental illness of the type we're dealing with here, effects 2 to 5 percent of the population, globally. That's a lot of people but you don't hear much about it if you're not affected. You'll hear about it now! Educate yourself. Dr. Bruce will get you started. And Oliver is fortunate to have such a loving father."

"And mother. I don't know if I should be the one to tell you this but Oliver's mother is an alcoholic, possibly bipolar. We're divorced."

"Well then, you've been around the block! You already know a lot about all this and that mental illness runs in families, right? That information about your wife is extremely valuable. Make sure you tell Dr. Bruce. No, I'll tell him."

John is stunned. What he's been through with Elizabeth he wouldn't call "going around the block."

Dr. Farrell, his hand on the door, was saying goodbye and good luck and good all of it. He seemed quite jovial as soon as John revealed some knowledge of mental illness. But what did John really know? He wasn't sure what he'd said except for the fact, the dirty big fact, that Elizabeth is a drunk and possibly bipolar. He didn't even know that bipolar disorder could be accompanied by psychosis like he'd just seen in Oliver.

Dr. Farrell opens the door when the lock buzzes and steps out into the hall, into freedom.

"Thank you, Doctor," says John. He turns from the door, hearing it slam locked behind him. Panic rises in his throat.

He stands in the psychiatric ward hall, alone. He knows he has to call Elizabeth, that he's waited much too long. He walks to the nurses' desk and tells her he wants to see Oliver.

"I'll take you," she says.

He follows her. They walk to room #2. She stands aside, gesturing to John to enter. He does. He's not prepared for what he sees.

Oliver is lying on a bed, his hands and feet each buckled into leather straps. His face is turned toward the door. John stops mid-stride, his legs go weak and he feels a wave of nausea.

"Why?" is all he can utter as he turns to the nurse who stands next to him.

"For his safety," she says to his stricken face.

"But . . ." John steps closer to Oliver. "Oh my God! I don't want him in these restraints!"

"I'm sorry, but we don't know what to expect when he wakes up. I thought Dr. Farrell explained that to you."

"Yes." John sits in the chair next to Oliver. He puts his face in his hands. "This can't be happening."

"I'll leave you." The nurse walks out of the room.

John stares at Oliver, whose eyes are glazed but open. John smooths Oliver's hair, he touches his cheek. He notices the beginning of a large bruise on his jaw from the security guard smashing his face into the linoleum. He holds Oliver's hand, noticing how young it is, how dirty with chewed fingernails it is. John puts his forehead on Oliver's hand and breaks into sobs.

Oliver closes his eyes, just a quarter open. A long string of drool escapes the corner of his mouth. John stands, kisses Oliver on the forehead, his hand lingering on Oliver's shoulder. He leaves the room.

7

THE WHITE COAT
PHENOMENON

John drives downtown to Elizabeth's coffeehouse. He had called to make sure she was there and not at home. Fortunately, one of her staff had told him she was in. Parking is usually dicey on Main St., but he found a space right away.

He walks in, nervous about what he would say and about how he would say it and how she would take it. She was downstairs in the dungeon of the basement office. He enters, knocking on the doorframe at the same time.

Elizabeth looks up. "John."

"Hi."

"What's wrong?"

"Ollie."

"Ollie? What's wrong with him? Isn't he with you? What happened?"

John, mortified, lets out one huge sob, almost a hiccup.

"Ollie is in the hospital."

"What? Where? Is he okay now? Can I go to him?" She came out from behind her desk.

"Lizzy. Wait! He's not okay. They said he had a psychotic break. He's in restraints!"

"What?" Elizabeth walks over to John and stands close.

"They shot him up with a drug called Haldol, and he's catatonic but still in restraints. They won't take him out of the restraints!"

John is sobbing, not caring if she sees him so broken, not caring about anything but the image of his son tied down to a bed in a psychiatric ward.

"What happened? What made this happen?"

"He wasn't taking his medication, Liz." John's grief swiftly turns to anger. "How could you let this happen? How could you not see? HOW COULD YOU? Wasn't it bad enough to put him above the garage? Did you ever climb the ladder to see what he was doing up there?" John yells at her.

Elizabeth walks across her office and closes the door.

"Your fucking customers, they come first, right?"

"Fuck YOU, John! Of course they don't come first! They pay the bills." She stands in front of John, challenging him. "How about Dr. Ritter?"

"Yes, he fucked up. He should have been monitoring Ollie much more closely than he did. There's a Dr. Bruce who's probably with Ollie right now. He's the resident psychiatrist. He'll be taking over. This Dr. Farrell who tended to Ollie at first in the emergency room isn't a psychiatrist."

"The emergency room?"

"Ollie punched the mirror in his bathroom. He had glass embedded in his hand so I took him to the hospital, then he attacked the doctor and security guards took him down."

"WHAT?"

"And they shot him with a drug called Haldol and now he's been COMMITTED, involuntary because he's eighteen. And he screamed and pleaded and . . ."

"And you couldn't call me?"

"Jesus, LIZ! When?" John is pacing around her office like a caged beast.

"When should I have called you? Between the bloody hand and the attack on the doctor or maybe I should have let them wheel him to the psych ward without me while I found a phone? I forgot my cell phone; there was blood everywhere! Is it possible that you can think of someone besides yourself? Then it was too late to call you, close to midnight by the time he settled, and I know you're pretty much out of it by then."

"I'm going up there to the hospital." Elizabeth stands, determined, as she and John glower at each other.

"I'll check in with my office then go back up there. And oh! Dr. Farrell told me that mental illness runs in families."

Elizabeth stares at John. Her fists are clenched, her fingernails pressing into her palms. "So, this is MY fault? You know it runs in families, John. You've known that for a long time!"

"You took him to that quack counselor who wanted to let him loose in the woods to 'find his way' and you took him to Ritter who, now it turns out, wasn't much better than the quack! Two quacks and now THIS! You should have known better!"

Elizabeth droops with each mental blow until she has to lean against her desk. John looks at her, his glare gone but still, the shaking of his head, the familiar disapproval she knows so well.

"I'm sorry. I'm so sorry. I thought . . ."

The phone on her desk rings. John leaves. She picks up the phone.

"Yes, you can order through us. We only sell Montana Coffee Traders beans."

Silence.

"Yes, you can order directly through them too. I'll give you that number . . . ready? It's 406-862-7633."

Silence.

"You're welcome. Bye."

Elizabeth hangs up. The call tips her energy back just enough to stand straight although she dreads having to walk up the stairs from her basement office to the coffeehouse above. Inevitably, a customer would stop her to ask a question or chat or a friend would be up there who she simply couldn't avoid. She was once told that if she didn't want to be stopped, no one stopped her, that she had an extremely effective "leave me alone" persona. Right now she feels too fragile to talk to anyone in the coffeehouse. She climbs the stairs then quickly walks through the coffeehouse, sunglasses on, and car keys in her hands.

Elizabeth arrives at the hospital. She's holding her breath, unaware that her shoulders are tight, her lips are almost white with tension. The elderly lady at the main hospital desk gives her poor directions to the Psychiatric Unit. Elizabeth gets the distinct impression that the old bag gave her a condescending, pitying look.

Fuck you, she thinks.

After turning wrong twice she finally arrives at the locked door and presses the button below the square speaker. She, too, notices the camera above the door.

"Yes, may I help you?" a female voice crackles through the speaker.

"I'm here to see my son, Oliver Moore." Elizabeth looks into the camera, trying to look sweet and motherly.

The door buzzes loudly and Elizabeth pulls open the door. She walks in and the door swooshes shut behind her with a bang and a clack. The locked ward door leads into a wide carpeted hallway. On the left an open nurses' station behind a high, wooden counter. Five heavy doors cover the wall opposite the nurses' station. Fluorescent lights, mounted in rectangular plastic boxes, form a line down the center of the hall ceiling. She notices a plexiglass covered "Pull In Emergency Only" fire valve set in the wall. Then she sees a nurse walking out of the door behind the nurses' station. She looks like a fairly mild-mannered woman, certainly not a cold-blooded Nurse Ratchet.

"May I see Oliver Moore? I'm his mother," Elizabeth whispers.

"Yes, certainly, but I must warn you that Oliver is in restraints because of his episode, and I have to leave him that way until Dr. Bruce does his rounds, which should be soon."

"Okay." Elizabeth doesn't really know what else to say. She follows the nurse into Oliver's room, then she stops dead in her tracks. Oliver is awake, staring at the ceiling. She sees his two hands strapped to his sides, one bandaged, his ankles strapped to the end of the bed.

"Oh my God," she whispers and thinks of John sobbing. "Oh my God, Ollie, I'm so sorry!" She walks closer.

Oliver continues to stare at the ceiling. She touches his arm. His eyes turn to look at her, his expression slowly gaining recognition. He turns his head to her now, his bruised cheek showing itself. His eyes fill with tears. She climbs onto the bed and holds him as best as she can. She's crying now too.

"It's okay, Mom," Oliver whispers.

She only weeps harder.

There's a knock. Elizabeth looks at the doorway and sees a man in a white coat who's walking toward the bed. She sits up quickly, keeping her hand on Oliver's arm.

"Dr. Bruce?"

"Yes. You're Oliver's mother?"

"Yes, I'm Elizabeth Moore."

"It's good to meet you." He extends his hand and Elizabeth accepts it with her left, the hand that's not touching Oliver.

"So, young man, I hear you had a rough night. I'm . . ."

"Would you please remove these shackles before you begin? Don't you think it's a bit humiliating to talk to someone while you're tied down?"

"Yes, of course, but I must tell you that these restraints were for his own good."

"I know, but he's fine now, don't you think so?"

"No, Mrs. Moore, he's not fine now. He's still feeling the residuals from the Haldol he was given last night."

Elizabeth doesn't want to believe this doctor even though she knows, deep inside, that John is right about her choice of doctors in the recent past. John never knew about the naturopath who gave Oliver drops of different types of oils, declaring that Oliver's symptoms all stemmed from anger—anger that was stored in his liver from John and Elizabeth's divorce. Dr. Ritter had been consulted before and after the naturopath. The Seroquel had seemed to take the edge off Oliver's crazy behavior, that is, when he took it. Then Oliver himself had told her he wanted a more natural treatment, that the Seroquel made him too sleepy. So, that's what they went for. But they didn't tell John. Before the Seroquel, Oliver looked emaciated from not eating and had huge black smears under his eyes from not sleeping. The naturopathic treatment had no effect. He stopped eating again, stopped sleeping again.

Dr. Bruce unbuckles the restraints. Oliver immediately pulls his legs and arms up into himself, a fetal position, as though a strong rubber band had been waiting for his release. His bandaged hand is now tucked under his head, the most protected position. Elizabeth stands, then sits further down on the bed and puts her hand on Oliver's calf.

Just watch and wait and watch and wait and watch and wait and watch and wait and watch and wait . . .

Oliver is mesmerized by a hairline fracture in the plaster wall and doesn't hear Dr. Bruce and Elizabeth talking through the repetitive words crowding his mind.

"We won't know his diagnosis for quite a while," Dr. Bruce says. "These illnesses tend to mock each other in the beginning. I'm afraid we can't keep Oliver here very long. This unit is primarily a crisis unit where we can stabilize a patient so they can then move on to either home or a full-care institution."

Elizabeth flinches. "Institution?" Her eyes grow wide with fright.

"I know. It's a word fraught with all sorts of prejudice but, for example, our State Mental Hospital at Warm Springs, employs some excellent doctors."

Elizabeth shakes her head, over and over, tears flowing down her cheeks. "Could this . . . could what's happening to Ollie . . . have anything to do with me probably being bipolar?" She has to ask. Fear and dread choking her words.

"Yes, it probably does."

Elizabeth doubles over in physical pain, taking her hand off Oliver's leg to hug her stomach.

"But wait. Mrs. Moore, wait. You wouldn't be bipolar unless someone a generation or two above you were also mentally ill."

"So, I shouldn't have had children, right? I caused this suffering."

Dr. Bruce shakes his head. "This is not your fault, Mrs. Moore. Do you blame your mother for having you?"

"No." Elizabeth's answer is small, tiny. "But I did take Ollie to two doctors who didn't know what they were doing."

"Did you know what you were dealing with?"

"No, but I should have."

"Have you ever been psychotic?" Dr. Bruce asks her.

"I don't know."

"Then how would you know what you were dealing with?"

"I just feel I should have known."

"What medications are you on?"

"I don't take medications; they make me feel like a zombie."

"Well, the zombie feeling would diminish quite quickly if you gave the medications another try." Dr. Bruce's voice turns business-like. "Oliver needs a chance at the right medications, a chance at a normal life."

Elizabeth raises her head, wipes her eyes with her hands. "Okay, yes, this isn't about me. I'm sorry."

"There's nothing to be sorry about, Mrs. Moore. Mental illness is a tough row to hoe. Your entire family is affected and there is an inherited gene. This won't be easy for Oliver or any of you. For now, I'm starting Oliver on Zyprexa. It's in pill form. He wasn't taking the Seroquel anyway so we'll eliminate that one. The nurse will dispense the Zyprexa to Oliver once a day. This drug can help with mania or psychosis so at this point, when we don't really know what Oliver's diagnosis is, it's a good beginning. We'll watch him carefully. There are a few other patients on this ward he will interact with. He'll be safe here with us. We don't want to continue the Haldol unless he doesn't respond to Zyprexa or any other anti-psychotics. Haldol is an extremely powerful drug with severe side effects if taken for long periods of time. We like to keep it in reserve."

Dr. Bruce looks at Oliver's chart. "I see here you have two other children. A sixteen-year-old son and an eight-year-old daughter. This will be hard on them. Keep the dialogue open. Do you have a therapist or a psychopharmacologist in town?"

"No."

"You need to find someone."

"Okay."

"This process will be stressful for all of you. Mental illness isn't particularly amenable to stress."

"Yes, I do know that. Thank you."

Dr. Bruce stepped over to Oliver who was still following the hairline crack up and down and up and down.

"Oliver?" Dr. Bruce called to him. "Oliver? My name is Dr. Bruce, and I'm here to speak with you."

Oliver keeps staring at the hairline fracture.

"Oliver?" Dr. Bruce makes his voice a bit louder and steps into Oliver's line of sight."

Suddenly, Oliver's bandaged hand shoots out from under his head. He looks around at the two of them, his eyes distant, suspicious. He looks at Dr. Bruce without seeing him.

"I'm not here to hurt you, Oliver," says Dr. Bruce. "I only want to ask what you remember from last night, from before you ended up in here?"

The people in white are evil and they know you're good. Even if you're the one who's evil and they're good, they're still keeping you out of the Real World.

Dr. Bruce notices that Oliver is becoming agitated. "What do you remember, Oliver?"

Oliver sees that Dr. Bruce's lips seem overly red and ready to devour him and his thoughts.

"Do you remember punching a mirror in your father's house?"

"Yes," Oliver says under his breath.

"Excuse me? I didn't hear you."

"Yes," Oliver says a bit louder.

"That's why your hand is bandaged."

Oliver looks at Dr. Bruce. Huge pupils, dead expression. Later in the afternoon, while writing his report, Dr. Bruce describes Oliver's expression as his affect, his type of affect as "flat." This, besides the psychotic break, were the first clues to Oliver's illness; that his illness was one of a few psychotic illnesses.

"Oliver, you need to keep that bandage on. The nurse will change it once a day while you're with us. She'll also be giving you one pill once a day to help you feel better."

Oliver stares at Dr. Bruce while thinking, I feel fine but I'll feel better when you leave and take this woman with you.

"I hope you sleep as much as you can," Dr. Bruce tells him. "I'll see you later." He turns to Elizabeth. "May I see you outside?"

"Of course. Just let me say goodbye." Elizabeth moves up to Oliver's head. "Goodbye, sweetie. I'll try to come back later this evening, okay?"

Oliver moves only his eyes to look at her. She's not wearing any white so she must be from the Real World. He hears her say, "I love you" and notices she's crying.

He closes his eyes, the eyes that are still preventing him from seeing the Real World.

8

THE ELEMENT OF BOOZE

Elizabeth drives home slowly. She is stunned into silence, her thoughts only for Oliver. She has a hard time concentrating on the road. Oliver as the shy, sweet young boy. Oliver as the boisterous young man full of joy and energy. Oliver, around sixteen, beginning to be the difficult son, the son who hurled insults, who punched walls and doors, who grabbed hold of her once, when it was she who went wild after he called her a bitch. In these past months when he was living above the garage she would hear the back door open and slam shut. She'd sit, afraid, not knowing what mood he was bringing into the house.

She pulled into the driveway feeling somewhat better but thankful Peter and Wren were not yet home from school. After setting down her purse, taking off her shoes, and making herself yet another cup of coffee, Elizabeth went into the downstairs bathroom, stood in front of the sink and looked in the mirror. Her dark, shoulder-length hair was unbrushed, her make-up smudged from crying, her cheeks pale. But it was her eyes that gave her pause. Unusually greenish-blue and clear, her eyes were foreign to her; they were darker and sadder than she was allowing herself to feel. She checked her watch. It was already 2:00 p.m., almost time to pick up Wren from school.

"What am I going to say to her?" she asked herself. "What am I going to say to Peter?" She walks up the stairs, slowly, feeling heavy, and changes out of her work clothes. She sits on her bed after dressing in old jeans and a loose blue sweater. She picks up her phone and calls John, knowing full well she's leaning on him more than he might want. Because of this morning, when John was so blaming and critical of her, she's unsure of herself and how to present Oliver's illness to Wren and Peter.

The US Geological Survey office where John works put her through to his office.

"This is John," he answers in his usual fashion.

"It's me," she tells him.

"What's up?"

His blunt question gets her heart racing but she takes the plunge.

"How should we tell Peter and Wren about Ollie?"

John's answer surprises her. "Together. I think we should tell them together."

Elizabeth feels such relief that her legs go weak and she sits down on one of the wooden kitchen chairs and starts to cry all over again, silently this time.

"When do you want to come over?" she asks, a slight tremble in her voice.

"I was going to see Ollie before five. I could come over after that."

"Okay. I have taco fixings if you'd like to join us."

"We'll see. Don't worry about me, Lizzy, and I'm sorry. That was uncalled for at your office."

"Thanks."

"Bye." Elizabeth hangs up, wondering, gratefully, what had come over John in the past hour or so. She searches her cupboards for taco mix, shells, the fridge for sour cream, tomatoes, guacamole, cheddar, and the freezer for ground beef. She sighs, relieved to find everything. She has an hour before Wren's school lets out so she pulls out a frying pan to brown the frozen meat, feeling great satisfaction as each layer browns and she scrapes to reveal pink underneath until all but a nub of frozen meat is left. She drains the grease from the beef down her drain knowing she shouldn't and puts a cup of water and a packet of seasoning in. Done. Elizabeth prefers to cook alone because, basically, she doesn't like to cook.

When Elizabeth and John were first married she'd cooked every day—breakfast and dinner and packed lunches for him and the boys when they began school. By the time Wren was school age Elizabeth bought school lunches for her and ordered pizza at least once a week for dinner. She knew this cooking aversion was pathetic but simply couldn't help herself. When she looked back on her glorious kitchen past it was a mystery to her. The only answer was that now, in the present, she spent her time making a living instead of being a full-time mom.

The end had come when Wren was two. Elizabeth and John had made it through the long infant nights together; he had even agreed to allow Wren into their bed for easy nursing. When the boys nursed, John and Elizabeth listened to those doctors who discouraged nursing in the parental bed. Eight years had made a world of difference as far as nursing attitudes were concerned. Everything with Wren was easier. But then Elizabeth's moods began fluctuating to such a degree that John became alarmed.

Elizabeth sought help from a local medical doctor and was given a drug called Imipramine that gave her night sweats and nightmares and then another drug called Wellbutrin, which didn't work for her. Then she began to drink alcohol to take the edge off the manic moods and try to bring a little cheer to the depressions. She would pour rum into her Coke before she got off work and be fairly friendly by the time she arrived back home. And she refused to continue medication, saying it made her feel sick.

When she was steady, all would be calm for a while. John, if he were asked, would have said he preferred the beginnings of her manic mood; she'd be fun, sparkling and productive, make great meals, and be super-sexual. This mood was her favorite also unless she got too high, and then it was torture in its own way. When manic she mostly felt pretty good, got things done, and had plenty of energy, but when the high was too intense she felt a pressure inside and would turn irritable, would pace back and forth, would talk very loud, yell at nothing, scream at the children. And this high was always followed by a low, a bone-crushing depression that made taking care of the children and a husband walking torture.

Then, in one of her manic episodes, Elizabeth stepped over the line. She had an affair. Someone tipped off John; he was devastated but told her he'd stick it out if she gave up the guy. She already had given him up but the mania and booze kept her defiant and pushed her back out the door into the excitement of partying. Her jaws were locked to telling John the truth. By the time the mania passed it was too late. John was gone and had filed for divorce.

Underneath her defiance she didn't blame him. If anything, shame was the overpowering emotion. Shame and guilt and the understanding that she wasn't worthy of John or anyone else really. Wren was two, the boys ten and twelve. Elizabeth attended AA meetings during the divorce proceedings that lasted almost a year. When their divorce was final she decided she didn't need meetings or sobriety anymore, that her excessive drinking was only because of her problems with John. And now he was gone.

9

THE UNHOLY TRINITY

John pulls into the hospital parking lot, locks his car, and sprints across the parking lot into the hospital. He walks fast to the locked ward, announces himself, pushes the door open as it buzzes and finds Oliver standing at the nurses' station, a small white paper cup in his left hand. Oliver's jeans are riding low on his hips, a blue t-shirt is tucked in halfway. He's barefoot and standing on the cuffs of his pants.

"Hi, Dad!"

Oliver's old smile is there, his crazy wavy hair is there, everything about him is there, again. Except now there is a bruise on his face and his right hand is bandaged. John's knees go weak with relief.

"Hey! You're up!" John walks up to his son and gives him a hug. "How're you feeling?"

"I'm walking! I have to take this pill . . . wait a sec . . ." Oliver tips the white cup back and downs the pill without any water. John wants to ask him to open his mouth to make sure the pill really went down but suppresses his urge toward suspicion. The nurse hands Oliver a small bottle of water.

"No thanks, I already swallowed it."

"Come on, water will help it dissolve," the nurse prompts.

"All right." Oliver downs the whole bottle of water, crumples the white cup and hands both to the nurse who gives him a wide smile.

"Your son has been quite lively this past hour or so," the nurse tells John.

"Is that so?" says John, suspecting mania.

Oliver walks to a narrow corridor, John following. This corridor leads to a cement room, barred windows, and cement benches jutting out of the walls.

"I can smoke in here!"

"Oh, great."

Oliver lights up. "Can you imagine if there was nowhere to smoke?"

John laughs. "No, Ollie, I can't! I'm so happy to see you so well!"

"Dr. Bruce came to talk to me again and said we'll try this new medication, the stuff I just took." Oliver sits on one of the cement benches, his back to the wall. He pulls his legs up, his bare toes hang off the edge and he holds his legs with his arms, crossed. A sitting fetal position.

"How's the hand?"

"It's okay. The nurse changed my bandage a little while ago. It doesn't really hurt."

Oliver's energy seems to drop a bit at the mention of his hand. John tries to think of something to get his energy back up. He thinks of mentioning home, of work, of the weather, of how good it is that Oliver is here, in the hospital, but he rejects all these options. Basically, he can't think of anything to say to Oliver that wouldn't risk putting him into a darker mood. Pins and needles. Familiar pins and needles. Eggshells.

Get your glasses!

Oliver jumps. He puts his feet on the floor and sits up straight. "Dad?"

"Yes?"

"Could you bring me my glasses?"

"Well sure, but don't you want new contacts?"

"No. My glasses would be better."

"Sure, I can bring your glasses." John is pleased there's something he can do for Oliver and he remembers Peter handing him the glasses from off the TV table in the loft. Peter knew Ollie would need his glasses. That brother thing. John wondered if he should let Peter visit Oliver in here. He'd store that thought away and discuss it with Elizabeth.

Oliver's vision, without lenses, is near-sighted so his father's face is soft from where he sits. He can't see the worry lines on John's forehead or the smile lines around John's eyes, the cleft in his chin, or even the gentleness in his expression. Oliver thinks the Real World, the one he can see without his contacts, is easier than the one he saw before and he likes it that way. He doesn't know why he needs his glasses particularly.

"Oh well."

"What?" asks John.

"Nothing." Oliver finishes his smoke and stands. "Let's go back. I'll show you the Common Room."

"Okay." John is relieved to get out of this dungeon. They walk back down the corridor, turning left toward the Common Room but stop before entering. Two patients, a young man and a woman sit on simple wooden chairs. A table sits in front of them, an unopened pack of cards the only object on the table, a huge white board hangs on the wall behind them. On the other wall, a built-in bookcase with magazines and random paperback novels; most shelves are empty.

John and Oliver stand and look into the room that seems clean and relatively comfortable. The patients sitting there do not look welcoming; their stares are intimidating.

John looks at his watch. It was almost time to go see Peter and Wren. He has just one question for Oliver. He puts his arm around Oliver's shoulders and leads him away from the Common Room. "How would you feel about Peter visiting you here?"

"Here?" Oliver freezes. "No way. Why would you want to do that? He and his friends already think I'm a freak, Dad. Why would you?"

"Ollie, it's okay. It won't happen. It was stupid of me, I'm sorry. I shouldn't have asked. Peter loves you, you know. He doesn't think you're a freak!"

"Yeah, right."

"He's your brother, and he loves you. You're his big brother."

"Well, he lucked out on that didn't he?"

"Let's drop it." John is kicking himself for bringing up this subject. "Listen, I have to go, but I'll see you tomorrow. I love you." He gives Oliver a big hug and kisses him on the forehead.

Now look what you did!

"I didn't do anything!" Oliver says, his teeth clenched, eyes looking down at the rug.

"Hey, I'm not blaming you for anything," says John. He puts his arm around Oliver again. "Don't worry, you don't have to do anything you don't want to. No big deal, really."

Oliver looks at him, distant.

John thinks, What happened? Where did he go? He doesn't know how to extricate himself from here, from Oliver and this god-awful place. He wants Oliver to revert back to how he was when John walked in only a short while ago. He wants to take back his question about Peter visiting. But better than all these wishes would be Oliver whole again, and all this mess revealed as a nightmare.

Oliver sees John to the door. After the door slams shut he feels relieved, torn, nothing. Nothing is how he wants to feel so that's how it is. He walks back to the Common Room and enters.

The two patients are sitting as they were but are no longer staring at the door. The young man, who looks to Oliver as though he's in his early twenties, sits with his head in his hands. His hair is long and dirty, his hands almost black with grime, and his clothes are torn and filthy. He's wearing leather-soled shoes without laces. Oliver watches as this young man exhales a long sigh then looks up at Oliver who can't avert his eyes quickly enough. They make eye contact and the young man smiles a slow smile.

"You part of the zoo or an observer?" he asks.

"Both." Oliver tells him.

The young man laughs. "Good answer. What's your name? Mine's Jude."

"Mine's Oliver."

"That woman there, the one with the burned face . . . I call her The Woman With The Burned Face. That's easy, huh?"

Oliver laughs. "Yeah, it is. What's her other name, do you know?"

"No idea. She doesn't talk. To me anyway. Maybe she'd tell you."

"I don't feel like asking."

"Well okay! Why are you here anyway?"

"I guess 'cause I'm crazy."

"The cops are why I'm here."

"Why?"

Jude begins patting his shirt pockets then his pants pockets and finds a crumpled soft pack of GVS cigarettes. "Wanna smoke?"

"Yeah, thanks."

They each take a bench in the cement room and smoke quietly for a few minutes. Oliver's feet are cold and he can't remember where he's left his shoes. He sits cross-legged and rubs one foot then the other. He can't remember how long he's been in the clothes he's wearing. He glances over at Jude and finds Jude is staring at him. He feels the hair on the back of his neck stand up but can't look away.

"Do you believe in God?" Jude asks him.

Be very careful.

If Oliver gives the wrong answer he doesn't know what Jude may do. Looking at Jude from Oliver's vantage point, the light coming through the barred window behind and above Jude, he looks like a crazy street person. His wild hair, his torn clothes, everything, even the musty scent that surrounds him.

"I believe in how I understand Him," Oliver says.

"How do you understand Him?"

"Well, I think God lives on this planet with us. I think Jesus does too." Oliver hopes this will satisfy Jude.

Jude's eyes get wide and he breaks into a smile. "Hey, man, would you believe me if I told you I've SEEN God?"

Oliver remembers God from the Emergency Room.

"Yes, I believe you." He doesn't trust Jude but maybe, just maybe, he's one of them, like Oliver is.

"Have you ever seen Jesus?"

"Not yet."

"I've got some theories that I'd love to chart on that whiteboard. Do you want to?" Jude is excited and is putting out his smoke. "Let's go."

Oliver stubs out his cigarette and follows Jude to the Common Room.

Peter and Greg had been friends since they were in diapers. Their mothers had been friends until a falling out that lasted even up until today but the boys were still friends. Greg jumped in Peter's Acura after school and they drove out to Cottonwood Canyon where they could smoke reefer and not get caught. The air was still cool in the late afternoons but the boys didn't want the smell of dope inside the car so they got out and hiked up a bit to an outcropping, one of their favorite places to sit.

And they sat, passing the joint back and forth for about ten minutes, not saying a word to each other. The lights of town were blinking on, getting brighter as the sun's light faded over the western mountain range. Peter flicked the roach and pulled his blue windbreaker tighter around himself. Greg wore a heavier fleece; he stuffed his hand in the pockets and broke the silence by chattering his teeth.

"Yeah," Peter says. "I can't wait for summer and climbing and mountain biking!"

"Rad," Greg says. "I hope I can get a new bike this year. Mine's too small."

"Yeah . . . and we've only got about two months of school left!"

Greg doesn't know how to broach the subject of Oliver. He was in the Acura the night Oliver acted out so destructively. He feels it heavy on his friend and, actually, on himself as well. Oliver has been a big brother to him, too, over the years. The three of them have palled around for as long as Greg can remember. Greg is an only child so his sibling interaction was relegated to Oliver and Peter, beginning when he and Peter were only one and a half years old. Both he and Peter are blond and, back when they were little, and with one of their moms out in town, strangers just assumed they were twins. They did everything together and Oliver was there, lording over them, being the big guy. Now, with something drastic going on with Oliver, Greg wants to talk to Peter about it but some instinct is keeping his mouth shut. He's never felt shut out of the Moore family before, but now . . .

Peter looks at his watch. "We better go." He jumps down from the outcropping. "I don't want to miss yet another crappy dinner at Mom's house."

Greg doesn't move. "Peter." It's all he can make come out of his mouth.

"What?" Peter's hair is blowing around his head and into his mouth. He keeps his eyes on the path, on the distant lights, everywhere but on Greg.

Greg makes a huge physical effort and pushes his question out. "How's Ollie?"

Peter answers much too quickly for this childhood friend to take him seriously. "I don't know, man. Not good."

"No, but, I mean, this is Ollie we're talking about."

"I don't want to talk about him."

"I mean," Greg pushes on, "is Ollie sick?"

"You know what, man? Ollie is MY brother and I don't know what's wrong with him except that he's crazy, but when I find out anything else you'll be the first to know, okay? Can we drop it now? Can we talk about something else?"

Greg runs his hand across his short hair and down over his face. If he didn't know Peter like he did, his feelings would be hurt but, he got what he wanted and he knew Peter would keep his word. Peter always kept his word.

"Okay. Thanks."

"Oh, and Ollie is living with our dad right now. You should see the mess up in the loft! Holy! Ollie had crushed all his pills with his shoes and the yellow powder is all over the floor. I should take a straw up there and snort it."

"Jesus, man, you don't even know what it is!"

"I'm kidding."

The boys chat all the way to Greg's home. As Greg exits the car Peter bends into the passenger side, his hair hanging long onto the passenger seat and says, "Thanks, man."

Greg knows what he means and gives him a thumbs up.

The whiteboard looks as though it hasn't been properly cleaned for a very long time. Jude asks the nurse for paper towels and cleaner and he and Oliver clean every dot, line, and smudge off what is to be their workspace. While they work, Jude prompts Oliver to tell him what he knows about Christ and by facing the whiteboard, by rubbing with his face so close to the surface and not having to look at Jude, Oliver tells him what he hasn't been able to tell anyone.

"Well," Oliver says, "Christ's blood is different from our blood because he's the Son of God and God is an alien and alien blood is different from our blood and our blood is the blood of the Real World." Oliver steals a glance at Jude who catches the look.

"Hey, it's good, man, keep going. I'm with you, man."

Oliver sprays more cleaner on his paper towel. He can feel The Woman With The Burned Face behind him but when he looks over his shoulder she's not looking at him. He continues.

"But Christ was human so he had our blood but he didn't live in the Real World because he was good and the Real World is evil, and I'm evil and these people are trying . . ."

"Wait. I need more paper towels, hang on." Jude walks out of the Common Room to the nurses' station and comes right back. "Okay, man, continue. You were saying . . ."

"Yeah, I was saying that I'm evil and these people are trying to use, analyze, kill, because they know I have Christ's blood but Christ was evil. I'm one of his angels and they don't want any angels because angels are evil too so it's hard to tell them apart but these people, the woman in white and the man who says he's my father want to kill me because they're evil really; I'm good. See?"

"Perfectly. You're lucky to have gotten away with almost losing your hand."

Oliver glances at his bandaged hand. "What?"

"Never mind."

Maybe he doesn't really understand.

The whiteboard is clean. Jude lines up the colors: red, blue, yellow, green, then he walks the blue one over to the whiteboard.

"Now, the way I see it is we're here, on Earth." Jude's filthy fingers hold the blue marker and draws a fairly accurate round Earth. "Get me a dollar, okay?" he directs.

"What?" asks Oliver.

"I want to show you something very important."

Oliver digs in his pocket and actually finds a dollar. He's surprised but gives it to Jude.

"Look at this, man, look at those arrows in the eagle claw; those represent the fact that aliens came to Earth and completely overthrew the Native Americans."

As Jude was telling Oliver this fact he was drawing an arrow on the board. Oliver thought he went a bit overboard on the feathers but, besides that, it made sense. The arrow pointed into the heavens where the Native Americans went; everyone knew that. Oliver watched as Jude crumpled up the dollar and shoved it into his left front pocket; he didn't care.

"Now, listen to this. It's very important. After the aliens came and went the first time, Jesus came to Earth because he'd been where the Native Americans went and there wasn't any room left. God owned all these planets." Jude picked up all the colors and drew round planets, one each color to make total of four. "God's favorite is the blue, which is why we're here but we weren't always here. We used to be on the green planet and we didn't have bodies. You follow?"

Oliver nods. He's holding his hand that has begun to throb since Jude mentioned it. He keeps pushing the bandage to feel his hand inside. He wonders why his hand is bandaged but can't remember, which worries him.

Suddenly, Jude is saying something Oliver finds especially compelling and he listens with renewed interest.

"You know that Bible story about Jesus coming back to life? What really happened was God, who is an alien, found Jesus in that cave and He drained the human blood from him and infused him with alien blood so Jesus was able to rise up and disappear into the heavens with God. People like us, who are able to know these things, are suspect. The humans don't want us to talk about these things and they give us drugs and lock us up so we can't spread the word! The REAL word." Jude's eyes are blazing with the truth. "Now, look at this . . ." He begins drawing arrows all over the board, arrows pointing to each planet, arrows intersecting the green and blue planets, circles with arrow points defining the yellow and red planets.

"If you die on this planet, on planet Earth, your soul will end up on the red planet because you still have Christ's human blood. If you can figure out how to get a transfusion of God's blood you get to go to the green planet where no one has a body and that's great!" Jude looks at Oliver. "You see?"

Oliver can almost taste Jude's energy. He feels it in his chest, on his skin. He wishes he wasn't barefoot as his feet feel vulnerable to this overpowering energy in front of him.

"Yes, I see," he's breathless now.

"Can I tell you a secret?"

"Sure."

"There are a few wise men out there who know how to change your blood without a transfusion but you have to find them, you have to know where to look for them."

"Have you ever found one?" Oliver leans forward, anticipating this great secret.

"I found one once, in Seattle, but I didn't know he was a wise man until I was already gone, hitching my way out here."

"Who told you?"

"Who told me what?"

"That he was a wise man."

"I figured it out on my own."

"Why did you come out here?"

"He told me that God was in the mountains east of Washington. I just kept going until I hit the Rockies."

"Did you find God?"

"Whattaya think? I'm in here aren't I?"

"What did you used to be?" Oliver dares to ask.

"I was my mother's son," Jude says without hesitation.

"But I mean, what did you do for money?"

"I was a brain surgeon," Jude says and laughs.

"No, really," Oliver persists.

"You don't take a hint too good, do you?"

"I'm sorry."

"I was a ward of the State of Washington until I decided not to be anymore. Okay? I find money when I need it except now they have me locked up, and I'm not sure where they'll send me next. I prefer freedom. I prefer panhandling and all the people I meet out there. People like us, who know God."

Oliver thinks, So he IS a street person!

The nurse, dressed all in white today, appears at the Common Room door. "It's time for medication, Jude." She looks at the board and doesn't register anything on her stony face. Then she turns to The Woman With The Burned Face. "Do you want to come with me?"

The Woman With The Burned Face stares at the nurse, she doesn't even blink. She brings her right hand up to her mouth and begins to suck her middle finger, like she's flipping off the nurse, but not really. Oliver looks over to Jude to see if he's seeing this and he's laughing, silently.

"I'll bring you your medication," says the nurse and turns away from the door and The Woman With The Burned Face. "You took yours earlier, Oliver."

"I know."

"Let's go," says Jude.

The two of them walk to the nurses' station, Jude almost hopping with energy. The nurse gives Jude a white cup with pills and a bottle of water. They start walking back to the Common Room. Oliver can't help but notice that Jude has many more pills in his cup than he had earlier.

Jude tips back his head and pours the pills into his mouth. "Yummy, yummy!"

"That sounds like Murphy from One Flew Over the Cuckoo's Nest," says Oliver.

"Give the boy a gold star!" yells Jude. "God, I love that movie! See, that movie is all about freedom. Everything should be about freedom but, sadly, it's not. What are they giving you?"

"I don't know."

"Hey, man. You should always know. Go ask that nurse. She has to tell you. You have a right to know."

Oliver goes back to the nurses' station. "Ma'am. Would you please tell me what's the name of the medication you just gave me?"

"Certainly, Oliver. It's Zyprexa."

"Thank you. And I need to see my hand pretty soon."

The nurse gives him a curious look then tells him she'd be fine with changing the dressing right before bedtime but not before.

"What time is bedtime?" Oliver wants to know.

"Eight o'clock."

"And what time is it now?"

"There's a clock right there," the nurse says and points to a wall clock behind her.

"Thank you."

Six-thirty.

Oliver really wants to find his shoes but he goes back to the Common Room to tell Jude about his medication. He finds him sitting near The Woman With The Burned Face.

"It's Zyprexa."

"That's an antipsychotic, heavy duty; stopped working for me a long time ago."

"What do they have you on?"

"Well, let's see, what are they trying now. Don't forget that I just got here too. We have lithium, a lot of lithium, Risperdal, Celexa." He pauses and looks down at his feet. His energy seems to have run out suddenly and it couldn't have been from the medication as Jude just took it. "They want to add a few grains of Haldol but I refused it."

Oliver has one question to ask before he goes to look for his shoes. "Why do you take the medication, Jude? I mean if you want to be free and all?"

Jude looks up at Oliver. His eyes are filled with the pain of everything he is: a homeless, family-less young man with too much time to tread before he dies.

"I take the medication because it gives me the means to be in their world long enough to figure out how to escape again. And . . ." Jude smiles a huge smile revealing missing teeth, "the food's not bad."

10

LOCKED OUT OF REALITY

Peter drives home from Greg's house feeling better than he has for a while now. He decides to drop by his dad's house to see Oliver and see what they're having for dinner since John is a much better cook than Elizabeth. He pulls the Acura into John's driveway but doesn't see John's car and notices that all the lights are off except for the porch light. He gets a weird feeling between his shoulder blades and jumps back into the car and races to his mom's house. Dad's SUV is there, in Elizabeth's driveway.

"Hey!" he says when he sees both his parents in the kitchen.

The house is warm and smells of tacos, one of his favorites. John and Elizabeth are sitting at the table but something's not right. Peter doesn't want to know. He wants this moment to be safe and real. "Where's Wren?"

"She's upstairs putting on a costume. She wants to do a dance for us but was waiting for you to get home," says John. "Where have you been?"

Peter feels guilty and hopes his eyes don't give him away.

"Greg and I drove up Cottonwood Canyon just for something to do."

"Uh-huh," says Elizabeth but decides to let it go. "Have a lot of homework?"

"Not too much." Then, to get the spotlight off him, Peter asks, "Dad, why are you here?"

"Your mother and I want to have a family meeting about Ollie so we thought doing it over dinner would be a good idea."

"Oh."

Elizabeth stands and calls up the stairs. "Wren! Peter's home! Come on down and give us a show!"

They hear a tiny voice from upstairs, yelling, as was their family habit although John doesn't care for it.

"Okay! I'm coming!"

They next hear the clack of high heels coming down the wood stairs accompanied by the clicking sounds of Jack's toenails coming down with her. She reaches the ground floor, scuttles to the kitchen doorway, and peers around into the kitchen to see who was there.

"Hey, you little weasel!" says Peter, his smile lighting up his thin face.

Wren comes into the kitchen. "You have to be in the living room," she says.

Elizabeth begins to say something but Peter interrupts her, "Sure!" he says and gets up, walks across the hall to the living room and sits down on the couch. Elizabeth and John follow.

"Now," says Wren to Peter, "will you say 'ta-da' and then I'll come in?"

"Certainly I will," Peter says, relishing this reprieve from the family meeting.

Once everyone is settled, Peter yells, "Okay!"

Wren, out in the hall, says, "I'm ready!"

Peter stands and cheers her in with a loud "TA-DA!"

Wren enters the living room on tiptoes inside her sequined high heels, spinning and spinning, her many layered pink chiffon skirt twirling around her. Her arms are up over her head like a ballerina and she has a huge smile on her little face. Her curly hair spins out from her head and she's singing a tiny tune, more to herself than to them. Her spinning takes her over to the bookcase then she stops, bends over, says, "Whew," and pants dramatically and spins all the way back to the hall.

Elizabeth, John, and Peter clap and shout and whistle. Wren comes back in and bows, says thank you, then it's all over.

"Let's eat," says Elizabeth.

Peter notices that his mother doesn't have her usual drink in her hand. He thinks it must be for his dad's benefit, noting she certainly doesn't make that effort for him or Wren. Or Oliver.

The four of them sit at the kitchen table and scarf up the tacos. There's little talk while they're eating. Only near the end, when they're stuffed, does John clear his throat and, pushing back his chair, he seems to be ready to talk. Peter wishes he could run or hold his hands over his ears, but he can't. He's going to have to hear about Ollie and it's not going to be good. He knows Oliver isn't at Dad's house and Oliver isn't here so this must be about where Oliver is. That's the part he doesn't want to hear.

John can't eat another taco. He can't think of anything he can do to postpone this terrible moment. He isn't prepared for the emotional fallout that will most likely happen once he's said the words he's going to say. He's exhausted, drained, afraid. He doesn't know how he can impart to his family at least a little confidence in the future for Ollie. He doesn't know how any of this works. How Ollie—who is eighteen and supposed to be going out into the world right now and who should be beginning to make his way in college, work, love—will ever find a meaningful way to live. John doesn't have a clue about a future for Ollie or, for that matter, a future for his family.

"It's obvious that Ollie is missing," he begins. "He is. But he's safe." John takes a deep breath. "Very late last night I had to take Ollie to the hospital. He wasn't well. He punched the mirror in his bathroom."

John looks over at Peter who's staring at the table.

"He cut his hand and the doctors fixed that. What they couldn't fix," John stops, licks his lips, wipes his eyes quickly with the back of his sleeve. "What they couldn't fix was Ollie's illness. The doctor told me that Ollie had to stay there, that it wouldn't be safe to let him be out. Safe for Ollie. So, he's up there, at the hospital. Safe." John glances at Peter who is still staring at the table.

"Pete?" John asks, "Are you okay?"

Abruptly, Peter pushes away from the table. He walks out of the room, down the hall and out the back door. They hear the door slam shut.

John puts his head in his hands. "I better go after him."

"Daddy?" Wren looks so small pushed up to the table as she is. "Can I go see Ollie?"

John's heart sinks. Everything about this little girl slays him but mostly her innocence. "I don't think so, Baby Girl, not right now anyway, right, Mommy?" John catches Elizabeth's expression of utter turmoil.

"Yes, Wren. Daddy's right. Not right now." Elizabeth closes her eyes and takes a deep sigh. "Thank you, John."

"Yes." John doesn't want to leave Wren but he needs to see where Peter went. He's pretty sure he went up to the loft. "Will you girls be okay? I'm just going to check on Peter."

"We'll be fine," Elizabeth answers.

"Yeah, we'll be fine," pipes Wren. She pats the top of Jack's head who sits close to her waiting for clean-up and scraps.

John walks down the hall and out the back door to the garage. The garage light is on, the ladder is down. He climbs the ladder and opens the door. Peter is sitting on the futon couch, watching the street below. He doesn't turn his face to John but speaks. "How many hours do you think Ollie spent staring at the street?"

John feels a kick to his gut. "I don't know."

"Why does this have to happen to us?"

"Lots of things happen to lots of people. This is an illness like any other."

"Oh, come on, Dad. It's not like any other. You know that."

Peter finally turns his head to see John. "You don't think I'm stupid do you?"

"Definitely not." John chuckles. "I guess it's impossible to hide much."

"Yeah. So don't give that 'it's like any other.' This illness makes people crazy! It's not like Ollie is up in the hospital with a broken leg or something. If he had a broken leg he'd have visitors and everyone would sign his cast and we'd joke and laugh. He could have even gone to his graduation. But this . . ."

John looks at this son who is so bright and sensitive and funny and prays he doesn't get sick too. That would be too much, he thinks, then says, "This is a big, huge thing that's happening to all of us. Our Ollie isn't here and it's going to take a lot of work on our parts, and Ollie's, to bring him back. He's going to need to know that we all love and care about him getting better. This is hard on him."

"Can I visit him?"

"Well, actually, I asked him that and he said that you and your friends think he's a freak and he doesn't want you to see him in the locked ward."

"It's LOCKED?"

"Do you really think he'd stay there if it wasn't?"

Peter laughs. "No, I guess not."

"I think Ollie is mortified by his situation. He doesn't know how he's going to get better. He might not even be thinking about getting better because he's so caught up in his strange thinking."

"Do you think he'd feel better if I visited him anyway?"

John let's out a deep sigh. "I have no idea. Let me think about it, okay? Sometimes, the way he looks at me, I'm not sure if he even knows who I am. He's pretty gone."

"Can I come live with you, Dad?" Peter interrupts. "I have a car and it doesn't matter if you're not home. I could go back and forth."

John realizes instantly that he's worried about Wren without Peter there to temper the atmosphere when Elizabeth is drinking. But that's not Peter's problem, it's Elizabeth's, and his.

"Let me think about that one too, Pete. I'm sorry I'm not full of answers this evening. It's like everything is upside down all of a sudden."

"Yeah." Peter smiles. "It would be cool though, don't you think?"

"Of course it would be cool; I love having you around! Let me think about it, okay?"

"Okay."

11

THE UNCOMMON ROOM

Oliver finds his sneakers. They're sitting quietly and neatly, the toes slightly under his bed. He's been given a room at the end of the hall, a couple of doors down from the restraints room, room #2. Oliver has no idea who positioned his sneakers in such a way but he doesn't mind. Both Elizabeth and John have neglected to bring him clean clothes so he's still wearing the white t-shirt with blood and the jeans he wore into the Emergency Room so very long ago it seems.

He tugs his sneakers on to his bare feet and walks back to the Common Room. Jude has pulled a chair over to the whiteboard and is staring intently at all the circles and arrows he drew earlier. Oliver feels Jude's energy, feels how much lower it is now that his medication has most likely had time to work. He decides he prefers Jude the way he was before the medication dulled him and wonders how long it will take to wear off.

Oliver sits down on one of the chairs and picks up the deck of cards from the table. He takes them out of the box and begins to shuffle. Neither Jude nor The Woman With The Burned Face flinch at the sound. Then The Woman With The Burned Face heaves up her large self to a standing position and stumps over to the refrigerator. She bends down and opens the door, taking out a red juice cup. She stumps back to her chair, sits and proceeds, painfully slow, to tear off the foil on top of the juice cup. Oliver and Jude both watch her intently. Oliver notices how the burned side of her face is melted, is red and black and dripping flesh, like lava when it's hardened. She raises the cup to her lips and begins to drink. Almost half of what she is drinking dribbles out of the burned side of her mouth. Oliver instantaneously sees that what The Woman With The Burned Face is drinking is not juice but blood, that blood is dripping out of her mouth and onto her blouse.

She's going to kill you after she's finished with the blood.

"Can you see that?" Oliver whispers to Jude.

"What?"

"Can you see what she's drinking?"

"No, man, she's just an ugly fuck drinking juice."

"No no no no NO! It's BLOOD!" Oliver screams and backs out of the Common Room into the hall. He sees the plexiglass covered "Pull in Emergency Only" fire valve and runs over to it. He pulls the metal ring that's set into the plexiglass cover. The plexiglass breaks. He takes hold of the handle inside the box and pulls. Nothing happens. Oliver runs back to the Common Room and picks up a chair. He walks back into the hall and proceeds to the nurses' station with the chair in front of him as a weapon. The nurse runs past Oliver and locks the Common Room door. Oliver drops the chair and dashes to the Common Room. Finding it locked, Jude and The Woman With The Burned Face behind it, he prostrates himself—an attitude of supplication. This close to the speckled carpet, he sees an eye in the pattern.

It's God.

He begins to pray.

"Dear God, now that I can see You and You can see me, please make this go away, please help me get away from these people, please, please, give me a transfusion so I can join You, please make all this go away."

Oliver feels heavy hands on his upper arms and finds himself pulled up into a standing position. He sees the security guards who smashed him into the floor the day before, one on each side of him. They are breathing heavily as though they just ran somewhere.

Oliver screams, "I just saw GOD, AGAIN!"

Then, to the guards, "But it's HER you should be taking, not ME!" Oliver tries to pull away from the two men who only hold him harder.

The security guards drag him into room #2.

Oliver sees the bed with the leather straps and struggles to get away.

"Come on, son," says the nurse. She's holding a syringe.

"NO! Please NO! You don't understand! She's dangerous! She's going to kill all of us!"

And drink our blood.

"Why can't you see? Locking the door won't help! I'm TELLING YOU!"

Oliver looks at the three people hovering over him. The security guards have strong-armed him onto the bed and managed to wrangle one wrist into restraints. Oliver's legs are kicking as hard as he can, his other arm is attempting to hit at whatever it can.

"NO," he's yelling. "I don't want to do this. Where did you come from? Who are you? LEAVE ME ALONE!"

The nurse asks the security guards to at least keep Oliver's one arm from flailing around, and she'll give him the shot in his restrained arm.

Oliver grabs hold of the headboard and won't let go.

Hit the guard this time!

The guards are on each side of the bed. The one who is near the free arm leans toward Oliver to get hold of the arm that is holding onto the headboard. Oliver sees his chance at taking a swing as well as he can with one arm tied down. He grazes the guard's chin before the guard wrenches Oliver's arm behind his back.

"You little . . ." says the guard. "Go for it," he tells the nurse, "I've got him."

The nurse sticks the needle into Oliver's shoulder and sinks the plunger.

"OW!"

The guards and the nurse take advantage of Oliver's pain and surprise to strap down his legs and other arm.

"Please," says Oliver, "please don't leave me alone. She'll come in here, I just know it!"

"It'll be all right, Hon," says the nurse. "I'll stay with you a while."

The guards leave.

"I have to change your bandage so I'll just go get supplies for that, okay? I won't be gone for more than two minutes."

The Haldol has an almost immediate effect on Oliver. He struggles to keep his eyelids open. "Okay," he slurs.

First, the nurse pages Dr. Bruce who is still in the hospital. Then she unlocks the Common Room door.

"What the fuck?" Jude confronts her, "I'm about to wet my goddamned pants and I'm having a nicotine fit!"

"I'm sorry, Jude. It was important we deal with Oliver without any interference. It really hasn't been that long."

"To you maybe! I wouldn't have interfered! What the fuck?" Jude stomps out of the Common Room and goes to his room to use the bathroom. On the way he looks in on Oliver in room #2. Oliver is strapped down and not there.

"Damn, Kid. You're not gonna get to the green planet like this."

Dr. Bruce sprints up to the locked ward and, with the nurse at his side, peeks in at the now unconscious Oliver.

"I'll call his parents. Do you have any idea what might have contributed to this?"

"He was ranting about Gladys being dangerous. He and Jude have been together all day, talking and smoking and drawing on the whiteboard. That's about it."

Dr. Bruce goes behind the nurses' station and finds Oliver's chart.

"He's on 10 milligrams of Zyprexa." He takes a pen out of his breast pocket. "Let's up him to 15 milligrams. And let's give that to him in the evenings." He signs the chart. "Now, the hard part." He finds John's number in the chart and, using the nursing station phone, dials the number. An answering machine picks up at John's house. He then dials Elizabeth's number. She answers.

"Mrs. Moore?"

"Yes?"

"This is Dr. Bruce at the hospital."

"Yes? Oliver?"

"He's all right, Mrs. Moore; however, he just had another episode and I wanted you and Mr. Moore to know about it."

"Yes, of course, what . . ."

"It's been a bit of a repeat situation. He's back in restraints and Haldol was administered again to calm him down. I've given orders to increase the Zyprexa. That should help. I'm sorry to have to tell you upsetting news but Oliver will be fine; we just have to find the right medication and the right dosage. He's safe here."

Elizabeth stands, not talking, only listening to the other end of the phone.

"Mrs. Moore? Are you there?"

"Yes, I'm sorry. I don't know what to say. You mean Zyprexa may prove to be the wrong medication?"

"It may. It's too early to tell."

"Oh, my Lord."

"Are you alone?"

"No, John and the kids, the other kids, are here."

"That's good. Then you'll pass on this news to Mr. Moore?"

"Yes, of course."

"Thank you. Don't worry, Mrs. Moore."

"How can I not worry?"

There's a beat of silence from Dr. Bruce. "I really don't know. Goodbye, Mrs. Moore."

Jude sits in the smoking room, finishing the second of two cigarettes in a row. He stands, hitches up his pants and walks to room #2. Without a pause he walks in, leans against the wall and slides down to the floor, ending up in a sitting position where he can see Oliver. He rests his chin on his knees. The nurse walks in with bandages, tape, and cleaning solution. She's startled when she sees Jude sitting there.

"What are you doing?" she asks.

"I'm sitting here."

"He doesn't know you're here."

"That could be up for debate."

"Well, it's almost time for bed."

"I'm not a child," Jude says, irritated. "I'm just sitting here."

The nurse doesn't say another word. She takes Oliver's bandaged hand out of the restraint and gently unwraps the gauze and tape. She cleans his wounds, puts antibiotic ointment on the cuts, and winds clean gauze and tape onto the hand. Then she buckles it back into the leather strap. She leaves the room.

Jude begins to whisper to Oliver. He whispers that he heard Oliver scream that he'd seen God again, he whispers that he saw Oliver praying outside the Common Room and saw the security guards pick him up and take him in here to room #2. He whispers that Oliver is a good guy and to just hang on and he'll be okay, that they can't take it all away from him. And he whispers his own secrets for only Oliver to know, that he's from Tucson and he's been on the road since he was sixteen and that his parents didn't love him like Oliver's parents do, so, Oliver was going to be okay. And, his most painful secret, a secret so huge he silently mouths the words, that he has a brother about Oliver's age who he left behind.

Peter and John climb down from the loft feeling much better than they did when they climbed up the ladder. They walk into the house to find Wren in front of the TV and Elizabeth banging around in the kitchen, cleaning up. Peter notices a short glass with ice and clear liquid on the counter near her. As soon as they enter, both smiling, she delivers the message from Dr. Bruce.

"Oh, my God!" says John. "Why?"

Peter goes into the living room to see Wren. He sits next to her and she snuggles up to him. Jack takes the other end of the couch.

"What are you watching, Weasel?"

"Something."

"Can I watch Something with you?"

Wren looks up at him, her tiny face breaking into a big grin.

"Of course, silly!"

12

GO FISHING

Oliver swallows his medication at the nurses' station. Dinner is on its way. The door will open soon and the heavy plastic cart will be pushed through with trays of food. He's still feeling the effects of last night's drama and the Haldol, now about to mix with Zyprexa. He knows the Haldol has probably worn off but it doesn't feel like it. He sits quietly in the Common Room. The Woman With The Burned Face has her back to him. He's positioned himself in such a way that he can see her but she can't see him. She moves slightly and Oliver immediately glances at her back. Today she's wearing a ribbed sweater, brown, and Oliver thinks she looks like a giant turd. Jude returns from the bathroom and asks Oliver if he would like to play cards.

"I don't know."

"Come on, it'll make you feel better."

"I doubt it, but I guess I could try. I'm just so tired."

"Hey, man, you don't want to TRY, you want to DO. So, what'll it be?"

"How about Hearts?"

"Go Fish."

Oliver stares at Jude. "You're kidding, right?"

"No. I won't play anything but."

"So why did you ask?"

"Just being polite."

Oliver laughs.

"Hey now," says Jude, "that's a good sound! You have to be polite, right?"

"Right."

Jude grabs the cards, knocks them out of the box and begins to shuffle. After dealing and making a sufficiently messy pond, Jude holds his cards close to his chest and looks at Oliver with an impenetrable look. "Hey, man, do you remember me sitting with you in room #2 last night? And talking to you?"

Oliver, splaying his cards in a fan, "No."

"Good."

"Why good?"

"Cause I told you a bunch of stuff I wouldn't want you to remember."

Oliver laughs again.

"Okay, man, let's get serious here," says Jude and he opens the game. "Besides," he says, "you can't let them hear you laughing too much or they'll think you're crazy!"

Before they're able to continue further, dinner arrives. They place their cards face down on the table, retrieve their trays and bring them into the Common Room. Being careful to not touch their cards or the pond, they position their trays on the table and take the round covers off their plates to see what's there. Mashed potatoes, meat loaf, peas, Jell-O, milk.

"Wow," says Jude. "Not bad!"

They eat in silence. Jude eats every tiny bit as well as the Jell-O. Oliver offers him his Jell-O and he takes it and eats that too. Finished, they return their trays to the cart and then pick up their cards and resume playing.

"I'm so tired," Oliver says.

"You can play a while, can't you?" Jude asks.

"I guess so."

Even though it's a school day, Peter decides to drive up to Hyalite Reservoir. He wants to be alone and to go somewhere fairly far from home, from both homes. Now that he's living with John, it's easy to gas up near the University. He grabs a tube of Pringles and a Pepsi and heads out. Peter knows there's a little weed under his seat along with his tiny glass pipe. The knowing gives him a feeling of security.

Peter hates everyone and everything. He simply can't make himself walk into the high school. There's a hole inside him that forces him to slouch when he used to sit straight at his desk at school and the dining room table at home. This force makes him walk slightly bent over all the time, his eyes to the ground, as though he's searching for something.

Peter turns left off College Street onto 19th Avenue and speeds up the long stretch of empty road toward the mountains. He opens the windows to feel the cool air on his face, to make his long hair blow around.

"I should be driving up here with Ollie," he thinks. "NO!" he screams, "I'm not going to think about him!" He pounds the black steering wheel with an open palm. "Ollie is DEAD DEAD DEAD DEAD!"

A sharp turn to the left and he enters Hyalite Canyon, a narrow track that leads him up and up to where the left side of the road becomes a steep mountain, shale rocks piled precariously on top of each other, the right side a rushing creek spilling out of Hyalite Reservoir. The landscape opens up unexpectedly, fields and campgrounds to the right, the creek now farther away, the steep mountain on his left becoming gentle swells with trees and trails where Peter had hiked and biked with Oliver many times. Peter keeps driving fast, the trees a blur on his left, the meadows and campgrounds flashing by on his right.

Peter glances at the Pringles tube sitting on the seat; somehow the Pringles sitting there make Peter extra lonely, make the seat seem especially empty. He allows himself to think of Oliver as though Ollie was sitting there next to him. He smiles.

Peter waits to see the reservoir, to see the water magically appear, the mountains rising up steeply on three sides of the lake once he's at the top of this long road. In spite of his anger he notices that he felt better for an instant when he allowed himself to think of Ollie, as he used to be. He decides to make believe that Ollie is with him, to pretend everything is all right for now.

Besides, Peter thinks, the Acura is half Ollie's so he may as well enjoy this ride even if he is locked up.

"Ha!" Jude throws down his cards. He's won his fifth game of Go Fish.

"You must be cheating somehow," Oliver tells him.

"No man, I'm good, that's all," Jude gloats.

"Then let's play Hearts."

"Don't know how and don't want to learn."

The nurse walks into the Common Room. "Hello, boys," she says to Oliver and Jude then, "Gladys, let's get your paperwork started so you can leave first thing in the morning."

The Woman With The Burned Face gets up slowly with the help of the nurse. She stumps her way out of the Common Room.

Jude and Oliver look at each other.

"Yes!" Oliver gives Jude a high five but Jude doesn't respond.

"I don't like that," says Jude.

"Why not?"

"Because it excludes."

"Oh. Okay." Oliver stands. He flips off the chair where The Woman With The Burned Face had been sitting.

"And I don't like that either," Jude says. "It's just mean. You can't be mean and survive out there, man."

"I'm going to my room." Oliver walks out of the Common Room and down the hall. He stops at room #2 and peers in. The leather straps are quiet, benign, but even so he feels a shudder go down his spine. Once in his room he lies down on the bed and closes his eyes. He thinks about what Jude said and has to agree. He doesn't want to be mean. Then he thinks of Wren and Peter. He sighs a deep sigh and slips into sleep.

John and Elizabeth rendezvous at the hospital for a meeting with Dr. Bruce in his office. He tells them he will have to inform Oliver about their meeting but he doesn't want Oliver overly stressed at the moment.

"We want to downplay what happened last night and help him be as calm as possible."

"But what happened?" asks Elizabeth.

"It seems he hallucinated that a female patient was drinking blood and that led him into another psychotic break."

"But that happened right on the ward, Doctor," says John. "Why can't we see him? It wasn't our doing."

"Because anything out of the ordinary right now would just upset him."

"You don't know that," says Elizabeth, flipping her hair out of her face.

"My opinion is the one that will open that door for you, or not," says Dr. Bruce.

"Well, if you put it that way, we have no choice."

"I'm sorry. I have to do what I think is best for Oliver. Let's allow him to stay subdued; he'll return home in four days anyway. Let's help him make that a positive transition, all right?"

John and Elizabeth don't say a word.

"Another thing," says Dr. Bruce. "I would highly recommend, and will provide the paperwork from my end, for the two of you getting a power-of-attorney for Oliver at least until he's well again."

"You mean, he'll be well again?" asks Elizabeth.

"I'm sorry. I should have said until he's maintaining well on a medication regimen. Which brings me to the second issue I wanted to bring up with the two of you. Have you given any thought to where Oliver will go after his stay here and after he comes home with you?"

"No." John's answer comes out very fast and very firm.

"I really haven't looked into it yet," says Elizabeth.

"I know you're both probably tired of hearing my opinion and also have opinions of your own, but Oliver is extremely ill and needs care twenty-four/seven, the kind of care you will not be able to provide. I would hesitate leaving him alone for any amount of time, and if your jobs make it necessary to leave him for long periods of time you could be facing a disaster."

"Thank you, Doctor, for putting it to us straight. We'll consider each issue, taking everything into account," says John.

"Does Oliver really have to come home in four days?" asks Elizabeth. "I mean, since he just had another psychotic break as you call them, shouldn't he be able to stay another ten days?"

"No, Mrs. Moore, it doesn't work that way. Unfortunately, the beds are limited and we have to get patients in and out with crisis treatment, just enough so they're able to move on to longer-term care if they need it. Sometimes they don't need it but in Oliver's case there's no question, in my opinion." Dr. Bruce stands up from behind his desk. "Thank you both for coming in. I would check out our State Mental Hospital at Warm Springs and the internet is a good place to begin looking for private hospitals if you can afford to go that route."

John and Elizabeth stand and shake Dr. Bruce's hand.

"Thank you," says John. "Please let me know how he is after you see him this evening, won't you? I'll pass it on to Elizabeth."

"Yes, that would be good, and thank you," says Elizabeth.

"I will." Dr. Bruce walks them to his office door.

Peter reaches the reservoir and drives over the dam. He keeps going until he spots a campground near the water. He drives down a short road to it and parks the Acura, turns off the engine, and gets out. He has the entire place to himself. The air is crisp. The surrounding mountain peaks are covered with snow. He pulls his windbreaker out of the back seat.

"Whattaya think, huh?" he asks the expanse of water and mountains. He knows Ollie would whoop and holler to hear the echoes come back without hesitation. He smiles to himself just thinking of it.

There was so much of Oliver that Peter thinks is so much more than himself. Oliver is louder, he wears his charm more easily, has more girls hanging on him, has a physique more built than his. Peter hadn't minded because it was Oliver, his big bro. Peter even attracted a certain status because of it. And now? How was he, Peter, supposed to fill in the gaps? How was he supposed to wait for Oliver to come back? He told Greg that this forced separation was good for him, but he didn't really believe it. From the day Peter was born, Ollie had been there.

"Shit!"

Peter walks down to the shore. He sits on the ground, finds small stones and throws them into the water. He imagines Ollie in a jail cell and he, Peter, crashing down the wall to rescue him. He visualizes Ollie pinned down by doctors in white coats and he, Peter, smashing his way through them to save Ollie from their needles. He sits there filling his head with ways to save his brother, none of which will work, and he knows it. His imaginings are derailed as soon as the scene is played out. He remembers what Elizabeth told him about the Four Steps of Grief:

Denial, Anger, Acceptance, and Advocacy. He hates it that she even told him. As far as he's concerned he's not grieving, he's just waiting and if it helps to pretend that Ollie is with him while he's waiting, then that's what he'll do.

Peter takes off his shoes and steps into the freezing water. The shock of it is welcomed. The pain erases all thought until his feet get used to it. He steps back on shore and takes off his pants, his windbreaker and shirt, his undershorts, then he walks, quickly, into the water up to his waist, gasping as he walks. Standing still, he shouts to the mountains, to Ollie, "FUCK YOU GOD!" and sinks under the water. He surfaces, screaming and laughing and returns to the shore as fast as he can.

"Holy Shit! That was for you, Bro!" Peter pulls his clothes back on as fast as he can over his wet goose-bumped skin, pulls on his socks and shoes. He jumps in the Acura, turns on the engine and cranks up the heat, still laughing. He reaches under the seat and retrieves his weed, pipe and lighter, and packs the bowl. He lights the pipe, pulling smoke into his lungs and keeping it there for a few beats; he lets it out in a whoosh. He puts the car seat all the way back, a smile plastered on his face, his wet hair stringy down to his shoulders.

"Whattaya say now, Bro? Are we still gonna fix up a bus and drive across the country some day?" Peter looks out the windshield at the lake and the mountains soaring above it. "Are we gonna go to the same college like we said?" he whispers. He takes another toke on his pipe.

Peter is disappointed with his high. He wants to keep his happy mood but begins sinking into melancholy, not a place he wants to go. "Fucking lousy shit," he says out loud, puts his window down and knocks out his pipe on the side of the car, then he opens the door. He swings his legs out and stands under the trees with the silence. He throws the pipe and weed under the seat and, pocketing his lighter, he walks up to the road above this campground. Abruptly, he takes off, sprinting as fast as he can. He runs until his lungs burn, until his breath is gone. He stops and is surrounded once again by the silence. Out of the blue he feels tears in his eyes, feels them spill over onto his cheeks.

"No, please, I don't want to feel this. I can't live like this."

He squats on his haunches but slowly collapses to the ground, his face protected from the dirt only by his hands. Peter sobs like he never has before, ever. He sobs for his brother and himself, for his loneliness and Oliver's imprisonment. For him not knowing how to behave without Ollie and for not being allowed to see him and for Ollie's loneliness behind the locked door. But mostly, for not knowing if Ollie is lost forever or not.

John receives two calls that evening. One from Dr. Bruce informing him that Oliver was maintaining well and another from the high school's recorded attendance machine communicating to him that Peter had missed all his classes that day.

"Jesus Christ! What the hell?" He immediately calls Elizabeth to fill her in.

"Where was he?" Elizabeth asks.

"How am I supposed to know?"

"You mean he's not home yet?"

"If he was home I'd know, don't you think?"

"Not necessarily." Elizabeth feels callous pleasure in hearing John so stressed out. She's finding it quite simple to take care of only Wren. "I will say that at this point it would be easier if we weren't divorced, don't you think?"

"Whoever would have known?" John says. "It would be easier but then we'd have to deal with each other on top of everything else."

"That's kind of mean."

"Oh, for God's sake, I wasn't implying anything. You know what I meant! Not 'dealing' with you but I don't mind sharing all this with you. Christ, Lizzy. We can't afford to fight right now, at least I don't have the energy for it."

"I guess we never could but we didn't know it."

There's a long silence on John's end of the phone, then, "Yes, you're right."

"What did Dr. Bruce say about Ollie?"

"Oh yeah, he told me that Ollie was quiet, he'd eaten and taken his meds without incident. He and that other young man, Jude, were playing cards for a while according to the nurse. Ollie was taking a nap when the doctor went in to check on him. Dr. Bruce also told me that Ollie has become quite attached to Jude. They're going to keep a close watch on Ollie because Jude leaves two days before him and they think he'll feel pretty lonely."

"Maybe we should visit him more after Jude leaves."

"Yeah, we should."

"How about that creepy woman with the burn marks on her face?" Elizabeth asks.

"She's leaving tomorrow."

"That's good! She's why he had that last psychotic break."

"No, I think if he was going to have a psychotic break he would have had one anyway," John tells her.

"Maybe you're right."

"Lizzy, Peter's here, I gotta go, bye." He hangs up.

Elizabeth hangs up. "Boy, am I ever glad I'm not Peter right now!"

13

EVERYDAY CYCLES

She looked at her watch, 3:05, and decided to walk to fetch Wren from the elementary school. The school was five blocks away, a pleasant stroll down the alley past funky old houses on the north side and along the creek that ran all the way through the small city. It was a cool day, April, the month that was her worst, her "fetal position month" as she always called it. It suddenly occurred to her that it was no surprise Ollie was so sick right now. She'd read somewhere that spring and fall brought on the worst episodes for bipolar illness. But her symptoms of bipolar 1 disorder were not like what Ollie was experiencing. She was confused by his actions and how completely out of his mind he seemed and the drugs that were prescribed to him.

Elizabeth reached the school and waited with the other parents for their children to be dismissed from class. Wren was in third grade and Elizabeth loved her teacher who loved Wren; it would be difficult to not love Wren. She was a solemn and sweet little girl.

Wren loved school, most of the time. If she could, she'd push for a day at home but mostly enjoyed going. Her friends were important to her and Elizabeth thought that friends were probably the only reason why Wren wanted to go to school at all.

Today, as Wren exits her classroom Elizabeth watches as she chats away with her friends.

These little girls already hug each other, she thinks. And how very honest they are.

Wren sees Elizabeth and grabs a little girl's hand and drags her over. "Mom! Guess what! This is my new best friend and her name is Mandy and I was wondering if she could come over? Please?"

Elizabeth begins to say no but instead asks Mandy if her mother was there. Mandy doesn't say a word but points toward an attractive woman who's making her way to them. She's blonde, young, wearing dangling earrings, and has perfect red nails.

Elizabeth feels herself shrinking; her bagged out jeans and dirty sneakers are her "at home" clothes and she most certainly had been at home. She steps up to Mandy's mother and says, "Hello! Our girls seem to be getting along!"

"Oh?" says Mandy's mother.

Wren pipes up, "Can Mandy come over to our house?"

Mandy's mother looks at Mandy who is nodding very fast. She then looks at her watch. "I guess that would be all right for about an hour or an hour and a half."

The two girls jump up and down, shrieking.

"My name is Elizabeth." She sticks out her hand and Mandy's mother shakes it. "We live only a few blocks from here. Wren, run back into your classroom and fetch me a piece of paper and a pen so I can give Mandy's mother our address."

Both girls disappear into the classroom.

"Julip," Mandy's mother says and holds out her hand.

"Excuse me?"

"Julip is my name."

"You mean like the drink?"

"Yes."

"That must be hard to live with."

A smile breaks out on Julip's face. "Yes, it is. Quite."

The girls come running and hand the paper and an orange crayon to Elizabeth. She writes their address and phone number in chunky, huge letters and hands the paper to Julip. "I guess you won't be losing that anytime soon!"

"I guess not," she replies and smiles. "It's been nice meeting you."

"You too. I'll see you in what, an hour and a half about? I walked today so Mandy will stretch her legs on the way to our home."

"Thank you. We just moved here and it's hard to find friends."

Elizabeth sees no wedding band on Julip's left hand.

"Well, it looks like these guys have buddied up pretty well," Elizabeth says. Then she thinks to herself, It would be fun to make a new friend but not now. She laughs a little to herself. Especially not now!

14

TIME GIVER

Oliver is sleeping when John and Elizabeth arrive at the hospital to bring him home. The nurse has paperwork ready and since his parents now have power-of-attorney, they are the ones who read and sign while the nurse walks down the hall to wake Oliver.

The past two days without Jude were not only boring but empty. Oliver paced the hall, back and forth. He wasn't manic. He simply couldn't think of anything else to do besides play Solitaire. A young woman had been admitted to the ward on the heels of Jude's departure. Oliver didn't like her. He tried to be kind, could hear Jude preaching to him but just couldn't force himself over the hump of his own criticism. Besides, she didn't speak when spoken to, so, what was the point? This girl was suffering with depression, had that awful stare into nothing that he'd noticed other depressives having. She reminded Oliver of his mother when she was depressed. This girl was a total downer, and he didn't even like having to see her. He took his meal trays to his room. He played Solitaire in his room. The two days before he was sprung dragged by.

The evening before his departure, Oliver asked the nurse for a plastic bag. She gave him a paper bag with handles instead. After packing his few things there was nothing to do but try to fall asleep, which, even with medication, wasn't easy.

Dr. Bruce walks on to the ward at 8:00 a.m. to meet John and Elizabeth and to speak with Oliver. The nurse, upon entering Oliver's room to wake him, sees the paper bag at the foot of his bed.

"Oliver?" The nurse touches his shoulder, shaking it a bit. No reaction. "Come on, Oliver. It's time to wake up!" She shakes his shoulder a bit harder.

"What?" Oliver opens his eyes, looks at the nurse.

"Your parents are waiting for you up front."

"They are?" Oliver's eyes open wide.

The nurse sees fear. "It's okay, Oliver. They're here to take you home."

"Really?"

The nurse smiles. "Yes, really."

Oliver dresses then walks down the hall with his paper bag. He detects the residual effects of Zyprexa sitting heavily in his brain. He rubs his eyes with his fists, changing the bag from one hand to the other. Elizabeth sees the sleepy little boy gesture and chokes up. She steps forward and takes Oliver in her arms. Ollie stands still, his eyes open and looking at the wall, his arms at his sides, the bottom of the paper bag touching the floor.

"Sweetie, it's so wonderful to see you!" She lets him go.

Oliver says nothing.

John touches his shoulder, "I'm so happy we can take you home today." He picks up Oliver's right hand. "And look at your hand. It's all mended!"

Oliver's grin is barely perceptible. He looks over at Dr. Bruce.

"We need to go over a few things, Oliver, then you're free to go."

Free to go, Oliver thinks and is reminded of Jude. He smiles.

"Dr. Bruce," Oliver asks, "do you know where Jude went?"

Dr. Bruce hesitates before responding, "I don't know for sure but I would suspect he's back out on the road."

"Yeah."

"Right now is about you, Oliver. I need your reassurance that you'll stay on your medication. Just so you know, I sent a good supply of meds with Jude and prescriptions for more. He wants clarity, the kind of clarity you can only capture with medication on board."

He's lying.

Oliver doesn't believe Dr. Bruce; he knows better when it comes to Jude and clarity.

Dr. Bruce continues. John stands with an arm around Oliver's shoulders, Elizabeth has hold of one of Oliver's biceps. It seems as though they're all listening.

"This may be difficult for all of you. Oliver, you are maintaining on the Zyprexa. I would like to introduce other medications but you would need supervision around the clock." Dr. Bruce glances at both John and Elizabeth. "I'm hoping your parents will find a good place for you where you can improve. I know you're still suffering from intrusive thoughts, and I'd like you to know that this form of suffering can be eliminated."

He's still lying.

What's he talking about? thinks Oliver.

He wants to leave. He wants this man to stop talking. As far as Oliver's concerned, Dr. Bruce is clueless. Jude would agree. Oliver stops listening to the words coming out of the doctor's mouth and tunes in only to the whine behind them.

All of a sudden Oliver is shaking hands with Dr. Bruce, hugging the nurse, and saying goodbye to the locked ward. He imagines he's saying goodbye to Jude but knows that doesn't make any sense. The door slams and clicks behind him and he's finally on the outside. John grabs Oliver's paper bag and sets the pace as they walk down the hallways on their way out of the hospital.

Elizabeth's arm is entwined in Oliver's. They walk and walk and finally are outside in the fresh air, under clouds opposed to ceilings and long fluorescent lights. His parents drove to the hospital in John's SUV; he fiddles with his keys and hits the button to unlock the doors.

"I'll get in the back," Elizabeth volunteers.

You don't want that woman behind you.

"No," says Oliver as he opens the back door.

"Well, okay," says Elizabeth.

John starts the motor. They're on their way. Oliver stares out the window; everything looks so new and strange.

"How long was I there?" he asks.

"Ten days," John tells him.

Oliver looks at his hand and the scars. Ten days. All healed in ten days.

The day before Oliver's release from the hospital, Peter finally arrived home the evening after driving up to Hyalite Reservoir. John was waiting. Attendance alerted him to the fact that Peter had been gone all day from school and John was scared. When Peter walked in the door he heard John hanging up the phone and then was right there in Peter's face.

"Where in the HELL have you been ALL DAY?!"

"I drove up to Hyalite." Peter dropped his backpack and windbreaker on the floor.

"All day? WHY? Why did you skip school?"

Peter stood his ground and only stared at his father. He had nothing to say. He didn't know how to explain what he'd done or what he'd gone through up there. It was his. It was all his and he didn't want John knowing about it.

"I just couldn't go to school, that's all."

"Did you have any tests today you weren't ready for?"

"No."

"Then why?" John stood with his arms crossed, his body leaning back slightly, his most severe body language.

"I just did, Dad. I can't explain it."

"Well you're grounded. You can take the damn bus to school. One week."

"It was only one day, Dad! When we were in elementary school we called them hooky days. What's the difference? My grades are good! You can't complain about that. How is making me take the damn bus going to teach me anything about going to school? I have straight As and Bs! What MORE do you want? If the school hadn't called you never would have known!" Peter's voice increased in pitch as he spoke, ending in as close to a yell as he would get when speaking to his father.

"But they did and I do know and you won't tell me why!"

"Can't I have some privacy?"

"To do what? Smoke weed all day?"

"As a matter of fact, no!"

"It was your mother who initiated hooky days."

The two were at an impasse. John wished he hadn't thrown out his punishment quite so fast as Peter's logic, as usual, made sense. He knew he was stressed out about Ollie coming home tomorrow. This was a bad time to have extra stress put on Peter but John couldn't go back.

"I'll make a compromise, Peter. I'll drive you to school on my way to work in the mornings and perhaps your mother could pick you up in the afternoons after she gets Wren. That's as far as I'll move on this. Ollie is coming home tomorrow morning and we're all stressed out about that."

Speak for yourself, Peter thought.

John ran his hand through his hair and turned away from Peter. "Let's see what we can come up with for dinner. Oh, and you better give me your keys."

Peter glared at John as he fished his keys out of his pocket. He wanted to throw them but knows better and hands them over.

"Thank you," said John. "Now, dinner."

The two walked into the kitchen. John opened the fridge. "How about grilled cheese and tomato soup?"

"Okay."

John grabbed a huge block of cheddar cheese from the fridge, found the cheese slicer, plugged in the electric frying pan. "Would you take care of the soup?"

Peter found a saucepan, a whisk, the milk and a family sized can of tomato soup. This was one of his favorite meals. He liked it better when there was snow on the ground but just about any time was good too.

"Pete, you know Ollie's coming home tomorrow. Your mother and I are trying to set up our schedules so he'll have very limited time alone. I wonder if you could cover us in the evenings when your mom needs to be back at work since she'll be gone all afternoon. I'll stay here with Ollie in the mornings, Mom will take over at lunchtime. Then, as circumstances will have it, she and Ollie will pick up Wren, then you, for a week, and you and Ollie can hang out here or at Mom's until I can pick you up or perhaps she can bring you here before she goes back to work. I don't know. When you get the Acura back maybe you could pick up Ollie from your mother's and bring him to my house until I get home. I should be home by seven at the latest. How does that sound?"

"Complicated. How about Wren?"

"She'll go to work with Mom and do her homework in the office."

"How long will we have to do this?"

"I don't know. We'll see if Ollie is getting better or not."

"I guess I can do that."

"Thanks!"

"But Dad," Peter said quietly, "what if he freaks out on me or something? What should I do?"

"You can call 911 and call me or your mother. I don't want to put you in a compromising situation but I do think he'll be okay. Keep the TV OFF. You can do your homework. He liked playing cards in the ward. We'll just have to see how he is."

15

HOMEWORK

John, Elizabeth, and Oliver arrive in town.

"How about if we stop and get something to eat?" suggests John. "Ollie, I know you haven't had breakfast. Are you hungry?"

"Yes."

"Let's go to Main Street Over Easy."

"That's a good idea," says Elizabeth. "What about you, Ollie?"

"Okay."

John drives down Main Street and pulls into the alley to park behind the restaurant. They walk through the back door. Oliver is very subdued. John finds a table in the corner. They sit and peruse the menu. Oliver looks around at the other customers then he puts his face in his hands and begins to rock back and forth, back and forth. John and Elizabeth look at each other with alarm.

Elizabeth touches Oliver's arm. He flinches. "Do you want to stay here, Ollie?"

"No." His answer is muffled.

"All right," says Elizabeth. "Let's go. You and Dad can make something to eat at home." She gets up as though it's the most normal thing in the world to come into a restaurant, sit, and then leave.

John and Oliver follow.

The waitress stops Oliver. "Is something wrong?"

Oliver stares at her.

"No, nothing's wrong," John says. "One of us is just feeling a bit sick." He puts one arm around Oliver's shoulders and steers him outside to the parking lot.

They drop Elizabeth at her home then drive to John's. John is worried about bringing Oliver back to where he punched the mirror, which still isn't replaced, back to the house where he was so sick, but there's nothing he can do about it. He's ordered a mirror; it just hasn't come yet.

They pull up to his house and get out. Oliver brings his paper bag and follows John.

"Let's make some breakfast, okay? Then we'll set you up in your room."

Elizabeth steps out of John's SUV and into her car. She heads to work. She knows how her house would feel after being with Oliver and doesn't want to experience the emptiness. Besides, if she's going to take over Ollie at noon, she needs to get to work now.

The coffeehouse is buzzing as usual. As far as Elizabeth is concerned getting to work is a good distraction from her thoughts. Upon entering she discovers that one of the young people who work behind the counter has called in sick and Susan, the manager, needs to be working in the bakery as they're one baker short for a few days.

Elizabeth steps up and takes over the cash register. She likes to think that the cash register is the "mouth" of the business; without feeding the cash register, no one gets paid. She gets on the phone and, in between cashing out customers, tries to find someone who would be willing to come in at 11:30 to cover for the sick girl.

Elizabeth likes working the counter; it's fast-paced and friendly, most of the time. The baristas are good, which makes ringing up orders flow. On the phone, she is able to coerce a young man to come in at 11:30 and, for now, she puts on an apron and welcomes the next customer in line with a big smile.

Peter is anxious for school to end. He's had butterflies in his stomach all day anticipating Oliver's homecoming and is eager to hang out with him while their dad is at work. Elizabeth, Wren, and Oliver will meet him at Wendy's across 11th Street from the high school. His day drags. At lunchtime he jogs to the Co-Op for a snack then hightails it back to school to get a bit of homework taken care of. The last bell finally rings. Peter shoulders his way through the crowds of students in the hall, finds his locker, gets what he needs, and he's out the glass doors to the street. A large group is already gathered at the crossing, many on their way to Wendy's to pick up rides. They move as one body across the road, dispersing when they reach the other side. He spots Elizabeth's red Camry and walks over to it, leans down to see who's inside and sure enough, it's the three of them: Mom, Wren, and Oliver.

"Peter!" Wren calls. "Look who's here!!"

Peter opens the back door and slides in, his legs almost too long for the back seat. He looks at Oliver, next to him now.

"Hey man. How are ya?"

"I'm good. Good to see ya too."

Oliver's expression is hard for Peter to read. He looks happy but cautious, almost frightened.

"Wren," Peter says, "how come you rate the front seat?"

"Ollie didn't want it, so there!"

"Oh."

Elizabeth speaks up. "Is anyone hungry? We could go to the Co-Op." She remembers Oliver's reaction to the restaurant but can't take her suggestion back now that it's said.

"Yes!" says Wren. "I want some soup."

"No thanks, I had lunch at the Co-Op."

"Ollie?"

"No."

Elizabeth drives two blocks over to the Co-Op anyway. "I'll take Wren. You two can wait in the car."

"Okay," says Peter.

Both boys watch their mother and sister disappear into the Co-Op. They sit, silently, their hands in their laps.

"It's good to see you, Bro," Peter says, shattering the tension.

Oliver doesn't answer right away. His eyes remain on the door leading into the store.

Say something you dumb shit.

"It's good to see you too." He glances at Peter. Even though Peter appears virtually the same as ten days ago, he looks different to Oliver somehow. He tries to see Peter without staring. Instead, he takes short, furtive snapshots and hopes Peter doesn't notice.

"Hey, what was it like in the hospital?" Peter asks.

Oliver's lag time answering is evident. He has to bring himself back to making conversation as opposed to plugging into all the stimuli around him.

"Boring, except when I was with this guy, Jude. He was a trip."

"Why was he there?"

"He told me he was there because of the cops but he must have been there because he's crazy, like me."

"You're not crazy."

Oliver keeps his eyes on the door leading into the Co-Op. He doesn't know what to say to Peter. He knows Peter thinks he's crazy. Why else would he have stayed away from the hospital? He decides to take a chance and forces himself to look right at Peter and say, "Yes, I am. I'm sorry, Bro. I didn't mean to be this way."

You wouldn't be if you weren't so fucking stupid.

"Don't they have a name for it? Like I've heard Dad say that Mom has bipolar, but the milder kind. Maybe. I don't know."

"I don't think so. Jude said he was schizophrenic but I don't know what I am."

Peter feels left out. He wishes he's met Jude. He wishes John had allowed him to visit Ollie in the hospital. He also remembers yelling at Wren about Ollie being crazy and telling Greg that Ollie was crazy. He's guilty.

"Do you know why I'm grounded?"

Oliver wears a small grin when he finally responds to Peter. "Why?"

"Because I skipped a whole day of school."

"How long are you grounded?"

"A week, starting today."

"That sucks."

"Maybe if I tell Dad that you and I want to be able to drive around he'll take it back."

A shopper walks up to the car next to them. He unlocks his door, puts groceries in the back seat. Peter watches Oliver duck his head, move his lips silently, and stare at the floorboards.

Oh man, he thinks. Ollie . . .

Elizabeth and Wren return with soup and a bag of groceries that they put in the trunk and get back in the car with the boys.

Wren turns around in her seat. She glances over at her mother before speaking, then, "Can I come to Daddy's with you guys?"

Peter glances at Oliver who hasn't responded one way or the other. "Sure, Weasel. Why not?"

Elizabeth smiles. "I'll pick her up later."

John hurries through the afternoon. Taking mornings off will be difficult but he has to do it. He gathers paperwork together to take home for tomorrow morning. He wonders how long they'll all have to sit with Oliver, if Oliver will begin to get better. His coworkers know what's up, that John's eldest is sick, that he just came home from the hospital. John has been vague about what's wrong. It's true he doesn't really know other than that it's some kind of mental illness, but no one knows definitively which one. No matter what he says to his family, he has little faith that the Zyprexa will keep Oliver in this world. John wakes with a knot in his stomach and falls asleep, when he can, with the same knot. He walks around with the knowing. Sometimes he forgets for a second then it comes back. The knowing. John has lost weight. He feels lonely much of the time. He loves having Peter with him but Peter is not adult company.

And now, both boys will be with him. Peter is grounded so he can't ask him to buy groceries for them. Maybe he'll have to lift the ban on the Acura. He did get his point across and he does need help. How will Ollie be at home? He wishes the punched mirror was fixed! He leans back in his chair, takes a deep breath and let's it out.

How am I going to do this? he thinks and glances at his watch. It's 5:30. Better go.

Oliver, Peter, and Wren are all in John's living room. Wren is sitting on the floor, her homework spread all over the coffee table. She's coloring in a geography assignment. Her math is untouched; she's hoping one of her brothers will do it for her.

Peter looks up from his history book. "Geez, Wren, I wish I could color in my homework!"

"Why can't you?" she asks in her little voice.

Peter looks at Oliver and they both laugh.

"Ollie, can you do my math homework for me?" Wren asks.

Oliver doesn't answer right away, then, "My handwriting would give it away."

"Well, I could write the answers if you could tell me what they are."

"I could do that."

"If you didn't want to, I could," says Peter.

"I'm not a retard," Oliver tells Peter.

"I didn't say you were a retard!"

Oliver stands up from the high-backed chair and looks at Wren's homework. "Wren, this is pretty easy. It's just addition and subtraction."

"It's not easy to me." She keeps her eyes on her map and colors more vigorously. "I'm almost finished."

"I'm going outside," Oliver tells them.

"But . . ." Wren says. She looks up at Oliver. "Can't you wait a minute? I'm almost done."

Oliver doesn't respond. He opens the front door and walks outside.

Peter looks over at Wren. "What are we supposed to do now?"

Wren looks stricken. "Should I not have asked him about my homework?"

"No, Wren, it's just Ollie. He doesn't act like other people. It doesn't have anything to do with you. He loves you."

"Will you help me?"

"Of course, but I better see where Ollie went. You want to come?"

"Yes!" She jumps up and takes Peter's hand.

The two of them walk outside.

Oliver's sitting on the top step of the stairs that extend to the sidewalk below. He's thinking about not being retarded and how much he feels like he is. He knows he has a mental illness, a brain disease, and wonders if people who are retarded think about their situation. He wonders if it would be easier to have Down syndrome than a mental illness. At least he wouldn't know it. Or maybe he would? Peter and Wren come out of the house and stand near him.

"Hey, Bro, what are you supposed to call retarded people ?"

"I think it's 'mentally challenged.' That's what they tell us in school anyway."

"And what do they call crazy. People, you know, like a word for a crazy person that's not nice, like retarded isn't nice for the mentally challenged?"

"Psycho?" asks Wren.

"Yeah! I've been trying to think of that word. Thanks. That's what they call me, isn't it?" Oliver looks over his shoulder at Peter.

"I don't think so, Ollie."

"Sure you do. It's okay. They can all go fuck themselves anyway."

Peter holds Wren's hand a bit tighter.

"That's what the boys call each other on the playground at school," says Wren. "It's not very nice, is it?"

"No, it's not," says Peter.

"Hey," he says to Oliver. "Wren's ready for your help with her math homework."

Oliver stands, walks halfway down the stairs to the sidewalk, then stops. He looks up at his siblings then comes back and into the house. Peter sighs a sigh of relief. He wouldn't know what to do if Ollie took off, not if Wren was with him anyway. He doesn't want Wren to see anything ugly.

A flash of headlights sweeps the house. John's home. A bucolic scene awaits him: Peter reading, Oliver and Wren working on her math homework. He's reassured. He brings shopping bags into the kitchen. He's stopped at Safeway and picked up two roasted chickens, a bag of salad and a bag of donuts, a gallon of milk, and some ice cream.

Wren jumps up and asks if she can stay for dinner.

"Of course, sweetie. Call Mom and let her know, okay?"

Peter and John hear Wren on the kitchen phone to Elizabeth. "Hi Mom! I'm staying for dinner. No, Daddy will give me a ride home. Okay, I love you too."

Oliver is sitting with a pad of paper; the numbers of Wren's math problems progressing down the left side of the paper, his answers next to them. He's enjoyed doing her assignment and wishes there was more to do. He hasn't had to speak or figure out how to behave while working on it.

"I'm finished, Wren," he calls to her.

"Oh goodie! Thank you!" She runs over to him and gives him a big hug.

"Pete," John says, "would you run Wren home for me after dinner?"

"Yeah, but . . ."

"I know. I need you too much right now. How about some outdoor chores to wipe the slate clean?"

"Like what?"

"I'll think of something."

16

SPIRALING

Peter and Wren leave John's after dinner. They get in the Acura and pull out of the drive.

"Ah! Back in the saddle!" says Peter.

"Whattaya mean?" asks Wren.

"I was grounded from my car and now I'm not."

"Why?"

"Because I skipped school for a day."

There's a little pause from Wren. "I like skipping school! Did you have fun?"

Peter thinks for a moment. "Not really, but it was good."

"Peter?"

"Yes, Wren?"

"Do you think Ollie will ever be Ollie again?"

"I don't know, Weasel."

"What if he isn't, what do we do then?"

"I don't think there's anything we can do. I guess we just love him the same as we always have."

"Well, yeah, but . . . he looks the same but he isn't the same."

"You have to love him, Wren. You have to! We're his only brother and sister and we can't abandon him. Maybe he'll come back someday. In the meantime, we have to love him so he knows it. I've been thinking, and I think it must be scary to be Ollie right now."

"Whattaya mean?"

"He knows he's different. I think he wishes he wasn't different. Whattaya think?"

Wren turns her little face to Peter. Her voice is very small. "I love him too. And you know what?"

"What?"

"I'm gonna punch those boys who say 'psycho!'"

"No, you better not do that, Wren."

"Why not?"

"Because they don't know any better, and I don't want you to get hurt," Peter says gruffly.

"I wouldn't get hurt! They're just pussies!"

"Now there's another word I don't want to hear you using!"

"Why?"

"Ask Mom."

"Okay, I will."

John calls Elizabeth around 11:30 the next morning to report that Oliver is still asleep.

"He's breathing slowly, in a deep sleep, and I don't want to wake him."

"I'll just come up to your house," Elizabeth tells him.

"Okay, thanks, that's what I was hoping."

"How long do you think we should let him sleep?"

"I don't know. The doctor says sleep is good for him so, whenever he wakes up, I guess."

"Okay."

Elizabeth arrives at John's house at 11:50. Her only hitch is she didn't have time to gather paperwork from her office or her book from her house. But she didn't know she'd need paperwork or her book.

John is ready to go. Once he's out of the house Elizabeth peers in on Oliver who's on his side, breathing peacefully, just like John said. She stands in the doorway gazing at him for a while.

He looks so untroubled, so . . . normal, she thinks. She begins to sink into that terrible place where thoughts of Ollie live. She stops herself and turns away from him, closing the door.

Elizabeth walks back to the living room and looks through John's books. She finds short stories by Jack London and settles into the high-backed chair for a read. She keeps putting the book down and thinking, first, how pleasant this is that she has some quiet time to herself then, what is she going to do with Ollie once he's awake. How long could she and John keep this up and what was best for Oliver. She remembers Dr. Bruce mentioning the internet as a place to search for private hospitals. She decides to look when she's home, maybe when Ollie was there with her? No, that wouldn't do. She picks up the book again and reads. The warmth coming in the window and the words on the page lull Elizabeth to sleep. She wakes with a start, her head drooping low, and still, no Ollie. She looks at her watch and sees it's 1:30. She walks to his room to check on him. He's still sleeping. She decides to leave his door open, walks back to the living room and sprawls on the couch with Jack London. She decides that if he's still sleeping by 2:30 she'll have to wake him. They must fetch Wren by 3:15 and that should give Oliver some time to get the cobwebs out of his eyes.

Elizabeth is trudging along in the freezing cold tundra with Jack London when Oliver appears in front of her in a t-shirt and boxers.

"What are you doing?"

"I'm reading."

"Oh." He walks into the kitchen and opens the refrigerator.

Elizabeth doesn't hear it close for quite a while. Next, she hears the cupboards open, the sounds of cereal being poured in a bowl, milk, spoon clinking. All she can hear is Oliver chewing. She looks at her watch, 2:15. Perfect.

"Ollie?"

"Yeah."

"We need to leave in forty-five minutes to fetch Wren, okay?"

"Do I have to go?"

"Yes."

Peter is hurrying out of school when he hears his name called. He turns and sees Greg running after him.

Greg catches up, out of breath. "You wanna come to Cameron Bridge with us?"

"I can't."

"Why not? What's going on with you anyway?"

Peter wants to confide in Greg but he knows Greg wouldn't be able to keep his mouth shut. Peter doesn't want anyone to know that he's babysitting Ollie every afternoon after school.

"I'm grounded."

"For what?"

"For skipping school."

"But that was a week ago!"

"I know. Hey, I gotta go."

Greg stands near the door and watches Peter run toward the student parking lot. He turns and walks back down the hall to the group of kids that are going to Cameron Bridge.

"He can't go," he tells them.

The late April skies are blue, reaching past the mountains. There are still no leaves on the trees and the fields are brown, but the warmth is making Peter and his friends antsy with spring fever. He pulls out of the parking lot and heads to his mother's house. He doesn't want to do this anymore. He wants to go to Cameron Bridge or anywhere, just not home to Dad's with Ollie. As far as Peter is concerned Oliver is not getting better. Peter struggles with the fact that they all have to pitch in to help take care of Oliver, but Peter is his brother not his parent. He knows his parents need help but this isn't Peter's responsibility. Then again, it is. This responsibility belongs to the whole family, even Wren. Maybe he could bring Wren with them this time. She always adds conversation and humor to the long hours before John gets home.

Peter pulls into Elizabeth's driveway. He feels a weight on him as big as the world. It's only been one week.

He walks into the house. "Hi, Mom."

Elizabeth is sitting at the kitchen table, paperwork spread out in front of her. "Hi, sweetie. How was your day?"

"Okay. Where's Ollie?"

"Outside."

"Are you sure?"

"Yeah, why?"

"I just don't know how much longer I can do this, Mom. I have no life."

"Yes, you have a life, it's just that you're doing this instead of other things."

"I would rather be doing other things."

"So would I, Pete. I don't know how long any of us can do this. I don't see Ollie getting better, do you?"

"No." Peter is relieved by the knowledge that his mother feels the same way he does.

"How about Dad?"

"Your dad has more fortitude than I do." She throws her pen down on the pile of papers. "He wants to keep it up for another week or two. I've been looking at hospitals. I don't want Ollie to deteriorate drastically before we can get him some real help."

"Then why are we doing this at all? Shouldn't he be in a place where there are other people like him so he won't be so afraid all the time?"

"Very well put. You might want to reiterate that thought to your father."

"Yeah. I'll go get Ollie." Peter stops in the doorway. "Do you think it would be okay to take him out to Cameron Bridge?"

"Absolutely not." Elizabeth knows what will be happening at Cameron Bridge on this, the first beautiful day of spring. Kids, lots of kids, drinking and weed.

Peter walks down the hall and out to the yard. As soon as he sees Ollie he feels sorry for complaining.

"Hey," Ollie calls. He's over by the creek, sitting in a chair. He smiles at Peter. "How're ya doin'?"

"Good. Whattaya doin' out here?"

"Just sitting, listening to the creek. I like this sound."

Peter squats on his haunches next to Oliver's chair. "So, what do you want to do this afternoon?"

"I dunno. I'm pretty happy right here."

Peter is itching to ask Ollie if he wants to go out to Cameron Bridge but knows he'll put him in an uncomfortable position if he does. Maybe, if he gets Ollie in the car, they could just end up there.

"You want to go somewhere, huh?" Oliver asks.

The hair on Peter's neck prickles. How could he know?

"Yeah."

"Where do ya wanna go?"

"Cameron Bridge."

Oliver doesn't speak. He turns away from Peter to watch the creek. Peter can see Ollie's jaw moving, like he's grinding his teeth. He knows he shouldn't have said anything; he shouldn't have put Ollie in the position of having to choose.

"Let's go," Oliver says.

"Really?" Peter thinks maybe he should take it all back. But he doesn't. "Awesome, man! There'll be some other kids out there, is that okay too?"

Oliver thinks for a minute. Other kids. That's not what he'd bought into but what could he say now? He says nothing. He gets up from the chair by the creek and walks to the house. Peter keeps in step with him.

"We better not tell Mom where we're going, okay?"

"K."

Both boys say goodbye to Elizabeth.

"Where's Wren, Mom?" Peter asks.

"She's at Mandy's house."

"Oh. Well, see you later."

17

BURNED BRIDGE

The boys get in their Acura and set out. Cameron Bridge is a good half hour from Main Street. Peter cranks the music. Oliver lights a cigarette. They don't speak the whole way out there. Once they turn into the Cameron Bridge road the tarmac turns to dirt. Peter slows down and opens his window wider. The day is warm, the Bridger Mountains are now situated across the Gallatin Valley, giving them a great view of the peaks still covered in snow.

Peter glances over at Oliver. "You good?"

Oliver is face forward and not talking. Peter considers turning around. He can only imagine the shit he'll get if John or Elizabeth find out about this, but they won't, he's sure of it. For the entire ride Oliver has said nothing and has only smoked. Peter doesn't know how many cigarettes because as soon as he flicks one out the window he lights another.

They approach the bridge. The parking areas are filled with cars. One area is on the right of the bridge, the second on the left. The left-hand parking is where they stop in the summer since it's close to the long rope swing they use to fling themselves into the Gallatin River. It's too cold yet for swimming and most of the kids are congregated on the right side of the bridge that leads to a large rocky beach. Peter knew there would be kids here but this is a lot more than he imagined. He parked in the left-hand area that wasn't as crowded in case Oliver wanted to stay in the car.

"Whattaya say? You wanna go over there?" Peter asks Oliver.

Oliver still isn't talking.

"Okay . . . well, I'll be back in a few minutes."

Oliver watches him cross the road and disappear into the crowd. He doesn't know what to do. He's exposed sitting here, can feel the kids talking about him. He hears them whispering: "Psycho boy" "piece of shit." Suddenly, Oliver jumps out of the Acura, ready to confront his tormentors.

They must think I'm a freak, he thinks.

Oliver was once the coolest boy in school. Now, because of his illness, he's not, and he knows it. His thick, wavy hair blows in front of his face—his battle mask. He touches his sunglasses to make sure they're on his face. He first encounters a group of girls, juniors he thinks. Oliver stares at them until they become uncomfortable; they walk away, leaving a wide space between Oliver and anyone.

Bitches.

He follows the path down to the rock beach. He's been here many times before. It seems like a lifetime ago. Someone has started a small fire and a crowd of mostly boys is gathered around, passing a joint. Oliver stands in the outer ring of kids, almost on the outside of the outer ring.

Peter looks across the fire and sees Ollie. His heart sinks. Ollie's expression tells Peter that he's there, but not, that look he's seen before when Oliver is in a dangerous, unpredictable place. Peter isn't sure what Oliver will do. He hopes he doesn't embarrass him. The joint comes around and he passes it on without taking a toke. He's frozen to the spot where he's standing and can't take his eyes off Oliver. He sees that Oliver is speaking to himself or maybe he's speaking to Peter. Peter raises his arm to signal Oliver who walks over to him. A couple of old friends and acquaintances see Oliver as he walks up to Peter. The kids don't know what to expect. They approach Oliver carefully. They're curious about what they've heard.

Most hang back. Their eyes give them away. Oliver can see their fear, taste their apprehension.

"Hey! Ollie! I didn't know you were here!"

Fuck you!

"Hey, man! It's good to see ya!"

"Look! It's Oliver!"

Fuck you all!

A group of the older kids, some of them Oliver's old friends and some Peter's age, including Greg, gather around Oliver to greet him.

You're full of shit.

Oliver can't hear the boys clearly. The voice inside his head is louder than the voices outside, the voices of these boys pushing close to him, suffocating him. Oliver is terrified and wants only to find Peter. He has to look for him again. He sees him standing off to the side, talking to one of Oliver's old classmates.

He's explaining why you're such a freak.

Oliver backs away from the well-wishers and walks over to Peter. "I don't want you hanging out with these fucking assholes," he says to Peter.

"What the fuck? They're happy to see you! Whattaya talkin' about?"

Oliver's pupils are huge, his skin clammy. "Fuck ALL of you!" he screams and lunges for the throat of an old friend who is taken off guard.

Peter jumps on Oliver's back and tries to pry his hands off the guy's throat but doesn't have much luck until both Oliver and the other boy are on the ground. Greg steps in to help Peter.

Peter can hear people saying "psycho," "out of his mind," "looney bin." Someone says, "Peter, take your psycho brother home!"

Greg yells, "Don't say that you stupid motherfucker!"

Peter finally pulls Oliver off the boy. He tries to take Oliver by the arm but he won't let him. Oliver struggles to keep himself free, breaks and runs for the car but veers off and runs down the path toward the rope swing instead. Peter and Greg run after him. Oliver finally stops and collapses near a log that's blocking the path. He sits on the ground and curls into a ball. Peter and Greg stand over him. They look at each other.

"Ollie? Hey, let's go home, okay?"

They see Oliver's shoulders moving up and down as though he's crying.

"Hey, it's okay. You're right, those guys are fucking assholes, right Greg?"

"Right."

"Come on. It doesn't matter. Let's just go home."

Oliver lifts his face to them, smudged with mud, wet with tears. But his eyes are what shock both Peter and Greg.

"Ollie." Peter stops. He has done something unforgivable to his brother and there's no taking it back. Underneath his shame, Peter is angry that Oliver is this way. Why, Oliver? Why couldn't it be someone else? Why does it have to be his big brother?

Oliver stands up. His look changes from pain to anger.

"Those fucking assholes," he mutters.

"Just leave it," Peter says. "I want to go home."

"Me too," says Greg.

The three of them have to walk to the road where they're certain some of the kids will see them.

"Let's move fast," Peter suggests. "Okay, Ollie? We'll walk right to the Acura and not talk to anyone, okay?"

Greg reaches the road first and sprints across to his car on the other side. No one is watching. Peter and Oliver reach the Acura, get in and peel out of the parking spot. Oliver lights a cigarette. Peter grips the steering wheel, hard. He hears Oliver muttering to himself.

All of a sudden Oliver yells, "I could've KILLED that motherfucker!"

Peter jumps then yells, "Why did you attack him? He wasn't doing anything to you!"

"He was going to KILL me! Didn't you see that?"

"No. No, he wasn't. He was just standing there! All of them were just standing there telling you how good it was to see you!"

Oliver flicks his smoke out the window and lights another one. "They all think I'm a freak."

"No, they didn't think that! They were happy to see you." Peter's beginning to realize that no matter what he says, Oliver won't believe him.

"They're all motherFUCKERS!"

"Why do you keep saying that?"

"Because they are! Didn't you see how they were looking at me? Like I'm a freak? They wanted to kill me! Couldn't you see that?"

"No, man, I couldn't see that." Peter is defeated. "Just don't tell Mom or Dad where we went, okay?"

Oliver doesn't answer.

The boys arrive at the house before John. Peter is relieved. He's kicking himself for taking Oliver to Cameron Bridge, kicking himself harder than John or Elizabeth ever could. He grabs his backpack and makes sure Oliver follows him into the house. He scrounges in the kitchen for a snack. Oliver isn't hungry and sits in the high-backed chair.

Peter wishes he could turn on the TV but knows he mustn't, especially now, with Oliver in this mood. He brings his snack over to the couch, glances at Oliver before settling in with his homework.

Oliver is wearing his dark expression, the look that tells Peter he's still not here. Oliver's forehead is furrowed, his mouth tight, his eyes blazing. It's his eyes the upset Peter the most. He wishes he'd never taken Ollie away from the creek behind Elizabeth's house. Oliver was happy, relaxed.

"What a stupid fuck I am!" he says to himself. "Why'd I do that? Why'd I think it would be okay to take him to Cameron Bridge?" He struggles to concentrate on his homework.

18

FUCKED NOW BUT NOT FOREVER

John drives up early. He walks into the house with a huge pizza and a smile on his face. Elizabeth called earlier to let him know how well Oliver seemed and John is looking forward to a stress-free evening, including a stress-free dinner. Peter keeps his face buried in his homework. He's afraid he'll give something away if he begins to speak. The pizza is a welcome surprise. John rarely buys fast food and helping with dinner is an expected chore.

"How're you guys?" John asks.

"We're good," answers Peter quickly.

Oliver says nothing.

"Ollie? How are you?" John puts the pizza down on the coffee table.

Oliver stares at John with that look they all now recognize.

John sits next to Peter on the couch and opens the pizza.

"What happened?" he asks Peter.

"Whattaya mean?"

"Look at me, Peter. Look at me straight in the eyes and tell me what happened. Tell me why Ollie's not okay."

"Nothing happened," Peter lies as he looks his father straight in the eyes. "Why do you always assume I did something wrong?"

"I'm not assuming anything. All I know is Ollie isn't right and he was fine before you picked him up."

Both Peter and John look over at Oliver. He's still sitting, staring at nothing, shut down.

"I'm not responsible for Ollie's moods," Peter tells him.

John recognizes this statement as one he had once told the boys when it came to dealing with Elizabeth.

"You're right, you're not responsible for Ollie's moods but you're responsible for him when he's with you."

"Dad, he's fine. Just leave him alone." Peter reaches for a slice of pizza but John stops him.

"Get plates and napkins first, okay?"

Peter walks to the kitchen.

John observes Oliver who seems glued to the chair. He remembers how quickly Oliver can move, even when he looks completely subdued.

"What did you guys do this afternoon?"

Oliver's expression doesn't change and John notices that his pupils are huge.

"Ollie?"

Peter brings plates and napkins. He serves himself and sits back down on the couch. John selects a slice, puts it on a plate and hands it to Oliver.

"Here, eat up."

Oliver refuses the food by shaking his head.

Peter and John eat in silence.

The phone rings. John takes the call in the kitchen. Peter knows it must be Elizabeth. He hears John describing Ollie's behavior, hears the words "hospital" and "Boston." He hands Oliver a piece of pizza, this time without a plate, and Oliver takes it. John walks back to the living room.

"Dad, look" Peter points out the fact that Oliver is eating.

"My God," John thinks, "We're treating him like he's a wild animal at the zoo!"

John gets up from the couch and walks toward the bedrooms. When he returns he has a glass of water and Oliver's medication.

"Here you go, Ollie." He holds the water and medication out to his son.

Oliver balances his half-eaten piece of pizza on his knee and takes the meds and water, swallows them down with no questions asked, not wondering why John is giving them to him early.

When Oliver finishes his slice of pizza he looks to Peter to hand him another. John hands him a napkin but Oliver lets it fall to the floor. After eating two slices Oliver finally vacates the high-backed chair. He goes to the bathroom. John and Peter hear the toilet flush then they hear Oliver's bedroom door close.

Elizabeth has spent hours on the internet looking for private hospitals and calling a few. She's spoken to her mother about the fact that most, if not all, private hospitals don't take insurance. Her mother said, "This is Ollie we're speaking about here. Anything he needs. Just take care of yourself, Lizzy, and Wren and Peter. Ollie will get the care he needs."

Elizabeth feels guilty that because of her wealthy parents she'll be able to afford sending Oliver to a private hospital, but not so guilty that she won't do it. She thinks of all the people out there who need this kind of care and can't afford it. She thinks how shamefully thin our mental health system is and how they could fix it. Money, politics, prejudice, and stigma. She called an old friend who lives in Boston to ask about Taylor Hospital and received glowing reports.

Elizabeth's father has also been researching hospitals and came up with Taylor on his end. Since Elizabeth's parents live in New York City, Boston wouldn't be too far away for them to visit Oliver when John or Elizabeth couldn't.

Considering the review her friend gave and the fact that her father chose Taylor, Elizabeth calls the hospital for more information. She has called four other hospitals before Taylor—one in Texas, one in Florida, one in Pennsylvania, and another in Massachusetts but she's most impressed with how Taylor Hospital handles her call.

On the Taylor call, she was transferred to a coordinator almost immediately. Once Elizabeth is speaking to the coordinator she's able to describe Oliver, what he's been through, the medications tried on him, the medication he's on right now. She's a bit embarrassed that she doesn't know Oliver's diagnosis but the coordinator tells her simply that if Oliver came to stay with them they would be starting from the beginning so it doesn't matter if she has a diagnosis or not. It's explained to her that if they choose Taylor Hospital, Oliver will initially be evaluated for two weeks in a separate facility called Wimberly House. The doctors will go over everything from an MRI, EEG, ECG, to blood work and psychological testing. Oliver will be allowed to rest in between testing, he'll be given good food, he'll have set times to speak to the psychopharmacologist whose office is in Wimberly House as well as to the psychologist who is assigned to his case. If Oliver stays longer than two weeks he will have the same psychologist for his entire stay. Elizabeth is also told that except for the inpatient unit and the drug and alcohol unit there are no locked doors at Taylor. Oliver will be free to walk outdoors and roam around the campus. However, she is told, security is very tight. They have a thirty- to sixty-second response for security matters as there are many security guards who traverse the hospital grounds all times of day and night.

Elizabeth hangs up from her call with Taylor Hospital feeling comforted that there actually is a place they could take Oliver where he would be not only be taken care of but also understood. She calls John right away. He's with the boys, eating pizza. Something was wrong but he couldn't tell her about it right then. She wanted to drive over there and get this decision taken care of. Maybe John had enough pizza for Wren? She asks if she and Wren could come over and to please save a slice for Wren.

"Of course."

Wren is thrilled to go to Daddy's and see her brothers. It takes them ten minutes to get there. Wren talks the whole way about school and Mandy and boys and the playground politics that Elizabeth always loves hearing.

Wren runs to John's front door, pushes it open and leaves it open for Elizabeth to follow.

Wren sees Peter first and flings herself on him.

"Hey, Weasel! Be careful there!" Peter laughs for the first time this day. Wren looks around, gives John a big hug then asks, "Where's Ollie?"

"He's in his room," Peter tells her quickly in case John steps in to tell her she can't see him. Oliver would never turn Wren away, Peter knows that. Maybe Wren is what Ollie needs right now.

"Can I go see him?"

"Sure," Peter says, "why not?" He glances at John who doesn't interfere. Possibly, Peter thinks, he knows Wren will be good for Ollie too.

The little girl runs to Oliver's room and opens the door quietly and closes it behind her. Oliver is lying on his bed, staring at the ceiling. She walks over and sits next to him. Oliver makes no effort to acknowledge her, keeps staring at the ceiling. She watches his face. Then she picks up his hand and holds it in her own. In her tiny voice, she whispers, "I love you." She feels Ollie squeeze her hand so she squeezes back. She stays with him for about ten minutes then returns to the living room.

"He's tired," she announces to the rest of the family.

No one says a word. Elizabeth scoops Wren up in her arms and gives her a big kiss. Wren notices tears in her mother's eyes.

"Why are you crying, Mom?"

"I guess just because I love you so much," Elizabeth tells her and looks over at John. "Shall we discuss this now?"

"Discuss what?" Wren asks as she takes a piece of pizza.

Elizabeth looks at John again. He nods. "We've found a wonderful place where Ollie can go to get better. As much as we love having him home we don't see much progress as far as Ollie is concerned. He's just not getting better."

"But . . ." Wren tries to break in.

Elizabeth nods at her, acknowledging the attempted interruption, but keeps talking. "At this place, he'll be with people who have the same illness he has and with doctors who know how to help him. He won't have to try to fit into our world out here, the way we do."

"No!" Wren says adamantly. "No! He won't be happy. He won't. He's just tired! I'm telling you!"

"Wren," John says, "he's not happy now. We're the ones who are happy with him around, but he's not happy. He's very sick and he needs more help than we can give him. We've tried and it's not working. Not because of anything we did but because of his brain illness."

Peter, listening, is overcome with guilt. He thinks back over the day and remembers, again, how happy and content Oliver was sitting next to the creek at their mom's, happy, that is, before he, Peter, stepped in and ruined everything. He knows that if Ollie is sent away his guilt will stay with him. He wants to tell and take the consequences but, the act of telling is so drastic that he keeps his mouth shut. If he was going to tell, he thinks, he should have told hours ago, certainly before he lied while looking into his father's eyes. But now he's just fucked, and so is Ollie. He owes Ollie for keeping silent. He owes him big time, now and forever.

19

LIFELINES IN HELL

That same evening, with Wren falling asleep on the couch and even after John lifts her up and tucks her into his bed, he and Elizabeth hammer out the details for getting Oliver back east to Taylor Hospital. Peter listens for a while but leaves his parents alone and goes to John's room where Wren has stayed asleep. He pushes her gently to make space for himself then lies down next to her and falls asleep, his parents' voices muffled from the living room.

Elizabeth repeats all she heard from Nan, the coordinator at Taylor. She assures John that this woman is confident they can help Oliver.

"I think we need to get him there as fast as we can," John says.

Elizabeth is surprised. "Really? Even though the airline tickets will cost double?"

"Yeah. He's not okay. I keep waiting for the next explosion, for another psychotic break. I'll pay for his ticket. Possibly we could get Dr. Bruce to write a medical order for the airlines. I don't really know how that works but it's worth looking into. For Ollie's ticket. Then we could split the difference."

Elizabeth is taken aback by John's sense of urgency. "If you really think he's that vulnerable right now, I could easily take off work to fly him back," she says. "Any time."

"That's what I was hoping for," John agrees. "Peter and Wren can stay with me."

"Why don't we call the airline right now and see what they have to say?"

John calls. He speaks to an agent who tells him that they do have health emergency tickets. All he needs for that special fare is the date they're flying, the name of the person who needs the medical service, the relationship to the other passenger, the name of the hospital they're flying to, and the doctor's name and phone number.

"Well, that's fairly straightforward," he tells Elizabeth. "So, when can you be ready to go?"

"How about the day after tomorrow?"

"Good. Let's do it."

"Okay, if you can get Ollie ready. And call Dr. Bruce about this. Maybe he could prescribe something in case Ollie does begin to freak out."

Elizabeth feels a punch of adrenaline to her stomach. What would she do, how would she handle it if Oliver had a psychotic break on the plane?

"I'll help Wren pack up," says John. "You can deal with Taylor Hospital since you already have a dialogue going with them."

"All right, I'll do that. Thank God for Susan at the coffeehouse! She'll take care of everything. I'll tell Taylor Hospital that we'll be there . . . what day is it today?"

"Tuesday."

"We'll fly in on Thursday. I know they have a room for him at Wimberly House. I'll have to get the name of the doctor who will see him right away for the medical emergency ticket. God, John, my ticket is going to cost a fortune!"

"Ollie's worth a fortune."

Elizabeth walks into John's bedroom to check on Wren. She's sprawled out, sound asleep. Peter is there, asleep too. She sits on the bed next to her daughter and leans down to kiss her. Her breath is Wren, sweet mostly, not so much tiny, little girl anymore but not the breath of a full-grown girl either. Elizabeth catches John's scent from Wren's pillow and buries her face in it, breathing him in. Taking his scent without him knowing makes her feel like a voyeur. If he discovers her doing this he would know she misses him. Missing him is so very complicated. She runs her hand over Peter's hair, bends down to kiss him, then leaves them and walks back out to the living room.

"As soon as you give me the name of the doctor at Taylor Hospital, and the number, I'll make a reservation."

"Okay."

"I don't think there's much more we can do tonight."

"Wren is sound asleep and Peter is next to her, asleep too. Would you mind if I sleep on your couch?"

John is surprised by the request. "But how about Jack? Won't he pee all over the house?"

"I'll run home and get him and some night clothes."

"Then why don't you sleep in Peter's bed and I'll sleep on the couch?"

John's voice is gentle, almost seductive. He realizes that he and Elizabeth haven't slept in such close quarters since she took up residence in the guest bedroom, so many years ago, before they divorced. He wants to mention this but thinks better of it.

Everyone she loves is right here, under John's roof, and she wants to stay.

"Okay, I'll sleep in Peter's bed."

John studies her face, sees her loneliness. "Sure, why not?"

"I better go home and get Jack."

With little traffic this time of night it takes Elizabeth only twenty minutes to get home, grab a quick slug of vodka out of the bottle in her freezer, fetch her nightgown and robe from the back of her bathroom door, get Jack into the front seat, then drive back. Upon arrival at John's, Jack jumps out of the car and runs to the front door. Elizabeth lets him in. Now, really, everyone is under one roof.

Today, Wednesday, makes tomorrow the day of departure. Elizabeth didn't sleep well in Peter's bed; she fought the urge to join John on the couch. She wanted another drink to mellow those feelings but John didn't keep booze in his house. She finally fell asleep by pretending John was lying next to her.

In the morning Elizabeth requests that everyone gather at her house for dinner so they can all get what they need before she locks up tight. She gives Wren and Peter rides to their respective schools then drives to her coffeehouse office to go over a few things with Susan. The fact that she'll only be gone for four days pales in the face of the onerous purpose of this trip. She calls Taylor Hospital from her office and speaks to Nan who gives her the name of the doctor who will be in charge of Oliver while he's at Wimberly House. She relays this information to John who has stayed at home to be with Oliver. John takes on the task of making reservations. Nan has told Elizabeth to not worry about transportation to the hospital as a car will be waiting for them at the Boston airport. She only needs to know when, what airline, what flight number.

John calls Dr. Bruce for tranquilizing medication for Oliver in case he panics on the plane or in the terminal. Neither mentions the possibility of a psychotic break.

Both Elizabeth and John are so busy with preparations that they don't pay much attention to Oliver who sits in the high-backed chair in John's living room, not eating, just staring. When John has finalized the reservations and put in the call to Dr. Bruce, he sits with Oliver.

"So, tomorrow is the big day. I'm going to wake you at 5:00 in the morning. Your and Mom's flight leaves Bozeman at 7:00. What do you think of that?"

Oliver looks at his father.

He's finally getting rid of you.

Oliver says nothing. He doesn't know what it is he's done to have to fly away somewhere.

"You do know that Mom is going with you, right?"

"Where?" Oliver finally asks.

"You're going to a hospital near Boston called Taylor Hospital where they can help you. It's not like the hospital where Dr. Bruce took care of you. It's a big place where you can walk around. There are other people there with your illness too."

"You mean people like Jude?"

"Yes, people like Jude."

"How long will I be there?" Oliver asks, warming to the subject.

"I don't know. I know they keep you for two weeks in the beginning and run all sorts of tests. But after that, we just don't know. They'll know more about what you're dealing with after all the testing."

Oliver sits back and looks up at the ceiling.

What they're dealing with?

"Let's get you packed, okay?" says John. "I need to go to work in a while so let's get you packed now and you'll be all ready to go. I'll drop you at Mom's on my way to work. And we're all eating dinner there too."

John and Oliver face the chaos that's Oliver's room. The floor holds everything that could be on a hanger or in a drawer.

"Wow," says John. "Maybe you need to do laundry before packing?"

"Ya think?" Oliver laughs.

John laughs too. How long has it been since I heard Ollie laugh? he wonders. He puts his arm around him. "You're going to be great! You know what? It would make more sense if you stuffed what you want to take into your suitcase and took it dirty to Mom's and wash it there. Okay?"

"Yeah, but what should I take?"

"Think threes. Three each of everything. That should do it. Except shoes. You only need two pairs of shoes. You do that and I'm going to clean up the breakfast mess in the kitchen, okay?"

"Okay."

John leaves Oliver standing on his mound of clothes, his suitcase open like a mouth waiting to be filled.

By evening all the preparations are taken care of. Elizabeth and Oliver will get their boarding passes at the airport the next morning. The laundry is done and packed. Wren's school knows she'll be living with her father for the rest of the week. John has picked up a prescription of Neurontin from Dr. Bruce for Oliver in case it is needed; the pills should calm him without knocking him out. Taylor Hospital knows when they'll land in Boston. The coffeehouse will run without a hitch with Susan at the helm. Wren has packed her pink suitcase with as many clothes as she could stuff inside. Jack's bowl and bag of food are waiting by the door next to Wren's suitcase.

The family is gathered at Elizabeth's house for dinner. Pizza and bread sticks. She apologizes but doesn't want to clean up a cooked dinner mess. She has a tall vodka tonic in one hand.

"Ollie, I hope you'll take care of Mom," says John. "She looks more nervous than you are!"

"I think I am!" She agrees.

Oliver, Peter, and Wren are quiet. Wren stays close to Oliver. When dinner is finished and the pizza box is broken down for recycling, the three siblings walk outside to the creek. Wren holds on to Oliver by slipping two of her small fingers into a belt loop on the side of his pants. Oliver lights up a smoke. There is no conversation as they listen to the creek. The water is rising farther up the banks as the snow melt from the high foothills fills the creeks below. Jack bounces around, a long stick in his mouth. No one throws it for him so he tosses it in the air for himself.

Oliver moves away from the creek with Wren still holding on and stares up at his old loft, at the dark window on the east end of the building. He pictures himself climbing the ladder and turning on the light switch right by that window. He turns his attention to the house and spots the TV antenna on the roof.

"You know why that's there?" he asks his siblings while pointing at the antenna.

"No," says Peter. "Why?"

"Because that's how they keep track of me."

"Who keeps track of you, Ollie?" Wren asks.

"Wren," says Peter. He catches her eye and shakes his head, glaring at her.

"What?" she asks him.

He shakes his head again. "Never mind."

Oliver ignores the give-and-take between his brother and sister. He sits down on the deck. "I wonder what it's going to be like," he muses.

"The hospital?" asks Peter.

"Yeah."

"Probably pretty nice."

Oliver lights another cigarette as Wren pulls her fingers out of his belt loop.

John walks out to the deck to join them. "We need to get going."

"We're taking Jack, right?" asks Wren.

"You bet," says John. "You know the plan, right? You're all coming with me. In the morning Ollie and I will pick up Mom at 5:15, and we'll go to the airport. I'll put them on the plane and come back home. We'll have breakfast and you and Peter will go to school and I'll go to work. Good?"

Peter nods, Wren says, "Yup." Oliver is silent.

"Okay then, let's go. Say good night and goodbye to your mother and grab your stuff."

20

THE DISTANT HOSPITAL

Four-thirty in the morning is much too early for any human to be awake. That's what John thinks anyway. He sits on the couch, feet on the floor. Wren is in his bed again. He can smell the coffee he set to brew at 4:15. He heaves himself up, pours himself a cup and then showers. Next, he wakes Oliver. Jack is sleeping on Oliver's bed and snuffles Oliver's cheek as John shakes his shoulder.

"Come on," he says, "we have to get up! It's time to go to the airport."

Oliver is out cold. He doesn't even stir.

"Ollie! GET UP!" he yells. Jack jumps off the bed while John shakes Oliver vigorously.

"Whattaya want?" Oliver mumbles.

"It's time to go to the airport," John tells him. "Come on. Up, up, up!"

Oliver groans and turns onto his back.

"I'll bring you some coffee." He goes to the kitchen and pours a cup for Oliver.

"Come on, here you go." He hands Oliver the coffee and stands over him while he drinks it.

"We need to get going. I know it's torture but we have to make the flight."

"The flight?"

"You and Mom are flying to Boston today, remember?"

"Oh yeah!" Oliver sits up straighter.

"All you need to do is jump in the shower then get dressed."

John stands in Oliver's room and waits until he's on his feet then goes to his room for clean clothes. Wren is sound asleep, her pink blankie, retrieved from Elizabeth's house, is wrapped in her arms up near her neck. John, as quietly as he can, opens his closet and chest of drawers. He can hear Oliver in the shower. He takes his clothes and changes in Oliver's room.

Oliver gets out of the shower, towels off then walks into his room. He finds John there, getting dressed.

"You excited?" asks John.

"I think so."

"I'm going to miss you. I wish I was coming with you." John feels himself choking up.

"Yeah." Oliver pulls on his clothes. "I'm ready!"

"Maybe you could brush your hair?"

"Oh." Oliver returns to the bathroom. He looks at himself in the new mirror while he brushes his unruly hair but suddenly he sees something move in the mirror behind him. He freezes, not knowing what to expect. The thing moves closer to him and he sees it's just Wren standing there, her blankie dragging on the ground.

"You scared me, Wren!!"

"I'm sorry."

Oliver looks at her closely and sees she's crying, quietly. "What's wrong, Weez?"

Wren throws herself at Oliver. "I'm going to miss you!"

Oliver picks her up, puts the toilet seat down and sits with her and her blankie, rocking her and holding her tight.

"I'll be back before you know it."

"But I'll miss you before knowing it!"

The prison inside Oliver breaks open against the softness of his little sister; the prison that locks up his emotions, his expressions, his self. He holds this little girl and he begins to cry, her fragrant blankie between them soaking up their tears.

John walks down the hall to find Oliver and sees, reflected in the mirror, the two sitting and holding each other. He looks at his watch. It's almost five o'clock. He feels helpless. He hasn't seen Oliver cry for such a long time. He doesn't want to break them up but they have to go. Five more minutes.

John walks out to the SUV, turns it on and cranks up the heater. Then, after re-entering the house, he pulls the quilt off his bed and grabs a pillow to make a nest for Wren on the couch. He turns on the TV to a cartoon channel. That should distract her and help her get back to sleep. He calls Jack and makes him get up on the couch. "Stay."

There was no more time. He returns to the bathroom and, feeling like an imposter, interrupts them. "Ollie, we need to go."

Oliver looks up at John. His face is wet with tears.

"You can carry Wren out to the living room. I made a bed for her on the couch with Jack."

"Okay." Oliver lifts Wren who keeps her arms locked around his neck. He carries her out to the living room and she lets him lower her onto the couch.

Jack licks her face, her tears, then settles back down on the quilt.

"I'll be back in an hour or so," John tells her and leans over to kiss her.

Wren looks up at him with more tears in her eyes. She nods. "Where's Peter?"

"He's in his room."

"Okay."

Oliver gets down on his knees and hugs her one more time. "I'll call you, okay?"

Wren nods fast. She twists her fingers into Jack's long black-and-white fur. "Come home soon," she says.

"I will."

Oliver and John walk out the door.

Peter hears the TV. He hears the end of the conversations, then the quiet after the front door is closed. He lies in his bed, hating himself for not getting up, hating himself for bringing Oliver to the edge and making it necessary that he fly away to a distant hospital. He loves Ollie for not saying anything about Cameron Bridge and knows what he's done to him by asking him to be silent. He stares up at the ceiling, feeling like a traitor. Then he thinks of Wren out there in the living room all by herself. He gets up, pulls a blanket off his bed and joins her in the living room.

"Hey!"

"Hi!"

"Whatcha watching?"

"Cartoons."

"Good."

The two of them, with Jack on their legs, settle in to watch Looney Tunes on the opposite ends of the couch, Peter's feet up by Wren's shoulders, her feet by his knees. Oliver is a palpable absence between them.

John and Oliver pick up Elizabeth at her house. John fetches Oliver's suitcase and Jack's food and bowl and they drive to the airport, parking on the curb near the Departures door. They enter the airport. John sits with Oliver while Elizabeth deals with their tickets. She beckons to Oliver when he has to show his ID. After that he returns to sit with John. She has to show all the medical information to the ticket agent even though the medical emergency ticket has already been issued. She has to point to Oliver, to finger him as the medical emergency passenger. She thinks the ticket agent is wondering what could possibly be wrong with this seemingly healthy, good-looking young man. She wishes for one second that Ollie was in a wheelchair so his disability would be obvious to all. Finally, boarding passes in hand, she and John and Oliver walk to the gate.

"Just hang on to me, all right?" Elizabeth says gently. "The only time you can't hang on is when we each step through the metal detector. Okay?"

"Metal detector?" Oliver's eyes open wide. He stands.

"It's all right. Why don't you stand up and see if you have any change in your pockets."

Oliver checks and comes up with a quarter. And he isn't wearing a belt.

"Here." He hands the quarter to John.

"You don't have anything to be afraid of," John says. "You don't have any metal on you. You'll sail through."

"I'm going now," John tells them. "You guys are on your way!"

"Okay," says Elizabeth.

Oliver has retreated back into himself. He's sitting with his elbows on his knees, his torso bent over, rocking back and forth.

"Ollie?"

No answer.

He's gone again, John thinks. He turns to Elizabeth. "Will you be okay?"

"I certainly hope so." She stands and opens her arms for a hug.

John responds and holds her tight.

"You call if there's anything I can do, even just to talk, okay?"

"I will."

"Ollie, I love you. Take care of yourself, okay?" John instantly thinks that was a stupid thing to say.

Oliver still doesn't respond.

The PA system announces their flight.

"Oh good," says John to Elizabeth. "Let's get him up and in line. Peter is with Wren. I shouldn't worry."

Elizabeth moves over to Oliver and puts both of her hands on his shoulders. "Ollie, we need to get on the airplane."

Nothing. He continues to rock.

Elizabeth kneels on the floor and takes Oliver's hands in hers. She peers up into his face. "Ollie?"

"Yeah." He stops rocking.

"We need to stand in line now to get on the plane. Okay?"

Oliver looks at her. She sees that his pupils are huge. She can see how terribly frightened he is.

John turns to Elizabeth. "I gave you his meds, right?"

"Yes, last night. I have the Zyprexa and Neurontin in my purse."

"Good."

"Come on," Elizabeth says and puts her arm through Oliver's. She hoists her large, black leather purse up to her shoulder and they move over to the line of passengers.

John stands where he is; stuck to the spot, his throat burning, and watches them move, inch by inch toward the ramp to the plane. He sees Oliver turn around to look for him. John waves. He wants to push through the crowd and grab Ollie and tell everyone it's a mistake, that his son is fine, he's just faking, that they'll work it out. But he doesn't. He fights an awful feeling that he'll never see Ollie again, that something terrible will happen to him at the hospital. He finally tears himself away and walks through the terminal out to his SUV, out of the airport parking lot and back into town. He would have liked to watch the airplane take off but thinks better of it. He needs to get back to Wren and Peter and work and everything that continues, unfortunately, even though Oliver is so sick.

21

GETTING THERE

Elizabeth and Oliver make it through the mobile tunnel to the airplane, find their seats, and settle in for the short flight to Denver. Elizabeth chats to Oliver about nothing, about how she wants to buy a book in Denver, how she likes the long moving sidewalks in the Denver airport.

"We'll be there for almost two hours so we can look around in the shops."

What his mother is saying sounds distasteful to Oliver. He doesn't like all these people around him, people in front of him, even a person on the aisle next to his mother. He knows they can hear his thoughts and it terrifies him. He stares out the window. He watches the luggage trucks pull away from the plane, hears the airplane's engines gather momentum as they pull away from the terminal. He puts his hands between his knees and squeezes hard. The pain takes his mind off his fear for a moment. They taxi to the end of the runway then turn, the engines roaring with power as they head down the runway and up, up into the sky where Oliver would like to live, up and away from everything that frightens him.

He smiles to himself, relishing this feeling. Maybe, he thinks, this is what death feels like. He sits back, his smile surprising Elizabeth who doesn't say a word but is glad to see him smile.

A flight attendant leans in to ask what he would like to drink. He doesn't answer and his smile fades. Elizabeth asks for a ginger ale for him and unclips his tray without asking. The uniformed woman places a bag of trail mix on his tray then pours his drink. He hears the fizz and the setting down of the plastic cup and the half empty can. He doesn't want them. He wants to be left alone, wants to relive taking off, the pressure to his chest, the roaring of the engines, the separation from earth. He doesn't touch the drink or the trail mix and stares out the window the rest of the way to Denver. Elizabeth drinks his soda and pockets his trail mix when it became evident that he didn't want it.

They arrive quickly. They inch forward as they exit the plane, Oliver quelling panic, a need to crawl over the tops of the seats to get out. Elizabeth is in front of him, which helps, but a large man who breathes heavily is behind him, adding to his panic. Once in the terminal they head straight to the Cinnabon stand and indulge in sugar.

"These are good, huh?" Elizabeth asks.

"Yeah."

"How're you holding up?"

"Okay."

"What shall we do for the next hour and a half?"

"Bookstore?" Oliver says, his mouth full.

"Well, I'd like to, but only if you're up for it."

"We can."

"Okay, well then, we'll go on the long moving sidewalk to get there. That's always fun."

They finish their Cinnabons then head to the center of the terminal. Oliver steps onto the moving sidewalk first, Elizabeth following him, stumbling a bit. Almost immediately, Oliver doesn't like it. He sees people coming at him fast, faster than he would ever want anyone coming at him. He holds on to the right-hand moving rail with both hands and stares down at his feet.

"Ollie? Are you okay?"

"No."

Elizabeth takes his left arm. She stands sideways with him, other people passing them without even a glance. Right before they reach the end she counts, "one, two, three" and they step off, making a smooth transition.

"We'll walk back."

"Good."

The bookstore is across from some tables by the huge airport windows. Oliver sits, content to watch the goings on outside the terminal. Elizabeth leaves him there and steps into the bookstore. She keeps an eye on him as she reads the book jackets and finally chooses two. After purchasing the books she sits next to Oliver.

"Would you like a book or a magazine?"

"No."

"How about something to drink?"

"Okay."

Elizabeth has gotten used to Oliver's monosyllabic answers but there's something about being in public that makes her want to prompt him, like she did when he was little, to add a "please" or "thank you," but she leaves it alone.

They get up and find some bottled water at a walk-thru deli.

"Let's find our gate and good seats to wait in near the windows and just hang-out. What do think?"

"Good."

The walk back to their terminal is a long one. The carts that transport people, that screech and beep as they push past, are unnerving; Oliver shrinks away from their frenetic energy. They're early at the gate and find many empty seats. CNN plays everywhere on overhead TV. Elizabeth tries to find a quiet spot behind a post away from them but it's a futile search. Oliver doesn't seem to pay much mind to them anyway. They finally find seats that face the windows and where you can't see the TV but you can still hear it. Oliver seems content to sit, again, and watch the outside world. Elizabeth opens one of her new books and begins to read.

Oliver hates boarding the plane. It seems as though the entire population of the world is trying to fight their way onto this flight. He doesn't understand why people have to stand so close to each other, why they have to be in such a rush, so impatient and irritable. He can feel them all around him and he hates it. He can feel them reading his thoughts.

Elizabeth wishes, when she hears the announcement, that she and Ollie could board first, but only passengers with young children, the elderly, and disabled people in wheelchairs are qualified. She wishes, once again, that Oliver was in a wheelchair or on crutches, just for this trip. She knows he's having a hard time. His lips are tight, his eyes smoldering with anger and fear. She has never before wanted to board a plane as quickly as now.

"Ollie. It's okay. We'll be in our seats in a minute."

Oliver looks at Elizabeth and almost doesn't know who she is. He feels himself slipping away, wanting to become part of the ceiling instead of being absorbed by all these people around him, people who are sucking his identity away from him. Elizabeth can feel him shattering, getting more and more angry and confused. She holds his arm and hangs on tight, as though she is the one who needs an anchor. They inch forward, half step followed by half step.

Finally, Elizabeth hands over their boarding passes and they're free to walk into the tunnel to the plane. Elizabeth continues to hold Oliver's arm but once inside the plane the commotion is worse. Elizabeth can't hold Oliver's arm anymore, they're squeezed between the seats down the aisle, people standing in the way, putting their luggage in the overhead compartments, taking forever to settle in and sit in their seats so others can get by. Elizabeth tells Oliver their seat numbers as he's in front of her. Even with giving him this distraction, she waits for him to deteriorate, to explode. The noise and chaos around them are fragmenting her, confusing any sense of purpose she may have had. She can't imagine what it's doing to Oliver. She sees his face but doesn't know where it is he goes inside himself. Thankfully, their seats are in the middle of the plane so they don't have too far to go. It isn't until they're in their seats that she takes a deep breath. Even though the plane is still sitting on the tarmac, she puts on her seatbelt and pulls it tight.

As soon as they settle in, Oliver asks Elizabeth to not put down his tray. He doesn't give her a reason but wants to experience the take off for as long as possible. He knows from the last flight that once they're airborne everyone around him will be able to hear his thoughts. By sitting very still and staring out the window he'll minimize the thoughts he's broadcasting to the passengers. He won't interrupt his vigilance by eating or drinking or talking.

During the first hour of the flight Elizabeth tries to get him to eat but he refuses. She tries to get him to speak but he won't respond. She finally gives up and decides to be grateful that he's not acting out. She asks the attendant for two pillows and puts one on Oliver's lap. She reminds Oliver that he can put his seat back, which he does without looking at her. Finally, after two hours, Oliver puts the pillow behind his head and falls asleep. Elizabeth, on the other hand, buys two tiny bottles of vodka and a tonic water. She's relieved when the alcohol hits her brain.

There's a man in baggage claim wearing a dark blue suit and carrying a sign that says MOORE. Elizabeth approaches him and asks which Moore he's waiting for.

"Elizabeth and Oliver Moore."

"That's us."

"Very good. Welcome to Boston. Let me help you with your luggage."

"And your name is?"

"I'm Larry."

They stand by the luggage carousel and wait for their bags. It seems an eternity, especially with a stranger standing next to them.

"There they are!" Elizabeth yells.

Larry hoists the bags off the carousel and carries them to the baggage ticket checker. Elizabeth has the tickets ready and they're out on the street in less than five minutes.

Larry puts the bags down, well away from the curb. "Wait here and I'll bring the car around."

Oliver lights a smoke the minute they're outside the baggage claim doors. He can taste the smell of the city and feels the humidity. He can hear cabbies yelling and car horns honking and suddenly these sounds become frightening. He knows the yells are insults directed toward him. He stands back against the building in the smoking area and watches Elizabeth and all the other people coming and going. He has a scowl on his face. A few others are standing near him, smoking. There seems to be no common denominator among the smokers; a businessman, an elderly woman, a student, and him. Elizabeth beckons to him as a sleek black car parks at the curb. Larry jumps out, the trunk of the car popping open. He grabs their bags, places them in the back, slams the trunk shut and motions for Oliver to get into the back seat with his mother. They pull away from the airport quickly and join other cars on the interstate.

Oliver is a bit excited now to see where they're headed. The number of cars on the road is impressive. He sees the Charles River, dock lights reflecting on the smooth water. In a half hour they're at the hospital, driving through the gates. They drive up and around a winding driveway and stop in front of a clapboard and brick house. Larry gets out and directs them to the entrance. Since it's after hours they ring the doorbell. The door opens immediately.

"Welcome! You must be Mrs. Moore and this must be Oliver. Welcome to Wimberly House. I'm Nan."

22

BEING THERE

Elizabeth and Oliver step over the threshold and follow Nan down a short hall to another door. A wide staircase to the left leads up in the opposite direction, the newel post thick and old, the banister heavy.

"You'll be seeing Dr. Svare while you're with us, Oliver," Nan says. "His office is right at the top of this staircase."

She opens the door at the end of the hall with a key. There's a window in this door embedded with wire mesh.

"Now, this door is locked after hours so no one can come in. It's not locked from inside so you're not locked in at any time." She looks at Oliver to make sure he heard her. He nods.

They step into a beautiful wide hallway, a dining room to their left, a long open space the width of two halls on their right, doors all along these walls with couches and chairs in between. Nan takes them into the staff room on their right. Two nurses are there, eager to meet Oliver. Ernest, a large African American man steps forward and takes Oliver's outstretched hand.

"Hey, let me show you around, 'kay?"

This nurse fascinates Oliver who was born and raised in predominately white Montana. Ernest takes Oliver to the patients' kitchen. Oliver has never seen so much food crammed into such a small space.

"We order dinner from any restaurant you all want every night," Ernest explains. "But you have to agree with the other patients. You can come in here any time of day and night to get a snack. Just like home."

They step out of the kitchen and walk down a back hall where Ernest shows Oliver the laundry. Reversing their steps he shows him a small room equipped with a TV off the wide main hall. A man, probably in his fifties, is sitting on the couch. He has long gray hair and looks miserable.

"Paul, this is Oliver. He's going to stay with us for a while."

Paul looks at Oliver without seeing him.

Oliver smiles. "Hi Paul."

"Now, my good man," says Ernest. "I'll show you your room."

They walk down the wide expanse toward the dining room. A door, almost hidden by the elaborate molding, opens into Oliver's room.

"Here you go. You can put your clothes in this armoire. Your bathroom is over there. If you need extra blankets or pillows they're right here in the armoire."

Oliver looks around the room. It's beautiful, comfortable but there's a TV right next to his bed.

"Where's my mom?" he asks Ernest.

"I think she's out there talking to Nan. Let's go see."

The two of them walk out of Oliver's room and find Elizabeth talking to Nan and the other nurse. They've been filling her in on the routine here, how meds are distributed, what's expected of the patients and what is not.

"Hi, sweetie," Elizabeth says when she sees Oliver. "This is quite a place, no?"

"Yeah. You wanna come see my room?"

"Of course. Let's go."

"I'm leaving now," says Nan. "I'll see you both in the morning."

"Yes, thank you so much," says Elizabeth.

Oliver is silent.

Elizabeth is puzzled when she sees a TV in Oliver's room. It doesn't seem right. She knows what TV does to him and suspects it does the same to other patients. But the room itself impresses her. She sits on the couch between his bed and the armoire while he unpacks his few things. When he's finished he lies on his bed and sighs deeply.

"You must be so tired," Elizabeth says to him.

"I am."

"I think I'll go check into the hotel then come back. I'm told it's not very far from here."

"Okay. Oh, Mom, did you meet Paul? He's another patient here and he's very quiet and gray."

"No, I haven't met him yet."

"Oh."

Elizabeth leans over Oliver and gives him a kiss on his forehead. She doesn't know what time it is but doesn't want to leave him for very long. She stops at the staff room and asks for a cab. They call one immediately. Ernest talks to her while they wait for the cab to arrive.

"You've got yourself a fine boy there," he says.

"Yes, I do."

"And he's eighteen?"

"Yes, eighteen."

"Handsome too."

"He is, isn't he? I'm so sad he has to be here."

"He'll be all right. We'll take good care of him."

"You know, TV scares him a lot. I wonder why there's a TV in his room. We've been careful to keep him away from it."

Ernest crosses his arms and Elizabeth notices his muscles. She thinks that if a patient got violent Ernest would be able to hold him or her down, no problem.

"Some patients are okay with it, others aren't. The ones who aren't, can learn to not turn it on. Oliver will learn about choices. It's not easy but it's necessary."

"But, when he's just beginning, when he probably isn't on the right medications, it makes me nervous that he has a TV in there."

"We'll keep an eye on him, don't you worry."

"I think I'll come back after I check into the hotel, all right?"

"Whatever you want. I'm not going anywhere."

The cab is waiting outside. "I'll see you shortly," Elizabeth says to both the nurses. She reaches to pick up her suitcase but Ernest picks it up for her and carries it out to the cab.

Ernest gives the cabby the name of the hotel where Elizabeth will be staying and a taxi voucher so she won't have to pay for the ride.

The hotel is only about five miles away. Once they arrive, Elizabeth asks the cabby to wait for her while she checks in. She walks to her room, quickly, and as she places her card key in her purse she discovers Oliver's meds. After ten minutes, maybe fifteen, they're back on the road to Taylor Hospital. As soon as they arrive at Wimberly House she tips the cabbie and jumps out. Ernest, who must have been watching for her, opens the door.

"How is he?" she asks.

"He's just fine. You only left a few moments ago," Ernest replies with a laugh.

"I forgot to give you his medications."

"Oh no, not to worry. Oliver's doctor in Montana must have called Dr. Svare because Oliver's medications were here before you were. We already gave them to him."

"How could I have forgotten that?"

"I'm sure you've a lot on your mind."

All of a sudden Elizabeth is dying for a drink but there's nothing she can do about it.

Elizabeth knocks on Oliver's door. No answer. She opens it and peeks in. Oliver is lying on his bed in a fetal position, the TV on. She walks over to him and see's he's trembling. She turns the TV off and sits on his bed.

"I saw a vampire," he whispers.

"Where was it?"

"First it was on the TV then it was in that window," he tells her and points to the window at the far end of the room.

Elizabeth stands. She unplugs the TV. She finds an extra blanket in the armoire and drapes it over the TV to block the screen.

"There."

She walks to the far end of the room and draws the curtains over the offending window.

"Don't tell them, okay?" whispers Oliver.

"Don't tell who, sweetie?" Elizabeth asks knowing full well who he means.

"Don't tell Ernest and that other nurse, okay?"

She sits on his bed again and puts her hand on his arm. "You're here because you have an illness that, among other things, gives you hallucinations. These nurses deal with," she pauses, wanting this to sound right, "they deal with patients who have the same symptoms as yours and hallucinations are a part of those symptoms. If you don't tell them what's happening, they can't help you. Do you understand that?"

"Yes."

"You can relax. That's why we brought you here; you don't have to hide or pretend or anything like that. You're safe."

"Are you sure?"

"Yes. Would you like me to stay with you tonight?"

"Yes."

"Okay, I'll tell Ernest. I'll be right back."

After speaking with Ernest, Elizabeth returns to Oliver's room and calls John.

"Hello?" John's voice sounds tight.

"It's me. "How's everything there?"

"We're great, but how about you and Ollie?"

"It's been a bit bumpy but we made it. We're both exhausted. I'm going to sleep in his room on a pullout tonight. This place is unbelievable!! If the care is as good as the facility Ollie will be home before we know it!"

"Pretty beautiful, huh?"

"Yes. How're you guys?"

"I'm okay, apprehensive, but Wren and Peter are good. They miss you and Ollie but some of the tension has evaporated."

"That's good. Give them my love, okay? And Ollie's. I miss you guys."

"We miss you too. Call me tomorrow, okay?"

"I will."

"Bye." John hangs up.

Elizabeth can imagine how stressed-out John feels and she's grateful that she came east with Ollie; the waiting on John's part must be awful.

23

A TOKEN OF COFFEE CAKE

The couch in Oliver's room is a pullout. Elizabeth sleeps the sleep of the exhausted and wakes up late morning. Ollie is still sleeping. She tries to smooth out her crushed clothes before she walks out of the room but they're beyond help. She was stupid to wear a linen blouse. She uses Oliver's brush in the bathroom and laughs quietly at her disheveled appearance.

There are two nurses on the floor, a large woman and a small woman, both brunette and both very accommodating. The larger nurse shows Elizabeth the patient's kitchen where coffee is waiting.

"Dr. Svare wanted to know when you were awake so he could speak with you. I'll call upstairs to let him know you're up while you have some breakfast. Help yourself to anything you see here. Eggs are in the ice box if you would like." The nurse opens a cupboard and shows Elizabeth a huge collection of pots and pans.

"Thank you. I think I'll just have some of this coffee cake and coffee."

Paul, with the long gray hair, joins Elizabeth in the kitchen. He is as quiet as a mouse as he pours himself a cup of coffee. She notices his feet are clad only in socks and observes that wearing socks probably helps him be quiet.

The large nurse enters the now crowded kitchen.

"Good morning, Paul," she says. He doesn't answer but does nod his head before scurrying away. She turns to Elizabeth. "I just spoke with Dr. Svare's secretary and she asked if you could come up to his office in fifteen minutes."

"Of course."

"If you'd like you could take your coffee upstairs to his waiting area."

"I'll do that. I only have a few bites left of this Entenmann's cake. We can't get this in Montana. I'm originally from New York and miss many of the culinary delights of the East Coast, to say the least."

"I'll take you to the stairs. You'll also meet our Program Director. She's the one to contact for almost everything that pertains to Wimberly House. Her name is Zoe Jarvic and her office is directly to the left when you enter before the stairs."

"Let's go," says Elizabeth. "That coffee cake is so good! I might not eat anything but that while I'm here."

The large nurse takes Elizabeth down the hall, past the staff room and out the door. She mentions that this door is unlocked, both ways, during the day. She opens it and points to the stairs. Elizabeth thanks her and begins her climb. There's a landing, a huge window above it, and a railing above the open space where she can see a grouping of chairs. No one is waiting. She climbs the rest of the stairs and arrives at the top, not knowing what to do now. The paneling is dark. A few doors stand silently with no indication of what's behind them. She decides to sit and wait. Almost as soon as she sits an attractive man with dark hair falling over his forehead comes out of the far-right door and asks her if she's Mrs. Moore.

"Yes, I am. But please, call me Elizabeth."

"All right, Elizabeth, I'm Dr. Svare. Please follow me into my office. I see you have some coffee already so we're set."

"Yes, thank you." Elizabeth's first impression of the doctor's office is one of clutter. His desk is near a window, facing into the room, a couple of chairs to the side of it. A large conference table is on the other side of the room, bookcases rising from the floor to the ceiling behind it.

"Please, sit." Dr. Svare indicates the chairs near his desk. "I understand you and Oliver's father have power of attorney so we're not breaking any laws here when we discuss Oliver."

"Correct."

"I would like this meeting to be a short gathering of Oliver's history, as you know it. I have his file from Dr. Bruce, but, even so, the more we know about Oliver the better."

"That makes sense."

"So, let's begin at birth. How was his birth?"

"Very difficult. I was in labor for twenty-one hours before a c-section. When they finally opened me up, they found the umbilical cord wrapped around Oliver's neck. His blood pressure dropped before they took him out so they dubbed it an emergency C-section."

"Was he a fussy baby?"

"No, not at all. He was very sweet."

"And he's the eldest? Of three?"

"Yes. He and his brother, Peter, are only eighteen months apart. His sister is ten years younger."

"What kind of young child was Oliver?"

"Ollie was shy, very shy but the sweetest ever. He was very cautious. He had to be pushed into things but once he was into them he excelled. He also got very silly and would charge around with Peter making a ruckus. Sometimes it was difficult getting him to settle down."

"Well, he was a little boy after all," says Dr. Svare, smiling.

"Yes, he was . . . a dear, sweet, darling little boy." Elizabeth stops her narrative and looks pointedly at Dr. Svare. "What do you think is going to happen to him?"

"Well, let's keep on with the history for now," he says, looking at her sympathetically. "What's next? How was he as a young adolescent, say eleven, twelve, thirteen?"

"Oliver was still shy but also very popular. Around my friends he was polite, considerate, confident. And he loved to talk! About almost anything. He had a curious mind. He was into sports and his friends. He had a lot of friends. Friends who don't seem to care about him anymore, at least they haven't been coming around to see how he is."

"He probably scares them."

"I don't know. I think it's hurtful to him. At least Peter has been sticking by him and his sister, Wren."

"So, how about his later adolescent years? Fourteen, fifteen, and on?"

"It seems that Oliver began changing around sixteen; he became aggressive, confrontational. He also became obsessive. No, wait, he was obsessive at a much younger age. He wore me down most of the time so I don't know if it was just habitual or if he was truly obsessive but he drove me crazy with it! Let's see. I know he began smoking weed around fifteen. And drinking. He was put on Adderall for ADD and Dexedrine, which seemed to make him crazy. He would become what I would now call manic. He also fell into depression and was put on Zoloft but, if my memory serves me right, the Zoloft only made him more manic."

"Tell me about the aggression."

"Oliver began acting aggressively toward me when I told him 'no.' At one point I went after him because he called me a bitch. He grabbed my arms and said he was going to kill me. That was scary. I was out of control myself and would have slapped him if I'd had a chance."

"That must have been difficult."

"Yes, it was. Just recently I was up in the loft where he was living and he screamed at me to leave and called me a bitch and I hadn't done a thing so, I don't know."

"Do you think he's been hearing voices?"

"Yes."

"Do you think he's been hallucinating?"

"Yes."

"And why do you think these things?"

"Because at times, actually most of the time now, when you speak to him he's just not there. It seems that he's listening to something other than you. And last night he had the TV on and was terrified because he thought he saw a vampire, first on the TV and then in the window. He's scared of people. Any person. He's just not on this planet anymore. Do you think you can help him?"

Dr. Svare scratched his head. "Yes, I do think I can help him. I'll meet with him this afternoon and we'll begin. It's a slow process. We need to eliminate certain physical considerations with blood work, MRI, EEG. These tests will take up much of the next two weeks. I'll visit with him every day. A psychologist, Dr. Greenwood, will see him every day as well and will begin getting to know him. His office is a short hike from here so it will be an opportunity for Oliver to get out and walk. Someone will accompany him until he's sure of the way. This will probably be tough on all of you as well as a relief. Oliver will be safe here with us. I'll most likely tweak his medication a bit. I like doing that while he's here, under my roof, so I can keep close tabs on him. Some of these medications take a long time to kick in while others kick in right away. Do you have any questions?"

"Oh, my God! Thousands! I don't know where to start so I guess I'll just wait to see what you come up with."

"Good." Dr. Svare stands. "It was wonderful meeting you. I reserve the right to interview you before you leave if I feel it's necessary."

"Yes, of course. Thank you."

Elizabeth finds her way out and back down the stairs. She feels a bit lightheaded from the interview, a bit out-of-body. She heads to the kitchen to eat another piece of the Entenmann's to bring herself back to reality. Oliver is standing in the kitchen, leaning up against the counter, eating coffee cake.

"Hi, Mom! Where've you been?" His smile is radiant.

"I was talking to Dr. Svare who you'll meet today. He seems like a good guy. When did you get up?"

"Just a little while ago."

"I'm so happy to see you so happy!"

"Hey, I found this back door here where you can see squirrels and chipmunks." Oliver walks out of the kitchen with his mom in tow and shows her the door.

"Let's take our food out there," Elizabeth suggests. "We could throw them some crumbs."

"Or whole pieces!"

Elizabeth wonders if Ollie is as relieved being here at the hospital as the family is having him here. Or is he relieved that this place is nothing like the crisis ward in Bozeman. Whatever it is, she'll take it. She can't even remember the last time she's seen him so joyful.

They step outside and spot the squirrels. Every once in a while a tiny chipmunk would pitter patter along the stone wall that encircled a small lawn. Elizabeth looks out and beyond Wimberly House and sees the road that they must have traveled on last night.

"Hey, you want to go on a walk?" she asks Oliver.

"Yeah!"

"How about if I go inside to check your schedule and see if we can, okay?"

"That would be cool, Mom. I'll wait here. Wait, wait, wait! Look! That squirrel took the piece of coffee cake I threw over there!"

"Yes, sweetie. What a treat you are! I'll be right back." She leans into him and gives him a kiss. "I love you so much."

"I love you too, Mom."

Elizabeth walks back inside Wimberly House to find someone about Oliver's schedule. She is stopped almost immediately by a small, energetic woman with short blonde hair who introduces herself as Zoe Jarvic, the Wimberly House Program Director. Elizabeth likes her immediately. They both go outside so Oliver can meet her.

"Ollie," says Elizabeth, "this is Zoe Jarvic and she'll be helping you with everything here. This is who we needed to meet as far as scheduling for you."

Oliver's energy drops, noticeably, but he walks over to Zoe and shakes her hand, unable to look her straight in the eye.

"Ollie and I wanted to take a walk. Do you have him scheduled for anything right now?"

"As a matter of fact, I do. I was coming to find you. Oliver, you have an appointment with Dr. Greenwood in twenty minutes. We can all take a walk as his office is probably a good, fast-paced five-minute walk from here. Why don't I meet the two of you outside the front entrance in say, five minutes?"

"Okay, we'll be there," Elizabeth tells her. "Maybe we could take an exploratory walk after that?"

"Yes."

24

ON THE MAP

Elizabeth and Oliver are waiting for Zoe outside the entrance in exactly five minutes. Zoe joins them and they head out, walking on a road that runs behind Wimberly House, not the road Elizabeth saw from the small lawn. Zoe keeps up a running dialogue about the history of Taylor Hospital and about the spring weather. When they reach a three-way fork in the road she takes them the straight route, through a large building into gardens where a huge tree shades picnic benches and a small pond. A few people are sitting and reading. Dr. Greenwood's office is close to this building. The three of them walk through an arched entrance and take the stairs up two flights. They're right on time. The doctor's office door is open so Zoe peeks her head in.

"We're here," she tells him.

"Excellent," he says and comes out into the hall.

Zoe makes introductions. "Dr. Greenwood, this is Oliver Moore and his mother, Elizabeth."

"It's good to meet you," Dr. Greenwood says to both Oliver and Elizabeth. "Oliver, why don't you come into my office and we'll get started." Then, to Elizabeth and Zoe, "We'll be fifty minutes. Oliver will be waiting outside the building after that."

"That's fine," Zoe tells him, looking at her watch. "One or both of us will be here."

"I'll see you in a bit," Elizabeth says to Oliver. She can see how he's withdrawn and wants to protect him but knows she can't.

She and Zoe walk back downstairs and out the arched door. They walk in silence back through the cafeteria building and out the other side. Zoe leads the way. Once they're outside she slows her pace to walk next to Elizabeth.

"It's difficult, isn't it," she says.

"Yes. He was in such a great mood. I haven't seen him so happy for a long time. Isn't that strange?"

"No, not really. He may feel less of a burden on all of you now that he's here. He may feel that he is finally getting some help and can let his guard down. Sometimes patients' symptoms get much worse before they get better because they don't have to hold themselves in check the way they do on the outside."

Elizabeth is now walking slowly, looking down at her feet.

"You couldn't have better doctors. Dr. Svare and Dr. Greenwood will work closely with Oliver to determine an appropriate diagnosis. They'll find what medications work and which don't. You can willingly entrust Oliver with them. And I'll take care of the rest along with the staff and Nan. Okay? I see how hard this is on families and I'm here for your support as well."

Elizabeth sighs deeply. "Thank you."

"Sighing is good." Zoe puts her hand on Elizabeth's arm.

The two women arrive back at Wimberly House. "Do you think you can find your way back?" asks Zoe.

"Yes, I can."

"Then I'll leave that up to you. Oliver has an appointment with Dr. Svare at 4:00. He may want to lie down for a while after you guys return."

"That would be a good time for me to go get cleaned up at the hotel."

"Just ask for a voucher. I'll see you later."

"Thank you. You've been a great help."

"I like to hear that." Zoe smiles and turns into her office.

Elizabeth sees on her watch that she has a half hour before she needs to begin to walk back again. She's anxious to hear how Ollie's appointment went and see how he is.

Oliver steps into Dr. Greenwood's office. The doctor directs him to a worn but comfortable looking blue chair. Oliver glances around the room. He notices kid art on the walls, mixed with other art, and wonders how young some of Dr. Greenwood's patients are. Dr. Greenwood settles himself behind his desk. It's not an imposing desk. Oliver can see the doctor's legs, see how he's crosses them, how relaxed he seems.

"Welcome to Taylor," Dr. Greenwood says. "What would you like me to call you?"

Oliver doesn't understand what the doctor means. "I don't know."

"What name would you like me to call you?"

Piece of shit.

Oliver takes a minute to answer. "I don't care."

Dr. Greenwood notices the confusion on Oliver's face. "I'll call you Oliver then. Is that okay?"

"Yes."

"Do you know why you're here, Oliver?"

Oliver pauses again, thinking about his answer. "Not really."

"If I told you that you were ill would you be able to describe your illness?"

"Kind of, not really."

That's a stupid answer.

"Well, let's start there. Give me one symptom of your illness that especially bothers you."

"Well, I think the only thing I've really noticed is that I don't have any friends anymore." Oliver glances at Dr. Greenwood to see how this statements sits with him.

"That must be a particularly upsetting symptom," Dr. Greenwood says calmly. "Do you know what it is about your illness that keeps your friends away?"

Oliver thinks about this. "Maybe 'cause they're all assholes!" Oliver's voice becomes forceful. "How should I know!?"

"They're ALL assholes? Is there one who isn't?"

"Yeah."

"Who would that be?"

"Greg. My brother's friend."

"And how about your brother?"

"No, he's not an asshole."

"So, you have two peers who understand what you're going through."

"Yeah."

"Do you know WHAT you're going through?"

What is this?! He's the doctor!

"The only one who makes sense is Jude."

"And who is Jude."

"I met him at the last hospital."

"And how did Jude make sense?"

"He knows why we're here on Earth and how we got here and the truth about Jesus and God. That's all I want to say." Oliver picks at a thread on the blue armchair arm. He wonders about the color blue, that this chair reminds him of the blue chair at his father's house. Perhaps there's a connection?

Of course there's a connection! You're such an idiot!

"Good," Dr. Greenwood is saying, "So you and Jude became good friends?"

"Yes. But he left."

"Do you know where he went?"

Oliver remains silent for a very long time then, quietly, he says, "Probably back out on the street."

"Have you had anyone else to speak with about these things?"

"No."

"Has it been difficult to stay quiet?"

"Not really."

"Who do you like to talk to?"

"My little sister."

"And why is that?"

"Because she's an innocent," Oliver says without missing a beat.

"Who else is innocent?"

"No one."

"Why is that?"

"Because they know the truth but keep it from me." Oliver looks defiant and glares at the doctor.

"And how is your sister different with the truth."

"She speaks it, she doesn't keep it from me."

Dr. Greenwood shifts in his chair. Oliver can see his legs uncross and cross again in the opposite direction. He notices that Dr. Greenwood is playing with a red paper clip. The red makes him nervous.

"Do you know why Jude was in the hospital?"

"He said he was there because of the cops but I'm sure it was because he's crazy."

"Are you crazy too?"

Oliver looks up at Dr. Greenwood. He sees that this doctor is sincere. He sees the red paper clip is lying on its side, is no longer being fiddled with, and no longer a threat.

How did he know? Oliver thinks. Then asks him, "What?"

"You said Jude was crazy, and I asked if you're crazy too?"

"I don't know. I guess so. I really don't know. I guess Jude and I couldn't be friends if only one of us was crazy. How can you tell if you're crazy anyway?"

"That's an excellent question! First off, I think we need to clarify the word 'crazy.' It's kind of a catch-all word. There are several mental illnesses that have their own names and crazy isn't one of them. Did you ever hear Jude's diagnosis?"

"Oh yeah, I did. He told me the doctors said he's schizophrenic."

"Good. Schizophrenia is a kind of mental illness. Another one is bipolar."

"That's what kids say to each other when one of them is behaving badly."

Dr. Greenwood smiles. "Another one is major depression, another is schizoaffective disorder. There isn't any mental illness that's just called 'crazy' except maybe in the movies."

"I know that. But most people call all of it crazy."

"Well then, most people are misinformed, wrong, or just plain mean."

The two of them sit quietly. This room is silent. Oliver looks out the window and notices a huge lawn sloping away into the distance. Massive trees, lightly green with small budding leaves stand along a stone wall encompassing the lawn. He spots a building that looks like it's out of a fairy tale sitting on a hill far away.

"What's that building?"

"Which one?" Dr. Greenwood comes out from behind his desk and looks out the window.

"That one."

"That building used to be an active part of this hospital. It's no longer used. Now that we have psychiatric medications patients don't have to stay with us as long as they used to. There are several abandoned buildings on this campus."

"Can I walk on that lawn?"

"Yes, you certainly may, provided you don't have any appointments."

"We don't have lawns like that in Montana."

"Yes, but you have mountains." Dr. Greenwood sounds wistful.

"I'd like to go now," says Oliver.

"All right. I'd say we did some good work today, wouldn't you?"

"If you call it work."

"Nan or your mom will be waiting for you outside. You can probably make it over and back by yourself tomorrow."

"Yeah."

"It was delightful to meet you, Oliver."

"Yes, you too."

25

INTREPID FOOL

Oliver walks down the stairs and out the arched door. He knows Dr. Greenwood let him out early. The lawn is beckoning and he sprints across the road and stands on the stonewall to look. He's never seen such a thing as this and itches to walk on it.

He hopes his mother comes to get him because they could explore.

Elizabeth meanders her way to Dr. Greenwood's office. She's a little early. The weather makes her homesick for the east. The trees, crocuses in bloom, the humidity. All of it. Fortunately, she knows that soon she'll be homesick for Montana but wishes she could stay here longer, maybe go to the Cape.

"That's not happening," she whispers to herself.

Once through the cafeteria building she stops for a moment by the huge shade tree. The branches are mature, long and low. She wants to climb up and lie along a branch like a cheetah but can't do that either. She decides to cross the road to see what's on that side of the hospital. Her footsteps are slow and she walks looking down at the narrow sidewalk. As soon as she comes to the road she looks up and spots Oliver standing on the stonewall, his right arm extended out, holding the oak tree next to him, his hip slightly bent, his entire being in a state of repose.

"John," Elizabeth utters under her breath, "this was the right thing to do." She returns to Dr. Greenwood's building and sits on the ground, leaning against the brick wall, inside the arch. Her back is to Oliver so he won't know she saw him gazing at the field of lawn. Her only concern is that he'll forget he's supposed to meet her here. She only waits a short while. She feels a finger touch her shoulder and looks up, sees his smiling face, his hair crazy wavy silhouetted against the blue sky.

"Hi Mom."

"Hi darling."

"Come here. I wanna show you something." Oliver puts his hand out to help Elizabeth stand. "You're not going to believe this!" He walks ahead of her, down the sloping narrow sidewalk. They cross the road. Oliver climbs up onto the stonewall again.

"Look!" He sweeps his arm, taking in the whole view, the lawn, the fairy-tale building, the trees on the left where the lawn disappears. "Can we walk into it?"

"What a wonderful way to put it," Elizabeth thinks. "Yes! Let's!" She looks at her watch. "We've an hour before your next appointment."

Oliver jumps off the wall and runs down the lawn, whooping and hollering at the top of his lungs. Elizabeth climbs over the wall and follows him. The grass feels wonderful even through her leather-soled shoes. She stops and takes them off. Memories of the lawn in Westchester County where she grew up flood her mind. No thistles like out west. Her feet sink into this grass. It's cushioned, not hard and lumpy like her lawn in Bozeman. She remembers hot, humid summers, picnic dinners, and fireflies. And the taste of milk when you drink it outside.

Oliver runs directly to the fairy-tale house. There's a huge portico and steps that rise to tall double doors. Oliver imagines horse-drawn carriages driving up to the stairs under the portico, fine ladies and gentlemen stepping out, the carriage tipping slightly as their feet touch the narrow, steel carriage step before they find the ground. He walks up the steps and peers in the windows that bracket the double doors and sees a great hall, trashed with dirt and leaves on the floor, tables on their sides, file cabinets sitting empty, their drawers open like hungry mouths. A great staircase leads up into darkness and Oliver suddenly feels the shadows of the place, the people who lived and suffered here. He hears a woman scream, and then another, a man this time. These are tangible ghosts that leave Oliver's neck pricking with trepidation. He backs away from the window, remembering the steps just in time before falling.

Elizabeth stands at the bottom of the stairs. She sees Oliver's apprehension, his close call with the stairs, and wonders what happened when he looked through the window. Something.

"What's inside?" she asks.

Oliver doesn't say. His face is pale, frightened. He's remembering what Dr. Greenwood had told him, that this building used to be an active part of the hospital, that because of psychiatric medications people don't have to stay as long as they used to. His vision of ladies and gentlemen, carriages and horses, falls, crashing into another vision of suffering and torture.

Elizabeth puts her shoes back on and sprints up the steps to look through the window. She sees what she would expect in an abandoned building. A mess. She wonders again what it was that Ollie saw.

"Come on, sweetie. Let's turn around and walk over there." She points across the lawn to a stand of trees, a path leading into the shade.

"No," Oliver says, his voice a monotone. "I want to go back to my room."

"Why don't we walk toward Wimberly House on the lawn instead of on the road? Then we won't have to walk through the cafeteria building."

Oliver doesn't respond. Elizabeth takes his arm and steers him away from the portico, back out onto the lawn. They walk slowly and as far as they can go, still close to the buildings. They come to a steep hill and climb up it, making their way through a long and narrow copse of trees. A church stands at the top of the hill, large, flat stones form stairs that lead to the road. Oliver sits for a moment on the top stair. Elizabeth sees him shiver and get up quickly. She wants to ask him what he felt but thinks better of it. Once on the road they find they're lost. Elizabeth spies a sidewalk of sorts across the road that begins near a three-story house. The name of the house is on a sign: Orchard House. The porch is full of patients smoking and watching them. Elizabeth feels uncomfortable. Oliver doesn't seem to notice them. They take the sidewalk that leads down some stairs and seems to continue in the direction of Wimberly House. The sidewalk merges with a road that Elizabeth realizes is the road she originally thought was the one that brought them here in the first place, by taxi. After about five minutes of walking they see the back of Wimberly House, recognizing it by the stone retaining wall that surrounds the squirrel lawn. They have to walk all the way around to get in.

Oliver goes to his room. Elizabeth goes to the kitchen for water and then to Oliver's room. She lets him know it's quarter to four, almost time for his first meeting with Dr. Svare. She is jonesing for a drink, a real drink, after this drama.

"I'm going to go back to the hotel while you're meeting with Dr. Svare. I think I'll take a nap, clean up, then come back to have dinner with you, okay?"

Oliver nods.

Zoe Jarvic appears at Oliver's doorway. "Hello you two! Oliver, I'll take you up to Dr. Svare's office this first time. We have about ten minutes. I'll come back to fetch you then. All right?"

Oliver looks at her as though he doesn't recognize her.

"I'll see you in ten," she says, unperturbed by his silence. She walks out of his room.

Elizabeth follows her. "Zoe?" she whispers. "Could I tell you what just happened to make him withdraw again?"

"What happened?"

"He was just fine, happy and upbeat, then we walked over to that big, abandoned building way on the other side of the lawn and he looked in a window and he changed, completely. He was scared of something. He wouldn't talk to me about it."

"If there's anyone who can get it out of him it's Dr. Svare. I'll try to get to him before Oliver's appointment." She looks at her watch. "I'll get him in a minute so we have an extra three for me to clue in the doc, okay?"

"Yes, thank you. I'm going to go to the hotel for a while but I'll be back for dinner."

Zoe knocks on Oliver's door while Elizabeth is in the staff room asking for a cab. Oliver gets off his bed and shuffles after Zoe. His body feels like it weighs a thousand pounds. He can't stop listening to the screams he heard in the fairy-tale house, he can't stop seeing how the stairs led up to darkness.

Zoe leads him up the stairs to the waiting area and asks him to wait a moment while she knocks on Dr. Svare's door.

"Come in."

"Hi, Doc." She steps into his office and closes the door. "I just wanted to pass on some information from Oliver's mother. She told me that he was happy and upbeat, full of energy after his time with Dr. Greenwood, then they walked to the abandoned building on the north end of the lawn and Oliver looked in the window. His mood changed dramatically after that. He's now withdrawn again."

"Thank you, Zoe. I'll take that into consideration." He stepped out from behind his desk and walked with her to the door and to the waiting area.

"Oliver Moore. It's good to meet you." Dr. Svare held out his hand.

Oliver looks up at him, doesn't take his hand.

"Let's go in my office and talk for a while, shall we?"

Oliver stands and follows. He sits in one of the chairs at the conference table. Dr. Svare doesn't miss a beat. He brings his notebook over to the conference table and joins Oliver there, three chairs away.

"So, you saw Dr. Greenwood early this afternoon, correct?"

"Yeah." Oliver slumps in the chair.

"And then what did you do?"

"My mom and I took a walk."

"Where did you go?"

Oliver looks at the doctor. He squints his eyes and looks at him through his eyelashes. "You know where we went."

"Yes, I do, but I want to hear it from you."

"Why?"

"Because hearing it from you gives it to me firsthand."

Dr. Svare leans back in his chair, tipping the front legs up a good eight inches from the floor.

"It's no big deal," Oliver says staring at the chair legs.

"Why don't you let me be the judge of that? Get it off your chest, so to speak?"

Oliver is silent for what seems a very long time, probably five minutes. Dr. Svare just sits as though he has all the time in the world. Oliver wants to tell him what he felt, what he heard, but he just can't get past the trapdoor in his throat.

"Can you say something?" he finally asks.

"Certainly. I would say that something scared you and that it would be helpful to get it out. Scary things aren't nearly as bad once they're out in the open."

Oliver takes a deep breath. "I heard screams. In that house."

"That house is very old, and I can imagine it being scary. Did you hear anything else? Like those screams?"

"No."

"Do you hear voices or smell scents that you can't account for?"

Oliver sits, mute.

"Do you hear voices inside your head?"

Oliver doesn't answer.

"Do you hear a voice that's like a thought but it's not you?"

"Sometimes." Oliver has pulled his green sweatshirt sleeves over his hands and crosses his arms. "I don't want to talk about this anymore."

"We won't then." Dr. Svare tips his chair back to the floor. "Do you think your mother hears voices?"

"No way."

"How do you know that?"

"You know why."

"No, I don't."

"Because she's one of you."

Dr. Svare doesn't hesitate. "And who are we?"

Oliver examines Dr. Svare's face, his cheeks and forehead, his chin and then, quickly, he glances at his eyes and mouth and sees that he really doesn't know.

You live in the Real World, Oliver thinks. You're not one of us.

Then, to the doctor, he says, "If you don't know I can't tell you."

"And why is that?"

He's a dick.

Oliver hesitates. He looks down at his lap and mumbles, "It's complicated."

Elizabeth asks the cabby to stop at a liquor store. She walks in, grabs a bottle of Sapphire gin, pays and walks back to the cabby. "Thank you," she tells him. "So much!"

When she gets to her room she opens the bottle and takes a deep swig. She loves the burning feeling as the booze runs down her throat. "Oh, my, God!" She lies down on the hotel bed and tries to sleep. Even with gin onboard she can't sleep. She decides to call John instead but when she picks up the phone, she hangs up almost immediately. She can't face speaking to anyone right now, not even John. It would not be a short conversation. She turns on the TV. Cartoons are playing and she leaves it there. Just in case, she calls the front desk to ask for a 6:00 p.m. wake-up call.

The phone rings at six and she's startled out of a deep sleep.

"Oh, my, God!" she complains to the ceiling. "I'm so tired!"

The next two days are filled with tests and sessions with Dr. Greenwood and Dr. Svare. Elizabeth accompanies Oliver to his MRI and the lab where they take a lot of blood. She feels like a fifth wheel and watches while Oliver seems to deteriorate. She remembers what Zoe told her, that patients sometimes get worse before they get better; it's hard to watch. His high energy is gone, has never come back after looking into the fairy-tale house. He's shut down. She wonders what it could be that he talks about with Dr. Greenwood every day. She mustn't ask.

These four days with Oliver seem to have gone by too quickly even though the hours when he wasn't with her seemed to drag by. She slept fitfully in the hotel but was eager, each morning anyway, to get back to the hospital. The morning of the fifth day Elizabeth is packed and ready, her tickets stashed in her purse, her dirty clothes stuffed in her suitcase. She takes a cab to Wimberly House one more time. A town car will pick her up there and take her to the airport for an afternoon flight. She should get into Bozeman around 10:30 that night.

This morning she feels as though she can't breathe, as though there are hands around her throat. There's a rock in her heart and her right shoulder is so sore she's actually aware of the pain. She knows she has to leave Ollie here but can't reach down inside herself to come up with any resolve. Not right now.

Elizabeth finds Oliver outside by the back door. He has a piece of bread and butter with him and is throwing small pieces of the crust to the squirrels and chipmunks. He seems peaceful, a welcome change from his depression of the past forty-eight hours. Elizabeth watches his profile through the door, tries to soak up each and every bit of him—his thick wavy light brown hair, his too thin and slender tall body and broad shoulders, his gentle, handsome face, his dimples, and his doleful blue gray eyes.

I should be leaving him at college, she chokes on the thought. No crying right now, she chastises herself, Buck up, Liz. She pushes the door open and Oliver turns to see who it is who's interrupting his interlude.

"Hi, Mom."

"Hi, sweetie. Any takers?"

"Oh, yeah! They love this crust."

"Ollie, do you remember I'm leaving today?"

Oliver doesn't respond. He throws a small piece of crust. "Look! That's the biggest squirrel! Did you see how fast he ran to that piece of bread?"

"I did. He's huge!" Elizabeth tells him. "I'm going to get a cup of coffee in the kitchen."

"Okay."

Elizabeth finds an almost full carafe of coffee in the tiny kitchen. She pours herself a cup then leans on the counter. Paul walks in. He finds a cup and pours himself some coffee too.

"Good morning, Paul," says Elizabeth.

He looks at her, seems to see her this time. "Good morning." He looks at the ground and begins to say something else, glances at her, but changes his mind and silently leaves the kitchen in his stocking feet.

She hears talking out in the hall and, taking her coffee, walks out of the kitchen. She sees Zoe with a young man who must be in his mid-twenties, a woman near him in her late fifties. The young man is tall with long dark hair down to his shoulders. He has a look in his eyes that she recognizes immediately: fear, confusion. Zoe greets Elizabeth and introduces her to the other mother.

"Yes, my son is here. I'm leaving for the airport very soon," she tells the woman. "This is a good place."

"Yes," says the woman. "I think they'll be able to help Sean here."

Elizabeth sees the pain in this woman and wonders if she, herself, is that transparent. She walks outside, back to Oliver, as quickly as possible without seeming to be rude. She doesn't care for introductions right now. She wants Ollie all to herself before she leaves. She sits down in one of the outside chairs by the door and watches Oliver. She can see his lips moving, can see him smiling and making small gestures to himself. She wonders where he is and wants to put her arms around him, rock him and cry.

"How am I going to walk away from him?" she asks herself. "How am I going to fly so far away knowing he's here?" She realizes that she doesn't really trust these people to take care of him. She doesn't trust that they'll know how to watch for his moods and help him when he's scared. But she has to go. She knows she and John can't take care of him. She interrupts Oliver's thoughts.

"There's a new person here, Ollie," she tells him.

He stares at her for a second then focuses on her. "What?"

"There's a new young man here. I saw him inside with his mother."

"Really?" Oliver grins. "What's his name?"

"Sean."

"That's good."

"I have to leave very soon," she tells him.

"I wish I was coming with you," he says.

"I wish you were too."

26

ANNIHILATION

Elizabeth and Oliver stand outside Wimberly House, on the steps, waiting for the town car. On the way outside Oliver got a glimpse of the new patient, Sean. Elizabeth saw him smile.

He must recognize himself in Sean, Elizabeth thinks. Like Jude.

The black town car drives down the slight incline to Wimberly House. Elizabeth's hands begin to shake. She takes hold of Oliver's arm in a vice grip.

"Oh my God, I don't want to leave you," she says to him.

"I'll be okay, Mom." He puts his hand over hers. She feels his warmth, his strength coming through his skin.

"I just don't know if I can do this," she says and begins to cry, grief enveloping her, making her nauseous, annihilating her resolve to be strong.

"I'll be home soon," Oliver tells her. "You'll see."

Elizabeth pulls away from him, then, up on her tiptoes, she puts her palms on either side of his face. She looks into his eyes and sees him. She kisses each eyelid, each cheek, his forehead and chin, just like she would when he was a little boy.

"Okay. I can go now."

The driver is waiting by the car, watching this farewell. Elizabeth greets him and indicates that her one suitcase is it. She and Oliver walk down the steps as the driver loads her suitcase.

"Say hi to everyone for me," Oliver says.

"I will. You can call whenever you want to, you know that, right?"

"Yeah."

"I'll call you when I get home. No, I'll call you tomorrow. I won't get home until after midnight Eastern time."

"Goodbye, Mom."

"I can't say goodbye. I'll just say, 'see you later,' okay?"

"Okay."

"I love you more than anything in the universe!"

"You too!"

Elizabeth pulls her door shut. She puts the window down but Oliver is already gone, up the steps and into the house. She's disappointed, hurt.

"Okay," she tells the driver.

They pull away and begin to ascend the short driveway. Suddenly Elizabeth sees Oliver busting through the back door, running, his thin body jumping in the air, his long arms waving, his heartbreak of a smile on his pale face, his hair lifting between each jump. She wants to ask the driver to stop so she can open the door and take Ollie with her. She strangles her purse straps with one hand and waves with the other. She's sobbing so hard she can hardly see and she doesn't care if the driver hears her. They drive out of view.

Oliver watches as the town car slips away over the hill. He stops where the lawn ends, allowing only the tips of his toes to touch the black pavement. He turns back, his feet registering the cold grass and small detritus from the overhead trees. He's curious that he just ran on this lawn and didn't feel the small, sharp needles, pinecones and seeds. He sits down in one of the chairs on the outside porch and watches for the squirrels. He thinks about the fact that his mom just left him here but tries to push the thought away. Pushing doesn't work. He feels restless, angry.

If you weren't such a fucking loser you wouldn't have to stay here, you could be home with your friends!

Then he thinks, what friends, which brings him right back to being a loser. He wishes his mom hadn't left. He isn't sure what to do with himself. He's curious about the new patient but doesn't want to speak. He wonders if he can get to his room without encountering anyone. Oliver opens the door and steps inside. His eyes follow the weave of the rug as he walks down the wide hall. As he nears his room, Ernest steps out of the nurses' station and almost bumps into him.

"Oh, hey man, I'm sorry!"

"That's okay," Oliver mumbles. He walks faster past the open door and slips into his room, shutting the door behind him, leaning his shoulder into it to make sure it has clicked shut. He looks around the room, as if for the first time. He notices how dark the room is, not the walls but the furniture, even the bit of the TV cabinet that he can see under the blanket Elizabeth put over it. The rug is dark too. The molding and walls are white. Elizabeth's absence seems to have shoved a curtain aside that allows him to see his surroundings more clearly. But he doesn't want to notice these things as they make him feel even more the stranger. He only wants to bury himself with his loneliness.

Oliver pulls back his bedcovers and crawls in. He curls up like an animal in its den and closes his eyes. Mercifully, there is nothing on the backs of his eyelids. Just black, a few stars. His back is to the door. The shades are down. He's warm and not unhappy lying here. He can hear voices on the other side of his door but can't understand what they're saying.

Oliver wakes up to the sound of knocking. He freezes, waits for the knocking to stop.

"Oliver?"

He holds his breath.

"Oliver, it's dinner time."

"I don't want dinner," he whispers to himself.

The door opens and Ernest peeks in. "Come on, get up, it's time to eat."

"I'm not hungry."

"You better eat a little bit. Come on, now."

"I was sleeping," Oliver says, angry.

"I can see that."

"Do I have to?" Oliver whines.

"Yes."

"I'll be out in a few minutes."

"No, up now, while I'm here," Ernest insists.

"Jeez!"

"You can come back in here as soon as you eat and take your meds."

Oliver throws his covers off and puts his feet down on the rug. "This is bullshit," he mumbles.

Ernest opens the door wider for Oliver. "All the orders are back in the kitchen. You go find out what you ordered, now."

Oliver, barefoot, shuffles down the hall to the kitchen. He doesn't appreciate Ernest's strong-arm tactics. He can feel Ernest's eyes boring into his back, between his shoulder blades, and turns to glare back at him. The hall is empty.

Paul is standing, socks on his feet, in the kitchen, reading the masking tape labels on the Styrofoam boxes that hold their individual dinners. His hair is wild, his expression unreadable. He hands Oliver a box labeled 'Moore.' Oliver accepts it without a word then takes a seat at one of the card tables outside the kitchen. He opens the box and sees salmon with bread and salad. He has to return to the kitchen for utensils but before he gets up Paul arrives with a knife and fork for him and sits at the same table.

"Thank you," says Oliver very quietly.

Paul doesn't respond but opens his box and begins to eat.

Oliver stares at the pink salmon. He picks up the bread and takes a bite but tastes something awful in the bread. He keeps staring at the salmon, knowing there's a connection between the bad taste in the bread and the fish. The pink salmon slowly takes on the look of human flesh, as though it's a slice of forearm, the top part, hair and all. Oliver thrusts it away. He stands so fast his chair falls backward. He looks over at Paul who's watching him. Their eyes lock for a split second then Oliver runs back to his room and slams the door. He takes the desk chair and puts it under the doorknob at an angle, lies down on his bed, facing the door this time, and waits. He can't close his eyes because of the image of the slice of arm in the Styrofoam box. The box bright white, the flesh dark pink and red, painted on the inside of his eyelids, on his eyeballs, soaking into his brain. He tries resting with his eyes open but that doesn't work. He's angry that Ernest forced him out of his room for dinner. But now, Ernest won't be able to get in. The chair will keep him out.

Oliver picks up the controller for the TV from the desk, sweeps the protective blanket off the TV cabinet and lets it fall to the floor. Then he plugs the TV into the wall. He switches it on and falls back on his bed, lying sideways, his pillow propped under his head. He feels comfortable for a moment, as though all is well, almost as if he's home watching TV after school, for a moment, until he remembers where he is. He glances at the door and the chair that's protecting him from anyone coming in. He gets under the covers, rearranges his pillow, punching it into the shape he wants it under his head. Then the sound of the TV enters his brain and squashes his thoughts; he pushes his head further into his pillow to rid himself of the feeling the sound makes but it doesn't work. Then, very subtly, he hears the sound of a snake hissing. He points the remote at the TV and turns it off. He lies still, frozen, and listens. He hears it again. The sound is concentrated near the bottom of his door. He can see light coming through the crack at the bottom of his door, light that shines out there in the hall. Oliver pushes his pillow away and turns on his stomach, his arms underneath him, his head turned sharply, his eyes fixed on the light. A shadow passes by and he hears the hissing sound again. This time it's unmistakable. He sits up, throws the covers off, his back against the bed's headboard. Then someone knocks, someone who was standing in the light, who, Oliver can see from the shadow, has two legs.

"Oliver?" A voice comes through the door. "Oliver? I'm coming in."

It morphed. Don't be an idiot! Don't let it in!

Oliver watches as the doorknob turns, as the door pushes against the chair that's propped against it. He's cold with terror, pulls his legs up into his chest and wraps his arms around his legs. The doorknob begins to shake. As Oliver watches, the back legs of the chair begin to hop with the vibration and move forward until the whole chair falls flat on its back and the door opens. Oliver covers his face with his hands. He hears someone or something walk into his room, drag the chair over to his bed and sit down. He hears Ernest's voice speak to him.

"You can't lock your door here, son, it's just not something we do." Ernest's voice is gentle and not what Oliver expected. "If you were allowed to lock your doors we wouldn't be able to help you when you were scared."

What's he talking about?

"Paul told me you took off down the hall like a bullet instead of eating your dinner. Anything you want to talk about?"

Oliver looks at Ernest through his fingers. "No."

"Are you hungry?"

"No."

"Tell you what. You come out of your room, get your meds, and I'll see what I can come up with that's more appetizing than salmon. How about that?"

Oliver finally lets his hands drop from his face. He stares at Ernest who gets up to leave, putting the desk chair back where it belongs. Ernest doesn't look at Oliver again but he does cover the TV with the blanket that's on the floor. He leaves the door open slightly as he steps into the hall.

Oliver puts his feet on the floor and sits up straight, facing the door. He listens to the sounds out in the hall and hears nothing but the muffled sounds of humans walking and talking in the staff room. He looks around his room, his gaze falling on the telephone that sits on his desk. He picks up the receiver and dials home, remembering to dial 1 and the Montana area code, 406. The phone rings.

"Hello?"

"Dad? It's me."

"Ollie? Are you all right?" John has been keeping his eye on the clock to make it to the airport in time to pick up Elizabeth. It's still early.

"Dad? The staff is trying to kill me!" he tells John.

"Oh, Ollie, I wouldn't think so . . ." John dismisses Oliver's fear.

"Dad!" Oliver yells, "I just heard a snake hissing outside my door and then Ernest walked in. He morphed, Dad, I swear to God, they're going to wait for nighttime then they're going to kill me!"

John doesn't know what to say. He hears the panic and fear in Oliver's voice and he wants to remain positive but this is such a crazy thought on Oliver's part that he's stumped. "I don't know what to say, Ollie. Are you still hearing the snake?"

"No."

"So, you think it went away?"

"Dad," Oliver sounds frustrated, "you don't understand . . . it morphed!"

"Oh, that's right. I'm sorry. I don't know what to say! I think it would be important to talk this over with Dr. Svare."

"You should have heard it, Dad! You should have heard the snake. First it was there and then all of a sudden it was Ernest and he was nice to me but I'm on to him. He morphed. I know he did! And they're going to kill me tonight!!"

"Ollie. Listen to me. I want you to go find Ernest and tell him about the snake and that you're afraid. Can you do that?"

John listens into the phone and doesn't hear anything. "Ollie?"

"Ollie? Are you there?" The sound of dial tone erupts in his ear. "Shit!" John tries to remember where he's written all the numbers for Taylor Hospital, can't place them in his panic and confusion. He calls information and is given the main number. Pacing madly from living room to kitchen he calls and asks for Wimberly House.

"Hello? Listen to me. This is Oliver Moore's father and he just called me and was going on about a member of your staff morphing into a snake, or the other way around, I can't remember, and then he hung up or we got disconnected and now I'm calling because he sounded so scared and I want you to check on him."

"Sir?"

"Yes?"

"Everything is under control, not to worry. Let me give you to Ernest."

"Okay."

"Mr. Moore?"

"Yes?"

"This is Ernest, and I'm standing here with your son, Oliver. Oliver told me that you told him to come find me and tell me about the snake. He did that and I'm very proud of him."

"Are you kidding me? He almost gave me a heart attack! I told him what I thought he should do and the next thing there wasn't any Oliver on the other end of the phone."

"That must have given you quite a fright, Mr. Moore. But I'm glad you encouraged Oliver to come speak with me. He may not have been able to agree with you verbally although he was able to agree with you in action. He'll be fine. He has a lot to learn here."

"Yes. Thank you, Ernest," John says, chagrined. "May I speak to Oliver?"

"Certainly, sir." Ernest hands the phone to Oliver.

"Hey, Dad." Oliver's voice is subdued.

"Hey, kiddo. I just wanted to tell you I'm proud you went to Ernest and that I hope you get a good night's sleep. I miss you."

John gets a lump in his throat.

"Night, Dad. I miss you too. I'm sorry."

"Hey, don't." John is crying but wipes his nose on his sleeve so Oliver won't hear him sniffle. "This isn't your fault. I love you, so much. Sleep. Remember? They say sleep will help you heal."

Elizabeth cries, intermittently, all the way to Denver, cries in a Denver Airport bar during the two-hour layover, cries all the way to Montana. She wonders about the mystery of tears and how it's possible to cry so much and not become dangerously dehydrated. Every time she thinks she's finished crying she sees the image of Oliver running toward the town car, jumping and laughing, and she begins crying again.

John is waiting for her at the gate. She spots him first. He looks anxious. Then he sees her and breaks into a smile and waves. She finally gets to him and they hug, tight. Elizabeth begins crying all over again.

"It's okay, Lizzy. He'll be okay." John keeps his arm around her. "Why don't you stay with us tonight?"

Elizabeth nods. "You know, John, I've wanted to be one of those people who cry easily but this is ridiculous! I can't stop!"

"It's okay. You've done a difficult thing." He gives her a squeeze with the arm that's around her. "Let's go get your bag."

Elizabeth and John stand, her shoulder against his arm, and wait with a small crowd for the luggage carousel to begin moving. Elizabeth is happy to be back in Bozeman's small airport. No kiosks, no Cinnabons, but less stress. After about twenty minutes they're on their way to John's car. The weather is crisp, clear. She can see the stars. On the way to John's she talks about Oliver and Wimberly House and Dr. Greenwood and Dr. Svare and Zoe and Ernest. John is especially interested in her description of Ernest. She could go on and on but they pull up to John's house and her heart jumps with excitement to see Peter and Wren. She can't believe it's only been five days and four nights; it may as well have been four months.

Everything is quiet when Elizabeth and John enter his house. Jack goes wild, whines and wriggles, his tail banging into the walls and furniture.

"Shhhh!" she says, trying to calm him. She hugs him and gives him a kiss on the top of his soft head.

"Wren is in Oliver's room," John tells her. "I guarantee she'd love seeing you when she wakes up in the morning."

Elizabeth pours a glass of water and takes a piece of bread, getting butter out of the fridge. "It's good to be home but I hate to think of Ollie all by himself, even in another time zone," she tells John who's leaning on the counter waiting to go to bed.

"Hi, Mom." Peter is standing in the doorway looking sleepy. His long hair is sticking out all over the place.

Elizabeth moves over to him and folds him into her arms. "Oh, my God, it's so good to see you! I missed you! You shouldn't be up so late."

"It's okay. I can go right back to sleep."

"Well, all right, I'll walk you back to your room."

The two of them go down the hall into Peter's room. He falls back into bed and she fixes his covers and sits next to him.

"Is he okay?" Peter asks.

"He's more than okay. He seems to like it there. Right before I left another young man joined him in the house he's staying in and I'm sure they'll get along. This young man seemed to have the same illness as Ollie."

"How would you know that?"

"His expression, his eyes."

"Yeah, I know what you mean." Peter sighs. "I'm glad he's okay. When do you think he can come home?"

"Well, he'll only stay in this house for two weeks. After that, I don't know. Pretty soon I guess. I really don't know."

"I hope it's not too long."

"Me too, sweetie." Elizabeth leans over and gives him a kiss on his forehead. Then she kisses his eyelids, his cheeks, and chin.

"Jeez, Mom, you haven't done that for years!"

"I know. I love you." She stands.

"I love you too."

Elizabeth turns and leaves the room before Peter sees her tears.

John is still waiting in the kitchen. "Lizzy, I just wanted to say one more thing before we go to bed. I wanted to tell you that Ollie isn't by himself. You don't have to torture yourself. He's where he needs to be. We all miss him but I think it's the Ollie before mental illness hit that we miss, not the one who needs care that we can't give to him. He'll be home soon. And he'll be better. Right?"

"Right. Thank you. And thank you to us for pulling together on this one. Now, I'm going to bed!"

"Me too."

Elizabeth takes her suitcase into Oliver's room. She can see Wren's little shape under the covers. She changes into her nightgown as quietly as possible and crawls in next to her. She can't resist kissing the little girl's soft cheek. Wren stirs ever so slightly but doesn't wake up. Elizabeth lies next to her and tries to fall asleep.

27

BUSTED

Peter loves getting stoned. He loves everything about it and now that Oliver is gone he's stoned most of the time. He doesn't understand why John doesn't see that he's stoned, or Elizabeth. He figures they probably don't want to see, that they've had enough trouble to deal with and don't want any more. Peter misses Oliver but not as much as he tells his parents that he does. He doesn't miss the Oliver who just left for the hospital at all. He didn't even know that Oliver and, frankly, doesn't even like him. He's angry with that Oliver, angry that Oliver has become a person who Peter doesn't know.

Peter doesn't skip school again but he doesn't come home after school either. He hangs with friends or goes for long rides. And smokes dope before and after school, anytime he can get away with it.

Two days after Elizabeth's return home, Peter is stopped for speeding. Elizabeth is getting ready to go to work when the phone rings. It's the police telling her they have her son, Peter, at the station and could she come down right away.

"What did he do?"

"He was speeding but the arresting officer smelled marijuana and arrested him for an illegal substance."

"Did he have anything on him?"

"Yes, ma'am, he did." The officer pauses. "Just under an ounce."

"Lord. Peter . . ." Elizabeth sighs into the phone. "I'll be right down."

"Thank you, ma'am."

"Yes." Elizabeth hangs up the phone. She sees Wren's soccer ball on the floor and kicks it as hard as she can. "SHIT SHIT SHIT!" The soccer ball ricochets off the kitchen cabinets and hits a ceramic bowl that flies off the counter and shatters on the floor. "FUCK!" She picks up the phone and calls John.

"Peter's been arrested."

"You must be kidding!"

"I'm going down to the police station now."

John sighs. "I'll meet you there."

John is waiting for Elizabeth outside the Law and Justice Center on the steps. They walk in together without a word between them, walk up the stairs and find a glass window on the right with a clerk behind it.

"I've come for my son," says John into the round voice amplifier.

"Your name, sir?"

"John Moore."

"I'll get an officer if you'll wait."

"What else are we supposed to do," John says in a low voice to Elizabeth, then, "This is crazy! Haven't we had enough already?"

"Maybe Peter just wants to get our attention," says Elizabeth.

"Well, he certainly did and I'm telling you right now, I'm not open to psychobabble at the moment."

"Fine." Elizabeth hopes the officer hurries up.

Suddenly, to the left of the glass window, a door opens with a loud buzzing and an officer is standing there. "This way, folks. He's in here."

The officer ushers John and Elizabeth into a locked holding room. Peter, his arms crossed, his forehead on his arms, doesn't move.

"Peter," says John.

Peter looks up. His face is creased where his sweatshirt had been pressing into it. His eyes are red and swollen as though he's been crying.

Elizabeth melts, wants to go to him, put her arms around his shoulders. But John stands between Peter and Elizabeth and she's not willing to push him out of the way. Peter puts his head back down on his arms.

"Stand up, young man," the officer tells Peter. "You can go home now, with your parents."

"With which parent?" Elizabeth asks, then feels like an idiot for asking.

"That's between you all," says the officer. "Come on folks, we got to get some paperwork taken care of."

"Where's Peter's car?" John asks the officer.

"It's been towed."

"So, how can I get it?"

"That's some of the paperwork I'm talking about." The officer leads them out of the small room and down a long, narrow hall filled with filing cabinets.

John takes Peter by the arm. "Haven't we been through enough shit lately without you pulling this?"

"I'm sorry, Dad," says Peter, "this wasn't meant to happen."

"You're damned right it wasn't! What the hell, Pete, what were you thinking! Did you want to get caught?"

"No!"

The officer interrupts John and Peter's conversation and proceeds to tell John that he would have to bring Peter to court, that he would be charged upward of $100 to $300 in fines, at the judge's discretion, plus court fees, and that Peter would also be assigned Community Service that would cost John even more money.

John looks stunned. He doesn't say anything for at least thirty seconds then clears his throat.

The officer was still talking. "Now you need to stop and talk to the clerk. Your son's car . . ."

"My car . . ." mumbles John.

". . . has been towed to a yard. You'll have to find out which one from the clerk, pay, then go get it."

"We'll do that. Thank you."

"And Mr. Moore," the officer says. "I just want you to know that your son was probably the politest young man I've ever had to arrest. I appreciate that."

"That's very good to hear, officer," says John. "I wouldn't expect less."

Elizabeth had taken a seat while John and the officer spoke. She could hear all that was said but wasn't feeling as rigid about the whole affair as she knew John was. She knew the cold-shoulder punishment Peter would be getting from John now. In a way she wished it had been her car Peter had been driving; she wouldn't be so severe, she'd allow the punishment doled out by the court to be the punishment. She watches the conversation come to an end and stands. The three of them follow the officer to the counter where he goes behind to tell a clerk who they are and to give her Peter's name.

The clerk is a round, short woman with glasses and thinning black hair. They watch her look through files until she finds what she needs. She waddles to the counter with the paperwork. "Now, first of all, the car," she says. "Your car is at Right Now Towing. They have the keys. Once you've paid me the fine, I'll give you a receipt along with your copy of this document. You take those papers down there and they'll give you your car. Their address is on this form. Now, let's see . . ." she peers down at the form then lets her fingers, without looking at it, work a calculator that sits on the counter, "you owe $187.00."

John, holding his checkbook, turns bright red. Peter thinks his dad looks like he's going to choke. "Who do I make this out to?" he asks quietly.

"Make it out to the Gallatin Valley Sheriff's Department." The clerk waits, her chin on one hand, elbow on the counter.

John writes the check and shoves it across the counter. Elizabeth jumps inwardly when she sees him shove the check. She knows he's close to erupting and it scares her. The clerk gives John the paperwork after carefully stapling the receipt to the form.

"There, that takes care of that," says the clerk in a singsong voice.

John hands the paperwork to Peter. "Hold this," he says. John's jaw is working furiously, his color still red.

Peter catches Elizabeth's eye and opens his eyes wide, making a grimace with his mouth. Elizabeth copies his expression. They both know how John can be when he's angry. Silent scary.

"This is your court date," she tells them. "The violation is written here," she points where to John, "and the court date is there." She points again. "It's best to be early to get in front of the line."

"Thank you," says John, "but can't I just leave him in jail?"

"No sir. We don't have a juvenile facility as of yet."

"I'm not all together serious," John tells her.

"Oh," says the clerk, clearly not amused.

The three walk out of the Law and Justice Center, John in front, Elizabeth bringing up the rear. As soon as they exit the building John turns on Peter. "You owe me all this money and then some," John snaps. "We'll get the Acura out of lock up but you won't be using it for a very long time."

Peter doesn't say a word.

Now that Oliver is safely at Taylor Hospital, Elizabeth sinks into a depression, helped along by an increased consumption of alcohol. She knows she needs to find a doctor but she puts off the search and continues to slide downward until she's paralyzed.

John comes by to pick up Wren a week after Elizabeth gets home from Taylor, a few days since Peter's fiasco. He finds her lying on the couch in a severely depressed state. The house is filthy with barely anything in the fridge and laundry piled high next to the machine.

"Lizzy, have you spoken to a doctor? I think you need help."

Former experience has taught him to tread lightly but Elizabeth is too far down to lash out.

"Yes." Her hand is over her eyes, protecting them from the light coming in the windows.

"What did he have to say?"

"To find a psychiatrist." Elizabeth doesn't elaborate, her speech is slow, slurred; John stands helplessly in front of her.

"And?"

"And nothing."

"Lizzy, you have to do something. You can't just stay this way!"

Elizabeth takes her hand away from her eyes and John sees they're filled with tears. "I'm just sad about Ollie."

"No, Liz. This is more than that and you know it."

She covers her eyes again with her hand.

"I'm taking Wren for the weekend," he says. "And I can't bring her back until you're feeling better than this."

"I want to stay here," says Wren from the doorway.

"Wren," John says, kicking himself inwardly for not spotting her. "Mom needs to rest. Peter and you will have a good time."

"Wren." Elizabeth speaks from the couch. "I'm okay, really." She pulls herself up on her elbows. "I'm just really, really tired."

Wren walks out to the hall and grabs her jacket off a hook in the entryway. She doesn't speak but stares at John and Elizabeth, tears in her eyes, her mouth a tight little line.

"We'll come see you on Sunday, Lizzie," says John.

"Bye, sweetie," Elizabeth says to Wren. "Gimme a hug."

Wren runs across the room and flings herself onto Elizabeth, hugging her tightly. She mumbles, her head buried in her mother's shoulder. "I love you. I'll miss you."

"I love you, too, my sweetness, and I'll miss you too. Have a good time, okay? Peter will be there so that should be fun, right?"

Elizabeth tries to keep an up tempo to her voice but it doesn't work very well. She holds Wren tightly and kisses her hair.

"Come on, kiddo," says John.

Wren pulls herself away from Elizabeth. "Bye, Mommy."

"Bye, sweetie."

John and Wren leave by the front door and Elizabeth collapses back onto the pillows on the couch. She's exhausted by the short interaction and closes her eyes, allowing relief to flow through her now that Wren is safely with John. She can stay on the couch, inert. Oliver is now safe, Wren is safe. And Peter? He's with John, safe. She falls asleep.

28

A THOUGHT DISORDER

Oliver has settled into the routine at Wimberly House. He's allowed to sleep in every morning then has breakfast. After breakfast the days are filled with seeing Dr. Greenwood, being taken to different buildings for tests such as memory, IQ, MRI, complete physical and blood tests. As his mother sinks deeper into depression, Oliver's stay at Wimberly House has almost reached its two-week mark. As promised, Nan calls John and Elizabeth regularly with updates on Oliver and their findings.

Elizabeth has, besides being depressed herself, been struggling under the burden of Oliver's phone calls that fill her with dread. Almost every time he calls, she then calls the staff room to let them know what's going on with him. She wishes, at times, that he was locked up, especially when he called to tell her he could stand in front of moving cars and they would just go right through him, no harm done. There was no reasoning with him, no getting him to see how impossible these stories were. It was as though, she thought, he was trying to drive her crazy too.

And then there was the Acura. Elizabeth began a repetitive delusional thought that Oliver is about to drive up, jump out of his car, and be the old Ollie. She listens for the car all the time. Since

Peter and Oliver shared the Acura she feels sick with guilt that she's let down when it's Peter, without Oliver, who walks into the house.

Nan calls Elizabeth the Monday after John takes Wren. Elizabeth rallies for the call and Nan doesn't suspect the depth of Elizabeth's depression or she may not have delivered the findings that she did. "We've seen the results of an MRI that shows us one slightly enlarged ventricle, which is indicative of schizophrenia or schizoaffective disorder. These findings juxtapose with what we found while interviewing Oliver—that he has a thought disorder as well as a mood disorder and that even though he sounds perfectly normal he makes no sense. He's psychotic. These two findings are probably the most important in making a decision for what will be best for Oliver's immediate future. We recommend that he be moved to Orchard House, a long-term facility, since he's far from stabilized. He's been in a mixed state since he arrived. Obviously, the medication he was taking wasn't helping him. Finding the right medication takes a long time. At Orchard House, he'll also learn, along with his peers, coping skills." Nan pauses.

"So he'd be with his peers?"

"Yes, there are all ages at Orchard House. I can't completely imagine what this means to you, Mrs. Moore. I don't have a son but I do have an inkling, and I'm so sorry to have to bring you these findings."

"Yes," Elizabeth whispers. "Who will tell Ollie that he can't come home?" She chokes and begins sobbing uncontrollably.

"I'm so sorry, Elizabeth," Nan says. "Is there anyone I can call for you?"

"No, thank you."

"Are you all right?"

"Not really."

"Is there anything I can do?" Nan asks.

"You can tell me he didn't get this from me."

"Why would you think that he got it from you?"

"Because . . ." Elizabeth sits up and reaches for her drink, "because I'm a drunk and a depressive."

"Mrs. Moore, Elizabeth, I can't say with certainty that Oliver inherited your condition but I can say that what he has is a thought disorder, not just a mood disorder like you're describing."

"Aren't they all mental illness?"

"Yes, but . . ."

"I just can't bear it, that's all."

"I know. It would help if you could talk to someone about this, face to face."

"Not now." Elizabeth swings her legs off the couch and sits, holding her phone in one hand and her drink in the other. "We've got enough going on with Oliver. I'll snap out of this, I'm sure, because that's how it goes."

"In the meantime, have you heard of NAMI?"

"No."

"NAMI stands for the National Alliance for the Mentally Ill. There's probably a NAMI group in your neighborhood. Find that group. They'll help you with what you're going through. Your whole family could go. This is not a picnic; this is hard stuff, painful stuff. No one expects you to present a happy face to the world but you do have to take care of yourself. I'll get back to you when I find a name of a psychiatrist in Bozeman. Okay?"

"Are you sure about the thought disorder part?"

"Yes, Elizabeth," Nan says softly, "we're sure. Call me any time if you want to discuss this or anything else, all right?"

"Yes. And you're sure you don't just want another patient?"

"I'm sure. We have more than enough patients, they come from all over the country and all over the world."

"Okay, I was just asking."

"That's fine. You can ask me anything you need or want to ask."

Oliver walks up the stairs to Dr. Greenwood's office. He now walks across the campus unassisted and today was feeling pretty good. He waits a few minutes on the bench across from the psychologist's door then a sad looking girl emerges. Oliver stands, anticipating an invitation inside.

"One minute," Dr. Greenwood tells him and disappears into his office again, closing his door in what felt like Oliver's face.

He doesn't want to deal with you. If you weren't such a dick he would have asked you in right away!

Oliver winces, puts his head down low, his arms on his legs, his hands together.

The doctor's door opens. "One minute is what I said and one minute is what it was. How are you my good man?" Dr. Greenwood greets Oliver.

Oliver is taken by surprise and looks up, a look of confusion on his face.

"Come on in," says the doctor, a bit less ebullient.

Oliver sits in the blue armchair and waits while the doctor settles himself behind his desk.

"So, how are things?"

That's a stupid question, thinks Oliver. He stares at Dr. Greenwood's legs and doesn't say a word.

"You've been here for almost two weeks, Oliver. We don't keep clients at Wimberly House for longer than two weeks and it's going to take longer than that to find the right medications to help you. We've finished all the physical testing, the blood work, and scans and all the other tests. It's going to take some work to get you on the right medications to help you get rid of these symptoms you're experiencing."

What symptoms?

"We, meaning Dr. Svare and I as well as the staff at Wimberly House, agree that it would benefit you to stay with us for a more extended period of time. We have an opening at Orchard House where many of our younger patients stay. I know it's not Montana, but it's safe and it's where we can continue to give you care. You have a stubborn illness and we can help you, but it will take time."

"Do you think Jude will show up?"

"No, I don't think so. But you'll meet other people like Jude up at Orchard House. Would you like to see it?"

How could there be other people like Jude? He's just trying to trick you!

Oliver stares at Dr. Greenwood for a long time before he answers. His curiosity wins. "Okay, I'll see it, but if I don't want to live there I won't."

"I can't give that to you, Oliver. Your parents have to decide with you."

"Do you think we could go see it?"

"I'll call Nan and she'll take you over there to see it and to meet the staff. I'll still be your psychologist but you'll have another doctor, someone different than Dr. Svare."

"Why can't I just go home?"

"Because if you just go home you may not get the care we can provide you. This illness is a nasty one, Oliver, as you know."

"Well, okay, but just for a few weeks."

Dr. Greenwood nods. "We can evaluate every few weeks. That's a good plan. In the meantime, I'll tell Orchard House to get your room ready."

29

TEAM OF INMATES

Peter can't stand not smoking weed. He can't stand being on the wrong side of John's good graces and he discovers, now that he's forced to be home and not stoned, how much he misses Oliver. He asks John and then Elizabeth if he could visit Oliver. They both say no. He considered running away, getting on a Greyhound Bus and traveling to Boston but realized his parents would figure that one out pretty quickly. Without weed, at least in the first weeks or so, Peter is jumpy, has no appetite, is irritable and intolerant. He's grounded from the Acura, even though it's now home in John's garage, for six weeks. John and Elizabeth have been chauffeuring Peter when the weather is too bad for him to use his bike. But, between school and community service, he hasn't been able to earn any part of what he owes John. School lets out June 10, and Peter will get odd jobs or work at Elizabeth's coffeehouse to pay his debt plus have some money for himself.

One month after the bust and a week after school lets out, John asks Peter if he would like to visit Oliver.

"Are you serious?"

"No, I'm kidding."

Peter ignores John's sarcasm. "You mean, by myself?"

"With me."

"When?"

"As soon as we can get reservations that aren't too expensive."

Peter hesitates, looks at the ground.

"I thought you'd jump at the idea."

"No, I am, I mean," Peter struggles to say "I'd like to, I just, I just don't know . . ."

"What to expect?"

"Yeah," Peter breathes out.

"I don't know what to expect either."

Peter smiles. "I wonder what it's like! One Flew Over the Cuckoo's Nest maybe?"

"I don't think so. As far as the facility anyway."

"Maybe some of the patients are like those guys in the movie, like the guy Nicholson plays."

"We'll have to keep a look out for him," John tells him, smiling.

"Thanks, Dad," Peter says.

"You're welcome, Pete. This has been hell on all of us."

"Is Ollie okay? I mean, why are we going back there?"

"I just want to see him. I miss him."

"Me too"."

"Yes, I figured as much. You can find a job when we return."

Oliver sits on the steps at Orchard House. He can hear the others behind him along with a boom box that sits on the deck. He's wrapped in the cloud of cigarette smoke from his own cigarette as well as everyone else's. Oliver is settling in. He's learning everyone's name and what they're in for, as though they're inmates at a low security prison. There is security here. White vans carrying guards patrol constantly. Oliver feels their eyes on him when they drive around the small circle in front of Orchard House, he sees how they look at him, knowing he's crazy just like all the others on the porch. Oliver wonders if they carry guns and, if they do, what kind of guns they are.

It seems that all the inmates smoke. They sit out on the worn wood steps and the benches, the boom box playing constantly, and they smoke. They speak to each other occasionally but mostly only when one of the talkative ones is absent, like Eddie. Eddie never shuts up. Ever. Oliver likes it when Eddie's out on the front stoop with all of them because there is no awkwardness, just Eddie talking. Oliver can tune Eddie in or out, it doesn't really matter. Eddie rips the filters off generic cigarettes and smokes them, one after another, while talking. Eddie suffers from treatment resistant schizophrenia. His wealthy family left him here, at Taylor Hospital, years ago and visit infrequently. Oliver wonders how Eddie feels about that, about being abandoned like that, but he won't ask. He's enjoying himself just sitting here, his cigarette in his own stained fingers, as one of the group. He takes a drag then ashes it and ashes it with his thumb, over and over. It's a satisfying feeling and he realizes he's not hating the day.

Oliver has been at Orchard House for a few months now. His hair is getting long. He ties a folded bandana around his hair to keep it out of his face, his feet are bare and his clothes are dirty but he doesn't care. He lifts his face to the sun's warmth.

Tagen walks out. The screen door squeals open then slams closed, two loud noises and there she is. Oliver cranes his neck around to see who came out. She flashes a smile at him that registers in his groin. Tagen is attractive, dark, and small with huge eyes. She's wearing tight jeans and a tight t-shirt covered with a gauze button down shirt. Oliver wishes Tagen was attracted to him. He knows that one of his symptoms is to not be able to read people and he wishes he didn't know that. He thinks that knowing that makes it even harder to read people. If he didn't know that he can't read people he'd at least be satisfied with thinking that he could. Tagen sits behind Oliver. He can feel her back there, hear her talking to someone. He wants to turn around and begin a conversation with her but can't make himself do it. His mouth is shut tight against not having anything to say, against his fear of saying something stupid.

Tagen suddenly appears at Oliver's side, her thigh quite close to his. Oliver's instant reaction is to pull away from her. He glances at her face and see's that she's glaring at him. He stands, walks up the steps, and disappears into the house. He runs up the stairs and down the hall, past the telephone booth and into his room. His roommate, Mike, is there, playing his guitar. Oliver lies down on his bed, facing the wall, and puts his pillow over his face and slips into overdrive. His thoughts are racing, about Tagen, her glare, what she meant by it, if it was really a glare, about how stupid he is, how ugly and stupid, how much of an idiot he must have looked just now, by running away from her, about this place and how homesick he is, about his roommate and how much he hates listening to him play the guitar and how much he wishes he could play guitar, about the doctors and the nurses and all the lunatics here and how much he doesn't want to be here. He throws his pillow on the floor and turns over onto his back. Mike seems oblivious to Oliver's presence and keeps playing his guitar. Oliver looks at his watch and realizes it's almost time to help in the kitchen. "Shit!" All the good feelings he had while sitting on the porch steps have evaporated. His energy is gone and he's pissed about it. He doesn't want to go back downstairs but knows that Virgil will come looking for him if he doesn't show up for his kitchen work detail. It's almost impossible to fake it; Virgil has seen it all.

Oliver likes Virgil. Virgil is what they call the House Nurse. He's a big guy, an older fellow, who gets along with most of the patients. He brings coffee cake on weekends. Oliver thinks it's like Christmas morning every weekend when Virgil brings that coffee cake. Virgil says that the residents of Orchard House are like his family and the residents feel the same way about him. But when Virgil has to get tough, he gets tough. He's been around people who suffer with schizophrenia, bipolar disorder, and major depression for so long that he knows what's up probably more than the doctors do most of the time. He knows what to expect when one of the clients is depressed or manic or delusional. He knows when you can fulfill your shift expectations and when you can't. According to Virgil, it's rare that a client can't do their shift.

Oliver decides to let Virgil come look for him. He stays still and stares up at the old, plaster ceiling. There are cracks and stains up there that take on all sorts of shapes and symbols that are disturbing to Oliver. One that bothers him the most is the one that looks like a ferret. It's wicked and gives him a bad feeling.

"Fuck you!" says Oliver to the ceiling.

"What?" asks Mike, his fingers poised over the guitar strings.

"Nothing."

"Did you say that to me?"

"Say what?"

"Say 'fuck you.'"

"No."

"Oh." He resumes playing his guitar.

Oliver feels nauseated and notices a pain in the back of his head. He closes his eyes and listens to Mike's guitar. It seems Mike has been playing the same song over and over but he can't really remember. He opens his eyes and looks at his hands; they look the same, maybe a bit smaller. Oliver doesn't know why his hands look smaller sometimes but they only look smaller when his mood slides down. He puts them at his sides. He thinks back to the morning and remembers that he didn't go to the group meeting he's supposed to attend every morning. Again. He just can't get up in time for it. He never really wants to get up. He knows he has to stay here in Orchard House while different drugs are being tried on him but he wishes he could just stay in bed the whole time. Then he thinks of Tagen. He thinks of her eyes and her shapely, muscular legs and small breasts showing through her halter top and he thinks about her sitting so close to him and he decides that maybe he could go downstairs but then he remembers how she glared at him and his energy drains back into the mattress.

"Fuck." He glances over at Mike who didn't hear him this time.

Virgil shows up in the bedroom doorway. "Come on slacker. UP! Time to work to earn your keep."

"Fuck you, Virgil," says Oliver, no vigor behind his words.

"Hey! We'll have none of that. Come on, I don't have all day to grease your pansy ass."

"Then do it yourself."

"I've got enough to do with lighting fires under you all."

Oliver figures he's played Virgil about as much as he dares. Virgil has turned him over in his mattress once and he doesn't want that to happen again.

"Okay, I'm coming."

"Put on some shoes."

"Yeah, yeah."

"Don't make me come back for you!"

"I won't."

"Mike," Virgil says, "what are you supposed to be doing?"

Mike stops playing and looks at Virgil with a scared expression. He pauses, then, "Nothing. I went on grocery detail this morning."

"Okay, good."

"I'll see you downstairs, Oliver." He leaves the doorway. Both young men can hear his retreat down the hallway, the old hall boards squeaking under his weight. Mike begins playing again.

30

WORK + DETAIL= FREEDOM

Oliver heaves himself up. His body feels like it weighs 1,000 pounds and he now recognizes, for a fact, that Mike has been playing the same song over and over.

"Christ."

He walks out on the landing and begins his descent down to the lobby. The stair railings have been extended upward for each flight to fill in the open space where someone, a patient presumably, could fling themselves down the three floors of stairs to their death. As necessary as this probably is, the sight of the tall railings always remind Oliver of suicide, which means they probably remind everyone of suicide which, actually, is probably pretty close to the surface anyway.

"Too bad."

He hits the lobby floor and realizes he's barefoot.

"Fuck."

He walks all the way back up, retrieves his shoes from under his bed and walks back out of his room on his way back down the stairs. Before he gets to the top of the stairs the phone in the phone booth rings. He stops and waits to see if Betty is going to come out of her room to answer it. Betty has bipolar disorder and has lived here in Orchard House for a long time. Her husband keeps her here. Betty has taken it upon herself to answer the third-floor phone and is always disappointed if someone else answers it. Sure enough, Betty's door opens and she comes out dressed in a cotton housecoat, her hair combed carefully. She picks up the phone receiver.

"Yes? Hello? I'll see if he's here." She lets the phone dangle by its short metal cord and walks to Jerry's room. She knocks. No answer. She returns to the phone. "Hello? He's not in his room at the moment. No, I don't take messages. Call the front desk. Perhaps he's downstairs. Yes." She hangs up and walks back to her room, leaving the door open.

Oliver has watched the exchange. He shakes his head and slowly walks downstairs. Virgil is at the bottom of the stairs, ready to come roll him out of bed if need be. Oliver is glad he's made it down. He tells Virgil about watching Betty answer the phone and that she doesn't take messages and that it was someone for Jerry.

"Well, they'll have to call the front desk, won't they? Now, you. You need to check the detail list to see what you're signed up for this evening unless you remember. Do you remember?"

"Yeah. I have to set the tables after I empty the dishwashers."

"Okay. I'll be around. Better get busy. Dinner's cooking."

Oliver doesn't mind this job too much, he doesn't have to talk to anyone. He finds a cart near the opening to the dining room and pushes it over to the dishwashers. Two dishwashers next to each other. He opens one, unloads the dishes and dumps the silverware from that one into a steel container, pushes the loaded cart into the dining room and begins setting the tables with the clean silverware. He piles the plates on the buffet table to the left of where the food will go.

Three patients are in the kitchen cooking dinner. It looks to Oliver like they're going to have meatloaf, green beans, and boiled potatoes. Janine is taking meatloaf out of the oven. Her hair is tightly braided, which means she's been home recently. Her parents live nearby and bring her home for regular visits. Oliver is pretty certain that Janine has bipolar disorder. He heard her recite some of her poetry once and was impressed. The thing about Janine is that when she hasn't been home recently she begins to smell like BO and her braids frizz up until they almost disappear into an Afro. Oliver knows to stay away from her when her hair is bad.

Maurice is spooning red potatoes into a huge colander from an even bigger pot of boiling water. He's working fast. Maurice always works fast. He's bipolar but mostly always manic. He's told Oliver that the doctors haven't been able to find a med to balance him out yet but he doesn't care. He likes being manic. Oliver has to agree with him. Oliver likes being manic, too, and wishes he was manic most of the time like Maurice. Maurice has a small mustache and long, black hair that he keeps in a ponytail. He's Hispanic and Oliver likes to hear him speak Spanish, fast, especially when Maurice is angry. Oliver knows that Maurice likes Janine and thinks it's curious they're on the same kitchen detail. He wonders if Maurice talked someone's ear off to get him and Janine on the same team.

The other person working in the kitchen this evening is Nason. Nason is Eddie's sidekick. He rarely speaks to anyone but Eddie and suffers with schizophrenia. In fact, Oliver has never seen Nason work before. He wonders if Eddie has talked to the staff before this and got Nason out of work detail. That seems unlikely but Eddie does hold a position of authority in Orchard House unlike any other patient. Nason is small and pale, almost elf-like. His hands, feet, and features are all small.

Oliver glances at the three in the kitchen while he sets the tables. He notices how slowly Nason works on draining the green beans. He hears Maurice yell at Nason to "get a move on!" Oliver is fairly certain that Nason will be reporting to Eddie and that Eddie will get in Maurice's face but Maurice won't care. Maurice is tough. Oliver would never want Maurice angry with him. Just thinking about it gives Oliver an uneasy feeling.

There are five tables with five settings per table. The staff eat with the clients. Oliver sets the tables quickly. He has to be careful to not forget the napkins and the salt and peppers and the pitchers filled with ice water. And the glasses. If it wasn't for those items he could set the tables very quickly. The pitchers take the most time.

The ice machine is out in the hall so he loads up the empty pitchers onto the cart, wheels it out into the hall, fills the pitchers with ice then wheels them to the sink in the kitchen, fills them with water, wheels them to the tables and he's done. Time for a smoke before dinner is called.

Oliver walks out the front door onto the porch. Tagen is still there. She looks up at him from the top step and pats the empty place next to her. He wonders if he's reading her signal right. She keeps looking at him and smiling so he figures he must be right. He sits down next to her. Before he has time to light up Virgil is out on the porch telling him he forgot to empty the other dishwasher.

"I'll do it in a minute."

"No, you'll do it now, before dinner," Virgil corrects him.

Oliver looks at Tagen. "I have to go."

"Apparently," she says. "I'll see you inside."

Oliver jumps up, a smile plastered on his face. He empties the second dishwasher in record time.

Dinner is an exercise in noise. Oliver has a difficult time with all the people and voices. He slips his sunglasses on. This evening he sits with Maurice, Tagen, Jerry, and Nason. Maurice keeps up a monologue. Oliver is thankful that he doesn't have to talk. Jerry tries to insert a few comments but Maurice just talks over Jerry's words. Oliver is concentrating on his meatloaf when all of a sudden Tagen is yelling at Maurice.

"Shut the fuck up, Maurice!"

"What you talking about, bitch?" Maurice yells back at her.

Virgil is standing by the table the next second. "What's going on here?"

"He won't stop talking!" Tagen screams.

"No one else is talking!" Maurice screams back.

"No one else can talk because you're just running off at the mouth!"

"Tell you what," Virgil says quietly. "Maurice, you come to my table with your plate. Kerry," he signals to Kerry, "will switch with Maurice."

Maurice just sits tight and glares up at Virgil. Kerry, the head nurse, arrives at the table with her plate.

"Come on, Maurice," Virgil says. "Come with me."

Maurice grabs his utensils and plate and follows Virgil. Kerry sits down. "Now, how are all of you?" she looks around the table.

No one answers her. Tagen begins eating again. They can hear Maurice talking at Virgil's table. Tagen catches Oliver's eye behind his sunglasses. She smiles. Oliver smiles back then drops his eyes back to his plate. He's not quite sure why Tagen is smiling at him. He thinks she's smiling at him because she thinks he said something stupid but as far as he can remember he hasn't said anything. He decides to keep it that way and keeps eating dinner while keeping his eyes safely behind his sunglasses and focused on his plate.

Jerry and Kerry are talking. Oliver listens to their conversation and wants to contribute but, his words get stuck in his mouth. Their words are all tangled up and he doesn't dare add more words to the mix. He steals small glances at Jerry. He watches how Jerry's mouth spills words, how his lips make shapes before each word comes out and how his mouth chews when he's listening to Kerry.

Jerry is a bit older than Oliver and also from the west. He's an outdoorsy guy who wears his blond hair in dreads. He's into reggae music and prefers sleeping in his sleeping bag rather than sheets. Jerry likes walking and hikes into town at every opportunity. Sometimes he walks out the front entrance of Taylor Hospital and crosses the road to the park that's situated on the other side of a stonewall. There's an entrance to the park but Jerry prefers hopping up on the stonewall then jumping down; he feels like he's getting away from the hospital more dramatically when he enters the park like that, as though he's scaling the wall, shutting out the road and the hospital. He appreciates the ducks on the pond, the waterfall, and the paths that lead deep into the woods. He'll sit on a boulder, hidden by trees. This afternoon he thinks about what it is that he's doing at Taylor. He smokes cigarette after cigarette but is careful to put the cigarette butts in his pocket after putting them out on the rough skin of the boulder. Jerry is trying to hold on to what he knows about himself. The feel of the rock beneath him, the trees around him, all take him back to Colorado where he grew up. He hadn't wanted to come to Taylor. He'd resisted his parent's plan for him by locking himself in his room then crawling out his window, leaving his meds behind. He'd hitched rides all the way to Ohio and wasn't found by his family until he was arrested for walking into a mall, naked. The police in Colorado Springs had put out a national APB on him and police everywhere were supposed to be aware of the fact that Jerry was mentally ill.

When Jerry walked into the largest mall in Cleveland he attracted all sorts of attention. Security was called immediately and a nearby store owner threw a brand-new blanket around Jerry's shoulders. Jerry stood rooted; he gazed up into the mall ceiling, his hands supplicating whatever it was that he saw up there. The blanket fell right off Jerry's shoulders. The store owner took off his own belt and handed it to the security guard to put around Jerry's waist.

"Just tuck the blanket in around the belt so it won't fall down," he told the security guard. "I'm going to look for his clothes." He then went out into the parking lot and searched for a pile of clothes but none were to be found. By that time the police arrived and mall security happily handed Jerry's fate over to them.

"He's just been standing there, naked, all quiet and such," security told the cops. "We can't find his clothes either."

"Whattaya think yer doin', Bud?" asked one officer.

Jerry smelled. He smelled like a human who's been on the streets for a long time. The store owner, when he got close to Jerry with the brand-new blanket, realized being a Good Samaritan might not have been such a good idea, but it was too late. If he took the blanket back now he'd look like an ass. He stood and watched.

Jerry kept his eyes on the ceiling. As soon as he was released, even though his hands were handcuffed in front, he continued to hold them together in the manner of prayer. The cuffs slipped down past his wrists.

The officers followed Jerry's gaze up to the ceiling. They almost expected to see something up there, so intently was Jerry staring. All they saw were the huge steel beams and girders holding up the mall roof.

"Where're yer clothes?"

Jerry continued staring up at the ceiling.

"This guy must be on drugs," said the first police officer, uncomfortable with Jerry's staring.

"That or he's nuts," said the second officer.

"Or both."

They began to load Jerry into their cruiser but the store owner stopped them, asking for the return of his blanket.

"Sure, but we can't take him in naked. We'll bring it back to you."

"Do you promise? How about if I come down to the station?"

The police officers looked at each other.

"If you want. Now, sir, we have to deal with this young man."

No longer important, the store owner stepped back to watch.

"How'd ya wanna do this?" the second officer asked.

"We need to get him outta here in case he blows!"

"Right."

"I'll put my arm around him and turn him toward the outside doors. You get ready with the taser, just in case, okay?"

"What if he doesn't want to be touched?"

"Can you think of a better way?"

"Well. No."

The first police officer stepped up close to Jerry. He put his arm around Jerry's shoulders and turned him. Nothing. Next, his arm still around Jerry, the second officer ushered Jerry out the doors to the waiting cruiser. Jerry's expression didn't change until he was outside and then the only change was that he squinted up at the sun.

And now Jerry was here, in the hospital anyway, facing the illness that took him to that mall in the first place. He looks across the table at Oliver, takes in the sunglasses, the wavy hair, the bandana, the handsome face. Oliver is one of the only residents here at Orchard

House that he feels comfortable with. Oliver is quiet, he's from Montana and he likes to hike.

"Oliver?" Jerry says to get his attention. "Oliver?" he says again.

"Yeah?" Oliver looks up and even though he's wearing sunglasses he looks confused.

"You wanna go for a walk into town after dinner?"

"Maybe."

"I'm gonna go," Tagen says.

"You weren't invited," says Jerry.

"So what? It's a free world isn't it?"

"Christ," Jerry says and shakes his head. "Never mind. I'm not going then."

"Well that's pretty shitty of you!" says Tagen, her voice rising.

"Why don't you want Tagen to go?" asks Kerry.

"I don't have to have a reason," says Jerry.

"Maybe he's gay," says Tagen.

"That's not necessary, Tagen," says Kerry.

"Fuck you, Tagen," says Jerry. "Why do you always have to be such a bitch?"

"Okay," Oliver says, still looking down at his plate. "I'll go."

Silence.

Oliver looks up. All eyes are on him. "What?"

"Nothing," says Jerry who notices that Oliver's hands are shaking. He doesn't know if it's just now or if Oliver's hands always shake. He makes a mental note to notice. And Jerry wonders if Oliver thinks he is gay. He tries to not care but the thought is disturbing and one he wrestles with all the time. He hates Tagen for bringing it up.

"I'm going for sure," Tagen says.

"No, you're not," says Jerry.

"Just let it be, Tagen," says Madeline. "There'll be other outings."

"Fuck that," says Tagen and pushes away from the table. She kicks her chair, spinning it around with a crash and walks away, leaving the dining room.

Oliver watches her go, his eyes peering over his sunglasses.

The evening was warm, the shadows long and black. Oliver and Jerry set out from Orchard House, leaving the smokers on the porch behind them. There was no sign of Tagen. They didn't speak. Jerry set the pace and Oliver followed. They walked across the road to the church situated between Orchard House and the field that would take them down to the road to town.

Jerry breaks the quiet. "Have you ever been inside this church?"

"Nope."

They skirted around the edge of the church and made their way down the steep slope and through a thin stand of trees before they broke free into the field. Jerry threw his arms out to his sides and ran, yelling at the top of his lungs, toward the road that cuts through the field. Oliver smiles but keeps up his walking pace, just putting one foot in front of the other. The sudden openness of the field scared him so he looked at the ground and kept moving. But even walking didn't help his fear. He stopped where he was and watched as Jerry walked away. He stared at the ground, hoping that by looking at his feet he'd come back to himself, come back from the huge sky that hung above him.

"Oliver!"

He heard Jerry calling him and looked up. Jerry was standing on the road, beckoning to him, impatient. Oliver's chest tightens.

"You okay, man?"

Oliver can't move, didn't want to move. He wanted to be back on the porch where all was familiar, safe, predictable—most of the time anyway. He tries to take in Jerry's face so he could tell him that he was going back but Oliver couldn't get a grip on Jerry's features. He feels as though he was sinking into the field, feet first, up to his knees now, then up to his rear. Jerry is standing over him, his hand out as though he wanted something.

"Oliver?"

Oliver can hear Jerry's feet as they walk around him, can hear his voice calling to him, but doesn't respond. He's caught in the cocoon of inert silence, vibration, and felt nothing else.

31

MONTANA BLUES

Elizabeth answers the phone before looking to see who's calling. She hears Oliver's voice on the other end and her heart begins to race, her hands shake.

"Mom?"

"Hi sweetie," she answers as calmly as possible. "How are you?"

"I need to come home, Mom. Will you send me a ticket so I can come home?"

"No, honey, I can't do that. What happened today?"

"Nothing. I just can't take this anymore."

"I know it's difficult but you'd be worse off at home."

"No, I wouldn't! I would live out in the woods and not bother anyone. Really!"

Elizabeth can't stand the tone of desperation in Oliver's voice. There's nothing she can do to help him. She walks into the kitchen and retrieves a bottle of vodka from the shelf above the dishwasher. Holding the phone receiver between her cheek and shoulder she opens the bottle then lifts it to her lips and downs a big gulp. After three gulps her hands stop trembling.

"Do you remember that Dad and Peter will be there soon to see you?"

"Like a freak in a cage . . ."

"Stop it, Ollie," she says as gently as this can be said. The vodka has tempered her words. "I know this is hard on you and believe me, if I could do anything to make it easier for you, I would. But I can't. I'm helpless and can't stand it either!" Elizabeth's voice rises even though she resists the temptation to scream.

Oliver can't hear the anguish in his mother's voice and can't respond to it. "Would you please send me a ticket, please?"

"Ollie, I can't and even if I could, I wouldn't because you need to be there for your own healing, your own good."

"But that doesn't make sense! They don't need me here! I'm just part of the freak show!"

Elizabeth wants to retort sharply but stops herself. "Haven't you done anything fun?"

Oliver pauses, then tells her, "We drove to the mall in the Orchard House van. Eddie came along and tried to boss everyone but Tagen and Jerry and Maurice and I didn't let him. That was kind of fun."

"You did what?" Elizabeth can't believe what she's hearing. "You drove to a mall in a van?"

"Yeah, it's the van we take on outings."

Elizabeth takes another gulp of vodka. "Who supervises these outings?"

"Virgil."

Elizabeth is suddenly nauseated and knows she must get off the phone. "Ollie, I have to go, okay? Get ready for your dad and brother's visit and try to enjoy yourself, okay? I have to go."

"Mom?"

"I have to go."

"I'll call you later then," Oliver tells her.

"Okay. Bye." Elizabeth hangs up the phone and runs to the bathroom where she throws up, again and again, tears streaming down her face, picturing Ollie in a van with a bunch of crazies going to a mall. After throwing up she goes into the living room and lies down on the couch where Wren finds her.

"Oh my God, Wren! I was supposed to meet you at school! I'm so sorry!" Elizabeth holds her arms out for Wren who merely sits down on the couch, close to Elizabeth's feet. "I was talking to Ollie and forgot about everything else. He wants to come home." The familiar wave of guilt hits Elizabeth. She sees the vodka bottle sitting on the hall table and wants to get up to hide it.

"Why wouldn't he want to come home?" Wren asks.

"Well, that's true but he can't come home, not yet."

"Why not?"

"Because he's sick!" Elizabeth raises her voice and immediately regrets it. She says, more gently, "He can't come home until they find the right medication to put him on, Wren. You know that." Elizabeth wishes she'd remembered to fetch Wren from school. She envisions Wren waiting for her at school then walking down the dirt road behind their house. She wishes she hadn't had a drink but at least her hands aren't shaking and she's glad that John will pick up Wren for dinner and the night.

"Come on, sweetie, let's get you a snack," Elizabeth says, burying her irritability for now. She heaves herself off the couch, picks up the vodka bottle, and walks into the kitchen. She returns the bottle to the cupboard. Now that she only has Wren after school the kitchen is much cleaner. She isn't eating much. There's a bottle of gin in the freezer, wine on the counter, the vodka in the cupboard— food doesn't play much of a part here.

"You know what, Wren?" Elizabeth asks.

"What?"

"When you come to stay with me while Peter and Dad are away we can go to the Co-Op for their already cooked dinners. Wouldn't that be fun? You could even do your homework there and I could help you or read. Okay?"

"That would be fun," Wren says. "We'll have Jack here, right?"

"Of course!"

"When are they leaving?"

"They leave in three days, the day school lets out."

"Oh. I'm mad they won't take me. I want to see Ollie too."

Elizabeth arranges crackers and cheese on a plate for Wren. She sits down at the kitchen table and watches while Wren sits.

"I know you want to see Ollie but that place isn't for little girls."

"If it's not for little girls then Ollie shouldn't be there!"

Elizabeth sighs. More conflict is the last thing she wants right now. She puts her face in her hands and shakes her head.

"Bring your plate into the living room and we'll watch TV, okay?"

"Okay. But still, I want to go too."

"And still, that's not going to happen," Elizabeth tells her, feeling her irritability surge. "That is just simply not going to happen!"

Peter is excited, apprehensive, eager to get out of Bozeman. He and John will catch a flight hours before school lets out for the year. Peter did well in his junior year despite the chaos at home. Schoolwork was easy for him, and he had found that it was also a good distraction from his personal life. He had become used to not smoking weed but was looking forward to vacation so he could take it up again. But first, this trip to see Ollie. He felt sorry that Wren had to stay behind but understood. He wondered though if it would be worse for her to stay with their mom. Elizabeth seemed more unstable ever since she came home from taking Oliver to Taylor Hospital. She was drinking a lot. He could smell it on her all the time. John wouldn't talk to him about Elizabeth; any mention of her got him exasperated. Peter didn't want to cause John to be in a bad mood so he didn't mention Elizabeth but he did worry, not only about his mom but also about Wren.

When Oliver heard that Peter and John were coming to visit his initial reaction was one of fear. He didn't want Peter to see him in this environment. But then, after a lengthy discussion with Dr. Greenwood, he changed his mind and was looking forward to it. Dr. Greenwood stressed how important it was that Oliver accept the fact that he had an illness, that he didn't have to apologize for it or make excuses about it. He was at the hospital because that's where he needed to be. Oliver could hear that from Dr. Greenwood. He could not hear it from anyone else.

Oliver and Tagen had begun a real friendship. After Oliver collapsed in the field with Jerry he stayed on the porch while his confidence grew again. Tagen stayed close and made it clear that she was attracted to him. Oliver, who hadn't had a girl interested in him for a long time, was buoyed up by her attentions.

"Hey, you wanna try walking to town again?" she asked after sitting near Oliver on the porch for almost a week. "Or maybe we could walk out the front gate and cross the street to the pond?"

Oliver looks at her while she's speaking. He was standing at the bottom of the stairs, she was three steps up, right in line with her big eyes.

"Whattaya think? Wanna go?" she asks again.

"Did I tell you that my father and brother are coming in two days?" he answers.

"You've told me about a million times! What does that have to do with taking a walk?" Tagen shakes her head, frustrated.

Joe walks out of the house and settles himself on the bench. He's been at Taylor for about a year. His hair is always severely combed to the side, the comb tracks visible. The younger people in the house make fun of him because of how he greets the other clients, no matter what. In fact, he won't speak to anyone except to say hello. Today, both Oliver and Tagen say hello at the same time. Joe gets back up and takes Oliver's hand and pumps it up and down, saying, "Hello. Hello. Hello!" and then does the same to Tagen's hand, smiling through it all. As soon as he sits back down, the smile is gone, the light in his eyes evaporates. Oliver and Tagen look at each other and try to not laugh. Joe rarely communicates unless it's to respond to hello, which he does, enthusiastically, even if he's seen you before, even only five minutes before.

"Okay, let's go," Oliver says all of a sudden.

"Where?" Tagen asks.

"Whattaya mean, where?"

"To the pond or into town?"

"Oh. Pond."

"Let's go!" Tagen jumps off the steps and takes off down the road.

"Hey! Wait up!"

"No! You catch up!" She looks back at him over her shoulder, grinning.

Oliver runs to catch her, smiling. He grabs for her hand but she pulls it away. Even so, they run down the road, laughing. The front gate looms. There's no gate, only stone pillars and a large sign announcing Taylor Hospital. Oliver stops. Tagen looks at him and walks off the road to the lawn. She sits cross-legged and watches Oliver. He stands perfectly still and stares at where the road goes through the gate.

Hey, shithead, what do you think you're doin'? You can't ever leave here!

Oliver glances over at Tagen. She's watching him and he can feel it. He's suspicious of being so visible. But he wants to go to the pond. He doesn't want to turn around to stay on the porch.

Tagen walks over to him. She takes his hand and leads him across the road and into the park. She leads him across a wooden bridge and up a path that leads into the woods. The boulders are granite gray, some almost flat on top with leaves and moss making inviting sitting places. Once across the bridge, Tagen drops Oliver's hand. Then she literally hops and skips up the path going quite a ways into the woods. Oliver follows. Coming around a bend in the path, they both see a huge boulder with what looks like handholds leading to the top. Tagen was on it before Oliver could even make a comment. He follows her and they discover, together, that the boulder has a deep indentation on its very top.

"Wow! Let's sit here!" Tagen is excited.

They lie down together on their stomachs and peer over the edge of the boulder.

"You could do some real spying from up here, huh?"

Oliver doesn't answer.

Black soil and moss lie under them. Leaves cover everything, and for every movement they make there's a rustling sound. The moss softened their hiding place. Oliver brushes the leaves aside to see underneath. He notices a bit of shiny and brushes the dirt aside to see what it is that's glinting at him. It's a piece of broken, blue glass.

"Look what I found!"

"That's pretty! Are there any others? Is it sharp?"

They both dig around in the loose, dark soil but don't find anything else.

Tagen laid on her back and gazed up through the leaves and branches to the sky above. Oliver laid on his back, too, holding the piece of glass up to the light. The glass, about one inch by two inches, was a very pale, almost purply blue, like Montana sapphires, and Oliver moves his head close to Tagen so she can see through it too.

"Look how beautiful this color is!"

Tagen moves her head even closer to Oliver's, until they touch. Oliver lowers the piece of glass and turns his face to Tagen. They look at each other and Tagen gently puts her mouth on his, pressing ever so slightly until they're locked in a deep, long kiss. Oliver slips the glass into his jeans pocket and then turns on his side to concentrate more meaningfully on Tagen. She flings her arms around his neck and Oliver somehow ends up on top of her. She can feel all of him through their clothes and suddenly gets scared.

"No, no more," she says.

"Okay. Phew!!" Oliver sits up while Tagen stays lying on her back, looking up at him.

"You are so handsome," she tells him.

"Thank you. And you're so beautiful!"

"Then we're pretty special, huh?"

"I guess so."

"I love it here," says Tagen. "I love how quiet it is. Orchard House is so noisy and there are so many of us there. I wish we could live in the woods."

"How did you know?" Oliver asks her, the hair rising up on his neck.

"What?"

"How did you know about the woods?" Oliver is getting scared, thinks that Tagen must have read his thoughts about telling Elizabeth that he wanted to live in the woods, that she must have read his thoughts to know something like that.

"Whattaya mean 'know about the woods'? What are you talking about?"

She's lying. How did she know unless she can read your thoughts?

Oliver is staring at her like he doesn't know who she is.

"Oliver? Everything's okay, isn't it?"

"I gotta go," he tells her and scrambles down the side of the boulder. At the bottom he looks back up at her, his face a picture of confusion and fear. She climbs down, too, but he's sprinted away before her feet touch the path.

"What the fuck?" she asks the woods and walks back down to the pond.

Oliver is nowhere in sight. The farther she walks the angrier she becomes. How could he just leave her out here by herself?

"What a jerk," she says to herself. She crosses the bridge then walks the long haul back to Orchard House, most of which is uphill.

Oliver walks, head down, fast, most of the way back to Orchard House. Knowing that Tagen had read his thoughts is terrifying him. He doesn't understand what happened, just that they were kissing, then Tagen had read his thoughts, something about the woods that he'd never told her.

"How could she know what I said to my mother unless she read my thoughts?" Oliver is staring down at his feet as he walks. First left toe shows then right toe shows then left toe shows and on and on. "And that's how it goes, left, right, left, right," he chants to himself. He keeps walking, glancing up only occasionally to make sure he stays on the road, to make sure no one is watching. At least he knows someone is watching, as always, but he has to make sure he can't see who it is. He passes the fairy-tale house in the distance across the expanse of lawn. He stops to stare at it but doesn't want Tagen to catch up with him. He looks back down at the gray surface of the road.

"What the fuck? Why did she have to ruin everything?"

Why are you whining? That bitch reveals she can read your thoughts and you're sad?

"Stupid bitch," Oliver mutters under his breath. "Stupid bitch thinks she can read my thoughts and me be okay with it!?"

Oliver arrives at Orchard House and sprints up to his room without saying hello to anyone. He kicks off his shoes and lies down on his bed facing the door so he can see if anyone comes in.

It's Virgil who arrives at his door. "Come on, get up for dinner," he tells Oliver.

"No."

"You want me to roll you out?"

"Can't you just leave me alone for once?"

"No, I can't. You know that too. Now, come on and get up or I'll put you on restriction and you'll be stuck here for a week."

"So? You think I care?"

"Come on, get up! This is my last warning."

Oliver heaves himself up and off his bed. He knows there's really no getting away from Virgil and as much as he doesn't care if he goes on restriction he doesn't want to give Virgil that power.

Oliver grabs a black knit hat and his sunglasses off his bureau, walks across the room and past Virgil. He jams the hat on his head and puts his sunglasses on. He puts his hands in his pockets as a sign of not caring and feels the piece of blue glass with his fingers.

Dinner is uneventful. Oliver wears both the knit hat and sunglasses and pointedly ignores Tagen. She, on the other hand, tries to get Oliver's attention by coming over to him, putting her hands on his shoulders. Oliver shrugs and she moves off, sitting down next to Maurice who, as usual, is talking fast and loudly. Oliver eats quickly so he can get back to his room but he glances over at Maurice and Tagen. She's listening to him, intently. Then he sees her glance over at him, Oliver. She tries to catch his eye through his sunglasses and pouts, her lower lip sticking out.

"What's that supposed to mean?" Oliver asks himself. He gulps the rest of his food then leaves the table, sprinting back to his room.

You are such a coward! You are such a piece of shit! Hear me? A piece of shit! She's laughing at you. Now Maurice will be laughing at you too!

Oliver collapses on his bed. He takes off his pants and throws them on the floor. Then he remembers the blue piece of glass and picks his pants back up, reaches into his right pocket and retrieves it. He gets under his covers then holds the glass up to the window above his bed. The color brings the afternoon and Tagen back and with it a sudden ache in his heart. He stares at the blue in his hand, up over his head, until his arm begins to go to sleep. He then holds the glass in his fist and drops his arm back to the bed. He notices how sharp one edge of it is and opens his fist to examine his hand to see it he's cut himself. There's a thin line of blood across his palm.

Nice! You could make it bigger perhaps?

Oliver licks the blood off his palm but it springs right back. He squints his eyes and examines the line out of focus. He opens his eyes wide again and notices that the blood line cuts across his lifeline.

Now you've done it.

He pictures himself walking out of Orchard House and crossing the road to the church. He sees himself sitting behind the church with the descending hill at his feet, the piece of blue glass in his hand and he knows that he'll cut his veins with it. He knows he'll feel blood coming out of him, warm, a lot of it, and he knows how good it will feel, how relieved he'll be, how perfect a reprieve he'll give himself.

Yes.

32

BROTHERS AND REFLECTIONS

John and Peter are getting ready to go. They've done all the laundry, fetched suitcases from the basement, packed what they can before last minute items like their toothbrushes. Peter is excited. John is worried. He thinks that perhaps he made a mistake by not letting Wren come along. There's nothing he can do about it now except maybe call Elizabeth all the time to make sure she's all right. He's angry that she continues to drink but his anger and worry are ineffectual, which makes him even angrier. If it wasn't for Wren he wouldn't have anything to do with Elizabeth. His patience for Elizabeth has vanished.

"Dad? Do you want to go say goodbye to Wren?"

"I wish she could stay with us tonight," John says.

Peter knows their flight, the 6:00 a.m. out of Bozeman makes their airport arrival time between 4:30 and 5:00 a.m. They simply won't have the time to deal with Wren so early in the morning.

"I wish she could go too," Peter tells John.

The two of them are out back in the yard, soaking John's vegetable garden in anticipation of their trip. The weather was still not great but John likes planting in early June, early for Montana anyway.

"Let's go over there soon so we can try to get to bed early-ish, okay?" John tells Peter.

"Okay."

"We might as well eat out, too, so we don't make a mess. Where do you want to go?"

"The Naked Noodle?"

"Good." John turns off the hose and they walk around the house to his SUV.

"Here, you drive." John gets in the passenger seat.

Peter stands, surprised for a moment, then gets in behind the wheel. "Thanks, Dad."

"You earned it. Just don't mess up again, okay?"

"I'll try not to."

"That's not good enough. Just don't, okay?"

"Okay."

Elizabeth meets them at the door with a vodka tonic in hand. "Hello!" she says, obviously tipsy.

"Where's Wren?" John asks.

"She's right inside. Why?"

Seeing the booze in Elizabeth's hand makes John revise his plan at the last minute.

"Let's take Wren to dinner with us," John says as an aside to Peter who is still standing outside.

"Well come on in then," Elizabeth says in a singsong voice. "We were just watching TV."

John walks into the living room and picks up Wren from the couch. "We're taking her to dinner," he tells Elizabeth.

Elizabeth's face falls.

"We'll bring her back before bedtime."

Wren doesn't have time to object or even say goodbye. John walks out of Elizabeth's house quickly, without looking back.

Peter lingers.

"May I come?" Elizabeth asks him.

Peter looks down at the ground. "I don't think so, Mom."

"Why not?"

Peter gives her a long look. He can't believe she doesn't know. "Because of that," he says, tilting his head toward her drink.

"This?" she says and holds up her drink. "This?" she says again, an unmistakable cynical tone in her voice. "Why, doesn't Dad drink? Does he think he's so much better than me? Huh?"

"I gotta go, Mom."

"No, answer me, Peter! Doesn't Dad drink?"

"Mom, stop," Peter pleads. He doesn't know how to manage this conversation and wants out. "He doesn't drink all the time." Peter hears these words come out of his mouth and he can't believe he said them.

Elizabeth is stunned and stands rigid, her face a mask of surprise.

"I'll see you when we get home, I mean, when we drop off Wren," Peter says and bolts, leaving Elizabeth in the doorway.

Wren is buckled in on the rear seat. Peter sees John get out of the car from the passenger side. "One second, Pete, I'll be back in one second."

John walks back inside.

"John?" Elizabeth says, smiling, from the couch. She gets up to see why he came back.

"I have one thing to say to you," John says, "if anything happens to Wren because of your drunkenness, I'll kill you. Do you understand?" He stares her down. As soon as she looks away, he leaves.

He gets into the SUV and says, "Okay, you two, let's get to the Naked Noodle! I'm starving!"

"Me too!" yells Wren from the back seat.

Oliver gets out of bed, pockets the glass, straps on his watch and walks downstairs and out to the porch. He smokes with everyone else. He looks as though he belongs. He knows he does not.

Virgil says good night and goodbye to everyone around 7:00. Oliver is still on the porch. He decides to take his meds at eight, keep them under his tongue, and spit them out as he's walking away from the meds window. He won't have any trouble waiting for an hour. This part of the world is on daylight savings time so he has to wait until there's some darkness to hide his walk over to the church. The security vans can't see behind the church, and he doesn't think the guards actually exit the vans to check.

Linda walks out onto the porch. Oliver loves being around Linda. She's treatment resistant schizophrenic and always extremely psychotic. Oliver can see her psychosis and he can see Linda. He sees that she's an intelligent woman in her thirties who is stressed and frustrated by her illness. She talks about the Real World and the physical world and there have been times when Oliver wonders if Linda is his real mother since they both know about the Real World. Linda will talk about the same things that Jude had spoken about: the real world, God and Jesus, and how Jesus had risen up to God. And Linda always has a bottle of water with her as though she's aware of her health. If so, it would seem that her health is the only thing she really cares about. Her health and clothes. She rides the van into the mall every week and buys clothes. Her room is filled with piles and piles of folded garments, the tags still on them. Every once in a while the staff goes up to her room to bag all the clothes and put them in storage, waiting for the day that Linda goes home. The part of Linda that Oliver likes most is when she's talking—she'll all of a sudden bellow, "GO AWAY!" or cackle a creepy laugh and holler, "GET OUT!" Oliver wonders to whom it is that Linda is talking. He loves it that she sees and hears things that he can't see or hear.

This evening the porch is full. Linda sits quietly in the corner, smoking. Obnoxious Eddie sits on the wood bench that faces the road. His sidekick, Nason, is next to him. Eddie's talking about whatever, Oliver can't figure it out. The screen door opens slowly and now Fredrick is out there with all of them. He holds the screen door guiding it until it's closed to not let it bang shut. Oliver likes Fredrick. He's short and balding and very agreeable. Fredrick is an identical twin whose brother is living on his own. Every evening, when the windows at Orchard House are dark outside, lit inside, Fredrick has a talk with his brother. Since they're identical, he doesn't have to make anything up. He talks to his reflection, tells his brother what he's done for the day, what he ate at dinner, and any other tidbits he wants him to know. Oliver finds Fredrick to be endearing, and he loves that Fredrick can speak to his brother every day. Fredrick smokes cigarettes like a cigar smoker; each intake comes back out quickly, not inhaled. The smoke stays in front of his face longer than a regular cigarette smoker's does.

Oliver rarely asks himself why he's here anymore. These people are familiar now, their illnesses reflections of his own. He listens to Eddie babbling away next to Nason. He keeps an eye on Linda because she's so unpredictable. He has a bottle of water and he practices how he'll pretend to swallow his meds. No one is watching him. Even if they were they wouldn't know what it is that he's doing.

Oliver is content to sit on the porch and wait for 8:00 p.m.

Peter and John return Wren to Elizabeth's. John goes inside with Wren and finds Elizabeth sleeping on the couch. He puts Wren to bed, sitting with her while she brushes her teeth, then tucking her in. Peter, waiting in the SUV, thinks that John and Elizabeth are probably fighting and is content to sit outside.

"I love you, sweetie," John tells Wren. "I'll let Mom know you're back and in bed, okay?"

"Okay." Wren stretches her arms to her daddy and they hug. "I love you," she says.

Downstairs, John shakes Elizabeth's shoulder, waking her. She stares up at him, a look of bewilderment on her face, drool wetting her chin.

"What?"

"I brought Wren home and she's tucked into bed." With that, John turns and walks out of the house.

Oliver glances at his watch. It's almost 8:00 p.m. He stands, walks into the house and down the hall to the medication window. He asks for his nighttime meds. He's nervous but excited to be doing something so illegal, at least around here. He takes the small white cup filled with his meds and tips his head back. They fall into his mouth where he makes them lodge under his tongue. He then takes the small bottle of water offered him and drinks, the water slipping over his tongue, the pills safe underneath. He walks slowly out of the meds room holding the bottle in his left hand. As soon as he's out of sight he looks around to see if anyone is watching, then spits the meds out into his hand, pocketing them in the same pocket as the piece of blue glass. He feels a sense of intrigue and excitement. The porch is emptying out for the night. Oliver watches as each person goes inside to get their meds or head to bed. Fredrick is one of the last to go but he stops in the hall, turns and finds his reflection.

Oliver decides to change into dark clothes. He runs up the stairs and changes as fast as he can, grateful that Mike isn't there. He wonders, for a split second, where Mike is but doesn't dwell on it and remembers to transfer the blue glass to his dark pants pocket.

Now, back on the porch in dark clothes, Oliver begins to execute his plan. He has no clue as to when the security guards come around. He resolves to hide behind the bushes that line the driveway to see how far apart the guards are. Or maybe, he thinks, he could wait behind the bushes until the guards pass by and at that time he could bolt for the church.

Yes, that's better, he thinks.

He walks off the porch and gets behind the bushes. He lies down on his side and begins the wait.

Waiting like this was harder than he thought it would be. He feels like his body is on a rotisserie, the turning and turning and turning around. Back, side, stomach, side, back. Dirt and the tiny, dropped leaves from the bushes stick to him.

This isn't pleasant, it's like lying on the mossy boulder. He sees several cars go by but none that turn into the Orchard House turnaround.

Oliver's patience is running out. His watch now says 8:45 and the sun wasn't nearly down as far as he'd like to see it before running to the back of the church. But he's sticking with his plan. Lying on his back is the most comfortable. He likes the view from his back better than the other positions. He gazes up at the sky, watches the wispy clouds up there, and, if he cranes his neck way back, the top of his head almost touching the ground, he can see the north side of Orchard House. He can hear Orchard House. People and music and TV. He can hear all of it but can't zero in on the individual sounds. He tries to imagine the dishwasher sounds and the sounds of toilet's flushing and doors closing. Orchard House is just one gigantic conglomerate of noise, held together by the skin of the house. It's breathing with the breaths of so many people.

Oliver begins to imagine each person breathing but, just then, the lights of the security guards sweep across the porch. It isn't dark enough yet for the guards to spotlight the yard or Oliver would have been seen. And then they're gone and Oliver is lying on his back. The house sounds pause themselves as the guards drive away and Oliver can't get them to start again.

He sits up, looks at his watch and sees it's 9:15 p.m., exactly. He stands. There was no telltale light from the van, either white or red. He walks to the tree at the center of the driveway turnaround and still can't see any light, except for what was coming out of the house. He walks down the driveway and turns left. He crosses the road and sprints down the huge flat stones that serve as stairs for the church. He passes the dark wood doors that lead into the church. They're locked, as usual, but Oliver checks anyway. Then he steps to the back of the church. The ground wasn't mowed here so the grass was tall. He walks to the middle of the wall then sits, cross-legged. Now that the excitement and waiting is over, Oliver doesn't quite know what to do. He leans back on the wall and feels the cold stones between his shoulder blades. The blue glass is in his pocket; he isn't sure what he wants to do with it. He doesn't feel the same degree of hopelessness that he had when he made this plan. He takes the glass out of his pocket anyway, just to see it. He holds it in his right hand and runs the sharp part over the veins in his left wrist, gently. A white line appears crossing over his whole wrist.

Push, you idiot! See blood! You can't even hurt yourself, you piece of shit.

Oliver holds the piece of glass with more determination and pushes a bit harder. The white line stays a white line and now there are two. The air itself is getting darker; he feels the coolness that approaches with night. He looks at his watch and sees it's only 9:35 p.m. He leans his head back against the church.

Why are you giving up? Why are you just sitting there?

Oliver covers his face with his hands and shakes his head back and forth. A sudden breeze rustles through the stand of trees at the bottom of the hill, it lifts Oliver's hair and brings him back. He puts his hands on his knees and raises his head to listen. He's happy for a moment.

The coming darkness and the breeze are soothing. He hates the noise in the house, the lack of privacy in his room. He wishes he could go home to Montana. He lies down in the tall grass, curls up like an animal and falls asleep.

"Oliver!"

Someone is shaking him.

"What the fuck? What do you want?"

"They're looking for you, Oliver," Tagen says. "If you don't get back to the house they'll lock you up when they find you!"

"That doesn't make any sense," says Oliver. He uncurls himself and stands, getting a head rush. "Who's looking for me?"

"Security, man," says Maurice. "Come on! I think we can get you into the house without them seeing you! But we have to hurry up, they're all over the place, man, come on!"

"Shut the fuck up, Maurice," demands Tagen. "Oliver, come ON!"

She takes Oliver's hand and leads him the way around the church. There were no steps on this side of the church, no door either. A small hill obstructs their view of the road. The three lie down in the grass, on their stomachs, and inch forward to peer over the hill. They spot several security vans parked across the road between where they are and Orchard House.

"Let's go back, go down the hill, and swing all the way around and come at Orchard House from the opposite direction," Tagen suggests. "Okay?"

Maurice and Oliver are mute and stare at her.

"Come ON!" She says forcefully.

A light shines in their faces before they get the chance to move.

"Oh shit," says Maurice. "Look, Officer, we were just going to walk over to Orchard House."

"Sure you were," says the guard. "Come on. Up."

He doesn't sound angry or even annoyed. Oliver responds immediately and gets up, looking at the guard carefully to make sure he wasn't mistaken about the guard's state of mind.

"You, your name?" the guard asks Oliver.

"Oliver Moore."

"Yeah, it's you we're looking for. Who are your friends? Do they live here or are they from town?"

"From town?" Oliver is confused.

Tagen stands up and takes over. "I'm Tagen and this is Maurice. We live at Orchard House with Oliver."

"Yeah." The guard turns to Maurice and Tagen. "You two get on back to Orchard House. I'll be taking Oliver to the Inpatient Unit."

"What? You can't do that! He's fine!"

"No, he's not fine," says the guard calmly. "Go on back to Orchard House." The guard takes Oliver's upper arm and begins to walk him over to the security van.

Oliver looks at the guard's face and sees a small mustache under a large nose. "What are you doing?" Oliver asks. He pulls his arm away from the guard's grip.

"I'm giving you a lift to the Inpatient Unit."

"Oh, no, you don't have to do that! I won't do this again!"

"I'm sorry, son. I was told to find you and take you there so that's what I'm doing."

"Can't I talk to Virgil or someone?" Oliver pleads.

"I got my orders from Virgil," the guard tell him.

"Oh." Oliver gets in the van, in the back behind the driver's seat. He spots himself in the rearview mirror and sees that he's pale, his hair is wild. He reaches up to his hair and finds grass and burrs in it.

The Inpatient Unit is not far. The guard takes Oliver by the arm again and walks him into the front hall of the unit. The male night nurse is ready to clock in Oliver.

33

DOOR #8

"I don't need to be here," Oliver tells the nurse. "I need to go back to Orchard House."

"Hey, I'm sorry, man," says the night nurse. "You were out past bed check, and it didn't look like you were planning on coming back for a while."

The security guard is still standing in the hall.

"I got it, man," says the nurse to the guard.

"No problem," says the guard. "Call if you need me."

"Will do."

The guard and his mustache leave and the door clanks shut. Oliver assumes it's now locked and he can't escape.

"Then how come Tagen and Maurice didn't have to come here?"

"Because they were in the house and, understandably, came out to find you when it became evident that you weren't there. They had a reason to be out. You did not."

"How do you know that?" Oliver asks.

"What were you planning to do out there?"

"Nothing."

Right, he's really going to believe you. You dumb fuck! Now look what you did!

Oliver looks at the floor. All his good feelings are gone and now he's stuck in this place; a series of rooms in a single-story facility that looks like a cell block from the outside, barred windows on both side walls, the hall at the front, and a small kitchen at the back. He's never been inside here before but has walked passed it many times.

"So, let me take you to your room for the night," the nurse tells Oliver and walks away.

Oliver stands still.

"Come on," the nurse says and Oliver, putting his hands in his pockets, follows him down the hall.

Oliver feels the blue glass in his right pocket. "Shit!"

"What?"

"Nothing. I just realized I won't have my pajamas."

"Pretty attached to them, are you?"

"No, it'll be okay."

They arrive at a door, number 8, and step inside.

"Here's your room for the night. I heard from the meds nurse at Orchard House that you took your meds at 8:00 p.m. tonight. Is that correct? Did you swallow them?"

Oliver doesn't say a word but walks over to the bed and sits down.

"I mean, you seem pretty wide awake to have taken those meds at eight. If you didn't it would be good to tell me so I can get you some more. If you did, then everything is cool. The problem with skipping a night is that you won't feel terribly well tomorrow and Orchard House tells me that your father and brother are arriving tomorrow."

Oliver remains mute.

"Tell you what." He pulls a small spiral pad out of his breast pocket. "You write down the real answer here, on this piece of paper, and I'll leave the room and shut your door, okay? Then you slip the whole pad under your door with the answer. Okay?"

"Here's a pen." The nurse hands Oliver a pen from out of his pocket.

Oliver nods. The nurse leaves.

Before writing anything down Oliver slips his hand into his right pocket and extracts the blue glass. He looks around the room to find a hiding place and spots a narrow locker. He opens the locker and sees a small shelf at the top. He puts the blue glass up there and pushes it to the back of the shelf. Then, with a sigh, he picks up the small pad and pen and writes "didn't" on the blank page, then slips the pad and pen under the door. He lies down on the bed.

The nurse arrives again, quickly. He hands Oliver a white paper cup filled with meds and hands it to Oliver along with a small bottle of water.

"Here you go," he says to Oliver. "Now you can go to sleep."

"Is there a TV room here?"

"No, no luxuries," says the nurse.

"Is there anyone else here or is it just me?"

"Yeah, there are two other patients here but not from Orchard House." The nurse moves over to the door. "Okay? You all set?"

"I guess so," says Oliver. "Oh, just one thing. When can I go back?"

"To Orchard House?"

"Yeah."

"I have no idea, man. You'll probably have to see your psychiatrist or psychologist before they'll let you go back."

"But my father and brother are coming tomorrow!"

"I know, man. Perhaps you should have thought about that first before you took off."

"Bullshit." Oliver lies down, his back to the nurse.

"You set it up, man, you set it up." The nurse closes Oliver's door, quietly.

"Fuck."

John and Peter enjoy their flight across the country. John sleeps the whole way, except when food is served. Peter relaxes in his seat. He has not only a movie to keep him occupied but the headphones offer a pretty good selection of music. The food sucks but that was to be expected. He thinks about what he's going to say to Oliver. He's excited to see him. He runs a few scenarios through his head like maybe them running across a road to each other or Oliver shouting a greeting as they exit the cab.

John wakes up when the plane lands. After retrieving their gear from the overhead bins they inch forward out of the plane. Humidity hits them as soon as they're in the tunnel that leads from the plane to the terminal. The terminal itself is busy but to Peter it's nothing like outside; the smell and sound of Boston assault John but Peter likes all of it. With John in the lead they cross the road to the taxi stand.

"Taylor Hospital please," says John once they're inside the air-conditioned taxi, their luggage safely in the trunk.

"Sure thing," says the cabby with a Boston accent.

John and Peter look at each other and smile.

It's only around noon in Boston so John calls his contact at Taylor to let her know he and Peter are on their way.

"When would be the best time to see him?" John asks.

"I'm afraid there's a temporary change of residence for Oliver," Nan tells him. "He left Orchard House last night without telling anyone and we had to call out security."

"Is he all right?" concern in John's voice.

Peter's face fell. John put an index finger up to let Peter know there would be more details, just wait.

"He's fine," Nan tells John, "but he can't go back to Orchard House until his psychologist talks to him and that won't be until around four o'clock today. But you could visit him in the Inpatient Unit if you'd like."

"Of course we'd like to visit him wherever he is," John tells Nan.

"All right, then why don't we hook up and I can take you over there," she suggests. "Can you meet me at the Director's Building in a half hour? The cabbie should know where that is."

"See you there." John hangs up. "Oliver got into trouble last night so he's in what they call the Inpatient Unit, which I think is just a polite way of saying lockdown."

"Shit," says Peter. "So, what are we going to do?"

"Well, Nan, the coordinator, told us to meet her at the Director's Building, whatever that is, in a half hour. She'll take us over to Oliver."

"Sir?" John tries to get the cabbie's attention. "Sir?"

"Yes?"

"Would you please take us to the Director's Building on the Taylor Hospital grounds?"

"Yes, yes, no problem."

Oliver stands in his room, tracing the lines of the concrete blocks under their pale green paint.

What are you going to do now, loser? You can't escape, you can't do anything right!

Oliver suddenly balls his fist and smashes his hand into the wall. "FUCK!" he yells, "that hurts like a motherfucker!" He lies down on the bed. He holds his injured hand and looks carefully at the cuts he just inflicted on himself.

There's a knock on his door. "Oliver? I'm the day nurse, may I come in?" she asks softly.

"Yes, okay." Oliver sits up on the bed.

The day nurse enters looking sunny and alert. "It's past breakfast, almost past lunch. You certainly had a good sleep!"

This nurse is a red headed, freckled alien. "I was just told that your father and brother will be visiting you quite soon, maybe in forty-five minutes or so?"

"I don't want them to see me in here!" Oliver feels panic rise and lodge behind his eyes and in his mouth; dizzy.

"Well, I can tell them that when they arrive." The nurse cocks her head and gives Oliver a vacuous look.

Oliver is taken back by her expression. She seems to be on autopilot, not quite there. "Okay," he answers. "Except . . ."

The nurse stands by Oliver's door, waiting.

Finally, Oliver says okay again but she stays standing where she is. "You need to go to the kitchen to get some lunch. Your room will be locked only at night, otherwise you can roam around."

Oliver doesn't want to roam around although he is hungry. He looks at his watch. It's 1:00. He doesn't want to interact with this nurse. He's never been fond of red hair and, even though he doesn't trust his instincts, there's something wrong with her. He bounces a tiny bit to hear the springs squeak, then gets up. His hand is throbbing but there's no way he's going to show the nurse. She spoke to him as though he was going to be here another night but that can't happen either.

"Dad and Peter are here?" He whispers. He heads down the hall and discovers the kitchen. Wrapped sandwiches seem to be what's for lunch—chicken salad or tuna salad written boldly with black marker on the white wrappings. He chooses tuna salad. Then he sees the nurse again.

"Oliver?" She says as she walks toward him down the hall. "You have an appointment with Dr. Greenwood at four o'clock, here."

"Okay." He unwraps his sandwich and takes a bite. He eats as he walks back to his room.

John and Peter arrive at the Inpatient Unit with Nan. The red-haired nurse tells them that Oliver doesn't want to see them while he's there.

"How long will he be here?" John asks.

"Only until he sees Dr. Greenwood, unless the doctor thinks it would be best for him to stay here."

"How long do you think that would be?"

"I really don't know, Mr. Moore. I have no way of knowing what the doctor will decide."

Peter listens to the conversation then slips out the door. He noticed, when they arrived, that the Inpatient Unit is built on one level. He wants to try seeing Oliver through a window. He walks around the side of the building and sees that the windows are set quite high and covered securely with bars. He's not deterred and realizes he can hoist himself up by the bars to look into each window. He heard the nurse say that Oliver doesn't want to see them while in the Inpatient Unit, but he doesn't care. He's here and he wants to see his brother. Peter has to take a flying leap to reach the bars and hang on tight once he connects. On the first try he makes it even though the lip of the window digs into his forearms. He's able to see into the room below him but no one is there. He lets himself down by simply dropping to the ground. There are leaves along the side of the building, leaves that came off the thick stand of surrounding trees over many seasons. His drop is cushioned. He walks to the next window. No. Next. No. Then he sees Oliver below him on the fourth try, his back to the window. Peter feels like he's spying on his brother. He feels his chest tighten. He watches Oliver eat his sandwich, sees how long his hair has gotten, sees the knot in the red bandana around Oliver's hair. Peter feels like a voyeur. Oliver's shoulders look vulnerable, the back of him seems sad. The room is bare except for the bed, a locker, and a small bedside table. The bed frame is metal like everything else. Dreary. And his brother is stuck here. Peter can't hold himself up much longer; it's taking great effort to see into the window. His arm muscles burn. He doesn't want to yell but he can't knock on the window while holding two bars. He suspends himself by one arm and knocks. He has to quickly grab the other bar before falling. Oliver looks up from his sandwich but doesn't turn around. Peter has to hold one bar and knock again. Oliver quickly turns this time and looks up. Peter sees the fear on him. He quickly yells out to his brother.

"Ollie! It's ME!"

Oliver climbs up onto the bed. He puts his face close to the glass and squints so he can see Peter.

"Hey, man!" Oliver yells.

"Hey!" answers Peter. "Can I come around?"

"Come around!" Oliver tells him.

"You don't mind seeing us?" Peter yells through the window.

"No, it's okay," Oliver says.

"Okay! I'm coming!" Peter yells.

Peter jumps down and runs to the front entrance. John, Nan, and the nurse are still speaking to each other.

"Dad! Dad! I just saw Ollie through the window and he told me to come around."

The nurse squints her eyes and asks Peter how on earth he's seen Oliver.

"I just grabbed hold of the bars and pulled myself up."

"And he changed his mind about seeing you?

"Yes!"

"Well, all right. I'll take you to his room.

But as soon as they begin to walk down to Oliver's room they spot him in the hall, running toward them, a huge smile on his face.

"Oh my God! Look at you!" John says. He steps forward and wraps his arms around Oliver. He takes in the scent of Oliver's hair, holds him around the shoulders and feels how tall his son is. He doesn't want to let go but Oliver pulls back and away, looking at John sideways. John had not known, until that moment, that Oliver was as tall as he was. John takes a deep breath and exhales.

Elizabeth and Wren, along with Jack, drive to the west end of town to the Co-Op for dinner. The Co-Op always has freshly cooked meals for dinner, all organic. Elizabeth likes eating there because everything is healthy. Wren likes eating there because it's fun. They take their trays upstairs to the eating area after choosing what they want to eat. Wren has brought some homework with her. Elizabeth brought a book. They sit quietly. Elizabeth isn't very hungry; drinking booze eliminates her appetite.

"How do you spell 'imagination'?" asks Wren.

"Try to sound out the beginning."

"I-m-?"

"That's right, then a-g-i-n-a-t-i-o-n. What are you writing?"

Wren leans her cheek on her left hand. "Trying to write why I like to write."

"Oh. Why do you like to write?"

"Because I can use my imagination!" Wren laughs.

It's the first laugh Elizabeth has heard out of her daughter since John and Peter left.

"How about dessert?" Elizabeth asks.

"Yeah! A cookie from over there," she says and points to the coffee counter where there's also a bakery display. "A sugar cookie with sprinkles, okay?"

Elizabeth stands and looks at her daughter. "I love you," she says and kisses Wren on the top of her head.

"I love you too, Mom."

34

REPRIEVE

It's difficult for the nurse to grasp hold of Oliver's shoulders and steer him away from his father and brother. The three of them sit in Oliver's room; Peter on the bed, Oliver and John on chairs provided by the nurse. They're laughing when she knocks on the door frame, the door being wide open.

"Dr. Greenwood is here to see you, Oliver."

Oliver takes his eyes off Peter and glares at this red-haired nurse. "I can't see him now," he says, irritated.

"You have to," says the nurse. "It's the only way you'll return to Orchard House." She moves behind Oliver and puts her hands on his shoulders.

"We're not going anywhere," says John. "We'll wait right here, okay?" He looks at the nurse.

"That would be fine," she tells him.

Oliver shrugs the nurse's hands off his shoulders and leads her out the door.

Peter looks at John and grimaces. "He doesn't seem sick at all!" he whispers.

"He's better isn't he?" says John.

"I don't think he needs to be in here."

"I don't think we should play psychiatrist, Pete," says John quietly. "He's in a controlled environment here, nothing's frightening, everything is predictable. I do think these doctors know what they're doing."

"I sure hope so!" Peter stands up and walks around the room. "I wonder if his other room is this bare. This is depressing."

Dr. Greenwood greets Oliver with a smile. "This is pretty great, no? Your dad and brother here?"

"Yes, it is," Oliver replies.

"How do you feel about them seeing you in the Inpatient Unit?"

"I don't care." Oliver slides down a bit on the slippery chair.

"Why did you leave Orchard House last night?"

"I didn't want to be there."

"And why not?"

"I have no freedom!" snapped Oliver, angry.

"Well, actually, you have quite a bit of freedom at Orchard House, certainly compared to here."

"Yeah."

"Were you going to hurt yourself?"

Oliver thinks of the blue glass, now in the locker in his room. He wonders if Dr. Greenwood can tell if he's lying. He wants to tell him the truth but can't. Too risky, especially with Dad and Peter here. He doesn't want their entire visit ruined by him being locked in the Inpatient Unit. He keeps the blue glass a secret, keeps the line on his hand a secret, and he makes sure he doesn't make eye contact with Dr. Greenwood.

"We're not jailers, Oliver," Dr. Greenwood says. "We simply want you to get well so you can go home."

"It doesn't feel like that."

"How does it feel?"

"It feels like, it feels like I'm being punished."

"Punished for what?"

"I don't know! Just punished!"

"Punished for being ill?" Dr. Greenwood asks.

"I don't KNOW!" Oliver yells. "You asked me how I felt and I told you. Why does it have to MEAN something?"

"Feelings usually mean something. But I'll take that. It seems that you're feeling punished for no reason. Is that right?"

"Yes."

"All right. How does it feel to see your brother here?"

Oliver looks up at Dr. Greenwood this time, makes eye contact. "It's embarrassing."

"Why?"

"Because," Oliver looks away from the doctor now, "he's my little brother."

"And."

"It just sounds stupid."

"What sounds stupid?"

"I don't want to stop being his big brother," Oliver says, quietly.

"You won't. You'll always be his big brother."

"Well, it doesn't feel like it."

John looks at his watch. "Pete, I'm going to have to leave you here and go up to Orchard House for a meeting. You stay here and wait for Ollie. Maybe he'll be able to come back to Orchard House after his time with Dr. Greenwood."

"I hope so! This place sucks."

"Well, I don't think it's supposed to make you want to stay."

Peter stretches out on the bed. He yawns. "See you later," he tells John. "Maybe we'll see you up there."

John is in the meeting with Dr. Matthews, the Orchard House psychopharmacologist, Leslie, Oliver's case worker, and Kerry, the head nurse.

"This all takes time, Mr. Moore. Physically and emotionally this is difficult on any patient but even more so on a young person. Oliver knows what he would be doing at his age if he wasn't here, if he wasn't ill."

"Yes, I can't imagine how it would be," John says. "He was so popular, had so many friends, and now they're nowhere to be seen."

"That's very typical, Mr. Moore. Young people get scared and flee."

"There is one boyhood friend," John says, "who's stayed around, who showed some concern, and wanted to learn more about this illness. But that's it."

Everyone is silent for a moment.

"Now, we don't really like to put labels on things. We like to treat the symptoms," Dr. Matthews continues, "but if I have to I will say that Oliver's symptoms lean toward schizophrenia, schizoaffective disorder, or bipolar 1 with psychotic features. Seeing Oliver for as short a time, relatively, as we have, it would be difficult to say which diagnosis will come out on top. A few months of observation is really just the tip of the iceberg as far as Oliver's diagnosis."

"How long will it take to stabilize him?"

"I wish I could give you a definitive answer but I can't. There's no way of knowing how the medication cocktail will work until he's actually trying the medications. It's not pleasant going off medications. We have to find the right combination and, as I told you, that takes time."

"Then he'll come home once he's stabilized?"

"Well," says Dr. Matthews slowly, looking John in the eye, " the medications are only part of the recovery. Oliver will need to take our in-house classes. Actually, Oliver is taking a few of the classes already when he's forced. We have a few groups that Oliver could participate in if he chooses to."

"He's been stubborn about joining in," says Leslie.

"That's interesting," says John, "because at home he was in a large group of friends who did almost everything together."

"Actually," says Dr. Matthews," that may be a big reason why he's holding back here. This group isn't anything like his friends; the young people here may actually feel like imposters to Oliver."

"He keeps to himself mostly but does love the art therapy group. He's an outstanding artist, isn't he?" Kerry asks.

"Yes, he's quite passionate about art."

"Perhaps," Kerry adds, "down the road, when he's more stable, he can enroll in Mass-Art as an off-Taylor campus activity. Building up his confidence is high on the priority list. Mental illness, severe mental illness, can strip the patient of everything. It's important that these patients, especially the young people, grow up and beyond their illnesses."

Kerry speaks up again. "We have a peer-to-peer group that I think would be helpful to Oliver. The young people get to vent their frustrations and also talk about managing their illnesses, their medications, their feelings. I've only made Oliver go to one peer-to-peer because he's so against sharing, and I don't want him to begin reacting against the groups because he's forced into them."

"But how is it that he comes across to us, especially his brother, as not being so ill anymore?" John asks.

"I hoped you'd see some progress," Dr. Matthews says. "He's got a pretty strong combination of medications in him right now. I dare say, however, that what you see on the outside is quite different from what's going on inside. Thought disorders are tricky, especially when paired with a mood disorder."

Dr. Matthew's soft but firm voice comforts John.

"I do think," he continues, "that Oliver probably has a thought disorder and a mood disorder, but that remains to be seen. Together they're problematic, as you can well imagine. That diagnosis would be schizoaffective disorder."

"How do you treat that?"

"With a lot of medication and therapy. It's quite a load for a young person to carry. But I'll tell you, the schizophrenic part of that diagnosis is a 'kinder' schizophrenia compared to paranoid schizophrenia for example."

"Will Ollie ever be able to live a normal life?"

Dr. Matthews chuckles. "Well, let's define 'normal.' He can live a good life full of rewards, personally and professionally. He'll have girlfriends and possibly a wife. He'll have to stay on medication. He may not feel well sometimes or may get tired of taking his medication. He'll need a psychiatrist to keep tabs on him and adjust his medication if need be. Living near family would probably be a good choice. When he turns twenty-one he'll have to deal with the booze thing and pot doesn't go well with serious mental illness, SMI for short. I guess I'd define normal as having a clean slate with the potential of living a good and full life, with parameters. But there are many illnesses that impose on their victims, diabetes for instance and Parkinson's."

"Well," John laughs. "I'm glad I asked. You just put it in a good perspective."

"Thank you. I've had a lot of practice. Most parents want to know the future. I would direct you to the present. Just the fact that he's here and participating in medication trials says that he wants to leave someday. And that's a good goal."

Peter lies on Oliver's bed, waiting. He feels out of place and wishes Oliver would come back quickly. Now that he's alone in this room he wants to be outside again but feels stuck in here, waiting. He sings a little song to himself, a made-up tune, no lyrics. Lying on his back he pats the bed with his palms and clonks his shoes together for an opposing beat. And this is how Oliver finds him.

He stands in the doorway and smiles. "Hey, Pete! Let's go!"

Peter rolls himself off the bed. "Hey, man. That didn't take so long."

"He let me off easy today. And he's giving the okay for me to go back to Orchard House. What a fucking relief! I hate it here!"

"Yeah, I can't imagine!" Peter looks at Oliver. "Let's get outta here, okay?"

"Yeah. But first I have to get my stuff." Oliver opens the locker and pulls out some clean clothes that Virgil brought. He prefers to stay in his dirty clothes. He looks sideways at Peter, sees he's not looking, and quickly grabs the blue glass from the high shelf. He has to feel around for a second before he puts his fingers on it. The cold of it surprises him. Cupping it in his right hand he pockets the glass, knowing it will warm against his leg. Then, as an afterthought, Oliver takes the glass out of his pocket again.

"Look," he says to Peter and holds the glass out to show him.

"What is that?" Peter looks at it and then at Oliver.

"It's a piece of glass I found in the woods."

"Oh. It's a really cool blue!" says Peter.

"Yeah, I just keep it in my pocket in case I need to use it."

"Whattaya mean, use it?" Peter asks him.

"Oh, I don't know. In case I have to cut something," Oliver answers.

"Like what? Why don't you just have a knife?"

"Because we're not allowed to have knives here."

"Why?"

"Because they're scared we'll off ourselves with them."

"I don't think that would be a great way to off yourself," Peter says.

"How would you off yourself?" Oliver asks quietly.

"I don't know. It's not something I think about much."

"Let's get outta here," says Oliver suddenly, pocketing the blue glass. "Where's Dad?"

"He went up to Orchard House for a meeting."

"Then let's go up there! I'll show you my crappy room."

Oliver has to sign out of the Inpatient Unit. The nurse walks behind the front desk and presides over Oliver's paperwork.

That done, he and Peter walk away quickly. "Oh man, I'm so glad I won't have to deal with that bitch of a nurse anymore!"

The brothers almost jog up to Orchard House. They spot several people sitting on the porch. Oliver is out of breath.

"Must be all the cigarettes," he comments to Peter and pulls a pack out of his pocket. He sits on the top step and lights up.

"Where have YOU been?" asks Eddie. He's sitting next to the boom box with Nason on the other side. Linda is sitting on a bench near the stairs. Oliver is happy to see her.

"Hi," he says to her. "This is my brother, Peter."

Linda stares at Oliver, then Peter, and doesn't utter a sound, but she smiles.

"I've been in the Inpatient Unit," he tells Linda.

Eddie perks up. "What did you do to get there?"

"It's none of your fucking business, Eddie," says Oliver.

Peter is taken aback to hear Oliver speak to Eddie that way but keeps quiet about it. "Let's go find Dad," he suggests instead.

"He'll come out when he's finished," says Oliver. "Lemme show you my room." He puts out his smoke then walks into the house with Peter following.

Peter notices the dingy white walls and worn carpeting. He follows Oliver up the stairs, touching the long bars between the banister and the ceiling.

"What are these for?" he asks.

Oliver laughs. "Those are there so no one can off himself by jumping."

"Jeez," says Peter and keeps on following Oliver.

35

MANNERS

John's meeting has come to a close. "Thank you, all of you. I'm so very grateful that Oliver is here, with you. I can't imagine a better scenario."

"I suspect Oliver is here, in Orchard House, right now," says Leslie. "He was given the go-ahead to vacate his room in the Inpatient Unit."

"Thank you, thank you very much, all of you," repeats John. "I won't worry as much now that I've met you and have seen where Oliver is living."

"I'm sure he'll show you his room now," says Leslie.

John leaves Dr. Matthew's office. He walks down the linoleum hall, past the kitchen and dining room. He enters the front hall where the staircase rises up to the rooms above and notices the door out to the porch is open. He heads out to the porch and takes in the group that's sitting there. He feels a wave of anxiety, realizing that Oliver actually belongs here, that his firstborn fits into this strange and unkempt group because of his illness. He feels lightheaded, out of body, then pulls himself together by sheer willpower and asks the group if they know where Oliver is.

"He and his brother went upstairs," Eddie, the large man with wild hair tells him.

"Thank you," says John and re-enters the house. He walks to the staircase and hears Peter and Oliver talking above him.

"Yeah," he hears Oliver saying, "I wish I had a room to myself. But Mike isn't all that bad. I could have someone like Eddie!"

"Hi, you guys," says John as the two reach the first landing. "How about if we go out to dinner?"

"Sure!" Oliver answers fast and jumps down the stairs, three at a time.

"Uh oh," John says to himself when he sees Oliver jumping down the stairs.

"Okay then, Ollie, let's go back upstairs so I can see your room and you can clean yourself up."

"Okay!" Oliver runs back up the stairs to his room. He finds a brush, pulls off his bandana, brushes his hair with three strokes and puts his bandana back on, already tied. "I'm ready!" he says to John who's just then entering Oliver's room.

"So, this is where you live," John says. Then, "Ollie, your clothes are really dirty."

"No they're not, they're okay," Oliver tells him.

John stares at this son for a beat then tells him, "All right. Let's go!"

"Whoooo!" Oliver yells. He runs down the stairs with Peter in pursuit and out to the porch. He announces, with everyone watching, that they're going out and no one else can come.

"Peter," John stops Peter from going outside. "Has he been high all afternoon?"

"No, not at all."

"Okay. I'll be out in a second. I have to call a cab." John walks back down the linoleum hall to the office. "Would you call a cab for us please? Also, I'm taking Oliver out for dinner. We shouldn't be too late. What time does he take his medication?" he asks the nurse behind the medication window.

"Between seven and eight."

"Thank you."

John walks out onto the porch. "Good evening, all," he says to the group.

Oliver sits on the middle stair and lights up a smoke. Peter sits next to him. John stands at the bottom of the steps and tries to not look at each and every one of the clients sitting on the porch.

"So," booms Eddie, "how long are you staying here?"

"Just three days," says John.

"That's not very long."

"No, no it's not," says John. "Better than nothing."

"My family stays away," says Eddie.

"That's too bad," John replies.

"Not really. They're pretty fucked up."

"Oh."

The cab shows up right then.

"Well, bye," John says to Eddie, relieved to be out of there.

"Why don't you bring us some ice cream or something?"

"Shut up, Eddie," says Oliver. "Why the fuck would he want to do that?"

"To be nice," Eddie says, "but you wouldn't know about that!"

"I'm nice! I'm just not pushy like you are!"

"Come on, Ollie, get in, let's go," says John.

"Eddie is such an asswipe!"

"Leave it, Ollie. It's not worth fighting over."

Oliver sits forward on the seat and emanates energy.

"Where should we eat?" John asks the cabby.

"Pizza, roast beef, what?" The cabbie answers.

"How about spaghetti?" Oliver says too loud.

"No, I'm sick of spaghetti," answers Peter.

"How about an Italian restaurant that serves spaghetti and other things?" John says.

"That would be Ferrari's," the cabby says. "I'll take you."

There's a line at the restaurant. John keeps his eye on Oliver and watches him slowly deteriorate. At first Oliver's mood is fun, albeit loud and energetic. Then he seems to notice how many people are standing next to him. He fishes his sunglasses out of his jacket pocket and puts them on. The restaurant lobby is dim and John wonders how Oliver can see anything. The sunglasses seem to give him a bit more confidence and he starts a conversation with Peter. John watches carefully but can't hear the conversation. For a moment he imagines that they're home in Bozeman and he's taking the boys out for a special meal after a ball game. But as he focuses on the boys, Oliver's sunglasses remind him where they are, not that he ever really forgot.

More people crowd into the restaurant lobby. Oliver stops talking to Peter and feels the crowd pressing in. He suddenly bolts but he's hindered by the thick stand of people. He pushes his way through and John follows him. Once outside, John watches to make sure Oliver doesn't run. Oliver takes out a cigarette and lights it, blowing the smoke up and into the darkening sky. He's muttering to himself, something John can't hear.

"Hey, Ollie, who don't we just get a pizza and go back to Orchard House?"

"Where's Peter?" Oliver asks suddenly. He looks at the doorway where people are spilling out onto the sidewalk and John sees him practically shudder.

"I don't know. I'll go find him. How about the pizza idea?"

Oliver doesn't answer but lights another cigarette off the red cherry of the one he's already smoking and throws the butt, still lit, on the ground. He leans against the outside wall of the building.

"Ollie?" asks John. "Wait here, okay? I'm going to find Peter."

John waits for a response from Oliver but doesn't get one.

"Oliver!" John is anxious, almost angry. "Will you please answer me?"

Oliver moves his face in John's direction, his eyes hidden by the sunglasses. His head turns so slowly that John is reminded of a reptile.

"I'm going to find Peter. Wait here!"

John swims his way into the crowd and finally finds Peter standing by the front, ready with a table. "We have to go. Ollie isn't doing too well. We'll order pizza and bring it back to Taylor."

"I'm starving! Are you sure?"

"Absolutely."

The two of them work their way back outside. John is anticipating an empty sidewalk but Oliver is still there, lighting yet another cigarette off the second one.

"Let's go," he tells Oliver. Then he remembers he needs to call for a cab.

After a twenty-minute wait, John and his two boys get into a cab.

"Could you tell me where we can find a good pizza shop?" John asks the cabbie.

"Yeah, right over there," the cabbie tells him.

"Would you take us over there and wait while we get a pizza then take us back to Taylor Hospital?"

"You want to pay, I'll drive, whatever you want, mister." The cabbie is smiling.

I'd be smiling, too, if I was you, John thinks.

Tagen is sitting on the porch when they return.

"Oh look! There's Tagen, the one I told you about," Oliver says to Peter.

"Oh!" says Peter, making his eyebrows jiggle up and down.

"Maybe she'd like to eat with us," John suggests.

"Hey, Tagen," Oliver yells to her. "Do you want to share our pizza?"

He's just antagonizing everyone, John thinks then, to Oliver, "Where should we sit?"

Oliver isn't listening. He jumps out of the cab and runs up onto the porch. He begins talking to everyone, gesturing, being loud. It's obvious to John that Oliver has slipped into mania and he's not sure what to do about it. He and Peter get out of the cab with the pizza. John had spotted a picnic table around the side of Orchard House when he was walking to his meeting with Dr. Matthews. He suggests, even though he knows Oliver isn't listening, that they go eat at that table.

"Pete, go tell Ollie that we'll be around the side of this building at the picnic table, okay?"

"I don't think he'll listen to me."

"Well then, announce it to the porch and someone will let him know when he cares to listen." John is exasperated and needs to breathe. He walks around the side of the building and sits at the picnic table with the huge pizza. His appetite is gone.

"Motherfucker," he says to no one and puts his head in his hands. His eyes burn with tears as he fights the knot growing in the back of his throat and mutters, "Why us? Why Ollie? Goddamnit to hell!"

"Dad?" Peter is standing next to him. "Are you okay?"

"Yeah, yes, I'm fine." John knows he needs to get a strong grip on himself. What he wants to say is "No, Pete, I'm not okay. I don't want Ollie to be here; I don't want this to be true."

Peter puts his hand on John's shoulder and says, "I know, Dad. This sucks."

Suddenly Oliver bursts into sight, Tagen on his arm.

"Howdy ho!" he yells. "We've come for pizza!"

"Well, that's what we've got," says John. "Is it Tagen?"

"Yes, Dad, it's Tagen," Oliver says.

"Yes, please." Tagen is speaking softly and it's difficult to hear her.

"Why don't the two of you sit down," John says.

Tagen lets go of Oliver's arm and sits. John hands her a piece of pizza on a napkin.

"Sorry we don't have any plates," John says. "Would you like a Coke?"

"No, thank you," Tagen whispers.

"Why are you whispering?" Oliver asks her and snorts. "You'd think she was quiet!" He sits next to her and asks John for a slice.

John is looking behind Oliver at a shape in the shadows who's moving closer and closer to the picnic table. Oliver watches John's face and turns to see what he's looking at.

"Holy fuck," he says and jumps up. "Get outta here, Linda! Go go go! You can't have any pizza because it's not yours, get it? Get the fuck OUTTA HERE!"

"OLIVER!" John thunders. "DON'T scream at her like that!"

"You don't know her, Dad. She's a mooch!"

"So what? I thought you liked Linda."

"I do like Linda but she's a mooch. You don't understand!"

"Yes, I think I do understand, but that doesn't give you the right to be rude!"

"Hey, you know what? I don't give a fuck what you say. You're not even my REAL father anyway!" Oliver stands. "You know what? My REAL father would never leave me in a place like this!" he screams at John and runs into Orchard House, leaving Tagen with John and Peter.

John is stunned and just stands and stares at where Oliver ran off.

"Don't worry about it, Mr. Moore," says Tagen quietly. "Whenever he's manic he picks fights, mostly with me but sometimes with Maurice or Mike."

"Oh, my God," says John then, to Tagen. "Should I go after him?"

"You asking me?" she says and looks around.

"Yes, I'm asking you."

"No."

"I agree, Dad. Let's go." Peter's voice is filled with resignation. "He won't be any different this evening."

"Okay. I'll call for a cab. Wait here, okay Pete?"

"Yeah."

John walks down the linoleum hall to the medication window. "Has Oliver stopped by to get his medication?"

"No. He certainly has not," she says and smiles at John.

"Well, you might want to make sure he gets them because he's not all right." He looks at the nurse.

"Yes, sir, I'll make sure he gets them. He'll be all right. Don't you worry."

"Thank you."

"He's in the right place," she volunteers. "He'll get better, you'll see."

36

HIDDEN POTION

After John and Peter leave, Oliver, Tagen, Janine, and Maurice walk into the woods and build a small fire. They listen to Janine's poetry and Maurice's story. Oliver is amazed by the poetry but thinks Maurice's story sounds like a third-grade assignment. He doesn't say anything to Maurice about it.

Tagen pulls Oliver aside. "I have a surprise for you in my room," she says.

"I heard that!" says Maurice. "I know what that means!"

"You're full of shit, Maurice," Tagen yells at him. "It's not sex!"

Oliver busies himself with the fire. He covers it with dirt and rocks since there's no water nearby.

"Where'd you learn to do that?" asks Janine.

"At home," Oliver tells her.

Tagen and Maurice are still fighting so Oliver and Janine head back to Orchard House.

"Hey! Where are you going?" Tagen yells. "Wait up!"

Oliver and Janine stop and wait. "Jeez," Oliver says under his breath.

The four walk into Orchard House and head down the linoleum hall to the medication window. They stand around with the other residents, shuffling feet, making jokes. Oliver is respectful of the older residents but Maurice is not and it bothers Oliver. Maurice makes fun by imitating some of the old people. Oliver doesn't participate but he doesn't say anything either.

After meds, Maurice and Janine head out to the porch for smokes but Oliver follows Tagen to her room. She closes the door and slips the back of a chair under the knob for safety, then pulls a bottle of vodka out from under her mattress.

"You see?" Tagen says, all smiles and excited.

"You wanna get kicked out?" Oliver asks.

"Fuck you," she says. "Maybe I do. Anyway, don't you think I know that? You want some don't you?"

"No," Oliver says. "I might not like it here but I don't want to get kicked out either." But mostly, even if he's not aware of it, he doesn't like the reminder of his mother's vodka.

"You're a pussy," Tagen says, unscrews the cap and takes a huge gulp.

Oliver sits on Tagen's bed until his medication makes him feel heavy, really heavy, like he's made of stone, and watches her get drunk. She talks and talks and Oliver find's he's not taking in a word.

"What did you say?" he asks several times and each time she just opens her eyes wide and says she won't tell him, that he should pay attention.

Oliver is relieved to get back to his room once she's had enough of his sober company and removed the chair from below the doorknob. Lying on his bed, dressed, he thinks about what he said to Tagen, that he didn't want to get kicked out. He may not want to get kicked out but he doesn't want to stay either. He begins to wonder how he could leave, by himself, and not be brought back like last time. He figures he'd have to leave long before curfew. Actually, right after curfew would be better because he'd have all night to get away and hide. He'll have to keep his plan secret, not talk to anyone about it, especially Tagen. She'd let the staff know for sure. He thinks of Jude and how Jude would land in psychiatric wards now and then to recover from the street. Oliver knows there isn't any time limit on his residency at Taylor Hospital. They can keep him here for as long as they want. And they can force him to take his medications. Oliver's eyes close. His breathing relaxes. As he falls asleep he decides he'll have to stop swallowing his meds, that without medication he won't be under their influence.

It's Friday when John and Peter return to Bozeman from Taylor Hospital. Even though it's 9:00 p.m., it's summer and they decide to pick up Wren.

Elizabeth hears Jack bark and comes to the door. She looks better than she did four days ago. John doesn't know why except that her hair is brushed and she's wearing lipstick; her face is still puffy from the booze.

"Hi!" she says to them.

"Hey, Mom," says Peter. He gives her a hug. "Is Wren up?"

"Yes, I think so. She's up in her room."

Peter takes the stairs two at a time and meets Wren, who heard their voices, in the upstairs hall.

"Hey, Weasel! I missed you!"

Wren throws herself into his arms, squealing. "Where's Daddy?"

"I'm down here!" John yells up the stairs.

Wren jumps on Peter's back and rides him down the stairs to John.

"Oh, Daddy! I missed you so much!" Wren says.

Elizabeth takes all this in. "We did have a little bit of fun while you were gone," she says.

"Yeah, we went to the Hot Springs, that was a LOT of fun," Wren chimes in. "And what else did we do, Mom?"

"We took Jack for walks in the park. Let's see . . . we ate dinner at the Co-Op."

"Yeah, yeah, yeah," says Wren, "and then we . . ."

"I'm so happy you had a good time, sweetie," John interrupts. "Now, do you have a bag packed?"

Wren looks at Elizabeth quickly, then says, "Yes. And can Jack come too?"

"Of course," says John.

Elizabeth is standing in the hall, practically invisible. John glances at her and sees that her hands are trembling. He thinks that possibly she's not drinking as her hands wouldn't be shaking at this time of night if she was.

"How's Ollie?" She asks before they can get out the door.

"He was manic the last time we saw him. Hopefully, they'll get it under control."

"They will, Dad," says Peter. "He's not much fun to be around when he's manic."

"No. I remember," says Elizabeth.

Peter turns to John. "Could we get something from McDonald's on the way home?"

"YEAH!" Wren chimes in.

"I guess so."

"I'll help you with your bag, Wren," says Peter who runs up the stairs and into Wren's room. She follows her brother.

"I think Mommy's going to be lonely," she whispers to Peter.

"She'll be okay," Peter says.

Elizabeth and John stand in the hall together.

"I've been talking with my doctor who thinks it would be good if I try AA," she tells him.

"That's really great, Lizzy! I hope it helps."

"Me too," she says and looks him in the eyes. He can feel the yearning in her, sees it in her eyes as they look into his.

"Shall we leave Jack with you?"

"No, I'll be okay."

"Are you sure?"

"Well, if Wren wouldn't mind too much, he is good company."

"Then we'll leave him," he says and smiles at her. "You're gonna get better, Lizzy, I know it. Come here," he says and takes her in his arms.

Elizabeth collapses into him. "I haven't hugged for too long," she says.

The kids come down the stairs and witness the embrace between their parents. Peter can hear Wren take in her breath. He helps her slide off his back and makes her follow him and her suitcase the rest of the way down.

"There," he says and drops Wren's suitcase on the floor next to his parents.

They both jump.

"Peter!" says John.

"What?"

John gives him a stern look then, to Wren, "We're leaving Jack to keep Mom company."

"Okay," says Wren.

"Bye, Lizzy," says John. "Call if you need to."

"I'll be fine," she says.

John doubts her statement.

"Thanks for Jack, Wren. I'll spoil him!"

"Bye, Mommy," says Wren. "I love you." She kisses Jack on the top of his soft head. And she kisses Elizabeth.

"I love you too," says Elizabeth. She sees them out the door, then locks it. She walks down the hall and locks the backdoor too.

Elizabeth hasn't had a drink all day and doesn't want to drink once her family leaves but, she can't steady her hands or calm her craving. She's thirsty and no matter how much water or soda or coffee she drinks she can't quench her thirst. She's craving the taste of vodka, craving the sound of ice going into her glass and the sound of vodka being poured over the ice.

Elizabeth wants to stop drinking but doesn't want to have to go to AA. Why would she want to hang out her dirty laundry for all to see? Why would she want to be stuck in a room with goody-goody recovering alcoholics? She doesn't want to be part of a group but, she feels hollow with loneliness. Her family doesn't want her around, and John knows how broken she is. Perhaps, she thinks, if she could stop drinking she could be . . . what? A part of the family again? She decides to look into AA tomorrow.

In the meantime, she can hear the vodka bottle screaming to her. She walks into the kitchen, two voices in her head, and the vodka wins. Urgently, she fills a glass with ice then pours vodka, straight up, to the rim. Her hands are shaking as she brings her lips to the side of the glass. Vodka spills over the rim onto her blouse but she doesn't care. She winces at the taste of pure vodka but feels much better for it, calm and warm. She walks back into the living room, the vodka bottle in her left hand, the glass in her right. She puts the bottle on the coffee table then turns on the TV. She curls up with Jack by her feet, her drink in her hand. She has a smile on her face. She doesn't feel lonely anymore.

37

LOST IN BOSTON

Two days later, on the weekend, Oliver and Tagen take the bus to Boston with Janice and Maurice. Oliver has thrown his medication away two evenings in a row now. His hands are trembling and he doesn't feel well. After they disembark the bus they walk along the sidewalk, kidding and talking. Oliver remains mute.

It's dinnertime when they hit Harvard Square and Tagen, Janice, and Maurice all want Italian food. The crowd is thick with summer tourists and Oliver's attention is suddenly drawn to the profile of a woman standing on the corner, about fifty feet away. She has a red scarf over her head, tied under her chin. He likes the bright red scarf then notices that she's wearing tight jeans and a t-shirt over a shapely body. As he looks at her, she slowly turns her head toward him. Oliver hears her hiss. He sees her painted lips slowly pull away from bloody vampire fangs.

Terrified, Oliver bolts and runs away from Tagen and the others. As he runs he can hear Tagen calling until he hears only his feet slapping against the pavement and his heavy breathing. He keeps replaying the woman looking over at him, replaying what he saw at first. He can't stop the vision of painted lips and bloody teeth.

Oliver's lungs are burning with the effort of running. He stops and takes his bearings: he's in an alley where there are no streetlights.

It's not very dark yet. He makes his way north, although he's not aware of the direction, walking the alleys only. The further he goes the dirtier the alleys become and soon finds himself among scrap metal and wood houses. He sees a man lying on an old mattress, half in and half out of a metal lean-to. Except for this sleeping man, Oliver hasn't seen anyone since he ran away. At one corner he peers down the road and sees car lights so he ducks back into the alley. He sees a flock of doves fly off a building roof to settle, like notes, on a telephone wire.

He keeps walking. Finally, he finds what looks like a sheet metal village. He sees a woman standing outside her shack. She gives Oliver a strange look, a look of suspicion and guardedness. Oliver, impervious, sits on the ground and watches her.

"What are you doing?" the woman asks him.

"Resting," Oliver answers.

"Then get the fuck outta here!" she screams at him. "Whattaya think this is, an amusement park?"

"No!" Oliver scrambles to his feet and wanders away, wondering if he should try to find his way back to Harvard Square. He thinks about Virgil at Orchard House and knows that the police will probably be alerted if he doesn't show up this evening. He knows he's experiencing withdrawals from his meds. He remembers the withdrawal symptoms he experienced when he was pulled off Zyprexa. He'd felt lightheaded and shaky and was extremely anxious for a few days. But now, out here on his own without meds, Oliver is scared about how he'll feel once all the medication is out of his bloodstream. He thinks about the words "bloodstream" and sees the blood running through his veins. He thinks about the kind of place he'd like to find to wait out the meds withdrawal, a place where he can figure out what he's going to do.

Oliver looks around the alley. Even though he's only slightly out of sight from the woman who screamed at him, he thinks he might just settle down in a corner somewhere. He's wearing tennis shoes and walking very quietly. He comes to a door and a three-step stoop that sticks out on both sides, like a cement foot stool. He sits, leans back into the doorway and takes stock of his situation. He counts his money and finds it's limited; he has forty dollars and some change. His clothing is thin but the weather isn't too cold. He has his sunglasses, which is lucky as he wouldn't want to be caught without them; too scary.

"I wonder, I wonder," Oliver says under his breath. "I wonder if Tagen and those guys are gone yet," he whispers to no one.

Suddenly, Oliver sees a figure walking down the alley. This person is walking as though he's full of purpose, like he belongs. Oliver tries to disappear into the doorway by pulling his legs up, holding on to them with his arms. It's a man, he sees, who's walking by. Oliver wonders if the man has anything to do with the woman who screamed at him. He watches as the man walks away and sees that he's very thin, his hair is brown and sticking up all over his head, his clothes are dirty, his shoes worn loafers. Oliver wonders where the man lives and if he, Oliver, could talk to him. But the man walks by and Oliver stays in the doorway. It's quite dark by now. The doorway is very dark and hides Oliver well.

"Water," is what Oliver wants and whispers to himself. He dares himself to stand. His legs are stiff, his back sore from sitting so long on the cold, hard cement. He sees light coming from the end of the alley and walks toward it. Several people pass him and he can feel them staring at him. Oliver feels out of his element but doesn't know where else to go. Once he reaches a street that's busy he walks the sidewalk, figuring that the dark will keep him safe. The road seems to stretch on forever but at least there are lights. He sees a bus approaching and quickly darts between two houses to remain invisible to the bus's windows in case it's carrying Tagen, Maurice, and Janice. He feels a pang of doubt, of missing his friends. He reaches a corner where the street crosses a boulevard complete with a painted meridian. There are quite a few people on the sidewalks. Oliver pulls his sunglasses out of his breast pocket and puts them on. There are enough streetlights to see even with his sunglasses. Now he feels safe and begins to look for a place to eat. He decides that he must be downtown as he's passing restaurants and bars. Most of the restaurants' interiors look dark and the bars hold no familiarity to nineteen-year-old Oliver. He sees a lit-up storefront on the corner right in front of him and recognizes the Dunkin' Donuts colors.

The inside of the donut shop is warm and bright. Oliver can see quite well in here. He orders coffee, water, and one glazed donut. He thinks the clerk is looking at him strangely but doesn't care because he's wearing his sunglasses. Oliver takes his order to a booth but realizes he needs something to read or he'll be too exposed. He notices a rack of newspapers and wishes it was closer to his booth. He has to muster the courage to walk across the room to the rack, select a paper then walk back to his table.

He can see that there are no other people in the shop except for one woman about his mom's age and, of course, the clerk. He feels safe again in the booth and opens the paper, the Boston Globe, August 1999. He stares at the three 9s and wonders if they mean something to him, something he's not getting. He remembers Harvard Square and wonders where it is and if Tagen and those guys are gone yet. He spots a clock on the wall and is surprised it's 10:00 p.m.

How . . .? He thinks. Certainly Tagen and Maurice and Janice are back at Orchard House. Certainly they've taken their meds by now.

Oliver smiles. He feels free and the caffeine has boosted his energy. He doesn't feel well enough to eat the donut. Then he thinks of his mom and dad and Peter and Wren and his stomach sinks. They'll be so worried. His mom will be crazy over it. He just wants to be free, wants to live on his own, and not take medication or talk to doctors. He thinks of Jude and knows that if he's thinking of Jude, Jude must be thinking of him.

Yes, that's how it works.

Oliver wonders where Jude is. His thoughts are running through his mind so quickly that he can't read, but the paper is a comfort and a companion for now; the kind of companion that keeps others away because they think you're occupied when you're really not, but you look like it.

Dr. Greenwood calls John's office that evening. The time difference is two hours earlier in Bozeman and John is still at work, catching up. Oliver's team at Taylor thought Dr. Greenwood was the best choice to deliver the news to John and Elizabeth.

"He's gone? What do you mean by that?"

"He took a bus into Boston with three friends this evening and he didn't return. I've interviewed his friends and they all say that they were in Harvard Square when Oliver suddenly bolted and ran off."

"And why didn't they follow him?" John asks, his legs feel weak and he has to sit.

"Well, one young woman began following him but the two boys held her back and Oliver didn't turn around. I think something must have frightened him."

"Have you told his mother?" John asks.

"No, not yet. How is she?"

"Very fragile."

"Then maybe we'll wait twenty-four hours to tell her, if need be. What do you think?"

John thinks for a moment. "I guess that would work but I want to know every detail of your search. He must be in Boston somewhere, right?"

"I would think so. We have the Boston Police alerted and our own security guards are combing Boston as well as they can. It's a big place."

"I'm aware of that. Why do you think he ran off?"

"It sounds to me like something scared him. I'll let you know everything I know. And you will notify us if he calls home?"

"Yes, of course," says John. "And thank you." He hangs up and combs his fingers through his hair. "Lord, what next?"

Oliver finally puts the newspaper back on the rack, then walks up to the counter. "Is there a pay phone here?" He's had to build up his nerve to ask but his sunglasses are on so it's safe. Kind of safe.

"Here?" the clerk asks. "No, there's no pay phone here, man, just donuts!"

Oliver heads out to the sidewalk after stuffing the donut into his pocket. He looks up and down the street but can't find a pay phone so he begins to wander. He doesn't have to walk very far before spotting a phone booth. He doesn't like the idea of standing in a glass phone booth where everyone can see him but he's anxious to call his mom. He squeezes into the booth, leaving the door open, and picks up the receiver. He pushes zero, then Elizabeth's number, and notices how cool the metal buttons are. He says his name at the prompt. He listens as Elizabeth accepts the call, just as she does when he calls her from Orchard House.

"Mom?"

"Hi! How are you?"

"Mom, I saw a vampire!"

Elizabeth's stomach sinks. She isn't feeling well enough to hear this from Ollie. "Oh, honey, I doubt it was a real vampire."

"Yes, it was! She even had bloody fangs! I'm telling you, it was REAL!"

Elizabeth wants to hang up, she doesn't want to hear any of this. "Ollie, I'm not feeling very well. Would you call your dad about this, please?"

There's silence on Oliver's end of the phone, then dial tone.

"Ollie? Ollie?" Elizabeth hangs up and dials the Orchard House number. "Hello? I'm calling about Oliver Moore. He just called me about seeing a vampire, would you please check on him and call me back, please?"

"Oliver Moore?"

"Yes."

"He's not here, ma'am," says someone on the other end of the phone.

"What? Where is he?"

"We don't know, ma'am. The police are looking for him."

"WHAT? This is his mother and I want to know where he is!"

"We don't know yet."

"And that's all you can say about it?" Elizabeth screams into the phone.

"Yes, ma'am. We'll call you when we've found him, okay?"

Now it's Elizabeth's turn to hang up the phone. She dials John's number.

Peter answers. "Hi, Mom."

"Did you know that Ollie is missing from the hospital?"

"Yes."

"Where is your father?"

"On his way home."

"Were you two going to keep me in the dark?" she asks.

"No. We didn't want to upset you."

"UPSET ME? You don't KNOW upset! How long has he been missing?"

"Mom, please call Dad. I don't know anything, really, just that he's missing, but just for this evening. He hasn't been gone very long."

Elizabeth slams down the phone and dials John. He answers. "So, when were you going to tell me that Ollie is missing?"

"As soon as I got off work," he tells her.

"Really? I don't believe you. He called me and, because I wasn't told, I thought he was at the hospital and asked him to call you instead. If I'd known I might have been able to get his location. If I'd known . . ."

"Elizabeth, shut up," John says, pronouncing each word in an exaggerated manner.

"He saw a vampire," she says, the words tight in her throat. "He was scared."

There is silence between them as they hold each other hostage.

"I'll call you when I get home," John tells her and hangs up.

Elizabeth breathes hard and is too upset to cry. She goes to the cabinet where her vodka bottle is hiding and reaches up to open the cabinet door. She stops and lets her arm drop to her side. "No," she says to herself. "Enough." She walks into the living room and sits on the couch, carefully. "Enough," she says again and clenches her hands together. "I can do this." She remembers speaking to someone in Alcoholics Anonymous, once upon a time, who told her tips on how to get through withdrawals. She doesn't want to but looks up the number for AA, again.

Oliver doesn't call John. He hangs up and continues down the sidewalk. A dark alley shows itself.

It's in there.

Oliver steps into the blackness as though testing cold water. He feels the road through his sneakers and, by reaching out, can feel a cinderblock wall with his left hand. He's frightened and knows that if he wasn't so afraid he'd prefer to be out on the sidewalk under the streetlights. He looks ahead and sees, over to the right, an orange glow. He hears voices. He sees, the closer he gets, that everything is bathed in the orange light. He hugs a tall building, peers around the corner, and sees men standing around a barrel, a fire licking the dark with tall flames.

This is Hell and these are devils.

Oliver, sick to his stomach, slides down the wall and sits on the dark side of the building. His whole body is shaking. He leans forward, on to his hands and knees, and pukes. He crawls up against the wall and curls up. His body is shaking violently with chills.

You're going to die.

Oliver wishes he was home in his warm bed. He wishes he was back at Taylor, anything but this.

Stop being a pussy.

He maneuvers himself away from the puke, then braces his back up against the building as a reference point. He puts his head on his outstretched arms and tries to sleep through the shakes. But every time he closes his eyes he sees monsters drawn in brightly colored lines with dripping fangs and terrifying eyes. He tries, again and again, to rest with his eyes open but it doesn't work. He changes position but that doesn't work either. Oliver is dripping with sweat and shaking. He wants to move away from this spot but is paralyzed with fear.

You SHOULD be afraid!

Oliver rolls over on his back and looks up at the sky. He can see clouds illuminated by the Boston city lights. He crosses his arms under his head and tries to shut his eyes again.

38

VODKA

The AA woman warned Elizabeth that during the first seventy-two hours of withdrawals she could be at risk for seizures. Elizabeth is grateful that Wren is with John and Peter. But she doesn't think she'll have seizures. She thought maybe she could go up to the hospital for the first two days, just in case, but rejects that plan almost immediately. She doesn't want to burden her family with more drama and thinks she'll be okay. Just in case, she calls Jane, a good friend who recently told her that alcohol was pushing her friends away. Elizabeth asks Jane to check on her.

"How about if I spend the night with you?"

Elizabeth is silent, then, "Maybe."

"Why not? I could sleep on the couch or on Wren's bed. Say yes! This is important. You shouldn't be alone if that's what the AA woman said. I'm sure she knows what she's talking about, don't you think so?"

"Yeah, I guess. I just don't want to be any trouble."

"For God's sake, Liz, you're more trouble when you're drunk! I'd be honored to help you through this. It's a big deal, you know? I'll probably not sleep wondering if you were all right."

"Okay. When do you want to come over?"

"How about around eight?"

"Okay, I'll be here."

"You know what?"

"What?"

"This is a really big deal, and I'm proud of you."

"Thanks."

Elizabeth looks at her watch. It's 6:00 p.m. The AA woman also told her to keep vodka handy in case she has seizures. Vodka, under those circumstances, would be needed. She doesn't know what to do with herself. She's not hungry so dinner is out of the question. She feeds Jack and sits at the kitchen table watching him eat. She's apprehensive, doesn't know what this process will demand from her and hopes Jane doesn't talk too much. She doesn't think she will. She wonders if she should take a drink before the process begins but realizes what she's saying to herself and laughs. Her hands are already shaking but they always do when she hasn't had an afternoon drink. She wonders how many days her hands will shake.

Jack finishes eating and they go into the living room. Elizabeth sees the room with a guest's eye and begins picking up. She folds the blankets on the couch, fluffs up the pillows. She wonders if she should vacuum and decides that anything to make the time go by is a good idea. She gets the vacuum out of the hall closet. Jack runs through the doggy door to go outside.

She wonders what it'll be like to have a visitor and no drink. She shrinks inside just thinking about it. She hasn't socialized without a drink in her hand for what, ten years? She didn't drink when pregnant or nursing so it's been eight years since Wren. But it's the past three that have been so difficult—not functioning without it, not sleeping without it, pretty much not even talking without it. Damn! And the vomiting that she has kept all to herself. She can't drink red wine anymore without projectile vomiting. And white wine gives her headaches. She has narrowed her alcohol down to vodka and gin. Everything else has turned on her. But the vomiting has another aspect, one so shameful that Elizabeth doesn't think she'll ever be able to tell another soul. When she and her friends go out, Elizabeth will go to the bathroom to get rid of the booze she put in her system by sticking her index finger down her throat. That way she can keep on drinking. Alcohol bulimia? What else could it be? She cringes with shame just thinking about it.

Jane arrives at eight on the dot. She's brought a six-pack of Dr. Pepper, a bag of chips, and some ice cream. She doesn't wait for Elizabeth to open the door; she walks in and puts everything down on the kitchen table. Jack comes scrambling down the hall from the back door, barking. Elizabeth hears from the bathroom and comes out.

"Jack! Stop! You know Jane, silly dog," says Elizabeth. "It's good to see you my dear. Thank you so much in advance!"

"No problem," says Jane as they hug. "How're you feeling?"

"Nothing yet, except for my hands shaking, but I'm used to that. I keep waiting for something terrible to happen but so far, zip!"

"What shall we do?" Jane asks.

"I don't know. We could watch TV?"

"I brought some goodies," says Jane. "Let's get the Dr. Pepper, I remembered that's your favorite, and chips, and see if there's a movie on.

Elizabeth fetches glasses from the cupboard and opens the freezer for ice. "This feels way familiar," she says. "Too familiar."

"Yeah, but you'll be pouring Dr. Pepper instead of vodka."

"I know."

The clinking of ice into the glasses makes Elizabeth's mouth water and she senses a huge, dark yearning opening up near her heart. She brings the glasses over to the kitchen table and sits, her legs weak with apprehension for what she's doing. She knows, at that moment, that her body will not cooperate with her resolve. She heaves a deep sigh and says, "I don't know. I don't know if I can do this."

"Sure you can. The feelings aren't bound to last forever," Jane tells her and touches on the almost forbidden, "and just think what this will mean to your children."

There's quiet for a minute. The two women can hear the light traffic outside the kitchen window.

Then Elizabeth says, "I guess I'm wishing Oliver would be found so I don't have to do this."

"That," Jane says, "is the addiction speaking."

Elizabeth looks up at Jane, quickly. "Addiction." She feels the word on her tongue, resonating in her teeth. "My God, what have I done to myself? And where is OLIVER!!" she screams then bursts into tears. "Maybe this isn't a good time to do this, Jane. I don't think I can do this. I need to know where Oliver is before I can do this!"

"No. You can do it, Liz. You're strong. Don't let the withdrawal symptoms preach to you."

"What the FUCK! I'm going to jump out of my fucking skin!"

"Lizzy, you told me to come over because you wanted to do this. You wanted to . . ."

"I KNOW! Please don't . . ." Elizabeth gestures with her hands, arms out, palms up.

"What happened to take away your resolve? We were just sitting here and all of a sudden you blew."

Elizabeth sits quietly for a moment, stops crying. "I think it was the ice," she says and laughs through her tears. She wants to tell Jane to go home but knows staying away from the vodka would be even more difficult without her friend. She decides to tell Jane about the vodka and where it is.

"The woman from AA told me I might need it if I get seizures."

"What's that called? Hair of the dog?"

"I don't know if that applies. That's for drinking to get rid of a hangover."

"Oh, well, maybe it works kind of the same way," says Jane.

"I don't think so," says Elizabeth feeling sudden and intense irritation. "Where do you think Oliver is?" Elizabeth bursts into loud sobs. "Goddamn him! Why did he have to do this?"

"Oh, honey, they'll find him."

"How do you know? He's not taking his meds, he'll be psychotic, and God knows who will get close to him. Maybe somebody will hurt him! He must be so scared! I can't bare this, Janey, I just can't bare this! Goddamn it. Goddamn it. Goddamn it!" Elizabeth jumps up and begins pounding her fists into the wall.

Jane isn't sure what she should do. She settles on sitting quietly and doing what Liz asked her to do, which is stay with her tonight to make sure she's okay.

When Elizabeth finally stops her tantrum she says, "You know what? I REALLY need a drink!"

"I know you do but you'll have to tough it out or go to the hospital."

"I never told you to take me to the hospital," Elizabeth snaps, angry.

"I'm capable of thinking for myself," says Jane.

"Who elected you Queen Bee?" Elizabeth sneers.

Jane gets up and walks to the cupboard. She opens the cupboard door and takes hold of the bottle of vodka. "Now, do you want to drink this?" she says and stares at Elizabeth. "Go ahead! Be the bitch, the one who can't handle staying away from this goddamn bottle, get drunk so if and when Oliver calls you'll be all fucked up. I've seen you sloppy drunk too many times to kid myself. You're an alcoholic, Liz, and you know it! Everyone else knows it too, especially John and your children."

"FUCK YOU!" Elizabeth screams at her friend then slowly sinks to the floor, sobbing. "What do you want from me? I don't know how to feel ANYTHING! I want Ollie to be well; I want John to love me; I want Peter and Wren to stop being disappointed in me. I don't know how to do this, Janey. I don't know how to feel so much without fucking VODKA!!!"

"Come on," says Jane and kneels in front of Elizabeth. "Come on, get up off this cold floor and go into the living room and get on the couch. I'll get you a Dr. Pepper and we'll eat those chips." Jane puts her arms around Elizabeth and lifts her to her feet. "You're skin and bones, Lizzy. You can eat now that the booze is gone."

"Is it gone?" asks Elizabeth.

"It is if you want it to be."

39

RIPPED OFF

Oliver hears voices above him and squints his eyes open. He sees shapes and can't make out what they are. Then they talk.

"Hey, man, you all right?"

Oliver hears the voice and the question but doesn't respond. He doesn't know where this question has come from. There are several shapes standing over him and he's scared to let them know he's awake. He rolls onto his side and groans. Feet move closer to his face. Oliver thinks he must have fallen asleep but doesn't remember. All he remembers is shaking and sweating and fear. He examines the shoes that are standing next to his face. He sees a loafer, a very worn loafer that hasn't seen polish for a very long time. It's one of the same loafers he saw on the skinny guy with messed up hair. He puts his hand up to shade his eyes and sees the man in the loafers.

"You all right, fella?" the man asks.

"I guess," says Oliver and manages to sit up and lean against the wall. He looks around and sees that they're in a narrow alley. His perspective is off because this isn't anything like he'd imagined last night. Last night he'd thought he was in a much larger area; them there, him here. He looks up at the group standing over him.

"Where am I?" he asks.

"In an alley," says loafers.

"No, but I mean, where?"

"In Boston?" says another guy.

Oliver looks at his hands and thinks, "Never mind."

"Are you hungry?" asks that same guy.

"I don't know," says Oliver.

"Do you have any money?" asks loafers.

Be careful.

"Yes," says Oliver.

"Then let's go get something to eat."

"What?" Oliver says and thinks he'd better stand. He uses the wall to help him get up off the hard ground. "I'm not hungry."

"Then give me money, and I'll get something to eat."

Oliver stares at the guy, his crazy brown hair, and notices he's wearing a filthy sweatshirt that announces Brown University across his chest. And when he looks at the guy's shoes he sees they're the kind of loafers that used to have tassels. He turns to the wall and fishes his cash out of his pocket. He gives the loafer guy a twenty-dollar bill.

"Do you have any change?" Oliver asks.

"What? I look like a bank? You can share the fire tonight if you're still here."

"Thank you," says Oliver, hoping he wouldn't be sleeping on the ground again.

"I'm coming too," says a third man.

"Sure, let's go."

Oliver watches the three men walk away from him without even a look back. "Who are those guys?" he asks himself.

They just ripped you off, you idiot!

Oliver wanders most of the day, sticking to the alleys. Every once in a while he looks out onto the streets. He wonders what happened to those three guys. He's still not hungry, still feels sick to his stomach. He now has a pounding headache as well and wishes he could sleep somewhere. At one corner he looks out to the street and sees a park. The trees remind him of home. He crosses the street. There are benches, two at a time, sitting around the perimeter of the park.

He sees people playing Frisbee, children running, dogs. He misses Jack. Then he spots an elderly man sitting on one of the benches, reading a book. The man is dressed in a tattered tweed jacket and a similarly weathered briefcase sits at his feet. He's wearing a battered fedora, the felt darker where the band should be.

Oliver sits, gingerly, on the end of the same bench and notices that the man is reading a Bible. He can see that the man is forming the words he reads with his mouth, like a child might.

The elderly man is wearing dress shoes, the kind with the little hole patterns on the toe like Oliver's grandfather wore except his were always polished and clean. This man's pair of shoes have walked many miles. He has one leg crossed over the other thigh, showing the bottom of his shoe to anyone who wants to see it. The heels are worn down, and this shoe has a big hole under the ball of his foot, showing dirty flesh. Oliver thinks he wants to sit next to this elderly man for a while. The man seems gentle and, because he's reading the Bible, all knowing. Oliver thinks that Jude would like this elderly man. Oliver thinks he may have found a wise man or God Himself.

He interrupts the man's reading. "Sir?"

The man lifts his eyes from the book and stares at Oliver.

"May I speak to you?"

The elderly man nods his head.

Oliver slides in closer to the man. He keeps his voice low. "What part of the Bible are you reading?"

"The part where it tells us that Jesus is an alien." The man continues to stare at him, his pupils so huge Oliver can't tell what color his eyes are. He then looks back down at his Bible.

"What did you say?" Oliver asks.

"Yes," the man says, "I'm wondering if you can hear the truth. As He said once, the truth will set you free or, depending upon whom you're speaking, will put you in chains."

Oliver thinks about this for a moment. "Do you know Jude?"

The man thinks momentarily then shakes his head.

"That's too bad." Oliver thinks of Jude and The Woman With The Burned Face and says, "He was probably the kindest person I've ever known."

"That's nice. Kindness is good."

"But" says Oliver, "where in the Bible does it say that Jesus is an alien?"

"The part where He goes up on the mountain with Peter, James, and John and they see Jesus bathed in light," the old man tells Oliver. "They talk a lot about the light, the bright, white light. And that's the proof."

"I've never heard that part but Jude knew that Jesus is an alien."

"How did this Jude know?" the man asks.

"I'm not sure."

"You want to see that part?" asks the elderly man. "It's right here in Matthew 17:2." The man put both his feet on the ground and read from his Bible: "'And in their presence He was transfigured; His face shone like the sun, and His clothes became a brilliant white.' I don't think you need much more proof than that. But then, in 17:5 it says, 'While He was still speaking, a bright cloud suddenly cast its shadow over them and a voice called from the cloud.' The cloud was really the space ship they traveled in."

"Wow" is all Oliver can say.

The two sit, comfortable in each other's presence; an immediate, tenuous companionship in the breath between them. They both watch the movements of the people and dogs in the park and each thinks his own thoughts. The elderly man looks back down at his Bible.

Ask him, dipshit!

Oliver sighs then takes a deep breath.

"Sir?" Oliver asks. "May I call you Sir?"

"Yes, of course, unless you want to call me Harold."

"Is that your name?"

"It's what I go by."

Oliver looks at Harold closely as they talk. His skin is dry and flakey, his yellow-white beard scraggly and stained around his mouth. He has age spots on his temples, reddish bags under his eyes, his eyebrows white and tipping over to slightly obscure his view. Oliver glances down at Harold's hands and sees the top skin is almost transparent, blue veins show through, age spots run riot; the skin of his fingers is shiny as though buffed and polished from a life long-lived.

"Have you ever been in a hospital?" Oliver asks.

"I'd rather not," says Harold.

"Whattaya mean?"

"I'd rather not be in a hospital."

"Oh . . . do you know about the other planets?"

"Of course," says Harold.

"Like what? Like what other planets?" Oliver asks, excited.

"I'm not sure of them individually, I just know there are other planets," says Harold, sounding bored with this subject.

He must be God, Oliver thinks.

"Am I?" asks Harold. He picks up his briefcase, closes the Bible, and puts it inside then hugs it in front of his chest.

He read my thoughts.

That's because he's God, you idiot!

Finally, Oliver asks the most important question. "Can you help me get into the Real World? People are looking for me, people from a hospital and if you can help me get into the Real World, I'll be safe."

Harold stands. He holds his briefcase by its handle, then looks over at Oliver. "Come with me."

Oliver follows Harold across the park. It isn't until they're in the street that he realizes they're right here, at Harvard Square.

This guy is leading you into a trap!

Oliver keeps his head down and looks furtively from one side to the other, searching for anyone who may be searching for him. He stays close to Harold. They walk and walk until the surroundings begin to look like where he spent the night, but here there are many people; mostly dirty, some acting crazy, some dancing and making their heads roll around on their necks, their eyes shining and vacant, dreadlocks swinging.

Oliver grips the blue glass in his pocket, fingering the sharp side. Harold stops in front of a dirty plywood shack built up against a brick building. He carefully places his briefcase inside the blanket door then offers Oliver entrance. Oliver gets down on his knees then crawls on all fours to get inside. Harold follows. A very thin mattress covers most of the floor. There are several paper-thin blankets folded neatly at the head of the mattress. Harold sits cross-legged near the entrance, silent.

Oliver wants to lie down and go to sleep. He feels protected inside this shack.

"You know," says Harold suddenly, "you can't see if you take their poison and live in their hospitals."

"I know that," says Oliver. "I've escaped."

The elderly man nods. "I know you have."

Oliver can't stop himself from sinking down on the thin mattress. He still doesn't feel well and he's exhausted. He wonders how it is that Harold knows he's escaped the hospital but compared to his fatigue, nothing much matters.

It's light outside when Oliver falls asleep, safe with Harold sitting in the entry.

Elizabeth hopes that sleep will come to her more easily than it does this first night without booze. She stays up very late watching HBO because she's afraid that sleep won't come. But it does, at about three in the morning.

She wakes up on the couch. Jane is gone and Jack is at her feet. She lies in the warm blanket on the couch for a few minutes before rousing herself.

"I did it," she says to Jack. "I got through the first night! Now, you can go to work with me," she tells him. She doesn't count on the energy she feels this morning and how annoying it is. She calls Orchard House and asks for Virgil.

"No, I'm afraid we haven't located him yet," says Virgil, "but we will."

"How do you know you'll find him?" says Elizabeth, angrily. "How many days has he been without his meds so far?"

"Just two that we know of. He may have been spitting out his meds while he was here but we don't know that for sure."

Virgil wants to hang up but can't. He's feeling desperate about Oliver. Tagen hinted that Oliver wasn't swallowing his meds for a few days before he fled. It could explain the vampire hallucination that scared him in Harvard Square.

"I'm sure we'll find him. He's still probably somewhere near Harvard. With all those students milling around it might be a bit difficult to spot him, but we will."

"Are you trying to be funny? To set me at ease?" Elizabeth is testy, pushing for a fight.

"Well," says Virgil, "I'm not trying to make light of the situation, Mrs. Moore. I truly believe that he'll be found soon.

Oliver is jolted out of his deep sleep by sirens very close to the shack. He's not quite sure where he is. He sits up abruptly, looks around and remembers. He notices a blanket thrown over his legs. He looks outside and sees light. He doesn't know if he slept all night or if it's still the same day. He wonders where Harold has gone. He crawls out of the shack and stands up. His nausea is diminished, replaced by hunger.

Oliver begins walking down the alleys, crossing street after street. He assesses each crossing to see if he's downtown yet. At one intersection he dares to come out of the alley and walks down the street.

They're going to find you and lock you up again.

Oliver finally spots another Dunkin' Donuts shop. As he's walking in, he glimpses his reflection in the window. His hair is wild, sticking up straight with dirt, but his face isn't giving away any hint of who he is behind his sunglasses.

You look like a damned freak! They're going to catch you.

Oliver walks up to the counter and points to a tray of glazed donuts. The clerk raises her eyebrows. Oliver holds up his hand, all fingers spread.

"You want five glazed?"

Oliver nods. "And coffee," he says quietly. He digs his last twenty dollar bill out of his pocket, pays, then looks around for a booth where he can hide. He discovers an empty one near the back of the shop. The walk from the counter to the booth seems to take forever. He feels the heat from coffee warming his hand, the donuts in their bag are heavy. Once he's seated he wants to get up again and grab a paper but is too scared to walk to the paper rack. He hears the clerk talking to another customer and he knows she's talking about him. He keeps his eyes on the table in his booth. He eats one donut then notices flies on the table, in the air, on his donut bag.

They're watching you. They're remote-control cameras and they're going to give you away, give you to the police.

Oliver picks up the hot coffee, grabs his bag of donuts, and leaves the shop.

40

BLUE GLASS GONE

Oliver follows the busy street to the park again. He isn't even amazed that he finds it. He sees Harold sitting on the same bench and feels a wave of relief. He walks over and takes a seat next to him. Harold isn't reading, is just sitting and watching the activity all around him. Oliver glances at Harold's profile; it's as stone-like as a statue. He doesn't know if he should talk to Harold or if Harold wants to be left alone. But there's a question Oliver simply has to ask. He screws up his nerve because he has to. He has to get away from this planet of cameras and pain.

"Harold?"

The elderly man turns his head so he's gazing at Oliver. "Yes?"

"Would you like a donut?"

"Yes, thank you." Harold takes the donut from Oliver's hand. He carefully breaks the donut in half, puts one half inside his jacket pocket and begins to eat the other half.

Oliver hands him another donut and watches Harold do the same routine with this donut but he's then left with two halves, one bitten in half. Oliver is trying to get up the nerve he needs to ask Harold the question. He hears Jude in the back of his thoughts, egging him on. "You can do it, man. Ask him!"

Harold seems confused by the donut pieces and is quietly sitting with a quarter donut in one hand, a half in the other. He looks over at Oliver, a tiny smile behind his beard.

"Eat that one," Oliver tells him and points to the quarter donut.

"All right," says Harold and pops it in his mouth, pleasure oozing from his grimy smile.

Ask him!

"Sir?" asks Oliver.

"Yes?"

Oliver puts his head in his hands and speaks to the ground, to his shoes. "Will you help me get into the Real World?" He squeezes his eyes together so tightly that he produces tears. He can feel his own heart beating. He hears nothing from Harold so he looks up and sees that Harold is staring across the park. Oliver follows his stare but doesn't see anything of great significance. He asks Harold again, just in case he hadn't heard him. "Sir? Will you help me get into the Real World?"

Harold whispers quietly, in fact so quietly that Oliver thinks Harold's words are somewhat like a breeze, so quietly that Oliver thinks Harold doesn't even understand the question.

"There is no Real World," Harold says.

"Excuse me?"

Harold turns his rheumy eyes on Oliver and dictates the words, as would an apostle, "There is no Real World."

"But you can give me God's blood without a transfusion, right?" Oliver begins to feel panic.

Harold is gazing at him, a vacuous expression on his face.

"But Jude said . . . and you're God, right?" Oliver implores.

"No," says Harold, "I'm just an old man who escaped."

Oliver glares at the elderly man and feels anger and fear overtaking him.

"Escaped from WHAT?"

Harold merely stares at him, then leans down to his briefcase and brings it up to his lap. He snaps the locks open, pulls up the lid and takes his Bible out.

Oliver sees that his Bible is the only thing in Harold's briefcase. He was certain that the contents were of great importance. He realizes, with a terrible sinking feeling of despair, that this man is not a wise man. He is not God.

Oliver stands and stares at Harold. "Fuck you, man!" He shouts at him. "FUCK YOU!"

He runs out of the park toward the Harvard Square shops.

Every time Elizabeth gets close to losing her resolve she thinks of Oliver out there, all alone, and that brings her back. Jane is keeping tabs on her and was finally able to wrest the vodka from Elizabeth and pour it down the drain. It seems evident that Elizabeth isn't going to have seizures.

"Any news about Oliver?" Jane asks as she walks in the front door.

"No, and this damn AA woman keeps inviting me to meetings."

"Why don't you just go?"

"I don't know," Elizabeth says. "This woman seems like such a Girl Scout. I really don't do well in groups."

"Oh, for God's sake, Lizzy, what's the harm in trying them out?"

"Well, maybe next time she calls I'll find out where the meetings are held."

"What if she doesn't call again?" asks Jane.

"There's a number for the local AA helpline I could call, have called."

"Have you seen Peter and Wren lately?"

"Well, not a lot, but they come by once in a while."

"Do they know what you're doing? Sobering up?"

"No. I haven't told them in case I slip up."

"Why would you do that? And isn't AA supposed to help you not slip up?"

"I guess so, Jane, I just don't know. I'd be so embarrassed if I told Wren and Peter that I'm sober and then screw it up."

"Wouldn't you be more embarrassed if John knew?" Jane shoots Elizabeth one of her 'I see right through you' looks.

"Maybe. God! You don't have to be so pushy!"

"Well, if I don't push, who will?"

"No one and that would be just fine!"

"Fine?"

"Okay, I'll call AA. But you have to leave before I do."

"Why?"

"Because, unless you want to go to meetings with me, this is something I have to do for myself. Just like deciding to stop in the first place, right?" Elizabeth's chin is jutting out.

"Okay, I'll go."

"Thank you," says Elizabeth and opens the front door for her.

"Call if you hear anything about Oliver, will you?" asks Jane.

"I will, I promise," says Elizabeth.

"And if you need support to walk into a meeting, call me."

Oliver stops running when he sees the crowd of people on the sidewalks. He reaches up to feel whether he's wearing his sunglasses and is relieved to find that he is. He walks to a small courtyard lined with shops, his hands shoved into his jeans' pockets. His right hand discovers the blue glass. He pushes his thumb, hard, on the sharp side, and recalls telling Peter that he kept the blue glass with him in case he needed to cut something. He recalls telling Peter that no one at Orchard House was allowed to carry knives. He thinks about why they aren't allowed knives, about the long railings on the stairs at Orchard House, and he thinks that maybe what they don't want him to discover is that the best thing to do, for him and his family, is to cut his own throat.

. . . the best thing.

He knows that releasing his blood would finally release the pain. Warm, gloriously dark blood pulsing out of him would absolve this unbearable pressure of anger, voices, and fear. He knows, as he stands there, that everyone around him can hear his thoughts. He watches their faces, sees their mouths form words he can't hear anymore. He is only conscious of the elderly man saying, "There is no Real World."

Oliver sinks to his knees, sobbing. He pulls the blue glass out of his pocket and, while shouting to the other God up in the sky, he cuts himself close to his left ear and under his jaw. Blood pours out of the cut, runs down his neck into his shirt, as warm as he knew it would be.

Tourists stand and watch. A local man pulls his cell phone out of his pocket and calls 911. Another man quickly pulls Oliver's hand away from his neck and pries the blue glass out of his bloody fingers.

"Call an ambulance!" He yells to the crowd as he puts pressure on the cut. "My God, son, what are you thinking?"

"NO!" Oliver screams. "Leave me ALONE!"

"I can't do that, son," says the man, his voice quiet and resonant. He kneels on the ground behind Oliver, put his left arm crossways on Oliver's torso, holding him tight while keeping pressure on the cut with his right hand.

"Leave me alone!" Oliver keeps screaming. "You don't understand. Let me GO!"

"I don't think so, son," says the man.

Sirens are upon them. Two police cars have responded to the call, their lights adding a certain hysteria to the gathering. The police run quickly over to Oliver and the man. Oliver sees them race up to him and stops screaming. He surveys their blue uniforms, the guns, and billy clubs. He stays silent, his eyes wide and helpless.

"Folks, folks, come on, move along now, this isn't a show." The crowd thins a bit, people wandering away, slowly.

"But he's so good-looking!" says someone in the crowd, someone who's taking her time to leave.

"What are you trying to do?" The first officer asks Oliver.

Oliver remains mute and it's the man who says, "He was trying to slit his own throat."

"All right, let's wait for the medics," says the first officer. "You okay?"

"Yeah," says the man. "I'm good."

The ambulance drives up and a team of two, a man and a woman, rush over. They assess the situation, see the man holding Oliver's neck, blood oozing through his fingers.

"Was the blood pulsing out?" asks the male medic.

"No, it was bleeding fast but not spurting," the man tells him.

"Okay, sir, you can take your hand away," says the female medic.

"Are you sure?" asks the man.

"Yes, I've got it." She puts her hand over the man's hand and he slowly pulls his bloody hand away. She and her partner hold the edges of Oliver's wound together with a butterfly bandage, then a bandage over that with gauze and tape.

The female medic tells the man that Oliver didn't cut his artery or there would be no way to hold the blood back. "He came pretty close though," she says, kneeling and smiling in Oliver's face.

"Come on, honey, let's get you to the hospital."

"NO! I don't want to go to the hospital!" Oliver finally speaks, fear written on his face.

"It'll be okay, I promise," says the female medic. "We just need to deal with this nasty cut on your neck."

"Ma'am?" Oliver asks, his eyes imploring her.

"Yes?"

"Would you please just let me die?"

The medic whispers back to him, "No, honey, I don't want to let you die. I think that in a few days you'll be happy to be alive."

The female medic stands and walks over to her partner. "This kid is depressed out of his mind," she says quietly. "We better have some Haldol pulled and ready. And we need the ER to put some stitches in the wound. That cut's pretty deep, and I'm amazed he didn't hit his artery."

The male medic finds Haldol and pulls up a syringe, keeping it close in his shirt pocket.

Dispatch squawks over the police radio that an eighteen-year-old male is missing from Taylor Hospital, that his name is Oliver Moore.

The medics have Oliver sitting in the back of their ambulance. One of the police officers steps up into the ambulance and sits across from Oliver.

"Are you Oliver Moore?"

Oliver turns his head quickly, wincing at the pain, and stares at the police officer. The officer sees what he wants to know but he has to get a spoken affirmation from Oliver.

"Is that your name?" he persists.

He's trying to trick you.

"Okay, I'll call it in," says the officer to the medics. "I don't think the kid's gonna talk but I'd bet my pension he's Oliver Moore."

"Will you guys communicate with Taylor about this?" asks the male medic.

"Yeah, we will. I'll get back to you," says the police officer.

"Then we'll run him to Mass General for stitches," says the medic.

"Okay then, we'll be in touch, and oh, hey, did you see the man who helped the kid? He seems to have disappeared and he must have taken the knife or whatever it was with him," says the police officer.

"No, we haven't seen him."

"Okay, thanks."

Oliver watches as the police officer steps down from the ambulance. He wants to lie down but the medics want him sitting up to help stem the blood flow to his wound. He's glad when the officer is gone. He heard the male medic saying that they'll be taking him to Mass General for stitches. The female medic sits close to him as the ambulance pulls away from the curb, lights flashing, siren announcing who they are and to get out of the way.

"You'll be fine," she says.

Fine.

John answers the phone at work.

"Mr. Moore?"

"Yes?"

"This is Officer Scott with the Boston Police Department. We've found your son, sir," says the voice.

"Where is he?" asks John.

"An ambulance took him to Massachusetts General Hospital to get stitches."

"Why? I mean, what is getting stitched up?"

"His throat," says the voice, quietly.

"His throat . . ." reiterates John. "He wasn't messing around."

"No sir, I heard from the officers on the scene that a bystander took it upon himself to pull your son's hand away from his throat and tried to hold the wound closed until the medics arrived at the scene."

"Do you know who that man is?"

"No, we don't know who he is. He disappeared after the medics took over before we had a chance to get his name."

"What did he use to cut himself?"

"We don't know. There was nothing at the scene. I'm very glad your son has been found, sir. You might want to call Taylor Hospital to see how they'll be transporting Oliver back."

"Yes, sir, I'll do that. You have a better day now," said John and hangs up.

John proceeds to call Orchard House. He gets the medication nurse on the phone and asks if she knew about the police finding Oliver.

"Yes, one of the resident doctors was just getting ready to call you. I'm glad you spoke to the police."

"When will you get Oliver?" John asks.

"Soon. Virgil took a cab into Boston to fetch him. And he'll have to return to the Inpatient Unit."

"Yes. Would you please call me when he's there?"

"Certainly. And you'll tell Mrs. Moore?"

"Yes. Thank you."

John sits at his desk. He puts his elbows on it and bends his head to cradle his face in his hands. "OLIVER!" he screams inside his mind. He slumps in his chair, keeping his face in his hands, and he sobs. "Oh, Ollie! Oh Ollie!"

Then he picks up the phone and dials Elizabeth.

41

EIGHT IS FATE

By the time John has informed Elizabeth, Oliver is on his way back to Taylor Hospital. Virgil had arranged a cab to bring Oliver from Mass General to Taylor, and Oliver's in it. He signs Oliver out and thanks the ER staff for taking care of him. He puts his arm around Oliver's shoulders on the way out to the waiting cab. He indicates to Oliver to get in the back seat, passenger side. Virgil walks around to the back seat behind the driver and sits with Oliver all the way back to Taylor.

"Here we go, right here," he tells the driver and they park in front of the Inpatient Unit.

Oliver hasn't said a word and allows Virgil to put his arm around his shoulders again and steers him inside. Once in, Virgil turns to Oliver.

"I've got some medication for you, Oliver, but you need to decide whether you want it the easy way or not. If not, we can give you the meds in shot form, or, if you want to participate with us to get you well, you need to swallow your medication in pill form. Do you understand me? What you did was terribly dangerous. You put many people at risk here at Taylor and you worried the piss out of your family. Do you hear me?"

Oliver tries to not look at Virgil but the longer Virgil speaks to him the harder he finds it to avoid his face.

"Yes, sir."

"So, you want pills?"

Oliver nods.

"None of us are going to give up on you, Oliver. You're going to get better one way or the other. It would be a shame to have shots every day, right?"

Oliver nods again. "Yes, sir."

Virgil nods to the nurse to give Oliver the pills and water. He swallows them down.

"Okay then," says Virgil. "You'll be back in room number 8 again."

They walk down the hall and enter the room.

"I've put some reading material in here for you, Oliver. I hope you take some time to read about your illness. All is not lost. Just hang on and things will get better, but you have to work with us."

Oliver is really only hearing a bit of what Virgil is saying to him. But he gets the gist of it. He walks over to the bed and collapses. It's so very comfortable. He glances up at the window where Peter had looked in. Then, putting his hand to his bandaged neck, he closes his eyes.

"Good night, young man," says Virgil. "I'll see you tomorrow. And I'm so glad you're back."

Oliver hears Virgil shut the door behind him and he hears the lock click into place. He doesn't even care.

John phones Elizabeth and finds her at work.

"They found him."

"Oh, thank God! Is he all right?"

"Yes, but he tried to cut his throat."

"WHAT? But he's alive? Is he safe?"

"He drew a crowd in Harvard Square. Some guy saved him by pulling his hand and whatever he was cutting himself with away from his neck. They don't know who it was and he supposedly took the knife that Ollie used. I think he prevented Ollie from hitting his jugular."

"Oh my God, John. He could have died! And the guy just disappeared?"

"Yes. I'd sure like to thank him but no one knows who he is."

"Should we go back to see Ollie?"

"I don't think so, not right now. Virgil says Ollie will be in the Inpatient Unit for at least a couple of weeks. Oliver's going to have to get with the program if he wants to get out of there. Oh, but Virgil told me that Ollie can come home for Christmas break. We can all look forward to that."

"How long will he be home?"

"I have no idea."

Elizabeth has to ask someone to hold on a second, someone who must have just entered her office.

"And how are you, Lizzy?"

"I'm good, thanks," Elizabeth says, smiling on her end of the phone in spite of herself, in spite of the fact that Oliver almost died.

"You sound good," he tells her.

"Thank you. And thanks for calling me right away. I'll let you know if they call me."

"Yup, " says John. "And let me know when you're ready for Wren over a weekend, okay?"

"Yes, thanks. Probably pretty soon."

"Okay then. Bye."

"Bye."

Virgil comes for Oliver the next morning. Oliver is groggy from beginning the medication all over again.

"This is what we're going to do, Oliver. You get to meet with both Dr. Matthews and Dr. Greenwood today. I'll take you up to Orchard House to Dr. Matthews office but there will be no sitting around on the front porch with your buddies."

"I'm too tired."

"Well, good. That means the meds are working. You know how it goes, Oliver. The drastic side effects leave in a few weeks. Dr. Matthews wants to speak to you about what he's prescribed, okay?" Virgil doesn't wait for Oliver to agree and walks out the door, indicating with his arm that Oliver should come with him.

Just as Oliver is about to follow Virgil the male nurse shows up. "Hey, Oliver. I'll change your bandage when you return, okay?"

"Okay," Oliver says, then scoots out the door after Virgil. He follows him up the hill to Orchard House.

There they were, the fellow nut cases sitting on the porch. In spite of himself, Oliver is really happy to see them, even Eddie.

Tagen screams and flies off the porch. "I've missed you SO MUCH!" She screeches and throws her arms around him. "Everyone did!!"

"Don't speak on my behalf," says Eddie, smiling.

Maurice walks down the steps and slaps Oliver on the back. "What the fuck, man? What's that?" He points to the bandage on Oliver's neck.

"Oh, nothing," says Oliver, embarrassed.

"It doesn't look like nothing," Eddie chimes in.

"Well, I'd rather not talk about it," Oliver tells them.

"Fine," says Eddie, "be that way!"

Virgil walks out of the house onto the porch. "Oliver, come on, Dr. Matthews is waiting."

Oliver follows Virgil inside and down the linoleum hall, past the medication room, and into Dr. Matthews's office.

"Hello, Oliver."

"Hello."

"I'll see you when you're finished," Virgil tells Oliver and closes the door on him and the doctor.

"So, you had quite the adventure I'm told," says Dr. Matthews.

"Yes."

"Would you like to tell me about it?"

"No."

"Why did you stop taking your meds?"

"I don't know."

"How was it without them?" asks Dr. Matthews.

Oliver flashes back, sleeping on the cold dirt, puking, Dunkin' Donuts, the extra loud voice. "Not great."

"You must have gone through some rugged withdrawals?"

"Yes, sir, I did." Oliver finally looks at Dr. Matthews. "It wasn't good."

"Oliver, how has the voice been lately?"

Be careful!

"Bad," feeling like a traitor.

"Oliver, I want to help in my capacity as your psychopharmacologist. I'm going to put you on oral Haldol for a while. I think two antipsychotics will help more than anything. We'll keep you on Clozapine but that's going to be a heavy hit, the Haldol and Clozapine at the same time. The side effects are going to be brutal for a few weeks but we'll let you sleep down in the Inpatient Unit. I'm going to keep you on the same antidepressant as before. Celexa is a good one but I'm going to increase the dose a bit. Then Lithium for mood stability. Okay?"

"I don't know."

"That's all right. All in good time."

"Thank you," says Oliver very gently.

"You can go now," Dr. Matthews says. "And don't forget how important sleep is and don't push yourself to stay awake right now. You'll be feeling better soon, I just know it. But you must know that when I say 'soon' I don't mean a matter of days. This is going to take months, okay?"

"Thanks." Oliver gets up and walks out to the linoleum hall, then outside to the porch. He doesn't see Virgil or anyone else so he sits on a bench. He's so tired that he leans his head up against the wall of the house and lets his body slouch. He closes his eyes. He feels someone sit next to him, quite close. He opens his eyes to slits and sees that it's Linda. She's simply sitting next to him. He likes it.

"There you are," says Virgil. "It's almost time to see Dr. Greenwood. Let's start walking."

Oliver rouses himself and stands. He looks back at Linda and smiles. She stares up at him, no expression on her face.

"Bye, Linda. I'll see you later."

"Bye," she says in a monotone and looks away.

Virgil and Oliver walk over to Dr. Greenwood's office. "He doesn't have time to come to the Inpatient Unit this time."

Virgil leaves Oliver outside the doctor's office door. "I'll be downstairs in a half hour," he tells Oliver.

Dr. Greenwood's door opens almost as soon as at the elevator door closes on Virgil.

"Greetings!" says Dr. Greenwood. "Won't you come in?"

Oliver enters the room and sits. Dr. Greenwood repositions himself behind his desk.

"So, young sir, what do you have to say for yourself? Trying to leave us, were you? That's quite a bandage you have on your neck."

Oliver takes in Dr. Greenwood's words and reaches up to touch the bandage on his neck.

"Does it hurt?" the doctor asks.

"A little."

"Why did you cut yourself?"

"I had to."

"What did you cut yourself with?"

Oliver sits quietly. He hears a rushing sound in his ears when he suddenly realizes that he's no longer in possession of the blue glass. He turns pale, his eyes widen.

"It's gone," he whispers.

"What's gone?"

"My blue glass! The one I found in the woods with Tagen."

"Is that what you cut yourself with?"

Oliver stares at Dr. Greenwood. "Is it really gone?"

"I don't know, Oliver. All I know is that the man who probably saved your life, disappeared. He must have taken the blue glass, maybe, by mistake."

Oliver looks at the ground. He clutches his hands together. He glances up at Dr. Greenwood.

"I've been thinking about this. I think that man was Jude. He didn't want me to die. And maybe it was his turn to have the blue glass."

Dr. Greenwood looks like he's truly pondering Oliver's statement. "You know, Oliver, I guess it doesn't matter exactly who helped you. It doesn't matter that he may have the blue glass. I hope it was Jude; that has a good ring to it, you know? I think what's really important here is that you understand what you need to do. From where I sit, you need to stick with your medications and you need to rest and you need to allow yourself to feel better. It's difficult to talk things over when you're still operating under a goodly amount of psychosis. Don't you think?"

"Yes," says Oliver. He's watching Dr. Greenwood's hands fiddle with a paperclip, yellow this time, which isn't bothering him.

"It's terribly unfortunate that there is anything like an illness of the brain. We need our brains to do just about everything. If you decide to get well, you will. We can help you with therapy and medications but it's you who has to do the work. Thinking that we're persecuting you doesn't help your brain get better. Running away from here doesn't help you get better. You have to do the work. If you really want to get better, if you want to stop seeing hallucinations and hearing voices, you get to do the work. You're so very fortunate to respond well to medications. How about the people who are medication resistant?"

Oliver thinks about Linda at Orchard House, then looks up at Dr. Greenwood's face. His eyes are on Oliver even though his hands are on the paperclip.

"You spoke about freedom the last time we met down in the Inpatient Unit. Those people, the ones who are medication resistant, will never be free. They'll be stuck inside their illnesses forever, unless a new medication arrives on the scene that actually works for them.

"You are free. You can be truly free by doing the hard work now to unshackle yourself from your illness. All you have to do is take your meds every day, without fail and without hesitation. And see to your activities and see me. That is your bridge back."

Dr. Greenwood sits back in his chair, leaving the paperclip alone. "Are you following me?"

"Yes," Oliver answers.

"You know, Oliver, there's an interesting dichotomy about mental illness. When you're taking medication you're free from most of the symptoms. Without medication you're trapped inside where all the psychosis lives. It's terrifying, right?"

Oliver looks up and sees that Dr. Greenwood actually wants him to answer.

"Yes."

"Suicide is the ultimate symptom. Without medication you could take your own life. You almost did! That's the ultimate trick of brain diseases. We all die eventually but suicide speeds up that process and leaves our loved ones blaming themselves. I think Jude would be proud of you. I think that a man like Jude, who doesn't have a family to see him through the hard parts, would be really proud of you, Oliver. I think he would encourage you to take advantage of the care that's offered you at Taylor. He would remind you of all the men and women who can't afford the long, drawn-out care that's imperative with mental illness. There are a few illnesses where the line is drawn so clearly between the haves and the have nots. I think mental illness is at the top of this list."

Oliver wants to get back to the Inpatient Unit and sleep. Dr. Greenwood's tiny office seems to be getting smaller the longer the doctor speaks. Finally, he stops talking.

"Time to go," Dr. Greenwood is saying.

"Really?"

"I'll see you soon."

"Okay," Oliver says and stands. "Thank you."

"Sleep!"

"Yes, sir."

Oliver finds Virgil outside the building. They walk to the Inpatient Unit where the red headed nurse is ready to change Oliver's bandage. She doesn't speak until she's done.

"Now, let's go to your room and get you in bed! I hope you sleep a very long time. You look exhausted."

Tagen, Jerry, Janice, and Maurice bring Oliver a big piece of Sunday coffeecake. It's as good as ever and Oliver thanks them by bringing them into his room and providing chairs for them all, except Tagen, who sits on the bed with him.

"How's it going in here?" she asks.

"Boring. I just sleep a lot," Oliver tells her.

"No TV even?" asks Maurice.

"Nope. Dr. Greenwood brought me a bunch of stuff to read about schizoaffective disorder. That's what they think I have."

"That sucks," says Maurice.

"Whatever," says Oliver.

The red-headed nurse pokes her face in the door. "Time to go, all of you."

"But we just got here!" says Maurice.

"I'm aware of that. It's still time to go."

Elizabeth doesn't have to ask Jane to walk into a meeting with her. She does it all by herself. Kerry, the AA woman, has told her about this noon meeting in the Baptist Church downtown. From the coffee shop all she needs to do is walk two blocks south and there's the Baptist Church. The sun is out, the air is getting a bit cooler as they pass the halfway mark of September. She steps out of her shop and navigates her way to the glass door into the AA meeting room.

"Oh my God," she thinks. "There are so many people!" She finds a place to sit, up against the wall, and waits.

A woman with dark hair comes out of the crowd.

"Are you Elizabeth?"

"Yes, I am."

"Welcome! Do you mind if I sit with you?"

"Good Lord, no!"

"Do you believe how loud all these drunks are?" Kerry asks her and laughs. "You know, don't you, that all these people are the same ones who sat on bar stools with us."

"I never really thought of AA people like that," says Elizabeth.

Their conversation is interrupted by a man sitting over at the grouping of tables in the center of the room.

"Okay folks! It's the top of the hour. My name is Dennis. I'm a coke head and alcoholic. Let's have a moment of silence to contemplate why we're here, followed by the Serenity Prayer."

Elizabeth sees Kerry bow her head for the moment of silence. She does the same.

Then Dennis begins the prayer and everyone joins in.

"God, grant me the serenity to accept the things I cannot change, the courage to change the things I can, and the wisdom to know the difference."

"Now," says Dennis. "Is there anyone here for their very first AA meeting? If so, please introduce yourself by your first name only."

Elizabeth raises her hand and says, "Hi, I'm Elizabeth."

Her raised hand invites a slew of people saying, "Welcome! Welcome! Welcome!"

Elizabeth presses her back even more into the bench, shrinking as much as she can.

Dennis asks if there is anyone who's in their first thirty days of sobriety. Elizabeth counts five people who raise their hands and introduce themselves.

"We should have a First Step meeting for Elizabeth. Anyone disagree?"

Elizabeth feels apprehensive and nervous about whatever this First Step meeting means for her.

"Well then, let's open the meeting."

It's mostly women who speak up. Their stories are shocking and very similar to her own. It is difficult to imagine this nicely dressed, bright looking woman as a late-night barfly. But she says she escaped it with the help of AA.

Or this woman who brought her crochet work to the meeting. She used to drink all day long while taking care of two young children who were eventually taken from her. She mentions that the only requirement for being a member of AA is a desire to stop drinking. Pretty simple. One day at a time.

Elizabeth has an epiphany and realizes that yes, John has been taking Wren because of her drinking. She knew that but she didn't know that. Her eyes tear up and she feels her face going red and she's horribly self-conscious. All these stories were directed at her. She'd never had so many strangers interested in her and she doesn't like it at all. She sees them try to make eye contact with her so she lowers her eyes and stares at the floor.

Kerry finds a schedule and passes it around the room where the women write their names and phone numbers. When the meeting is adjourned Elizabeth is the target for hugs and words of encouragement to keep coming to meetings. She does not like all the attention from so many strangers. She wants to throw their hugs back at them and run away. But she thinks of Oliver.

After the meeting Kerry suggests that Elizabeth begin every day with a new commitment to not drink for the next twenty-four hours. And that's it. Don't bother thinking about tomorrow.

"I like that," says Elizabeth. "So, today, I won't drink."

Kerry hands her a thick hardback book. "This is the Big Book. Start reading it and show up. You won't get that much attention again, don't worry!"

After a couple of weeks at the Inpatient Unit, a subdued Oliver returns to Orchard House. First, before he's allowed to go upstairs to his room, he's ushered into Dr. Matthews's office. Both the doctor and Leslie, Oliver's case worker, greet him and show him a chair. He sits.

"Oliver, Leslie and I want to talk to you about attitude now that you're back with us. Dr. Greenwood suggested that you find freedom to be an especially difficult concept when applied to mental illness. I think it's pretty simple; while you're taking your meds you gain freedom from the disease that controls your mind.

"When you don't take your meds you're free of the meds but the disease has you in its clutches. Do you know the meaning of the word 'disease'?"

"No."

"It's really very simple. Dis-ease, meaning no ease. And there's dis-order meaning no order. But all that is beside the point. You choose one of the following: You swallow your medication and get with the program here and eventually you're able to return home. Or don't swallow your medication, don't be a part of the group, lose your mind again, and find yourself in lock up. I think it's important that you see what happens to you without your meds. Do you remember a time when you had similar experiences?"

"Well, yeah. Before I went to the hospital in Bozeman for the first time." Oliver fights feeling trapped. He suddenly recalls what the not-wise man had said about poison. "Do you think these medications are poison?" he asks.

"Some people think medication is poison but I would say those people aren't mentally ill or don't work with the mentally ill."

"But won't these pills shorten my life?" Oliver pulls himself upright in the chair.

"I think you almost shortened your life, drastically, by being off your meds. I think I can say with confidence that your struggle with freedom would be greatly diminished if you committed suicide." Dr. Matthews grins. "Don't you think so?"

"Well," Oliver laughs a quiet laugh, "I guess so!"

42

THROUGH THE KEYHOLE

Oliver wakes up. It's nine in the morning. Group is at ten. He swings his legs on to the floor and groans. It's cold, a damp east coast cold, unlike the dry cold of the Rockies. He's slept in a fleece pullover and his jeans so it's relatively easy to get up.

Oliver is getting used to the routine and his medication side effects are dumbing down. Three months since his attempted suicide, the best part of the morning routine is that upon waking Oliver knows there isn't anything to "get," that he can simply take things at face value. This is new and exciting for him.

After sticking with his meds and forcing himself to be part of the group meetings, Oliver begins to have short moments of clarity that give him a glimpse into life without psychosis. Taking things at face value is a huge win over psychosis. He begins to laugh again. It's only a couple of short weeks until his moments of clarity become longer. But he does continue to sabotage himself at times by trying to hold on to an idea that isn't real. Dr. Greenwood says that holding on to an idea that isn't real is a habit for Oliver, one he needs to break, but also one that medication and talk therapy will eventually help him squash.

Oliver has a meeting today with Dr. Matthews and Leslie. They'll be speaking to him about his upcoming trip back to Montana. But first he has to eat and go to group.

The dining room is quiet. A few people are sitting at tables, mostly alone. Oliver picks out bacon and a cinnamon roll and sits at an empty table.

"Hey! Oliver!" It's Maurice.

"Hey."

"What are you doing?"

"I'm eating breakfast, what does it look like?"

"Going to group?"

"Yeah."

"Okay, see you there," Maurice tells him and walks out of the dining room.

That was kind of weird, thinks Oliver. He crams the rest of the cinnamon roll into his mouth and gets up. He pours himself some coffee from the carafe on the buffet table, adds at least half an inch of cream, and two packets of sugar. He gulps this cup then fills it up again, same routine. Now, he's ready for group.

Oliver can hear loud voices coming from the room where group is held. He smiles to himself. He can hear Maurice loudest of all and then Tagen's shrill voice. He arrives at the open door and walks in.

"Come to attention, people!" yells Jerry who is running the peer-to-peer group meeting today. "Do you have anything to say for yourselves?"

Oliver, feeling confident, announces that he's going home tomorrow.

"We knew that," says Tagen.

"Well, now you can know it twice," Oliver shoots back at her.

Jerry speaks up. "I think many of us are going home for Christmas. Why don't we talk about what we're afraid of?"

"Gee, Jerry, you sound just like a shrink!" says Maurice.

"Thank you, thank you," Jerry stands and takes a bow.

"Okay, I'll be first," Tagen says. "I'm afraid that I won't come out of my room and that I'll fight with my parents."

Silence.

"Okay," says Jerry. "Who's next?"

Janice pipes up. "I'm afraid my cousins will treat me differently because they know I live at a nut house."

"Do any of you object to Orchard House being called a nut house?" asks Jerry.

"No," says everyone.

"Okay, that's good," Jerry says. "Does anyone hear an underlying message?"

Oliver raises his hand. "Fear of going home?"

Maurice chimes in. "Fear of not coming back?"

Tagen says, "Fear of being at home, alone?"

Jerry raises his own hand, halfway, and says, "I like Tagen's. That's how I feel about it. Home alone, without any of you guys to let me know I'm okay."

"How do your parents treat you?" asks Tagen.

"Like I'm a freak but they also tell me they love me all the time so it's kind of confusing."

"Maybe we should exchange each other's phones numbers to take with us?" Oliver suggests.

"That's a really good idea," says Tagen. "Here, let's do that now."

"Anyone have paper?" asks Jerry. "And a pen?"

"That's a really good idea, Oliver," Maurice tells him.

"Thanks, man." He looks at the wall clock. "I gotta run to see Dr. Matthews. See you later."

"See ya," says everyone, collectively.

Oliver books it down the linoleum hall to Dr. Matthews's office. He knocks and Leslie opens the door.

"Hi, Oliver. Thanks for being on time."

"No problem."

"Hi", says Dr. Matthews. "Well, this is an exciting meeting, no? How long has it been since you were home?"

"Almost eight months," says Oliver, not missing a beat.

"Wow! Well, congratulations for a job well done."

"Thanks!"

"Leslie and I want to go over a few things with you. I see you'll be leaving tomorrow and be gone from December 23 until January 4. That's," he pauses, "that's thirteen days. So, tonight, when you get your evening meds, they'll give you all the meds you'll need for the dates you'll be gone. Next, we need to write up an emergency sheet that you can access if needed."

Leslie brings a copied piece of paper over to Oliver and sits next to him on the second chair. "Okay, the heading really isn't necessary as you know who you are, right?" She chuckles.

"Yes."

"Then these headings can be filled in and we'll be done. So, this asks what you should do if you become overwhelmed. What do you do, Oliver?"

"I need to find a quiet place without noise or people."

"Good. Now write that down. Okay, now, medications."

Oliver hesitates for a moment. "I need to establish a time to take them and not forget." He writes this down under the proper heading.

"Good. If you panic and can't get yourself back?" she asks.

"I should call you or Dr. Matthews or Dr. Greenwood."

"Right, and we can all be paged from the main number, okay?"

"Right."

"Yeah, how about Virgil? Could I call him instead?"

Leslie glances over at Dr. Matthews who nods his head.

"Then you would ask the switchboard for Orchard House, then ask for Virgil, okay?"

"Right."

"Now, always travel with your medication in a carry on. Don't ever put it in a bag that you'll check. If you panic in the airport, call one of us, okay?"

"Yup."

"I just know you'll do really well, Oliver," Leslie says. "You've worked so hard these past few months and I think it shows. I think it's important that you know I'm considering you for enrollment in an art class at Mass Art when you return from this holiday. So, that's it!" She stands as does Dr. Matthews and Oliver.

"Good luck, mister, and have a great holiday," says Leslie.

"Yes, Oliver, have a good holiday and we'll be anxious to hear how it all goes when you return," says Dr. Matthews. He shakes Oliver's hand. "I'm really gratified by the work you've done, as Leslie says. Don't hesitate to call if you need or want to."

"Thank you," says Oliver, beaming. "And that's really awesome about Mass Art!" He folds the emergency paper into small squares and fits it into his shirt pocket. "I'll see you."

Elizabeth and Wren are jumping up and down excited about Oliver's return for Christmas. They all decide to have the Christmas tree at John's as that's where Oliver has a room that isn't above Elizabeth's garage. Elizabeth and Wren bring their decorations over and mingle them with John's as they dress the tree. John, Peter, and Wren have chosen a beautiful blue spruce from the National Forest. John warms cider and adds a cinnamon stick to each mug. He found maple sugar cookies at Costco and puts a pile of them on a plate.

When the tree is finished, John speaks. "We know Olllie is coming home but we don't know how he'll be. Eight months is a long time, especially when you're nineteen. Your mom and I attended a NAMI meeting last week, for local support. And Dr. Matthews from Orchard House told us to have a quiet room ready for Ollie where he can escape if he needs to. I hope we won't take it personally if he has to retreat to his room. His quiet room will be his bedroom so I just ask you guys to not knock on his door or call to him if he goes in there and shuts the door, okay?"

"Yup," Peter and Wren say in unison.

"Will he look different?" asks Wren.

"Gosh! I don't know!" says John. "He was pretty scruffy at the hospital. We'll just have to wait and see. Tomorrow is coming very slowly, don't you think?"

"YES!" yells Wren.

Oliver can't stand waiting inside the airplane for everyone to disembark. He has a window seat and is cramped standing under the overhead bins while people seem to take their time getting off. He is so excited he almost feels sick.

Elizabeth, John, Peter, and Wren wait inside the airport, looking through the glass where they'll see Oliver emerge.

"What if I don't recognize him, Dad?" asks Wren.

"Ollie? Of course you'll recognize him!" says Peter. "Wait, here come some people. Here Wren, let me pick you up." Peter scoops up Wren and holds her tightly while they watch the travelers disembark.

"THERE!" yells Wren. "There he is, see?"

She's pointing to a young man carrying a red backpack, hair to his shoulders, wearing a navy and white bandana.

"Oh my God!" says Elizabeth. "That's HIM!"

Oliver looks up and sees them standing there. He smiles and waves and they all do the same.

"His hair is so long!" says Wren.

"That's eight months of hair growth," says John.

"He looks perfect," says Elizabeth.

"Aaaaaaawwwwww, Mom!" says Peter.

And then Oliver is standing there, waiting for their arms to be thrown around him. "I can't believe this," as everyone hugs him. "Am I really home?"

"You betcha!" says John.

They walk down the stairs and wait for Oliver's luggage to come in. He feels awkward just standing with his family, doing nothing. They take turns hanging on him. He picks up Wren. She throws her arms around his neck then says, "Ollie, what's that?" and puts her fingers on his scar.

"It's just an old scar from a cut," he tells her.

She touches it. "It's kind of squiggly, and bumpy."

"Yeah, it is, isn't it?" Oliver tells her. "I'm glad it's all healed."

Elizabeth has been watching this and gets tears in her eyes. She walks over to them. "Let me see it too," she says. She holds one of his arms and looks at the scar. Her stomach feels queasy looking at it. "Ollie, you've been to hell and back, sweetie."

Oliver looks at her. "I'm pretty good now, Mom."

"It certainly looks it! I'm so very proud of you."

"Thanks."

"Here, the bags are coming," says John.

Oliver puts Wren down and waits close to the carousel.

"Here we go," he says and lifts up a stuffed blue duffel bag. "I guess I don't need a luggage tag here in Bozeman, right?"

"Nope" says John. "We're still sort of a small town."

"We're parked out this way," says Peter and takes the lead.

They walk across the road and into the parking lot and hear barking.

"Jack! Did you bring Jack?" Oliver asks.

"Of course we did!" says Wren and she takes off and runs to the SUV. "JACK! Look who's HOME?"

John pops the locks and Wren opens the door and lets Jack out. He comes bounding over to the rest of the family and suddenly realizes that Oliver is there. He leaps and whines and wiggles.

"JACK! God, it's so good to see you!"

"He's going crazy, Mom!" Wren yells.

"Of course he is! Ollie is HOME!"

They all cram into the SUV, Jack sitting on Oliver's lap.

Back at John's house, Peter makes them wait at the door while he goes inside and plugs in the Christmas tree. Then they make Oliver walk in first. He takes a few steps then stands, like a pillar, as they walk in behind him. John looks at Oliver's face lit by the Christmas tree lights. He sees that Oliver's cheeks are wet with tears. He chokes up and puts his arm around him.

"I love you," John says. "This has been hell, hasn't it?"

"Yeah," says Oliver. "Hell." He walks over to the tree and begins looking at the decorations. "I remember so many of these," he says, quietly.

"Are you hungry?" John asks.

"Yeah, I guess I am." Oliver wipes the tears off his face. "Dad?"

"Yeah?"

"Would you mind making a grilled cheese sandwich? I've been craving one!"

"Sure, anything you want! And yes, we're going to spoil you while you're home."

Oliver picks up the red duffel bag and walks down the short hall to his room. He passes the bathroom on the way and glances inside to see if the mirror was ever replaced. That was so long ago. His room feels welcome and he bounces on the side of the bed for a moment. No squeaks.

"I stayed in your room for a while," Wren says from the doorway.

"You did? How come, I mean, I don't mind, I . . ."

"Because Mommy was sick," Wren tells him.

"She was sick?"

Peter sticks his head into the room. "What's up?"

"Wren was just telling me that she stayed in my room because Mom was sick. What was she sick with?"

"It was alcohol," Peter tells him.

"Alcohol?"

"She was drinking way too much but, she isn't drinking anymore."

"That's awesome!" says Oliver.

"Yeah, it is," says Wren. She kicks at the wall with her bare foot.

"Hey, Ollie, you want to go skiing tomorrow?" Peter asks.

Oliver sits on his bed. "I don't know, Pete. Who would be up there?"

"I don't know. Maybe some of the guys."

Oliver skips a beat. "I don't want to see any of the guys."

"How come?"

"I just don't," is all Oliver will say.

Elizabeth sticks her head into the room. "Grilled cheese ready!"

"That was quick!" says Peter.

"Wren? I'm going home now. Do you want to come with me or stay here? You'll have to sleep on the couch."

"That's okay, Mom. I'll sleep on the couch." She looks furtively at Oliver.

"It's Christmas Eve tomorrow!" says Elizabeth. She walks into the room. "I'll never be able to express to you how grateful I am that you're home." She takes Oliver's face between her hands. "I just love you so much." She kisses his forehead.

"Thanks, Mom," Oliver says. "But I have to go back, you know."

"I know. But you're here now."

They hear John yell, "Come on all of you! Your grilled cheese is ready and hot!"

The four of them walk into the kitchen. John is in there, holding a spatula. He hands each one a golden grilled cheese on plates. "Now, I'm going to get some wood."

"Damn! This smells so good! Just like home," Oliver crows.

"It's my favorite," says Wren.

"What time is it?" Oliver asks.

"Ahh, let's see," Peter reads the time off the microwave. "It's 7:30."

"I think I need to take my meds. Leslie wanted me to remember that Boston is two hours ahead of Bozeman," Oliver says.

"Who is Leslie?" asks Peter.

"A nurse at Taylor," Oliver tells him then heads to his room.

"I'm going to an 8:00 meeting and then home," says Elizabeth.

"See you tomorrow?" Peter asks.

"Of course! It's Christmas Eve!" she says. "I love you guys."

"Love you too Mom."

John creaks open the door and walks in holding a huge load of wood in his arms. He dumps it on the hearth, standing several of the snow-covered logs on end so they'll melt quicker.

"Would you guys light a fire and bring in more wood please? I'm going to the store to get a few things we'll need for Christmas Eve dinner tomorrow. I won't be long at all."

"We'll be okay, Dad. Don't worry," says Peter.

Elizabeth has stuck to her vow. She attends AA meetings regularly. She cringes when newcomers arrive at meetings because she remembers how mortified she was during her First Step meeting and is glad she's on the other side of it now. She thinks to herself that not wanting to deal with another First Step meeting is a good deterrent. She doesn't see her old friends much anymore. She's noticed that Wren takes tiny sips of whatever she's drinking when they happen to go to a restaurant or to the house of one of those old drinking friends. She doesn't let on to Wren that she knows what she's doing. Wren's behavior with the drinks is also a good deterrent.

Oliver walks into the kitchen. He gets a glass of water and drinks down a handful of pills. He turns around from the sink and looks straight at the cupboard that he'd searched so frantically a year ago. He feels scared for a moment, then realizes he's safe, that he hasn't heard that voice for a long time now. He sits with Peter and Wren and eats his grilled cheese then walks out to the living room. He sees the teal chair he sat in way back then, the chair that's in front of the tall window. He doesn't want to sit in it now. He pulls out a cigarette and sits on the ledge in front of the fireplace. He glimpses a reflection of himself in the glass doors of the fireplace. He opens the glass doors, narrowing the reflection, then lights the cigarette. He blows the smoke up the chimney. He decides to sit in the teal chair once he's finished his smoke.

Peter walks into the room. "Whoa! Did you ask Dad if you could smoke in here?"

"No."

"He might be pissed if he smells smoke," Peter says and walks to the couch, then flops down.

"That's okay," says Oliver. He puts the cigarette out inside the fireplace then closes the insert doors, leaving the butt inside. He stands and walks across the living room to the teal chair. He lets himself down into it, slowly. The view of the living room and doorway into the kitchen bring back such visual memories that he freezes, rooted to the chair. These memories have a physical aspect to them that Oliver hasn't encountered before; he feels as though someone has kicked him in the stomach.

"Want to watch TV?" Peter asks.

Oliver stares at Peter, can't open his mouth. He nods, slowly. Peter looks back at Oliver and sees in his brother's eyes that he's not there.

"You okay?"

Oliver closes his eyes.

"Wren?" Peter calls. "Wren?"

"What?" She calls back from the kitchen.

"What are you doing?"

"It's a surprise."

Peter hears dishes clanking and the fridge opening and closing. He smiles.

Oliver opens his eyes and stands. "I'm going to bed," he tells Peter.

"But Wren is preparing a surprise for us. Can you wait a minute?"

Oliver, still not quite there, says, "Okay, I'll wait."

Wren walks into the living room with a tray carrying two bowls of ice cream with spoons and napkins.

"Oh boy!" says Peter as he takes a bowl off the tray. "You're quite the great Weasel!"

Oliver stands. He walks over to Wren and takes his bowl off the tray. She hands him a spoon and napkin. "Thanks, Wren. I'm going to eat this in my room," he says and walks away down the hall.

Wren looks at Peter who shrugs his shoulders. "It's okay, Weez," he tells the little girl. "Let's watch TV and now get some ice cream for yourself and we'll sit on the couch."

"Where's Jack?"

"He must be outside or maybe he went with Dad."

"I'm going to draw," she tells Peter. She goes to the cupboard near the TV where her art supplies live.

"Hey, turn the TV on, would you?" Peter asks.

Wren turns on the TV, then reverts her attention to her art supplies. She chooses a piece of yellow paper and a huge box of crayons. She places the piece of paper on the coffee table in front of the couch, then sets up the box of crayons, the lid open.

"Hey, would you get me a piece of paper too?" asks Peter.

"Sure! You wanna draw?"

"Why, yes, I do," he says, grinning.

Wren fetches a piece of white paper for Peter then focuses entirely on her drawing. She draws two houses. Then, in between the houses, she draws Jack, Elizabeth, John, Peter, Oliver, and herself.

"What are you going to do with that?" Peter asks.

"I'm going to give it to Ollie," she says. She writes "I love you" under the family.

"Wow, that's a really, really awesome drawing, Weez," Peter tells her.

She folds the drawing, biting her lower lip, then brings it with her down the hall to Oliver's room. She carefully slips it under his door.

EPILOGUE

At the first signs of spring, in April, Oliver comes home to stay. Leslie, the nurse and case worker at Orchard House, wanted Oliver to stay in the Boston area to begin his studies at Mass Art. But Oliver wants to return to Montana and promises Leslie he'll continue studying art at Montana State University in Bozeman.

Two years to the month after he first flew to Taylor Hospital with Elizabeth, Oliver comes home to Montana and his family. He now relies on his brain instead of being afraid of it. He displays good hygiene, communicates well with his family, and is able to run errands on his own. Even though Oliver still wears his sunglasses he's sometimes able to enter stores without them.

Peter and John take it upon themselves to get Oliver out into the woods and mountains that surround Bozeman. They hike up trails they hiked before and camp in places that Peter and Oliver grew up in and love so well.

Oliver feels whole once again and talks with ease about the mysteries of the universe that once became so muddled with psychosis that he lost sight of everything and everyone, including himself.

One late afternoon in June, the brothers hike up Cottonwood Canyon to the outcropping where Peter and Greg sat so long ago when Oliver was first sick. They find a dry rock to sit on and gaze out over the whole Gallatin Valley; the town lights twinkle, the sky is a very dark blue and the far away Tobacco Root Range indicates the edge of the world.

Oliver, quiet and happy, comprehends now what the Real World really is and, although he doesn't say it, perceives it's sitting right here, next to him, embodied in Peter, his brother and best friend.

ACKNOWLEDGMENTS

We wish to thank our family for supporting the
writing of this book, especially Glenn Close who
founded, with others, BringChange2Mind.

We also acknowledge our mental health supporters,
Dr. Anna Stan and Dr. John Wimberley.

We also thank Thomas Flannery of Vigliano Associates
for finding a home for our manuscript.

Printed in the USA
CPSIA information can be obtained
at www.ICGtesting.com
JSHW020951251124
74077JS00001B/1